WEST KILL CREEK

WEST KILL CREEK

SHAWN PURCELL

Published by
The Troy Book Makers
291 River Street
Troy, NY 12180
www.thetroybookmakers.com

Printed in the United States of America

-Detail from map *The State of New York with Part of the Adjacent States* by John H. Eddy (NY: James Eastburn & Co., 1818) reprinted with the kind permission of the David Rumsey Map Collection.

-The poem "The Barefoot Rank" from *"Pray Tell, Private Hell": Extracts From the Confessions of a Civil War Soldier* by Steve Bartel (Los Angeles, CA: Hellbound Press, 2007) reprinted with the kind permission of the author's family.

-A passage from *The World of Sex* by Henry Miller (NY: Grove Press, 1965) reprinted with the kind permission of Grove/Atlantic.

-An excerpt from *Mammals: A Guide to Familiar American Species* by Herbert S. Zim and Donald F. Hoffmeister (NY: Simon and Schuster, 1955) reprinted with the kind permission of Simon & Schuster.

-The proverb on fishing from *Reeds' Lilliput Maori Proverbs* by Aileen E. Brougham and A. W. Reed (Wellington and Auckland: A. H. & A. W. Reed, 1976) reprinted with the kind permission of Penguin Books NZ.

-Excerpts from the March, 1944 issue of *The Schoharie County Farm Bureau News* reprinted with the kind permission of the New York Farm Bureau.

Many thanks to numerous past and present local historians and other specialists, first reader Keelin Purcell, close reader Carol Reid, editor Marcus Trower, and Jessika Hazelton and company at The Troy Book Makers.

Cover photos by the author.

The text of this book is set in Palatino Linotype, the epilogues in Garamond, and the titles and chapter headings in Boycott.

To Mary Kim

ONE

Dar didn't *need* to know the approximate true artificial date, but it helped. He placed the thirtieth pebble on the second sill and felt yet again the mild embarrassment of never having learned how many days belong to each month. The young man decided from the beginning of his confinement to calculate the passage of time using the rounded-off ancient Egyptian standard that only added up to 360 days per year, tacking on an extra five at the end, as they had, if he made it that long. He understood better than most how these divisions of time evolved to begin with—from prehistoric skygazing to the estimable calculations of early civilizations right on through the papal fine-tuning of the Gregorian calendar—but the allotments themselves had never been fully committed to memory.

He thought it a good thing that they weren't uniform, and had always used simple devices to recall other schemes. He still remembered his first ever, Never Eat Slimy Worms, for the four compass directions. Roy G. Biv arced over HOMES, My Very Educated Mother Just Served Us Nine Pickles was a harmonic planet mnemonic, and I Value Xylophones Like Cows Dig Milk helped with Roman numerals when he first got into the antiquarian book business, but something strangely niggling prevented him from being able to recall and recite one of the many versions of the standard little ditty most people employed for the duration of the months. "Thirty days hath September," April was usually next, and then *blank*. Perhaps he had missed school that day back in his formative stages, or was this subjective medieval dirge on the wheels of time simply too chaotic? There was really no reason and little memorable rhyme to it, and the "hath" had always distracted him from the tathk at hand.

Starter September and probably November rather than December hath thirty days for sure. February had twenty-eight, and an extra on leap years, but how would you keep track of when that was? Did they coincide with what used to be presidential election years, and exactly when were leap years leapt once in a great while to make things come out correctly? No easy way to look stuff like that up anymore. Most of the rest had thirty-one even. April had thirty, as did either May or June. And he did remember Daffy Duck slobbering, "Thirty days hath September, April, (whatever), and Nebraska."

That was just enough uncertainty to justify the thirty-day average. This little mental deficiency hadn't hampered him all that much before the downfall. Back in his school days some girls even thought it cute. But now he would better himself, like an illiterate tired of hiding the truth, and there was no calendar, newspaper masthead, or working computer or device to sneak a peek at, and nobody to ask. Actually, there was a spent calendar with its next-year-at-a-glance page upstairs, but that was not among the handful of essential items grabbed on the way down.

Thus a second full month was marked in his sealed dirt-and-cinder-block cellar tomb in upstate New York. Pebbles on the shaded sill for the days, his "dim sums," and for the months, carved into a sturdy horizontal support beam, deep "buenas notches" one could feel in the dark. A careless sleeve had accidentally swept most of the pebbles off one time, obliterating the geologic time scale, as it were. After this mishap they were relocated away from his main window on the world to the darker sill with its thick, dormant bushes just outside. Small substitute bits of shale he imagined to be distant descendants of Arcadian and Adirondack scree were less likely to roll, but certain favorite pebbles were retained to note what passed for new Saturdays. These micro-markers had to be placed in somewhat random fashion, should a powerful flashlight ever pick up this tiny clue of life within, but the likelihood of visitors seemed more remote with each passing day.

Although the recluse customarily averted his eyes from the hideous stain on the floorboards above as he turned away from the window, this time it triggered a sad mental recitation of the chain of events that led to his cave-creature existence. It all began with alarming news reports of highly lethal epidemics sweeping through an increasing number of major European and U.S. cities. A knee-jerk trust in science saving the day was quickly dashed when it was revealed that particularly nasty biological warfare–type agents were at work. Death was relatively swift. There were no reported cases of successful treatment, and no clear proof of natural immunity.

Amid the panic and evacuations, word came over the airwaves one evening that there had been a brief, bewildering exchange of nuclear weapons in the Greater Middle East and Central Asia, with scant information as to cause and effect, and not long after that things just blinked off. As this one-two sucker punch sunk in, the thin veneer of civilization peeled off in a wave of shock and violence that washed clear around the planet. Who could blame everyone for leaving their stations in the face of disaster? Humans rise to the occasion by nature, but unlike supercolonial worker ants they know when the cause is lost, and in general would rather make a last stand at home than perish on post in brainless toil for a dead queen.

Moderately steeped in the literature and lore of post-apocalyptic form and function, and enjoying certain logistical advantages of underemployment and bachelorhood—as in free to swing into action, and only one mouth to feed—Dar stocked up on provisions within a day of the first widespread virus reports. There was only one sizable grocery store within easy striking distance. He had noted faux panic in advance of one-day snowstorms, let alone possible Armageddon, anywhere he'd ever lived in the Northeast, so he thought it prudent to compose a quick shopping list and make the nearly half-hour trip to town. All seemed fairly calm there those first few days, but soon stores were closing one by one, posting advisories such as "We don't know if and when there will be more deliveries." People huddled in deep conversation, and true panic was in the air now. Polite looting followed, as compared to reports from other areas of the country.

Gasoline disappeared first, before food, and the other smart thing he did on that initial day of realization was to top off the tank of his van and to fill up four five-gallon containers before the quotas kicked in and the supplies ran out. There was an old metal can from the cellar with graphics good enough to sell as an antique, a dull plastic job his father had employed during the 1973 gas shortage (as had been related to him many times), and two cheap shiny Walmart numbers he'd purchased a year earlier with some remorse over not supporting the local hardware store instead.

Home was a rental cabin near the confluence of two long dirt roads on the side of a heavily wooded hill that would have been considered a de facto mountain in most states. The locals joked that their zip code was EIEIO and their longest season was Mud. Dar's move two years earlier was a strategic retreat from living with his transplanted parents a couple of counties to the west. Decent work was scarce there, and leaving the nest was a good five years overdue anyway, as with so many Millennials. He had a vague late-twenties desire to become a master at some clean trade, like woodworking, but an apprenticeship in that field did not work out. Dar was barely meeting his bills selling books and collectibles online and renting space in antiques centers, both of which required steady investments on the supply side of the pipeline. His mother had been forced by declining health to give up her sideline of haunting every yard sale in the county for fun and profit, and most of the great stock she'd picked up years ago on the cheap and donated to his cause was now long gone.

Landlord Mel was a rather conniving lapel-puller whose single-minded daily pursuit was coming out on top in all things great and small. His ad in the Albany newspaper caught Dar's eye, with promises of seclusion and natural surroundings, and $600 a month was quite reasonable for a house of one's own in the woods. He was pretty much sold at first glance. From the road you mainly saw a long white extension to the left of the driveway, and as you pulled in, the slightly set back original pine-clad cabin presented itself. The windows and roof were bordered in red under cinnabar shingles. It looked trim and happy on the outside and was smallish but clean on the inside, in the overall shape of a pregnant shotgun shack. There was a tiny serviceable kitchen to the right as you entered, a relatively spacious living room with knotty pine paneling and two large windows that looked out back over a distant soggy field dotted with young trees, and a narrow hallway that extended back toward the road leading to a bare-bones bathroom on the right and two small bedrooms to the left and at the rear. A more primitive door off the living room led to enough back yard for a rope clothesline before plunging down into thickets and through the vernal fen.

The property was set into a saucer that seemed a bit unnatural, as if the sand and gravel there had been scooped out to construct this section of the road a century earlier. Even though the house was just to the left of the crossroads looking uphill, it was situated at the end of a long, half-grass and half-red-shale driveway, and shielded from traffic by a ridge that wrapped right around past the kitchen. Nearby residents had little reason to pass by, as straight up and down from points above and below was usually a quicker way in and out, so it truly was secluded.

As for being surrounded by nature, no false advertising there either. Going back the way he first arrived on what he came to call the Up Road—because the actual names of roads on this hill sometimes confusingly gapped out or gained an "Old" on certain stretches, and because he wanted to go blank slate up there anyway—it was all hardscrabble hanging to the side of the hill, with rather exceptional properties carved out here and there wherever it leveled off for a bit, half of them second homes, most on the rustic side, some featuring tannin-stained brooks with small pools, and one or two with enough sunshine for an actual vegetable garden. Go east at the top of this dirt road and you were heading for the Massachusetts border and the picturesque, trendy town of Great Barrington, with its very own functioning castle, while due west would drop you down through dairy land toward humbler Chatham, with its great old movie theater, cozy eateries, and railroad-crossing culture.

Back at the bottom of the crossroads coming down to the rental, a left on the Middle Road brought you out through high grassy fields again toward Chatham, and the land here had the look of being almost for sale, waiting only on a few crusty stewards to give up the ghost. A right past Dar's driveway brought you 250 feet or so and then dove straight downhill again dogleg left, darker with close overhanging trees than ever. Mel's sprawling modern home was perched above the elbow of this turn. Actually, the Middle Road did continue past his house, but it seasonally dead-ended before long just past a big, active beaver pond.

The other natural feature worth noting was a splendid stream that coursed year-round down to the Kinderhook Creek and, like everything else in these valleys, eventually out toward the Hudson River. It was only tamed once at the top, plunging through a wide underground culvert near the peak of the Down Road by Mel's place and then past Dar's rental, on the other side of the quiet country lane. Its smooth bluestone banks were deeply cut and invisible from above, especially when the leaves reappeared, and its leaping waterfalls and kettles and flights of cool dark water were magical in appearance. One bathing pool in particular was just right for his sturdy six-foot frame, lined with small pebbles and clean as a whistle, though he never drank of it with the beavers above. There were even some sun-dappled stretches where one could read or lie down in peace next to this proverbial babbling brook on warm stone that was softer and certainly cleaner than many mattresses. Although it was a little high up for trout, minnows and water bugs abounded, and stalwart orange-brown wood turtles flourished along the banks in terrain that was ideal for them. Once, toward sunset, when the biting and stinging insects were just getting ready for business, a fox hunting its way up the streambed came into view, stared hard for a moment at the interloper, and melted away down some contour. Most marvelous of all was a little ancient graveyard of white and gray speaking stones set down there, almost low enough to be out of sight from the road but sufficiently elevated so as not to be washed away by floods. Smart like that they were back then.

These nice summer things were not at all apparent in the dead of winter, however, and Dar had immediate misgivings upon moving in. The dwelling was cold and drafty. The ticking baseboard heaters smelled like fried dust, and he needed to keep the electric bill down. There was a small wood stove, but the landlord was being a jerk about letting him cut even dead standing wood in the middle of this gigantic forest. He could have it, but he would have to work it off.

Dar was surprised at what a difference the higher elevation made. Every time four inches of snow fell in the area, they would receive a full foot up on the hill. His van got stuck once and he had to hike nearly two miles to reach the rental. Another time he noticed the dim top register of flashing red lights over the bank at the bottom of the intersection and climbed down to find a car had slid clear through the saplings and grill-first into the creek. He expected to discover a frozen body, but footprints led off toward Mel's house. It was farther away than Dar's place but must have been more invitingly lit up.

The power was off for six days once, which meant huddling near the wood stove, punctuated by a few trips to town. Mel checked in with him toward the end but there were no offers of a generator hot shower or other assistance. Worst of all, he couldn't even get the usual fairly decent antenna signals from a handful of local networks in Albany and Schenectady. Cable was said to be coming by the landlord, but the tenant learned later from the regulars at the coffee shop that this had been delayed for years now. These roads were simply too boondocky. It would not pay. Dar made notes on things that needed checking as they occurred to him, and was able to get most of his Internet work done in local cafés and libraries without too much inconvenience.

His first face-to-face meeting with Mel was rather disconcerting too. The landlord related how the previous renters were lesbians, and that he'd enjoyed watching them from up in the woods through a rifle scope, particularly at night when they showed up through the windows better. Dar hoped he was not referring to undressing and lovemaking, but this was still a most curious thing to admit to the new occupant.

Mel also shared his plans for this large neck of the woods, which he'd inherited from his father. He might be putting another rental house in the nearby field, as wet as it seemed down there, and he'd finished a sap house and sawmill up the hill a little that he hoped to turn into commercial ventures. Dar's place then was just within sight of Mel's house down and off to the right, especially when the leaves were gone, and barely within earshot of his new operations up the hill behind him. He gave a brief history of the rental cabin, which had started off as a hot dog stand in nearby Ghent and was hauled there decades ago for use as a small hunting shack before being expanded to its present form. It felt a little cosmic cooking franks there after that, like the joke about the Dalai Lama telling the hot dog vendor, "Make me one with everything."

When spring came, the charm of the spot really sunk in. A rock garden set into the shielding ridge across from the front door and extending around past the kitchen window burst into forget-me-nots and perennial herbs and flowers, and the hills were ablaze with rich pink and white rhododendrons. Even the grass up there smelled sweet, dotted with buttercups, clover, and those small red-orange sunbursts lifting off the lawn like rockets he assumed were poor second cousins to the dandelion until he discovered it was actually orange hawkweed, a noxious foreign invader. By picking his way straight up through this rock garden over the back ridge and banking left, Dar could reach the pond without any glimpse of roads, structures, or people, and he watched the muskrats putter and beavers toil by the hour. The birdlife up on this hill was highly interesting, including preternaturally scarlet scarlet tanagers he hadn't seen in many years, and more muted denizens of the deep forest such as vireos and catbirds that were quite engaging in their own modest way.

Sitting in a faded blue shell-back lawn chair just behind the house, completely out of sight, Dar gradually trained a resident chipmunk to eat right from his hand. Reading, relaxing, and getting away from everyone telling him what to do was just what the doctor ordered. Dar calculated he could afford to pull this off for another year or so, coming out at the other end with a firm plan for his thirties. He missed Internet access at home, hundreds of TV channels, a dog, and a girlfriend, in some order that kept changing, but those things could wait a bit.

The aspiring hermit had been through the normal assortment of relationships. His first serious inamorata in high school was great in the beginning, and a natural educator, but she turned out to be kind of loco, and wanton, cheating with his best friend, and with triplet brothers—two of them anyway, and not at the same time, at least—even claiming she was pregnant during the tumultuous breakup. Since then he'd been much more selective. As Dar went through his late twenties he noticed an increasing emphasis on potential marriageability that did not fit in with his immediate plans. "Peter Pan Generation" muttered one companion disapprovingly toward the end. If that meant he wanted to enjoy life a little first, avoiding some of the common mistakes and regrets of their parents, he was guilty as charged, and the economy sucked anyway so what was the big difference? It was more than that though. If matchmaking really worked, he would have been a tough placement in the modern market. All things considered, he was a little challenging, and somewhat lacking. It would have to be just the right girl.

In the looks department, Dar was easy on the eyes, but more along the lines of the third buddy in a beer commercial, back near the pool table while the super handsome stud up front was hitting on the hottie. He had a pleasant mug, like a fresh-faced New England boatbuilder. His brown hair had been longish in the past but was now quite cropped; usually complemented by a short full beard. And although he'd been a little soft coming out of college, he had worked himself back into top shape.

In one instance Dar's firewood barter work for Mel involved hoisting shingle bundles up a ladder to the top of a new outbuilding among the many that dotted his baronial spread. It was hot, backbreaking work, though he did get to meet the family for the first time. Mel's wife was decidedly above her husband's physical station, taller, with wide doe eyes, long wavy brown hair, and what his brother would have referred to without hesitation as a killer rack. She was polite enough, and even seemed to take note of his rugged good looks, but their brief conversations never rose above what one would expect to transpire between lady and servant. Mel's mother was even more aristocratic, with the added burden of a lifetime of baggage in tow, and some apparent uneasiness in her current living arrangements on the compound.

The son and daughter looked like little hellers, with their father's ruddy complexion, squint, and dark wiry hair. He'd seen them tearing around the dirt roads on their bikes, and beating a frog to death with sticks in a puddle once, but they did not seem like country folk. Mel didn't either, for that matter, but there he was, terraforming the land into a series of buildings and businesses right out of an old stumps-and-smoke Currier & Ives print.

At the end of that task Dar said he would rather pay for a load of seasoned firewood out of the back of the *Chatham Courier* than barter for it, but Mel said don't worry about it, whatever that meant, and he "repaid" him a couple weeks later with a face cord of over-the-hill logs and a baby food jar of homemade maple syrup. Other small, essentially one-way favors followed, like "keeping an eye" on workmen when the whole family was away, and stacking long slabs of fresh-cut pine at the sawmill.

One summer day Mel asked if he could top off Dar's garbage can with a few items he said would not fit into his own fleet of receptacles. The only thing he added was a topless can of leftover turpentine that should not have been discarded in that manner to begin with, though Mel's father would've just dumped it into the stream and chucked the can into a hollow, so there had been some progress. Naturally it spilled down the side to the bottom during pickup, permeating the black plastic with toxic fumes that were pure death thereafter, especially in the simmering heat. These were small, annoying impositions and outrages, but they were becoming common and they added up.

ΩΩΩ

In July, Mel made a proposition. One of his businesses concerned a mammoth warehouse down in Yonkers that had been converted into a storage facility. He needed somebody to watch it for one full week, spelling the regular sap. The duties would be simple. You were to guard the premises, you let people into their space if they needed access, and you had to activate some kind of systems alarm when you went to sleep. He called that process "walking the dog," as it involved pulling a small piece of machinery on wheels by plastic jump rope from its protective housing and plugging it into something else for some reason that escaped Dar when first explained. For this week of life he would make $550 under the table—the $50 going toward gas and food—but Dar needed the dough so he agreed.

The monstrously large, stiflingly hot facility was in a bad part of the city. Mel confided that a major portion of the operation was devoted to housing the seized assets of organized crime, including cars and boats, all of which paid up to four times the going rate—our tax dollars at work. As a result, there was not much need for access and for staff, so this was a real cash cow for him, as it had been for his father.

On that first orientation day before Mel returned home an older black man and his crew showed up to remove a big pile of debris that included filthy crumbling sheets of asbestos. Mel asked what he wanted for the job on the off chance it was lower than his offer. The laborer named his price, the landlord laughed and said if they didn't want $75 for half an hour of work he would find somebody else who did, and the poor guy knuckled under. When the truck was loaded up and Mel extended a handshake to the sweat-drenched and contaminated crew chief, he simply stared him down until the phony gesture was replaced by a nervous grin in what was the most potent "Ef you whitey!" Dar had ever witnessed in person. "I know you'll dispose of that asbestos properly," was Mel's final shaft as they pulled away.

When evening fell he followed the simple closing procedures, but once the big front doors were shut he felt overwhelmed by the sheer volume of the closed space and its probable legions of roaches, rats, and ghosts. The little staff room in the middle of the facility was like a bomb shelter, but at least it had a small fridge, cable TV, and box of tissues.

As he made his rounds in the near dark later, voices could clearly be heard echoing through the dead air of the largest chamber on the ground floor. Creeping toward the commotion in calm terror with an iron bar for protection, Dar was relieved to find they were coming from the other side of the big roll-down doors of an obsolete loading dock. Inspecting this area on the side street the next day, he found a ratty sofa, an assortment of weather-beaten chairs, and a small rusty barbecue pit. Hypodermic needles and beer and liquor bottles were scattered among the high parched weeds. He ventured out at night once for a cold six-pack and could see about a dozen men back there whooping it up and cooking something delicious that smelled like pulled pork. Dar spent several nights on the inside of this bay listening to their colorful conversation, eavesdropping on something he could normally never be a part of. The men sitting against the door were just inches away, but the most immediate danger of detection was something like dropping his beer bottle or sneezing, and even then they would have been hard-pressed to breach that steel and concrete fortress even if they wanted to.

One night Dar was suddenly awakened by shouts and tromping feet. The TV was still on, and he jumped up in his boxers in panic and confusion, fumbling for his crude weapon, to be confronted moments later by half a dozen burly firemen squeezing into the tiny sleeping quarters. He had forgotten to "walk the dog" that night and whatever the hell it was supposed to do it didn't, so an alarm went off. They busted his balls, and Mel called the next day and did the same, but more like a boss. Dar decided that was the last work he would ever do for this prick. He brought the topic up shortly after returning.

"Thanks again for the money, Mel."

"You earned it," the landlord said, clapping a hand on his shoulder. "I know it was a little hot down there this week."

"Yeah, a little, but some nights it cooled down into the nineties. Listen, I like renting this place," Dar began, "but I was drawn to your ad because I was kind of looking for a retreat. I know I'm not working full-time right now, but I need to concentrate on what I want to do next, my parents need help back in Schoharie County, and I don't really have time for lots of small chores and things. I know that sounds blunt, but there are probably plenty of people around who would be happy for a little work, like that guy with the truck down at the warehouse."

Mel stiffened at the thought of paying some local yokel who

would undoubtedly become too familiar with his kingdom and its booty, and then wondered if there was a dig in there somewhere. Before he could manipulate the conversation back to his advantage, Dar drove the point home.

"I've lived in some crowded places, and to tell you the truth I came out here to be alone. I would actually love to build a small house off the road above the beaver pond if I could ever afford it. I pictured just sending a check to the landlord once a month."

"Why waste a stamp on that? We practically live next door to each other."

"What I meant is I pictured the landlord living somewhere else."

"Well . . . okay," Mel replied, "but I've been renting this cabin out for about ten years now, and most of the tenants were happy to help out a little. I scratch your back and you scratch mine."

"Right, except that isn't how *I* want to do it, and that was not part of the contract."

Mel could see the uncharacteristically agitated tenant would not bend for now, and he offered a surprisingly open justification in retreat, as if it might be his last chance to set the record straight.

"No problem, I understand. Look, I'm maybe ten years older than you, right? My dad got me started, but I work very hard for what I have, I don't hurt anybody, and I just want to take care of my family. You'd be surprised at how quickly you can get behind and lose everything. Especially with those assholes down in the city."

Dar contemplated this disjointed confessional later that night. It seemed impromptu but was so practiced that he felt he was getting a glimpse into the private Big Lie gyroscope at the core of his being. Mel's father did more than just get him started, there was some hard work but most of the income rolled in by itself while he played a young Ben Cartwright, he screwed people because he liked to—not because he had to, the family scene was not all that warm, and it takes an asshole in the city to know one. Dar remembered a cowpoke's disparaging remark from an old episode of *Bonanza* that went something like "To get that big you gotta stomp on somebody along the way, and that's a fact."

Later that week he found a note in his mailbox that read: "Hey

Dar, when you have that firewood delivered, please get it dumped as far back in the driveway as possible. Make sure it's seasoned too, as green wood is not good for the stove. Thanks, Mel."

He saw very little of the landlord after that, with one exception. An unfortunate article appeared glossily proclaiming this very town to be one of the top ten places to live in the state due to its scenic beauty, Norman Rockwell hamlets, great schools, low crime rate, and proximity to the Berkshires, Boston, and Montreal. Above all, it was within easy striking distance of New York City. Fancy cars were cruising the Middle Road within days, and they came in droves the next few weekends. Mel smelled a rent increase when the lease ran out in December, and he just wanted to give "fair warning."

"Do you really think you can get a thousand dollars a month or whatever for this place?" asked Dar. "Most of these people probably just want to buy empty lots and build, and this isn't exactly in a prime location. They want vistas like you get farther toward town. I might be able to go seven hundred tops if you really need to do that, but I won't know until then."

ΩΩΩ

They left it at that for the time being. As the cool, moist hanging gardens of Dar's hilltop getaway began to dry out in early August, his father suddenly succumbed to a stroke. Dar's older brother and sister lived out of state, and it fell upon the whelp of the family to help their mother keep the house running. The trip was about eighty miles each way, so he would often stay overnight. The property was quite large, and it took hours just to mow the lawn and whack the weeds. His father's huge garden was in full bloom too. It had been brought along enough for self-sufficiency but did need watering during dry spells. Father's peaceful solution to pests and raiders was to overplant like hell so there was plenty for all.

Mother dutifully canned this last crop of a lifetime, and there was barely room for it all in the cool cellar of the Plain Jane but proud Federal-style house that looked out over chartreuse-spectrum fields cascading off darkly forested hills as far as the eye could see. His father had planned on sledging down the now-useless cistern wall in order to expand the cellar storage space, but that was just one of those things he never got around to. Late fall laid all that reaching garden greenery into sodden brown heaps.

Dar and his brother, who wanted to sell the house, began to squabble about what to do with Mother, who was resolved to stay out of the local nursing home. The weekly trips began to weigh on him, but the matter was suddenly settled late the following summer when she slipped on the cellar steps one day, fracturing skull and bones against the cinder-block wall and lingering for days. Before the sumacs turned crimson they buried her as well, too soon, just shy of sixty.

Dar was tiring of his housing situation, the second-year lease was almost up, and he could suddenly picture himself moving back to the twenty-acre property as master and commander, in spite of the recent shocks there. It had been a cheerful hop farm in the last century, with two large fields in back sloping gently up to wonderful woods and waters beyond. A local farmer was paying a token amount for the sweet hay they now produced.

There was a monumental boulder at the very top of the hill, like a small boat, off to the side and rather out of sight. This glacial erratic provided a sweeping panorama of the blue house and broad valley below. The entire family sat on it once in happier times, and he imagined aborigines hopping on top, for a vantage point if nothing else. Dar had buried a family dog right at the wood line there. The round border stones he used were so perfectly laid out that he calculated the plot would get dug up someday out of curiosity. His noble companion, so stiff in his arms on their final climb together! How long would the collar and tags last?

A huge, gray Yankee bank barn with massive timber framing and a foundation of uncoursed fieldstone sat not far behind the house. Smartly following the lines of the hill, it could be accessed on several different levels, though that was seldom necessary in relic status. Swooping sharp-winged barn swallows showed up around the same day every spring, bolts of steel blue with off-white underparts back from South America to nest in various corners of the old structure amid hand-hewn posts and beams, launching themselves out open windows to harvest insects all day long. There was an elevated earthen "barn bridge" on the left side that accessed the upper level. Big double doors decoratively trimmed in white paint slid open to the middle of the ground floor, directly behind the house. Every stout iron nail and old shelf or tool in this structure had a tale to tell, to those who would listen.

There was a low, secluded work area underneath the right side of the barn, with smaller livestock bays directly above, that was open to the elements at the rear. Dar chainsawed and split firewood for hours on end in this old agricultural setting, his taut body conducting vibrations down through the earth and out into the sky like a human Tesla coil. This wooden island, with its weathered barn boards, wide chopping blocks, and sawdust footing, was surrounded by a sea of tall fragrant grass that bent and whipped about on the winds, breaking at his feet like waves. The young man looked out over the bobbing seed heads during breathers and wondered where he would end up someday. Toward evening, towering white clouds became tinged with coral and orange, violet twilight gave way to showers of the brightest wheeling stars, and the dark swallows were replaced by darker bats.

Dar had once contemplated the market for locally grown hops. One might enquire with regional microbrewers regarding supply and demand, learn the venerable trade, secure funding, and come out after some years of trial and error with a great business model that could serve as the beginning of a boon for the whole region. Heck, you could even remind the barn what hop dances were like, be on the lookout for redeemable "kissing loop" vines during the harvest, and sneak off to do some sparking under the hazy moon in the Swedish summer of upstate New York, though the peak era of local hop production over a century earlier was such a flushed age of innocence, unlikely to be repeated on either score. And he wasn't getting any younger either. He would settle for a respectable job and a happy marriage. This county was fertile, famous for serving as the "Breadbasket of the Revolution" in earlier times, and it was once bale-rich in heady hops as well. Where he lived now was soothing, but the landscape was too shady, the soil too sandy, the rocks too red, and the local politics too flinty. Perhaps it was time to come down from the evergreen heights to the rolling hills and sunny plains and college bars. Beckoning hop poles over twenty feet in length were piled along one inside wall of the massive barn, and he envisioned their triumphant re-erection after decades of dusty slumber. He remembered an old local saying that Schoharie County was noted for "raising hell, hops, and Democrats."

This was all a bitter dream, of course, as his siblings wanted to sell as soon as possible and he was in no position to buy them out. They were already on bad terms over recriminations regarding how well their mother had been cared for, leaving Dar incensed and outspoken at the sheer effrontery of such charges. The housing market was down, and as ever if you have to sell quickly you lose even more, but between those split proceeds and two life insurance policies all three of them would gain a nice bump in their fortunes. In Dar's case this would pay off his outstanding debts and float his present humble lifestyle for another several years, but the question remained of what to do next. Time to bust a move.

As the youngest, his wishes did not apply to other matters as well, and settling the estate became an increasingly rushed and ugly affair. Dar could not take the larger furniture he was interested in, including an enormous Dutch kas and some wonderful primitives his parents stole at auction years earlier before pieces like that got so hot. His antiques center spaces were already reduced and crammed, and there was no other practical place to store such items. His brother communicated with the realtor and a high-end antiques dealer, and Dar was left to deal with the lesser hyenas of the estate sale and clear-out trades. He made numerous trips in advance of the closing, always returning with loads of two seemingly inexhaustible commodities more valuable than he could have dreamed at the time—canned goods of all varieties from the hands of his beloved parents, and books from his father's library—in addition to several decent guns the others also showed no interest in.

Grocery store produce department banana boxes with still-flattened and ultimately reusable U.S.P.S. 0-1097 Priority Mail boxes for sturdier bottoms were perfect for transporting the books. There were over five thousand titles to sort through, and as they were rather carefully selected by his father to begin with, there wasn't much dreck to weed out. Nevertheless, Dar did manage to part with more than half the stock right at the house, leaving them for the clear-out crew. Two handy maxims he'd taken to heart about the used, out-of-print, and antiquarian book trade are that you have to handle and make decisions on a million or two books before you can even begin to know what you're doing, and "Booksellers are people who help solve problems created by books." The transported boxes filled both bedrooms of the small dwelling, they lined the hallway, and they took up a good portion of the usable space in the living room, all stacked at angles two or three high. Most of the books were not highly valuable, though he would need Internet access to check on certain titles. It might have been smarter to leave them, but his antique center bookshelves were getting bare, and these would help pay the rent there five or twenty dollars at a time.

The canned goods in all manner of smaller boxes took up much of the rest of the living room. Dar wasn't exactly sure what he was going to do with all that food, and he knew the landlord would not approve if he spied it there, but he just couldn't bear to see it pitched into dumpsters. There was a mixture of old Mason jars with wire-clamped glass tops and somewhat smaller modern ones with screw tops, all carefully labeled by contents and date. He knew stewed and whole tomatoes were the leaders of the pack, but the inventory included beets, asparagus, peas, beans, corn, peppers, pickles, and sauerkraut. There were also apples and pears from the property, and more types of jam than you could shake a stick at. A beautiful specimen of pickled carrots with a large wand of dill pressed against the side brought him briefly to tears for the first time since the accident. Oddities included "silky apricot butter" and "chocolate raspberry sundae topper." Rounding out the haul were a few sacks of potatoes and some cabbages. His father always hacked off colossal sunflower heads to save as a winter seed treat for the birds, thrown out on the ground or nailed up whole, and some of those were brought to the dark hill that knew no sunflowers as well.

The Schoharie house sold in short order, the monies came in, and things settled down nicely. There was an unspoken agreement between the three siblings that there would be radio silence for a while. Still, Dar was uneasy. He'd pictured himself out of the rental cabin and into a new lifestyle, but that had fallen through big-time. He had a slight prejudice against upcoming November. Dog shit on dead leaves. Looming Christmas stress. Cold winter ahead whose back would not be broken until late March at the earliest. And just then, all hell broke loose.

The Barefoot Rank

I am a lowly private,
and grateful every day
that in this vast misjudgment,
I shall have no say.

They can't blame me for starting it,
their hate aroused my hate.
So soon we'll rot and be forgot,
what a stupid fate.

I hope to never answer
for what's bein' said and done . . .
just put me in the line, boys,
and hand me up my gun.

"Pray Tell, Private Hell": Extracts From the Confessions of a Civil War Soldier by Steven Bartel (Los Angeles, CA: Hellbound Press, 2007)

TWO

BY THE END of the first week of this modern plague (not really the right word but in common use nevertheless), it became apparent that the virus spread rapidly through human contact, acted quickly, and was widely fatal. Speculation and spotty reporting ran rampant. One talking head postulated that it was also transmitted as an airborne disease. Another claimed there were signs that it was not moving as speedily through colder climates, though that may have been a simple function of population. Gaia types ruminated that this was all a natural corrective, evangelicals recognized it as the Apocalypse, and survivalists locked and loaded.

Dar stayed glued to the TV and radio. He missed the CNN-type coverage that cable would have provided, but the networks and locals were all-news-all-the-time now anyway. The contagion did not appear to be weaponized, but it had all the characteristics of germ warfare—an efficient delivery system, high virulence and infectivity, and the absence of effective vaccines. It may have arisen naturally in a back corner of the world, perhaps traceable to birds or mammals, or it may have been introduced by design. Nobody knew for certain.

Some of the big anchors broadcast for a while, but most of the news channels were operating under chaotic conditions that worsened every day. State and federal authorities began to take over, but their reports sputtered in frequency, reduced at times to crawls at the bottom of a static screen listing online resources and urging calm. One station hosted a guerilla segment, where anyone with a video camera and working connection could submit responsible reports. Cases began to appear in upstate New York, and Dar decided it was too risky going out again, though by this point it would have been more for information and consolation than for supplies that could no longer be passively acquired.

He spoke with Mel right in the road at first, trading reports about what they heard on TV and saw in town, but after a while there wasn't much left to say. The only other neighbor he knew stopped by one afternoon. John lived about halfway up the hill, and they had chatted at the sawmill once. The elderly, unarmed gent parked out on the road and slammed the car door as if to announce his presence. He held a handkerchief over his mouth at first, and was intercepted by Dar in the middle of the long driveway. Mel joined them shortly with his shouldered rifle, which confirmed that he was probably scouring the roads from his raised vantage point. Their visitor was running short of food already and wondered if it might be time to start breaking into some unoccupied homes. His wife would be in need of prescription medication soon as well. A quick glance between the two younger men confirmed that they did not wish to join any raiding parties, and that if things worsened this couple was probably done for. They parted with best wishes for a return to normalcy.

Dar had been careful not to mention his large cache of preserves stacked up in the living room, and now resolved to relocate it. The cellar was reached by means of slanted steel hatchway doors at the back of the house that led to concrete steps running down to an uneven dirt floor. There were piles of old tires in one corner, and crude wooden shelves against the walls held cans of solidified paint, fusty linoleum tiles, rusty tools, dusty tarps, and numerous other examples of broken-down bric-a-brac. The better yard items were kept in a small metal shed on the precipice of the back yard, and this cellar was just a junkyard. A copper pipe under the kitchen side provided gravity-fed springwater at the turn of a spigot, and it was cold and clean as could be. Other than that, it was lifeless down there.

Mel only mentioned this cellar to the prospective tenant as a bogus selling point, never showing it to him. Dar had only been down there once, some weeks earlier, finding conditions unsuitable for his books and canned produce, but that was then and this was now. The shelves were emptied and swept, the jars were stacked, and paint cans and empty boxes were arrayed along the front in disguise. This clandestine operation was all accomplished in the wee hours one night, with nothing but a back-corner candle for light, and the operation left Dar spooked and exhausted. He kept some tomatoes upstairs with the whole fruit and potatoes from home and took stock of the rest of his store-bought supplies, which consisted of regular canned goods like soup and baked beans, cereal, rice, some chip group items, peanut butter, frozen goods, red wine, and a case and a half of 46′er Pale Ale, his newest favorite when he could find it.

All through early November only a couple of cars passed by, as safely witnessed from inside the house. Fearing marauders, he began leaving the lights off at night and shielding the increasingly useless TV so as to contain its nocturnal flares. His blinds and curtains were closed at all times now. The lights had flickered in recent days, and suddenly it seemed the power might be off for good. Dar immediately began to cook freezer meat and slices of frozen pizza right in and on the wood stove, saving some dried steak strips in empty canning jars. Finishing the last of the chicken with some wine in dark solitude one night, he had a double flashback to Vincent Price maintaining a generator-powered meat locker as *The Last Man on Earth*, and to his father, illuminated by the fridge, going for a quick midnight TV commercial snack to the tune of Tom Waits' raspy *"He's got a snake skin sportshirt / and he looks like Vincent Price / with a little piece of chicken / and he's carving off a slice."*

The amenities of modern life began falling like large catalpa leaves the morning after a cold snap. Electronic information and entertainment, light on demand, easy heat, the wonders of the kitchen, and the convenience and civility of modern plumbing. On this last score, the kitchen sink still dribbled some water out, but the toilet now had to be filled from the slow cellar pipe in order to flush, or from the stream across the road and down the steep bank, which was too much work and exposure. There had also been a nasty backup that ran right down under the cheap linoleum.

Dar could utilize the far corner of the back yard instead, au naturel, as it pitched straight downhill into a notch that would not be stumbled upon or otherwise detected, at least in winter, but he did have to keep his eyes and ears open for people or cars. With little foliage left, he imagined binoculared Mel making him out from some window of his fortress, eliminating in his general direction, so he favored times when it was misty or dusky, storing pee in a bucket to cut down on the number of trips.

Dar was well stocked in the clothing department, with warm comfortable apparel and a variety of quality footwear. He'd been wearing a heavy college sweatshirt with the hood up but this cut down on his hearing and peripheral vision, so he eventually switched to a thick wool cap. Firing up the wood stove in the evening brought some life back to the living room, and on the coldest nights he retired at its iron feet, lulled asleep by the gentle hisses and settlings of molten wood.

Looking back, one mistake Dar made during the estate clear-out was rather unfortunate. His mother had never met a candle she didn't like. Squat self-standers, or seated in glass, pottery, and lowborn metal; crude novelty numbers and elegant white tapered jobs; gels, floaters, votives, tealights, and of course, birthday candles; waxy beacons of every shape, size, and color, picked up in kitschy shops, forced bus-tour stops, living museums, gifted and especially re-gifted, since people knew she liked them, squirreled away in the farthest reaches of many pieces of furniture—she could have opened a candle museum. Some were pure as the driven snow, made with high-grade vegan soy wax and infused with only the purest essential oils, but most were scented with God knows what actual ingredients—always nauseating to Dar, especially phony bayberry—and he was happy to donate them by the bagful to the local Goodwill. He did keep a hoard of her emergency candles, but it would not be big enough for this one.

It seemed unlikely that the power would crackle back on. No local or governmental relief crews appeared, but neither did the thieves and murderers who so deeply occupied his thoughts now. Dar had ended up in kind of a near-perfect remote location for this, like those dark empty streets kids didn't bother with on Halloween, though nothing short of a military base could really hold out for long against superior numbers of desperate men. He imagined the virus laying low the human race, and natural death and violence chopping down survivors one by one, eventually leaving large parts of the planet like Easter Island. If he and his immediate neighbors had survived this long though, there must be others. It would just take them longer to reach this spot, especially during winter. Would they be friendly? A fifty-fifty chance if he had little to offer, he thought, depending how much further all of this went, and much lower odds if he wanted to keep his excess foodstuffs, gasoline, and weapons.

ΩΩΩ

To bide his time and to make the house look less occupied, Dar began going through his father's books. A rough triage plan emerged. He would keep the cream of the crop in twenty bankers boxes of the type usually used to haul inventory to the antique centers. They were smaller than banana boxes, but they had tops, and would stack and store better. The remainder was sorted by category, labeled with neon Post-it notes secured with packing tape, and stacked in the two curtained bedrooms. Dar pulled his mattress and set it up by the wood stove now that winter was firmly at the doorstep, and both beds were flipped against the wall to make more room. This also rendered the place slightly less hospitable to those who would flop there.

The keepers were a good mix, though naturally limited by his father's taste, and by considerations of size, weight, and usefulness. Mostly nonfiction, and more about where we had been than where we might be going. How-to, reference works, and natural history made up the bulk of what he kept. For writing—not because he was especially good at it, but out of interest, and to help keep it alive— among other items, a dictionary, concise encyclopedia, and thesaurus, all in softcover; the two-volume *Compact Oxford English Dictionary* complete with its own slipcase and magnifying glass (the heaviest book by far); and the probable ultimately penultimate edition of his preferred style manual. For his possible travels, an original edition of French's *Gazetteer of the State of New York*, dated 1860 and deemed to hold up better than the crappy modern reprint; a tour book and large-format atlas of the state in softcover; some local histories; and a small collection of upstate maps and camping, hiking, and fishing guides. Guilty pleasures included world history, travel works from Thoreau to Theroux, books on books, some letterpress, and some thin, interesting esoterica. Rounding out the lot, a couple boxes of classic literature, more for enjoyment than preservation. And at the last minute he'd brought down half a dozen banana boxes of biography, to love them and leave them.

Sorting through these books forced Dar to think about his next move. Everything came back to the same question: Would order be restored, or was this to be a basically brutal evolutionary bottleneck? "Chance humankind will be completely eradicated based on current data," he droned out loud in that computer voice from *Star Trek*, "four-point-six percent." Modern humans would probably survive after a fashion if the virus went away somehow, but in a highly diminished state, and possibly back from near scratch.

Books would survive a temporary disaster, though many would fall to their traditional executioners—water and fire. But in the event of an unremitting emergency, as in place your head between your legs and kiss your ass goodbye, large collections of physical books were doomed. Nice to think of Burgess Meredith puttering around the stacks in that old *Twilight Zone* episode (were his crushed glasses a metaphor for too much reliance on technology or a warning about getting what you wish for or just singular bad luck and a boffo ending?), but books would vanish at about the same rate as people who still cared about and for them. As for digital access, if it could be awakened someday, great . . . if not, *nice going* tech pundits and e-reader peddlers and quick-fix library bureaucrats who impugned the perfect technology and staying power of printed books. Your e-books were now 0-books. For Dar's immediate purposes, however, although books would probably not be very good for barter, he would save those he could, for himself if nothing else.

Of post-apocalyptic works—a nearly mined-out genre right up there with vampires and zombies—he'd read quite a few, but the only true specimen still in his possession was a paperback edition of *Earth Abides* by George Stewart, published in 1949 but only recently discovered on a bargain shelf in a big used-book barn. The hero probably survived that airborne disease because he was bitten by a rattlesnake in the opening passage. There was another good bit about primates being the only animals dying in zoos at first. It was an enjoyable effort, though rather quaint now in some respects. Ish (short for something, meaning something else) could have turned a small group of blacks into willing slaves but he had better things to do. Traveling all over the country by car seemed implausible, as did the discovery of the bored socialite couple in Manhattan. The author was fixated on bad tires, gas supplies, and failing auto parts. He would have been impressed with the engineering advances that made the high-octane world of *Mad Max* possible a mere three decades later.

There was a library scene in that one too, wasn't there? A university library. Ish was the only survivor who could still read, and nature was prying at all the openings. And the gradual demise of the hero and the progress of his tribe were lacking on some level. Still, a great entry in the category, and apparently influential from what he read in the introduction to this much later reprint. Why hadn't they made a movie out of that, with somebody like Ray Milland?

More recently, Dar had read and seen Cormac McCarthy's *The Road*. It was suitably depressing, riveting, and with two small exceptions, spot-on. Pushing a shopping cart of belongings through such a blasted and threatening landscape for that many miles would be far more trouble and danger than it was worth. And—spoiler alert!—leaving that well-stocked bomb shelter so soon was almost as incredible as stumbling upon it to begin with.

Filmic treatments of the post-apocalypse were legion. Dar's favorite was probably *On the Beach* from 1959. Director Stanley Kramer and company brought dignity, nuance, and even a little humor to the project, and the acting and Australian locations were topnotch. There was only one really dumb scene, when Gregory Peck and Ava Gardner go on that comic-relief trout-fishing trip. The author's battles with the makers of the film were highly typical, and he ended up losing control of his own creation, though it's a miracle it came out as faithfully as it did, considering the era. As for the U.S. Navy, it refused to cough up the true nuclear sub that would have been provided in an instant for a more gung-ho patriotic vehicle.

An obvious question about this book project slowly dawned on Dar. Why separate out twenty boxes? Where were they going? What would he do with the vast remainder? If things got back to normal maybe they could be sold someday, but he didn't bother penciling in prices because that was a pipe dream. He couldn't live in this glorified hot dog shack forever. It was on a road . . . a crossroads. Even if a few local survivors were peaceable, their days were probably numbered. What to do? Out of the frying pan and maybe into the fire, or stay put and hope for the best, like an Irish monk in an island beehive hut, brained or disemboweled sooner or later and rolled into the sea by a thick boot past startled puffins.

ΩΩΩ

Now that the return of the Dark Ages was making significant gains nearly two months into the downfall, Mel suddenly began to visit again, cutting rapidly across the seasonal road by his place and dropping down from the ridge in back, rather than risking the short stretch of open road. Dar had to let him inside so they could both stay out of sight. Mel eyeballed the younger man before entering, always wearing his sawmill cartridge mask now, only lowering it to speak from some distance, and all the while casting furtive glances and making nervous jokes. The one time Dar turned the tables and showed up at his door there was no answer. They traded a large jar of canned tomatoes for some syrup in a small wax cup, but he decided not to engage in any more bartering after that. Mel asked what he would do if his food ran out, and Dar gestured toward the loaded Savage 30-30 leaning against the side of the couch.

"I know hunting season is over, but who's gonna stop me?"

"Hey, not me," replied Mel, absorbing the gist of this half jest, "but just be careful where you point it. The quieter the better back here too. Right now I don't think there have been any local invasions, but if things keep on this way we can expect that. As long as we're talking about it, it would be better if you don't start shooting up the woods."

"Well I've heard some shots toward your house. Have you been hunting?"

"Not much, but if things don't get better I may trap for muskrat and beaver in my dam." He didn't own that piece, and the *my* of this was not lost on Dar. "They wouldn't be bad with seasonings. How are you fixed for food?" Mel asked in a more direct fashion.

"I'm almost out of store goods. I figure I can kill a deer and make that last a pretty long time. There's plenty of squirrels around too."

"Pick a windy day then so the sound will carry most in one direction. Due east is probably best. And clean up any signs real good, okay? Sorry I can't help but we are low ourselves, and I have four to feed."

"Four?"

"My mother was out of town when this broke, too far away to reach."

"I'm sorry. I didn't know that. You never said."

"It's been tough."

"I don't hear your generator anymore."

"I'm rationing my fuel, but it's also better to keep quiet, and that thing's noisy as all get-out. I can run the wood stove, but only at night because of the smoke. You should do the same."

"I pretty much am. Aren't your kids going stir-crazy? I haven't seen them out at all."

"They're doing okay. We just have to hold on until things get better. They understand that. Listen," said Mel, changing direction, "I've been down the hill"—referring to the tiny town about a mile below—"and I don't see anybody. No signs of life outside anyway. I smelled something though. It could have been a big dead animal, but I think there are bodies in some of the houses."

"You probably don't want to go knocking on any doors to find out," replied Dar. "You scare the hell outta me when you do that here," he said, glancing at the rifle again. "I'm actually pretty surprised nobody has been by on the road. We might have some fast and tough decisions to make if they start going house to house."

"I think it was the plague down there," Mel replied, "but I'm expecting trouble too. Winter's coming, and I don't want to leave footprints everywhere. I'm going to hunker down. I'll probably shoot at anybody coming onto my property too, so be careful. If you're out and about, stick to the deepest woods. Don't be walking on the road, okay? And I want to be up front . . . I can't take you in or give you food. You might want to consider heading out somewhere, like to your other house, before it snows too deep. Chances are it's empty. What about the rest of your family?"

"I spoke to my brother and sister briefly when the phone still worked, but they live far away," Dar replied, hiding his mounting alarm at the slant of the conversation. "I guess I could make a run for it if things get too bad, but you don't have to worry about me imposing on you."

"I mean, technically speaking, you *are* on my property, and in some ways you're a security risk."

"I hear you on that, but I might be a help too. Safety in numbers, or maybe you'll hear them slaughtering me and have better time to prepare. And if it's the back rent you're concerned about—"

"I'm not kidding around, Dar," Mel shot back. "This is serious business. You wouldn't believe what people will do when they're that hungry. First they get grumpy, then weak and nervous, then desperate, and then murderous."

Just then there was a loud report from the wood stove, startling both men, and as the landlord turned to look Dar noticed the glinting butt of a concealed handgun under his coat. All of this marked a big turning point in their relationship, and was in fact the last time they would ever speak.

"Happy Holidays if I don't see you before then," the landlord said on his way out.

"You too, Mel, and say hi to the family for me."

It had been a relatively mild early winter so far, though rather gloomy, but snow was in the air now, and Dar realized that Mel was quite correct about leaving signs and trusting in the goodness of man. Woman, maybe, but not man. He had a strong desire to do some scouting himself, in all four directions, and some serious hunting, but was reluctant to leave the property unguarded.

Dar began to sit up on the ridge in deep contemplation, glad to be outside even in the deepening cold. On the third or fourth such outing, sitting still as can be in case a deer happened by, he caught some movement below and off to the right. It was *Mel*, dressed in camouflage and taking up a prone position facing the rental. Dar realized in a flash that this was probably the same vantage point used to spy on the previous renters. Mel was sighting through the scope the way he said he watched them through the open curtains. Twenty minutes passed. Dar was cramping up, and he needed to pee. Jesus! Stiffening, his thoughts ran to age-old military calculations. The high ground. The cover of descending darkness. The advantage of surprise. And then Mel suddenly slid away like the Ghost of Christmas Yet to Come, alarming some dark-eyed juncos in the process. Maybe it was all harmless curiosity.

ΩΩΩ

It was time to get down to brass tacks, as his father used to say. He didn't know what that actually meant, though he *had* looked up the meaning of "dead as a doornail" once, another of his common pointed expressions. Leaving the cabin seemed out of the question, with deep winter just around the corner. Dar could still make a break for it, perhaps trading food for shelter, but he just couldn't rid himself of the premonition that such a move would hasten his demise. On the very next afternoon the question was settled for him by the sound and then sight of two big off-road vehicles passing directly in front of the cabin. They made the corner and parked on the Down Road just below Mel's compound. Through thickening snowfall he observed four or five men circling around the back of the house from both sides, followed by the muffled but unmistakable sounds of forced entry.

This was it then! Balls-to-the-wall home invasion. Was he next in line, or did they somehow know that Mel's house was occupied and well provisioned? Dar laid out his weapons: his pump-action deer rifle; a sharp-looking Winchester Wildcat .22 of undetermined origin (not a family gun—probably something his father picked up from some widow of a friend), also scoped; his childhood Ithaca .410 shotgun; and a heavy, deadly-looking P250. There was a good supply of ammo for all except the latter, including a ridiculously large number of .22 cartridges handed down from dead uncles and such. Dar had run a few of the estate guns through a local auction early on. Who needs three .22s, for example, when one will do? And he was happy with his own 30-30 as well. They always put the guns up first thing at country auctions, so those twitchy buyers didn't have to sit through collections of teapots or Hummels. The auction hall refused the ammo, however, and the more Dar cleaned house, the more he found. He meant to bring all the odd bullets to the local police station, but on second thought and with time running out he left it all in a dense box for the clear-out guys to marvel and celebrate over.

Mel's generator kicked on. The men started bringing smaller items out in boxes, presumably food. He zeroed in on them with his scope. Their faces had seemed odd-looking, and now he could see that they all wore white particle masks. Their demeanor was rough but fairly relaxed, like at the end of a hunt. No shots had been fired, at least that he could hear, and there was no sign of family members, unless they were being held inside. Had they been evacuated by Mel already? Did they run in time? Did they have a hidden room? Dar thought of Mel's wife. She was the haughty queen of her sunny back yard not that long ago, a fully drawn bow of femininity possessing all the tools necessary to make a fool out of most males, deigning to hand over an iced tea to a coarse peasant who would've liked to get all up into that. Who could have imagined the suddenness of the present reversal, where the physically stronger were now so much more likely to dominate?

The invaders seemed all packed up and done with their business. They stood on the road next to their vehicles making plans. One pointed directly at the cabin, causing Dar's heart to leap to his throat. Early winter twilight was descending, and there was a good three inches of fresh snow on the ground already. Unless they were an ever-prowling pack, which did not seem to be the case, they must have been concerned about getting back to their home base. Everyone knew how bad these hill roads were in the winter, and that was *with* plowing and sanding. After some discussion they ended up going downhill instead of back the way they came in, probably because that was safer driving and the paved road was closer. Just before they left, one man went back into the house and killed the generator. As the lights blinked off he realized how transfixing they'd been.

"Crunch time," said Dar out loud. What to do? Which path to take? This wasn't just idly figuring out what to do with his life—this was how to freakin' *save* his life. Slow down. Don't panic. Fear is the mind killer. Fear is the little death that destroys. When was the last time he was scared enough to summon that approximation from *Dune* up? Settle down. "Thimk before you mess things up." That old bumper sticker on his father's car brought a smile to his face. He remembered another he had: "Be alert . . . the world needs more lerts." They may have hit Mel's because it was the biggest house around. They may have heard his rifle out that way and come to investigate. They swarmed the house carefully, but not military-style. Perhaps they didn't expect to find any survivors so far from town. How had *they* survived? Those masks were the first bit of real news Dar had in weeks. They were not to mask the smell of the dead, because they stayed on the entire time. Either the virus was still doing its dirty work, or they at least thought it was.

Night fell, and he didn't dare cast even candlelight in case the men came back for some reason. As Dar drifted off to sleep, something jerked him back into consciousness as surely as Thomas Edison's balls hitting the floor. What was that thing that might save him? It had crossed his mind in some context only a few hours earlier. Get your bearings, man! And just before the pearly gray fog crept back in, he had it. Fumbling for a small pad, he scribbled the words down for safety's sake. "Hidden room."

Dar had been an incurable night owl in the previous life but was now naturally early to bed and early to rise. This morning he awoke later than usual, however, sitting up with a start. "Fucking idiot! You *tryin'* to get killed?" There was no activity out on the road. The snow had stopped but the skies were still steely and foreboding. Coming back from the window, he saw the pad and remembered its message. "Great idea, *not*," he muttered. A frozen, dark, dirty cellar was a lot different than a hidden room. Dar paced between all the windows, hunger gnawing at his belly. He'd lost a good ten pounds now from a frame that was lean to begin with. Oh to wake up from this nightmare and go out for breakfast at some cozy diner—eggs over easy and a mess of crispy seasoned home fries with buttery wheat-bread toast and endless perfect coffee all served up by some sassy or sultry or businesslike waitress—where he could read the morning paper at a corner table or right at the counter and leave a nice tip on the way out!

Dar cracked open the back door and decided against peeing down the bank, as that would leave obvious tracks across the yard. And then it hit him like a ton of bricks. It's too late to run, and stay in the house and you are super vulnerable. Look what happened with Mel. Death could descend at any time. Go down to the cellar for three or four months and make a break for it in early spring. Do it now before the snow gets any deeper, or you'll leave signs that will lead right there. That's the way to go!

From that moment on, Dar was like a man possessed. Treating himself to some of the last snacks—in the form of wood stove–crisped pretzel nuggets and a single can of Chinese take-out Dr. Pepper saved all those weeks—the first order of business was making a quick list of what to do, starting with outside chores. He trudged out to the storage shed and retrieved some of the better tools kept there, in addition to tarps of all sizes. On the return trips he carted over cellar junk likely to be in the way. After the final run he used a hard rake to fill in his tracks with fresh snow as well as possible.

Half an hour was spent on the van. Dar had tucked it around back weeks ago, right next to bushes of nearly the same color, pointing out. Now he removed the front left tire and propped that end up with cinder blocks, and he gave the interior a panicked look. Finally, he started it up for the first time in days, let it run awhile, and then removed the battery and brought it down to the cellar along with the tire.

Time was spent on the cellar windows. Successive washings removed years of soiling from all three, and it was just enough above freezing to get the job done. This felt fussy, but these would be his windows on the world for some time to come. Dar needed a KEEP OUT sign that demanded serious attention. He painted large, rough, red X's on the white cabin extension and the front and back doors, implying virus trouble within.

There was time for one last visit to the high ridge above. Looking down through a hissing curtain of thickening snowflakes, all seemed peaceful to Dar. The roads were mere soft outlines, the useless telephone lines seemed out of place in those vertical-wooded hills, and there were just a few splotches of muted man-made color here and there. He left a deep trail coming back down, but it was in folds that would get filled in soon enough.

Next came whisking everything down before much more fell. The whole idea was for the cellar doors to remain under a thick carpet until spring. Any disturbance to natural settling of the snow there would betray him in an instant. Otherwise, chances were nobody would bother looking for survivors or useable items in such a primitive cellar. Living down there would be bone-chilling and ghastly, but he could make it work. One could endure almost anything for a few months. He used to watch prison shows with "Lockup" in the title and knew most of those guys would trade up to being their own boss in a dirt pit for a relatively short stretch like that without hesitation. Darkness came quicker than ever, but by early evening the move was complete. He said goodbye to what little was left of the moon, and the double doors came down with a cold clang in the gathering gloom.

The Forgotten Books
by Thomas S. Collier

Hid by the garret's dust, and lost
Amid the cobwebs wreathed above,
They lie, these volumes that have cost
Such weeks of hope and waste of love.

The Theologian's garnered lore
Of Scripture text, and words divine;
And verse, that to some fair one bore
Thoughts that like fadeless stars would shine;

The grand wrought epics, that were born
From mighty throes of heart and brain,—
Here rest, their covers all unworn,
And all their pages free from stain.

Here lie the chronicles that told
Of man, and his heroic deeds—
Alas! the words once "writ in gold"
Are tarnished so that no one reads.

And tracts that smote each other hard,
While loud the friendly plaudits rang,
All animosities discard,
Where old, moth-eaten garments hang.

The heroes that were made to strut
In tinsel on "life's mimic stage"
Found, all too soon, the deepening rut
Which kept them silent in the page;

And heroines, whose loveless plight
Should wake the sympathetic tear,
In volumes sombre as the night
Sleep on through each succeeding year.

Here Phyllis languishes forlorn,
And Strephon waits beside his flocks,
And early hunstmen wind the horn,
Within the boundaries of a box.

Here, by the irony of fate,
Beside the "peasant's humble board,"
The monarch "flaunts his robes of state,"
And spendthrifts find the miser's hoard.

Days come and go, and still we write,
And hope for some far happier lot
Than that our work should meet this blight—
And yet—some books must be forgot.

Ballads of Books by Brander Matthews, editor (NY: George J. Coombes, 1887, No. 45 of 100 printed in the large-paper edition)

THREE

Stretching, Dar smiled at the thought of a girlfriend who used to tuck the sheets in far too tightly at the bottom. "Can't you leave my half out, just when I stay over?" Next came the sensation of cold shoulders, and a pervasive smell of cold soil. His eyes opened slowly under the brow of his restored hoodie. They beheld frosty breath, crystallite spicules of mold-like white stuff in the dirt inches from his nose, and beyond that vague piles and cinder-block walls under dull windows. Not exactly an "I'm going back to sleep for a while" first encounter with the day. No shit/shave/shower before work. No *Morning Joe* or old movie or Sunday newspaper with breakfast in bed. No cuddling, or walking the dog. He was getting used to those losses anyway, but there had been a certain routine and modicum of comfort upstairs, where the wood stove had become his warm best friend. This was more like a grave just before they threw the dirt over you.

Climbing out of his sleeping bag, sore from the day before, Dar uncapped his big-mouth water bottle, took a large swig, pulled on his work boots and heavy coat, and sat up to survey the situation. As he was snipping the fingertips off a pair of extra mittens, he had a sudden, somewhat incongruous flashback to the housed memory of a small item in the paper once about a Vietnamese family that had rented a cheap self-storage unit in California and actually managed to live there for some months before being discovered and turned out. That would be even more claustrophobic, he thought, with no windows, and deadly hot in the summer. Deadly cold was better. It's kind of a rotten feeling, but you don't crave water so badly, you kind of drift off at the end, and it's far quicker. They had each other's company, but that meant more worry too. Dar had only himself to watch out for. They probably landed in the social safety net once the story broke, or perhaps they were deported. His alternative was post-apocalyptic pinball. They had clean concrete and sheet-metal surroundings rather than a grim pit, but at least dirt was natural, and it gave a little.

Then he mentally dredged up an old *Hägar the Horrible* comic strip. The wife is sweeping like crazy, commenting on how hard it is to get the floor of their hovel clean, when Hägar informs her that it's a dirt floor, as in hence impossible to clean. In another, she thought-bubbles fine birthday presents from her behorned husband, only to be presented with a new muckrake instead. Those wacky Vikings!

First things first, after an old, cold, energy bar. The three windows were cleaned from the inside now, which improved the view and lessened the murk. There was nearly a foot of welcome fresh snow on the ground, nicely obliterating signs of Dar's recent activity outside. These were old, steel-frame, hopper-style windows, the size of four cinder blocks. They were terribly inefficient, but the trade-off was some good oxygen exchange. The two along the side of the house facing the driveway were at about eye level from inside the cellar, and a foot or more above the ground on the outside. They afforded slightly different views toward the road out front. The one on the left gave the better angle and was less obstructed by shrubbery. The third window on the opposite side of the cellar was a bit lower for some reason, with a sloped sill. From there Dar could see along the back yard toward Mel's, including the section of the road where the marauders had parked and hobnobbed. All three windows appeared to be overpainted and rusted shut; attempting to open them would probably break their glass.

A low opening in the wall near the cellar steps led into a long, windowless, dirt crawl space that ran back under the hallway and bedrooms. The ground had not been excavated as deeply there, so you stooped about halfway in and crawled uphill at the very end. It was a creepy and essentially unusable space, though Dar knew this would be the best place to dispose of his garbage and his waste.

This then was his newly drawn rectangular quarters. Down the steps; ten feet or so to the right until you hit the north wall; turn left past the crawl space entrance until you come to the long west wall; turn left past those two windows until you hit the south wall underneath the kitchen and living room, with its copper water pipe and crude shelves; and then a final left past the single back yard window and more shelving, back to where you started. There were four thick metal jack posts in the middle of this space, which was otherwise unencumbered, and a number of shorter such posts propped up the sagging structure from the crawl space as well.

Although this was all poor construction technique, and no doubt added to the chill and draftiness of the rooms above, it must have made sense to cut corners back when this was used as a hunting camp for just a couple of weeks each year, before it was expanded out. The ground wasn't wet, and most of the soil up there was part sand, which helped with drainage and moisture content, but it was certainly cold and clammy.

Dar examined the white spots in the dirt he'd noticed earlier, unable to decide if it was dangerous mold or the first baby steps of some strangely deposited or extruded cellar-type stalagmites (he *was* in class the day his science teacher said that stala*ctites* hold "titely" onto the ceiling). Perhaps it had taken decades to form these minuscule incrustations, and he was thoughtlessly wrecking them, like some douche bag explorer in a virginal cave system.

At any rate, Dar decided to spruce the place up as best he could. The entire north side of the floor was cleared of all objects, and loose soil and small bits of junk were raked into a pile, shoveled into a strong cardboard box, and dumped far to the rear of the crawl space. Normally this would have stirred up dust that floated around for hours, but even that seemed leaden in this cold pit where down was the order of the day, not up. A very large green tarp was laid down over this half of the space, flush with the driveway wall. It did what rugs do for decrepit floors—help to hide or forget what lies beneath— and hopefully it would take the damp off a bit. Cuts were made to accommodate the jack posts. He did the same for the other side of the main floor, choosing a blue tarp for contrast. Rather than covering up every bit of dirt, he left it exposed near the rear and water pipe walls. Tarps on the floor viewed through a window would not necessarily give away his presence, and everything else was arranged to look more like careless storage space than planned living quarters.

This activity warmed Dar in body and spirit, and he took time out for his first underground lunch. More than half of the canned food was in the form of tomatoes, and he felt a duty to chip away at those rather than be left with nothing but at the end. Tomatoes were not very filling and not that great for his stomach, but there was nutrition there, and they mixed well enough with certain other morsels. In the now-constant preoccupation with food, Dar missed refined grains, meat, junk food, and fresh fruit and vegetables the most. Fish and oils too, though he treated himself to an olive every third day or so.

He had done well in the supermarket sweep, mere hours before those things started running out, but his supplies were dwindling. Items that got stale or moist had been consumed weeks earlier before they became unusable. The best stodgy food left in any quantity was close to a dozen large cans of different brands of baked beans, some bragging on their bacon or pork flavor. Once opened, they were transferred into Mason jars and relished a spoonful or two at a time in their "tangy sauce with brown sugar & spices" or whatever that particular label called it.

The other proven comfort food was Cheez-Its, which stayed quite fresh in their inner bags, tightly wound and triple-clothespin sealed. These were rationed out a few at a time as well. He put things on them that might not taste very good by themselves, like something his mother labeled "pumpkin butter." Eight large boxes of those were left. As for meat, only a few jars of homemade smoked jerky strips remained. They were suspicious-looking enough to warrant high heat before consumption. He often lamented not thinking to purchase an entire box or even a small case of normally objectionable Slim Jims, and from time to time wondered how surviving vegetarians would be making out. Juice mixes, more tea and honey, and instant coffee would have livened things up too.

Calculating how few hours of cellar winter sun were left, Dar turned next to setting up sleeping quarters. He erected his roomy veteran tent to the right of the second window, in a corner location that would be relatively hard to spot by anyone peering in, and he covered it with a dirty shredded tarp for camouflage. The front entrance faced the steps, not far from the crawl space opening. Inside, there was room for the better single mattress from upstairs. That would be a lifesaver down there. He wanted to be as close to the driveway as possible in order to hear any approach or commotion, so his head would be toward the west wall, with his feet pointing out toward the tent entrance. A sleeping bag on top, extra blankets and quilts, and a good feather pillow completed the bedding, next to which was laid a pine "cup board" for night water, a hospital pee bottle, and a flashlight. Dar was right-handed, and he slept on his stomach. Just beyond the board at the bottom of the tent wall was the perfect place for an iron poker and the two best guns. The others were laid in the narrow space between the tent and the wall in long wallpaper boxes, and the extra ammunition was boxed and wrapped against moisture right alongside.

Having wrestled some primitive concerns to the ground and operated on his environment rather successfully, Dar felt a great sense of accomplishment after only one day's work. Perhaps this would not be so bad after all. Upstairs, there hadn't been much daily purpose other than firing up the stove when it was safe to do so and sorting the books. He'd been mostly glued to the windows, far too paranoid about invasion to relax. This early evening, for the first time in quite a while, Dar cracked open a beer and a book and read in the tent by the weak light of his nearly discharged solar lantern. He heard a few ticks and creaks, probably caused by the weight of the snow on the roof, and what sounded like a little scurrying, but all in all this felt safe and restful, and he drifted off peacefully, all things considered.

Come morning, Dar took breakfast and then set about making piles of items grouped by category. He had the boxed books; the four guns, ammo, and assorted knives, including a survival model at his belt; all his clothing, some of which could be turned into rags; some kitchen items; camping and fishing gear; a basic set of tools; a small but heavy antique oak machinist's chest filled with screws, washers, nails, and other hardware; a chainsaw, fuel mix, and bar oil; the gas cans; a variety of live traps; and a couple of still-silent radios.

The main things Dar left upstairs were the rejected books, kitchenware he couldn't use, and a swell LP collection, mostly vintage jazz from a single estate purchase he'd made. There were very few personal items. Just a small box containing a rather unusual assortment of artifacts and memories, from a megalodon tooth to his external hard drive. In case deep cold could kill his hibernating laptop, and as a silver sliver of hope, he reserved space for that under a corner of his pillow. His sister had borrowed all the family photos, papers, and videos in order to make digital copies, and unless her family survived *and* humankind could miraculously pull out of this nosedive, he would certainly never see those again. Sad.

Not long after the big blackout of the previous winter, Dar went on an online spending spree, picking up some items that would be invaluable to him now. The most crucial purchase was a new Svea camp stove, normally most suitable for one or two people out on the trail. Small, cylindrical, made in Sweden of solid brass, it was the perfect marriage of form and function. The aluminum lid came with a detachable handle and served as a cooking pot; the fuel/flame key was attached by a chain so it couldn't get lost, and adjustment wrenches were stamped right into the key; and a built-in cleaning needle in the burner jet automatically broke up soot deposits. There were only those two moving parts, the key and the needle, and nothing was made of plastic. The burner was self-pressurized, and the only tricky part was getting the stove to start by pouring a little fuel into the primer pan and lighting it. Dar had a large can of stove fuel, but the Svea also burned regular unleaded gas, though not as cleanly.

He'd also looked into solar lanterns, picking out a compact LED model. It never seemed to fully recharge down there, even near the sunniest of his three windows, but the low-light setting was usually all he dared use anyway. Dar cut out rough pieces of cardboard to fit over the windows on those nights when he stayed up late, but feared they would betray him, there one time and gone the next. He wished he could see how much light escaped his closed tent from outside the cellar, in order to determine if the cardboard was necessary. The other indispensable item was a survival flashlight that ran three ways, though cranking would be the only fail-safe method. How relatively miserable those six days without power had been. He couldn't have imagined such a phenomenal upside at the time.

Over the next couple weeks Dar began to put his subterranean affairs in order. First up was converting the crawl space to his needs. The best place to bury solid waste would be in the farthest corner, as high up as he could squeeze. Using a spade, Dar dug down about two feet. His crapper was a short blue bucket with a handle, and his privy area was across from the tent entrance, near the concrete steps. This maintained some semblance of normalcy, and the crawl space opening was conveniently close.

He'd only picked up a single four-pack of toilet paper in the shopping spree, as it was going fast, and more would have filled the cart too much, but using wet rags that could be rinsed out did the trick. His "slops" as he came to think of and term them were dumped down the hole, a black plastic garbage bag was then laid directly over the waste for suppression, and a folded tarp was placed over the surface for decorum. Even in freezing temperatures, he automatically breathed through his mouth when going through this routine. When the hole was nearly full he dug another just to the left and used that dirt to cap the old hole, being careful not to break through the dividing wall.

These rows could be extended across and then down the slope as needed, as long as they didn't get too close to his living quarters. "Shit goes downhill," he chuckled to himself. This area was named the "poop deck," and when he could finally leave someday it would remain as mildly hazardous "brownfields" in one of the many puns and word plays that helped get him through the day. A bigger pee-only hole at the top of the hill simply drained down, especially when warm, and did not require further relief wells. What little regular inorganic trash he generated was stored in plastic garbage bags and piled in the other high corner. Dar ran a tarp up the middle of the hill to keep his clothes clean, and he usually multitasked during these quick visits. He hung a gray wool blanket above the doorway that more formally separated the two spaces, and might even hide the entrance from outside view if he ever needed to retreat there.

After much deliberation, Dar decided to store the books on the lower end of the crawl space, against the wall, taking care to enrobe them on all sides with tarps. It was probably a bit colder and damper on that side, but otherwise they would be underfoot, and that many uniform boxes or a covered mound of that size might arouse interest if spied through a window.

The next big project was dealing with the preserves, which were subject to freezing. He excavated a deep pit in the center of the floor where the tarps met, lining it with additional tarps and blankets, and sunk the stacked boxes and alcohol into that. Once every few days he retrieved an assortment of food and stored it in the tent, where his body heat would help at night.

Tiny footprints and nibbled packaging gave away a marginal colony of mice, whose living quarters and exit tunnel were probably underneath the shelving. The smallest live trap baited with a bit of precious peanut butter yielded three of them, one night after another. Although Dar would have liked to keep one as a pet, it was safer to eradicate them. With no common nest to snuggle in, these quiet creatures perished fairly quickly in the cold trap while he slept anyway, and made their inglorious farewell to the world of live air from the bottom of the slops hole.

Although cellar life was shaping up to be relatively comfortable, Dar wondered if he had made a mistake. The plunderers had not returned, the roads seemed impassable, and it would be very nice to reactivate the small wood stove just feet over his head. The amount of time spent staring out the three windows was reducing every day, though he did have a nightmare about deep snow covering them up for good. Unless he happened to be looking at the right moment, he would have to depend on hearing or perhaps headlights for an alert.

To combat lethargy and prepare himself for a return to the outside world, the detainee began a rigorous exercise regimen. It was drawn largely from gym and karate class routines, with some aerobics and lifting thrown in. Despite weight loss from eating far less (and far healthier), Dar was in pretty good shape, with no ailments to speak of. He yearned to stretch his legs on a big walk more than anything. There were occasional bouts with depression and claustrophobia, but that was to be expected. Mentally, he was disturbed by the utter silence the most. The only sounds he heard that were not self-generated came from crows and blue jays, or the wind, or dripping water, and they were highly muffled. The complete stillness inside was barely relieved by the sight of swaying branches or drifting snowflakes.

Then there was the mortal fear and unholy dread of the dark we'd been trying to conquer forever, from the primitive abject terror of a solar eclipse to crucial fires that failed to a blown bulb to losing your cable connection. This shouldn't be happening! Let there be light!

Then there was the filth we'd been trying to crawl out of forever, from bogging muck to shite to a sudden stain on your favorite garment to the sight of a rodent racing along the wall at a fancy restaurant. This shouldn't be happening! Out, damned spot!

Physically, what concerned him the most about the cellar was the relative dampness. Was mustiness the same as moldiness? Would something bad settle into his lungs?

He only got drunk one night, on cheap wine. Painting the rusty jack posts with trees from different climates and seasons under happy skies seemed like a good idea in the middle of that, and they didn't turn out half bad, for him. The only real vegetation he had were a few dried flowers that had fallen out of a book over a century old, faded pressed roses in the dead of winter, probably placed there by some hopeful young thing with no inkling they would outlast her and then some.

ΩΩΩ

The weather had cooperated so far. Cellar temperatures hadn't dipped below twenty degrees, as confirmed by a retro thermometer removed from near the back door on the way down. Dar had a good portable filter from his backpacking days, but the copper pipe continued to provide excellent water. Although it came in below the frost line, the exposed section was wrapped in former heat tape and further protected with insulation. If this pipe failed him somehow, or burst behind the shutoff valve, the game would be up. He stored water in whatever plastic receptacles got emptied out, burying them deep underground in a separate location, but those would not last long at all.

A few weeks into this ordeal it dawned on Dar that the skies had seldom cleared, going all the way back to November. This realization seized him by the throat. He couldn't remember an all-blue day, just a patch of sunny sky now and then. Could this be from the nuclear exchange reported on the other side of the world as the virus was just ramping up? If this was some form of nuclear winter, wasn't it supposed to be colder than normal?

Shortly thereafter, as Dar hunkered down in the tent one night, his throat felt sore, and the next morning he awoke with full symptoms. Severe chills alternated with feverish spells, a bad case of the trots lived up to its name, and he had no appetite whatsoever. Things got worse on the second day. He began to imagine this might be the virus at last. Even if it wasn't, why fight anymore? Who was he kidding? He yearned to drive into town, looking for help or companionship, but would have been physically unable to deal with reactivating the van, which would have gotten stuck in the snow within feet anyway. As if on cue, the temperature dipped below zero that night. He was shivering uncontrollably, panicked for the first time. Just when he'd finally fallen asleep, in the middle of a bizarre fight-or-flight dream, an explosion of broken glass yanked him awake with a start.

Dar reached for a gun but found the poker first. He froze, focused on identifying the threat at hand, and sat stock-still for a full five minutes, but there was no follow-up noise. As his senses cleared, there was a stinging sensation in his right hand, and his face felt sticky. Shielding his flashlight to the maximum, a quick, muffled halo revealed blood spots and bits of glass everywhere. Had he shot himself somehow, or been shot right through the window? He often read about shock and adrenaline taking over at first. His heart pounded wildly. Playing the flashlight around a bit more, he burst out laughing in great relief. There was the culprit, the remaining bottom half of an icy jar of tomato sauce. It had not been partially consumed like the other preserves on his board, or brought into bed like his water bottle, and with no room for expansion had simply burst in the sub-zero night close to his exposed hand.

It was dawn now, under a vanilla sky that looked through his deteriorating window on the world like white cake drizzled with the thin dark chocolate of countless slender tree branches. Dar made the supreme effort to rouse himself and restore order. His stained hoodie and sweat-drenched clothes were stuffed into a plastic bag and tossed back toward the steps. He'd been washing underthings in a plastic bucket when conditions were right, with hot stove water and a little soap, and these things could be cleaned up another time under better circumstances. Next he gave himself a good once-over with a wet washcloth, taking care not to embed any remaining slivers of glass even deeper. Shivering so strongly that his back began to cramp, Dar put on a dry, clean change of clothes, pulled his backup sweatshirt and big coat on over that, and set about making some rare orange tea. Sufficiently calmed and warmed, he cleaned up the tent as best he could. As the sun briefly reached directly in through the rear window on its daily rounds, the frigid cellar lit up like a crystalline cave.

Whatever was besetting him was persistent. He told himself he must perdure, per Dar. He needed some distraction. Swimming into the crawl space at the pendulum point between chill and fever like it was a wrecked sailboat plummeting toward the ocean floor, Dar quickly found the Travel box and retrieved a volume that had aroused his interest through two sorts already, more so because his father had a near-complete collection of this author's output. It was *A Vagabond Journey Around the World: A Narrative of Personal Experience*, by one Harry A. Franck, undertaken around 1905 and published in 1910. Franck was quite a character. According to the introduction, he set off to explore the world, inspired by some idle boasting among undergraduate students, with nothing but a Kodak camera and $104 in funds. This sum quickly ran out in Europe, and he labored for transit money the rest of the journey, making exotic stops and trenchant observations on life as he found it all along the way.

"It is easy and, alas, too often customary for travelers to weave fanciful tales," admitted Franck. "But a story of personal observation of social conditions can be of value only in so far as it adheres to the truth of actual experience. I have, therefore, told the facts in every particular, denying myself the privilege even of altering unimportant details to render more dramatic many a somewhat prosaic incident." These disarming and often somewhat calculatedly self-effacing introductory assertions are a dime a dozen, especially back then, but that is how Franck's writing struck Dar, as quite honest. It was sprinkled with some common prejudices, and the author had an especial problem with perceived laziness, but there was also much that read well and rang true. He was sucked into this book by the adventurous Art Nouveau-style panels of stamped decoration on its green covers, bodily carried through hundreds of encounters and exploits spread out over a year and a half in lands and waters far and wide, and expelled out the rear on page 502, where the final seven words are enough to describe Franck's ultimate return, when he "entered the portals of my paternal home."

Most of this read was accomplished with his head just outside the tent. As the light faded he retreated inside and swapped ends, employing the lantern. What a thrill, doing nothing all day but reading a great, good-smelling old book, with a long doze-off nap in the middle! He recalled a couple of Internet pages on Franck consulted when trying to figure out the mystery of his father's interest. There were a dozen or so similar titles spread out over a long career, most published by The Century Co. with simple but wonderful embossed covers, and his wife wrote a book of her own called *I Married a Vagabond*. When the romantic age of globe girdling and tramp steamer transit was on the wane he made a couple of trips that did not produce the expected travel book, and later in life he wrote too candidly for publication about his World War II experience as a trainer and in the field.

Were his other books as good as this first one—such a rare thing? Dar remembered another factoid, about his only other bestseller. Something about a stint as a policeman in the Panama Canal Zone, so the contemporary buzz of that setting must have given it a commercial boost. If Dar could ask him a few questions, they would be these: "Where did you learn to write so well?" Franck's background, as far as he could tell, was cattleman. "What bad things happened that you decided to leave out?" After all, he was in some very rough places and tight spots, like seedy ports, deep jungles, and high mountain passes. "This is perhaps an indelicate question, but did you make any close acquaintances with women in your many travels?" "Did you have any intimate relations with others?" would have been too direct. Discretion was probably the better part of amour with him, but there was nary a frank word on the subject, and enquiring minds wanted to know. This journeying soul had left much. How many today could do what he did, the adventures *or* the written record, in *either* century?

ΩΩΩ

Dar's generation had come of age right on the cusp of the online revolution, as earlier crops had at the dawn of printing and radio and TV. Although he had fond memories of doing things that didn't require a cable in the back of your neck, like coloring in front of the fireplace on a rainy day, he was truly addicted to the Internet himself. He hadn't quite got the damn thing on his phone yet, but its seemingly unlimited potential (he once heard Quincy Jones or somebody talking about staying awake for three days in a row at the initial wonder of it all) and the handiness of computer applications and the vast, unblinking, oft-delicious smorgasbord laid out by several hundred channels of cable TV all had him by the nads.

Nevertheless, he'd wondered how future generations would see and shape the world. "Only connect!" indeed. Yes, kids not much more than half his age were already far past what he had needed or wanted to do online, but they often seemed enslaved by the technology and infatuated with owning the latest gadgets and versions. He observed them rudely checking their messages every few minutes in the movie theater, ruining the communal escapism up on the big screen, or opening up devices one step outside the classroom, like nicotine addicts lighting up upon touchdown. These kids would have been decrying presently unimaginable youthful behaviors themselves in another five or six decades, like the sweet irony of once-rebellious graffiti artists with sagging tattoos getting their own property tagged in old age. "Get off my lawn you cyberpunks!"

On the other hand, social networking has always enriched our lives, doing your own deep or shallow research or good or bad business is enormously empowering, it tooketh away time but also gaveth it back in spades, real-time uncensored information was giving Big Brother a run for his money, etc., etc. Where had it all been heading? Damn! It was like dying in early 1942 and never knowing how the war turned out. Was there live TV or Internet anywhere in the world now, Dar wondered. "Many of your questions can be answered by visiting our website."

The night fever was back, stronger than ever. Assuming a fetal position, Dar cradled his testicles in one hand. They felt foreign, like blistered marshmallows about to fall off the campfire stick. Shaking uncontrollably, sweating profusely, he fired up the Svea for tea and company on a piece of paneling right inside the tent. This was unsafe on several levels, but the little jet roar of the burner was greatly relieving, as was the happy blue flame. Boiling water had a multiplier heating effect, though he imagined the outside skin of the tent might ice up on such a bitter night. A yellow flame meant the four ounces of fuel would last for hours, as opposed to only seventy-five minutes at full throttle, but it didn't strike the flame spreader and boil the water that way. During a lull in the shakes Dar made a dutiful trip to perform his toilet, losing two hours of warming up in that two minutes. Settling back in, too beset to fall asleep, too cold and desperate to extinguish the stove, and too bleary-eyed to read another book, his mind wandered deliriously, advancing and testing theories in a manner that provided some distraction.

Though Franck was more of a wanderer than a wonderer, reading him triggered the three big questions: Whence? Where to? And Why? And this always reminded Dar of the young Woody Allen character in *Annie Hall*, worrying about the expanding universe instead of his homework. "What is that your business?" asks his mother. She tells him he's in Brooklyn, and that Brooklyn is not expanding. "It's something he read," she explains to the visiting doctor, who allows that Brooklyn won't be expanding for billions of years and we've got to enjoy ourselves while we're here. Either you can understand the questions and work on them—even amateurishly, as Dar did—or the questions are over your head, or you grok them but choose not to waste any effort pondering them because you have better things to do, or because you know you can't change or even understand anything that big anyway.

And to stretch what Einstein said a little, either you think everything is sort of a secular or spiritual miracle or you think nothing is close to one, at least outside the framework of dogmatic religious instruction. How to explain it all! How to cast off insular blinders! Einstein also said "Common sense is the collection of prejudices acquired by age eighteen."

We are all complex yet simple bags of blood, tissue, bone, and waste product, and most of us are self-absorbed. Selflessness and parenthood and companionship can be wonderful, but you can't really *know* what it is like to be someone else. Elizabeth Cady Stanton referred to "the isolation of every human soul and the necessity of self-dependence," as well as the need to identify and reject *all* forms of bondage. We are sort of self-sovereign, as she pointed out, and you are almost always virtually alone at the very end, as she lamented.

Another barrier to mental and evolutionary progress is the theory and practice of survival of the fittest, more modernly thought of as looking out for number one, which had become easier than ever for physical weaklings who may have been weeded out quicker in the past. That's another big question though—is survival of the fittest a path or a barrier? Social Darwinists say pure path, while progressives might argue that it was a useful teacher in the beginning but now it's high time for Evolution 2.0.

Dar had spent about seven years smoking good pot (or was it ten?), and one lasting benefit of that phase, in his case, was the ability to rise up and look down at the proceedings with dispassion, largely free from prejudice and hearsay, rather like a mammalogist or entomologist in a scientifically unexplored, superstition-riddled jungle. Outwardly too. The doors of perception, and all that. The planet and probably the universe were living organisms of sorts, strung together in a way that may or may not have been figured out with more time and study. Things got the way they are and still happen the way they do thanks to science and chance. As for the human ant farm, most of us do indeed lead lives of quiet desperation. Why not cast off the yoke of oppression and save two birds—the planet and ourselves—with one stone? But nooooo!

Back to the miracle thing, it is a zillions-to-one shot that *any* of us are even here. If your mother died before you were successfully born, no exact you. Most would agree that the same goes for both sides of your family going back generations. If some ancestor had not survived this or that war and come back to mate, you would have missed out. (And what a brilliant thing, making that feel so good, to make sure it keeps happening. Does it work like that for the "lesser" creatures as well in ways that are not obvious or can't be measured, or is it just programmed in, like finding your way back solo from the ocean to the roey, milty salmon stream of your birth, or like birds building perfect first nests?) Most, however, cannot or do not make the logical mental leap that this lifeline extends all the way back to the first cellular organisms, the earliest fishes, etc.

To simplify matters, consider a primate ancestor from tens of millions of years ago, or even anatomically modern humans from hundreds of thousands of years ago, and fast-forward with your universal remote. There is a straight line from them to you. That's a lot of individual survival before mating and birthing. That's a lot of almost getting slaughtered by man and beast, living through floods and fires and droughts, nearly freezing to death, dodging infection and disease, and committing and consuming unspeakable acts and meals just to stay alive.

Most would agree that only a tiny percentage of human history has been *recorded* in any way, using that term loosely, and the vast majority of that is not very useful. How then to study and consider all that came before? Again, just so he could even wrap his head around it, Dar stuck with early humans, as distinct from earlier incarnations or other species.

We are born. Our parents usually provide the best care they can, mothers especially.

Some spark was kindled along the way, perhaps by use of the opposable thumb.

We created and employed and perfected tools.

We invented language far in advance of how other animals communicate. Yes, whales can send nuanced sonic messages for miles, but let's see them compose, record, and publish (in a trilingual edition) *XII Sonaten für Altblockflöte oder Violine und Basso continuo*, or draw up plans to retaliate against Japanese and Norwegian whalers.

We invented religion to explain things we didn't understand, and to help ease the sorrow once we became aware of our own mortality. While it could be comforting, and even liberating, religion was often used to control others rather than to help them. Hell though, possibly the whole thing *is* divine in some way—and the biggest traditional argument for that is how did it all start to begin with? Which in turn makes you wonder how many planets host natives that sit around and think about this stuff, percentage-wise. But the Supreme Being is more likely to be everything than one thing (especially a bearded guy who directs cancer cells and tornadoes in mysterious ways or keeps stables of virgins on tap). And although it would seem that what happens on Earth stays on Earth, it may be that its myriad forces and even the actions and feelings of its life forms help to create some kind of useful universal energy! Most likely, though, our home planet is just a grain of sand on an endless beach, buffeted by cosmic winds and waves, as good dead as alive.

At some point we stopped following game migrations and settled down, inventing agriculture. Staying put allowed us to accumulate greater amounts of covetable possessions. It was the same with now-permanent plots of land, and then entire territories, the natural features of which often formed political boundaries, and the natural resources of which are often finite. All this led to greed and struggle, and to small and big nationalism, and to regional conflict and finally worldwide wars.

We journeyed far from Africa, pushing the envelope in every direction, and changing colors to suit the climate. We moved relatively rapidly from basic stone tools to great pyramids, and from simple weapons like atlatls to atom bombs.

How many important civilizations had there been before the ones we know about? How many events have transpired in the sweeping pageant of human history, let alone planetary history, that are completely lost? How many birth pangs and death throes?

Dar once saw an animated online map of World War II showing the rise and fall of Nazi aggression, like time-lapse photography of some aquatic nuisance plant taking over a pond in the summer and then dying back to its point of origin in the fall. The difference with early humans is that not much contained or thwarted them—other than ice ages, disease, the lack of food and water, and past planetary cataclysms—so with us it was more like twists and turns than a predictable rise and fall.

How cool would it have been to create such maps for the spread of bipedal hominids, with statistics to back it up? Changes in physical characteristics, such as cranial capacity and height (including weird pockets like that dwarf race reduced to three feet tall by "island rule"), interbreeding among the main species, migration patterns, birth and death rates, population figures, the development of tools, etc. Some of that might have been possible through DNA and other studies, though the timelines and divergences often changed with new discoveries, and important related metrics like the prehistoric rise and influence of language were seemingly beyond our means to quantify. In Dar's green utopia, the problems of the world would be squarely addressed on one front, but academic enquiry would be just as prominent on another, with armies of historical and scientific researchers forming a significant part of the global economy.

Pallid and torpid inside the carapace of his dimly illuminated tent as he ruminated over these things for the thousandth time, Dar pressed ahead. In trying to work out human history, and to crack larger codes, he was infused with an intense general awareness of all that had come before. Scientists and specialists comprehended pieces of it far better, mega-historians could regurgitate their understanding of the whole enchilada at will, and poets could express vignettes and vistas with more pathos and grandeur, but there was some kind of curious visionary circuitry in his head that *got* the whole sweep of late human history. Not the exact details of everything these people did, of course, or exactly what was on their minds, but the physical struggle, the questioning, which seems to make us different from other animals, and the evolutionary trajectory. He paid homage to the strife, joy, and very existence of these people by reflecting on the journey of humankind rather a lot. One way to do this was by imagining and summoning up countless unrecorded but highly probable scenes featuring our predecessors. Little non-dramatic things irrefutably common to us and them, like yawning or stubbing a toe or finding a misplaced object or feeling threatened by somebody, but more specific events too. As silly as they sounded, he could make them up all day long, and most would really have happened just like that. Be there or be square.

A small band of quizzical cavemen come upon birds that are drunk from ingesting fermented berries. What's up with that they think, gesture, grunt, or otherwise articulate. (Ha, little did they know their grunting descendants would get shit-faced in man caves someday watching sports teams named after birds and other animals!)

A black panther breaches a thorn barrier in what is now Ethiopia and carries off a child, resulting in fear, grief, fence strengthening in that spot, and oral history of some duration.

In the ancient Indian city of Dwarka, one child pushes another on some temple steps, resulting in a chipped tooth or a broken arm.

Passing each other in a busy old crossroads marketplace in present-day Korea, a teenage boy zigs into a girl of the same age when he should have zagged, they smile, their nostrils flare, and their heart rates quicken.

A large fiery minable iron meteorite pierces the sky and skids to a stop in the Arctic Circle, standing in bold relief for hundreds of Stone Age summers before being discovered by intrigued Inuit.

Polynesians on what is now the island nation of Tuvalu watch the sea recede in fascination, as elders frantically warn them to seek what passes for high ground there.

A Roman soldier stops to pee in the forests of Germania and is pierced through the temple by a tribesman's arrow.

Here was a thriving Norse village (Vikings again!) near the blue water. The bearded and burly warrior chief is cut down far too young by a mysterious illness, and there is great regret and consternation among his followers as their thoughts turn toward the politics of succession.

Early Iroquois Indians wake up to warm temperatures in January, they discuss the unusual weather as we would today, and one of them jokes about planting their crops right away. (That one might be a stretch, but hey, who can say?)

A Norman lass survives the invasion of her small settlement, and is brutally raped in a cold muddy field. Afterwards, she sobs and averts her eyes while awaiting her fate.

A gigantic Dark Ages Slavic church door breaks off its hinges on one side, under bells destined to be melted down for bullets by future czars, and after much beard stroking the town fathers conclude they no longer have the resources or know-how to effect immediate repairs, that being the Dark Ages and everything, so the townspeople only use the side that still works for now.

That reminded Dar of a joke. During a solemn church service in a medieval village, a crazed man bursts through the front door, and before he can be detained by officiants and parishioners, runs up the bell tower stairs. Once on top he crashes headfirst into the largest bell, staggering back dizzy and bloodied. Before the horrified pursuers can react he repeats the process, this time stumbling out the narrow belfry window to his death on the cobblestone street far below. A crowd gathers. The local constabulary asks if anyone recognizes this man. The priest replies "I don't know his name, but his face sure rings a bell." He remembered another from a late-night comedian. Something like "Why are church doors so gigantic and heavy? So the altar boys can't escape."

Roman jokes. The whip-cracking overseer of a slave galley announces "I have good news and bad news. You can rest awhile, but after lunch the emperor wants to go waterskiing." And another.

Caesar is visiting the Northern Alps for the first time, reviewing his troops. Small pellets of ice begin to pelt the entourage. He turns to the centurion next to him and asks "What is that?" "Hail, Caesar."

Dar used to be the life of the party back in the day, with a comprehensive mental rolodex of corny, dumb, clever, and indecent jokes, but the austere version got back to the task at hand. Think of the millions of things that happen to you in a lifetime, and multiply that by some innumerable number of years and beings throughout the long course of human history. Some of these older, flickering scenes would be so unfamiliar that we'd be hard-pressed to understand them at first, but there would be much we could relate to. On the happy side, untold riches of positive human experience. On the bad or sad side, feeling their fear and pain and remorse well after the fact doesn't help *them*—though he liked to think many would appreciate the late commiseration—but it could help *us* get through tough stuff. *Zounds*, if they could stand that, I can certainly stand this. And then there's the saying about not learning from mistakes of the past. Finally, there's the huge debt. What they paid to pave the way.

Again, this visceral awareness of what came before was all distinct from the tiny sliver of recorded history, whereby the closer we get to the present, the more we really know. To pick one thing that was roughly the same in prehistoric times as now, say toward the end of the Stone Age, the more wolflike domesticated canines serve well. What can we learn about the relationship between those humans and their dogs? Cave and rock paintings, fossilized footprints, bones, and frozen or otherwise preserved remains will tell part of the story, but there are few hard facts about how we befriended each other. A Paleolithic pooch discovered in Belgium seems to have pushed dogdom back from 14000 to 31700 BCE in a single leap. We don't know how early they started naming and selectively breeding their dogs, and we don't know of the individual exploits of these faithful companions. We know more *details* about the names and breeds and history of Hitler's dogs than we do about the first twenty thousand years' worth of dog life. (This reminded Dar how he and his friends would stay up all night debating things back in those heady college days, gradually establishing the observation that the first one to work Hitler into the argument was often victorious.)

We even know that one of Hitler's favorite dogs, Blondi, his last, was mounted by Gerdy Troost's German shepherd Harras and gave birth to a litter of five in the Berlin bunker around April 4, 1945 (would Dar even be in his own bunker now if that maniac had stuck to watercolors?). We are told that Eva Braun hated Blondi and kicked her under the table, and it is recorded that when Hitler did not trust his doctor's suicide pills and ordered that they be tested on his own pet, Blondi's death was more upsetting to some members of the remaining inner circle than Braun's subsequent suicide. Reportedly, Hitler's dog handler then took the puppies from the Goebbels children (before they were murdered by their own parents) and shot them up in the garden before administering lethal injections to Braun's two Scotties and his own dachshund. The Soviets even dug Blondi up and took photos. What specific breeding history or irrefutable exploit–type facts do we know about the dogs of the entire sweep of prehistoric peoples? How much was that doggie in the limbo? *Vox audita perit, littera scripta manet.*

What about when there is a historical record but no surviving physical evidence? We know something, for example, about the famous Colossus of Rhodes, one of the Seven Wonders of the Ancient World, of which only the Great Pyramid of Giza survives. It was around 110 feet tall astride a fifty-foot-high marble pedestal, it cracked at the knees and fell in an earthquake in 226 BCE, having stood for only fifty-six years, and they let it lie there as a tourist attraction for about eight centuries, after which its superstructure was finally dismantled and its bronze panels hauled away for scrap. Pliny tells us something close to "Where the limbs are broken asunder, vast caverns are seen yawning in the interior." The main things we don't know about this statue are exactly what it looked like and exactly where it stood, though the myth about straddling the mouth of the harbor has been debunked. If light or other rays that bounced off the planet could have been caught and played back in some way someday, by someone or something, or if we could have peered back through time in some noninvasive manner, perhaps those things could have been found out. Or maybe they *were* fully known, in other quarters.

What about surviving physical evidence with no historical record? To use a famous architectural example, mute Stonehenge has been studied to death, and unanswered questions still abound.

As for mystery artifacts that pop up, as opposed to bones and building projects, early Irish brooches sparkle the imagination. Who made them? Who owned them? How did they get lost? All we know is what they are made of, how they were probably manufactured, and in the case of the most famous example, the Tara Brooch, where it was found—on a beach, supposedly, or perhaps on the grate of a inland peat fire.

Something was wrong! Dar had finally slumbered, and the camp stove water had all boiled off, blackening the small pot enough to produce a burning smell. "Fuck! Stupid stupid mistake. Don't blow it. Get through this!" Pouring a little water in to cool the pot, the violent reaction this caused rendered him wide awake again. Dar carefully placed the stove outside the tent and ran a cool washcloth over his face and neck. He wanted to change his wet tee shirt, but there were too many layers to peel off, and he was weak with exhaustion and hunger. There was nothing to do but try and get back to sleep, to ponder and perchance to dream.

A new old memory swung in now from out of nowhere, from age twelve or so. He was sitting in a tree, fittingly, ripping through a paperback edition of Jack London's *Before Adam*, which touched on some of these issues. Perhaps this book would seem hokey now, and he wished he had a copy to consult, but either way, London's dog tales and other adventures were often more than they appeared to be, capable of setting the rustless hook of humanism for life, though London was by no means without sin. "I have written a wicked book, and feel spotless as a lamb," Herman Melville said of *Moby Dick* in a letter to Nathaniel Hawthorne, though at least London knew how to make a name and a buck out of it in his own lifetime.

Different tribes of primitive hominids struggled for survival. There was a neat passage about falling out of a tree in your modern dreams and waking up just before hitting the ground. As a child Dar hadn't realized how common this dream was until he read it there. In the book, if he remembered correctly, it was explained that those ape persons who died had no "racial memory" to pass on, but those who caught a branch in time, or who hit the forest floor but did not perish, did. Almost getting killed made a big impact on them, you might say, and this was passed down to us. Or maybe London was wrong about all that, and we are just dreaming about being dropped as infants, rolling out of bed, or tipping our own high chairs over.

Could it be though that these memories and glimpses of past life were passed down similarly in our marvelous brains, and that some owned or could access them better than others? This was an intriguing possibility, but ultimately it did not matter to Dar. The general scenes he imagined were extremely close to events that had actually occurred—*had* to have, with that many beings and that much time—and that was good enough.

When you are doing genealogical research, you're probably the only person on the planet at that moment thinking about a particular common person who lived in the early 1800s or whenever. Dar liked to think that these ancestors would appreciate this. He happened upon an old passage once about a frontier woman in an untamed forest who was sweeping her one-room cabin out when a breathless fawn ran in through the door, leaving pursuing wolves just outside. That's a marvelous thing for her to have recorded. He did not know her face. Neither did he know the face or name of the early Incan who began to slide off a peak and caught some vegetation just strongly rooted enough to save him from certain death, but he knew that had really happened sometime somewhere. Close one, fawn and Incan dude!

Dar was drifting off quicker this time. What was that other aspect? Oh yeah. With the exception of widely acknowledged backsliding, like the Dark Ages or the destruction of your village, or futile underachievement, like being a Chicago Cubs fan (this too would have passed), most generations think they are "with it" and their predecessors weren't. That is to say, they kind of imagine those who came well before them thinking, Gee, we're more primitive than we'd like to be, but people will have it better off in the future. Many in the more modern era know or hope that will be the case, intellectually, but it doesn't inform their everyday behavior. It's easier to look backward than forward because there is real experience to draw on. Denizens of a particular Viennese coffee house in 1900 looked down in some ways on their fellow habitués from a century earlier—for their old-fashioned customs or funny pants or whatever—little realizing how primitive they themselves would seem to their year-2000 counterparts. John Fiske put this prettier when he wrote: "There has probably never existed, in any age or at any spot on the earth's surface, a group of people that did not take for granted its own preeminent excellence," not just over other groups, but over earlier times. We often impudently think we are the first generation to be on the cutting edge. When bureaucrats and business leaders talk about *reinventing* something, they act like it was invented once in the past and they are the very first to reinvent it, though that's usually an ongoing practice. We are alive right now, and in the moment, but that's the only *real* difference—though there could hardly be a bigger one—between us, and those who came before us, and those who haven't appeared yet.

That old *Twilight Zone* episode with Buster Keaton suddenly materialized, though he was fading fast now and was not sure if it fit in. Janitor Keaton steals the time travel helmet a scientist is working on to escape the 1890s, which he loathes (cleverly shot as a silent film). He visits the modern day where he's even more miserable, what with all the noise, the faster pace, and the higher prices. He meets a historian enamored of the earlier era who tries to go back alone, but Keaton latches on to him just in time. They arrive together, Keaton happy, the romantic quickly dismayed and soon dispatched back. The grass is often greener on the other side, and distance lends enchantment.

And what of the recent present? Poli sci major and history buff Dar understood U.S. and world events pretty well from about the Great War on. The interwar years held much fascination for him. There was want and oppression, joined by widespread economic misery, but in America the government reacted to the Depression in an effective manner, setting the stage for growth, dignity, and achievement. Look at the interesting furnishings and clothing and designs from that era, and how well things were made. Old black gooseneck desk lamps from eighty years ago worked better now, still, than modern plastic jobs produced by overseas slave labor, which had to be replaced every six months when the knob twisted off in your hand. Anything was possible then. It was an age of marvel and excitement. Look at the movies, especially before the Hays Code kicked in. Look at the thrilling magazine covers and stories. Dinosaurs in the swamps of the Congo . . . could be. Flying cars and a return to prosperity just around the corner . . . why not?

The Second World War was the defining event of the century, of course, and how many centuries had a single hinge date like D-Day? The Allies eradicated one instance of evil, but the Cold War stifled forward progress in many ways. Wartime communications had been set up in virtually every corner of the globe, remaining in place and multiplying in ability, revealing or debunking the world's mysteries one by one. Surprises from later in the century and reports of Ripley's Believe It or Not-type oddities paled in comparison to earlier wonderment. Only seven or so large "new" mammals had been discovered (by white guys) since 1900, the last of these an ox and a deer in Northern Indochina. The final holdout Japanese soldier surfaced in 1974. Interesting, but hardly as thrilling as the Labors of Hercules, or finding King Tut's tomb. We landed on the moon, but that was more of a technical achievement than a new discovery. We made great *advances*, but the mythological had become the mundane.

The 1950s through the 1970s are fascinating decades in their own way, but America often acted in its own self-interest, as per the blueprint for emerging superpowers, creating some prospects for widespread health and wealth and happiness but ruining many others. Kennedy's chance death begat Nixon, and Watergate kicked off an unrelenting, escalating blood feud between the two political parties. There was sort of a single moment around 1978 or so when the waves of progressive change began receding, beat back by Greed Is Good and abetted by the overreach and factionalism of the left. Cue the disco music.

The 1980s and beyond seemed to usher in a final loss of Old World purity and innocence—not that things were perfect before, by any means, but in the broader sense—with mixed results. Postmodern irony and cynicism became our common currency. We achieved too much self-awareness, like Skynet. The world was becoming smaller— not more diverse, as most held, but less so in many ways (dying languages, for example)—and the Internet would finish the job. In terms of changing cultures, it's all there in the pages of *National Geographic* magazine, which began in 1888. Dar remembered reading somewhere about some explorer piercing some last wild place like New Guinea only to find a Budweiser can woven into the headdress of the chief. Such incursions were not all that new. One of the photo captions in Franck's book read: "Sellers of oranges and bread in Jerusalem. Notice Standard Oil can." But the virtual global village created by electronic saturation and planetary homogenization *was* something new, though perhaps not so inevitable after all.

As the century closed out, hardball geopolitics, screwing others for profit, and relying on fossil fuels came back to haunt us. True weapons of mass destruction and the blind hatred of fanatical religious movements threatened stability on a worldwide basis. On the home front, the anti-government anti-intellectual Reagan Revolution sowed seeds of dissent and distrust that flowered decades later beyond its wildest wet dreams. We could no longer get our act together. The balance of power was shifting. The West was in decline, for better or worse.

More bolts from the blue as he drifted off, this time in retro cartoon format, slumbering on his laptop as a movie clip. Human existence is like that frenetic eight-second scene at the end of each episode of the witty 1960s *Rocky and Bullwinkle Show* somebody hipped him to. Lightning, angry black clouds, ominous music, a highly stylized moose and squirrel run for their lives this way and that but the blasted ground splinters and gives way, they rise as outlined apparitions against a vaguely religious mosaic background as the music brightens, a smiling sun fills the screen, the shot pulls back to reveal puffy white clouds over a barren field and things look right at last, a bumper crop of big yellow flowers bursts up rapidly back to front accompanied by brisk triumphant marching music, our evolved fully drawn heroes pop out of the soil front and center at peace and unscathed (though stupid moose is still half-buried), and there is a moment of silence for the first time, followed by a final comedic musical boink (the virus?) and then fade to black.

The late part of human existence—when we should have known better—is like good old Bugs Bunny burrowing up into bad places and realizing, "Hmmm, I knew I shoulda taken that left turn at Albuquerque." What if one great commonsense person or movement had come along and steered us away from the worst ravages of religion, nationalism, and the permanent upheaval of rampant capitalism (which jettisoned Adam Smith's prerequisite of a moral framework, spawned communism, and then confused that with socialism)?

As for wrecking the environment, it isn't easy to stop an ocean liner coming full speed into port at the last minute. Perhaps this virus was a timely corrective. You can have a healthy planet without people, but people without a healthy planet not so much.

Earth and the humans who crawled up through its mire had survived many deadly storms. There were fewer regular natural cataclysms now, but we had created our own, spewing poison, raising the temperature, eradicating interconnected life-forms, and surpassing an unsustainable and rapidly rising population of seven billion souls. These things he knew before. They'd chastened and hardened him. He'd studied the tactical mistakes and buffoonery of the left, and taken note of where well-meaning reformers went wrong. But just as he once realized he wouldn't be visiting as many countries and corners of the globe as previously imagined—to name one unrealized to-do list of many—Dar had gradually resigned himself to the fact that he couldn't make much of a difference after all, and would never even amount to much, save perhaps through instilling his beliefs in a strong daughter or son who might do better.

This led to a certain melancholy. He sought a better balance with the world as he found it, and girded his loins for responsible economic survival. He was in the process of putting away childish things, folding up maps, and forgetting about medals. Let somebody else be the pained pain in the ass Thomas Paine. Then came the passing of his parents and the bitter estate business that followed. Introducing a deadly worldwide pandemic on top of all that would put a crimp in anyone's evening, but Dar now felt those early stirrings again, as if perhaps he *could* make a difference of some sort in this new world.

It is my conviction that what we choose to call civilization did not begin at any of those points in time which our savants, with their limited knowledge and understanding, fix upon as dawns. I see no end and no beginning anywhere. I see life and death advancing simultaneously, like twins joined at the waist. I see that at no matter what stage of evolution or devolution, no matter what the conditions, the climate, the weather, no matter whether there be peace or war, ignorance or culture, idolatry or spirituality, there is only and always the struggle of the individual, his triumph or defeat, his emancipation or enslavement, his liberation or liquidation. This struggle, whose nature is cosmic, defies all analysis, whether scientific, metaphysical, religious or historical.

The World of Sex by Henry Miller (NY: Grove Press, 1965, the first American publication of the complete Paris edition)

FOUR

AND SO the underground weeks turned into months, and a fourth was notched at the end of the third week in April, give or take a day or two. Although there had not been many long runs of frigid weather throughout the winter, gray skies persisted. Dar grew quite certain this was due to the reported nuclear skirmishes lifting tons of particulate matter into the jet stream. If you don't like the weather in the Northeast, just wait a few minutes, it was said. The temperature and wind and precipitation still varied in normal ways, but he was a close student of the fantastic palette above, "our daily manna," and it was downright unnatural to see so little yellow and blue enlivening the skies for months on end.

The great thing about this area of the country was this changeable weather *within* the gloriously changing seasons. In winter, for example, upstate New York often recorded the coldest temperatures in the land. Crunching around in those conditions was mentally and physically challenging, and it even helped you forget about global warming a little. Yet there was not a single winter day when it couldn't hit fifty or sixty degrees, unleashing seemingly fragile winged insects from their sundry places of refuge. There were also big snowstorms and bitter weather in October and even May, of course, but all this kept things interesting.

While Dar had longed for companionship in his cold, lifeless cell, sharing this space with someone else may have proven difficult. As for pets, he greatly preferred dogs, but any self-respecting canine would have been miserable down there, deprived even of windows unless he constructed an elaborate ramp, and a single bark might have given them away. An aloof cat may have fared better, with some provocative places to prowl, but the caretaking-to-fellowship ratio militated against such a plan even if he could have lured or snatched one in time. For a cat person, however, it would have made all the difference. Looking back, he wished he'd kept some of the poor mice.

With late March came the first surprising signs of life within. Several spiders appeared, weaving wondrous webs in the windows, though the pickings were pretty lean at first. When other bugs somehow made the scene and their pantries appeared full, some of the captives were cut free out of mercy, though it was difficult to totally remove the ensnaring bonds without crushing delicate features. More than a few were damaged beyond repair, but a quick death off the web seemed preferable to the god who intervened on their behalf.

Large crickets showed up in early April, though they became dormant again whenever the temperature dipped. He didn't like how they felt on his skin, especially at night, their interest in his food, and the feeling he was being watched, and did what he could to eradicate them before they bred further. He'd smashed the first with a biography and left the body where it lay, until he noticed others feasting on it the next morning. The best method for mass extermination involved placing buckets and plastic wastepaper baskets in all of the corners, which caught them by the dozens. They couldn't climb or hop out as long as the pile of bodies didn't get too high. He was deeply thankful he didn't have to eat them to stay alive.

On one particularly warm day later in the month he noticed tiny puffpalls of pollen falling from the yew shrubs just outside the windows like little clouds of drifting artillery smoke, one after the other. There was nary a breeze, but some mechanism had been triggered. Funny he'd never noticed this phenomenon before. It was probably over shortly after it began, like missing your child's first steps because you were at work that day. Normally he would have looked for video of these pollen clouds, on YewTube perhaps, he joked to himself.

Dar was greatly invigorated by such signs of nature. He'd kept a cellar birding list, but they were all common species. At a distance he was sure of red-tailed hawks, crows, and blue jays. White-breasted nuthatches as well, a bit too far away sometimes through the obscuring windows, but verifiable, as that is the only bird in the region that follows tree trunks down toward the ground headfirst. The short tail and powerful beak were good giveaways too. Up close, just sparrows, chickadees, and juncos, though confusing spring warblers and wrens were just arriving, as were brilliant yellow and black goldfinches. One time an entire shrub outside the second window near his tent came alive with chirping sparrows, always a happy sight. You don't see hermit thrushes animating bushes like that. There was a hamlet downstate a bit, in the town of Deerpark no less, that was probably named after this phenomenon. One pioneer must have said to another, "Let us call this place Sparrowbush."

Some of the books in Dar's traveling library were his own, and among those was a nearly complete set of the basic Golden Nature Guides, many authored by Herbert S. Zim. Not *Stars* and *Sea Shells* and such reachier treatments, but the animal ones. Illustrated guides to "familiar American species" such as *Reptiles and Amphibians*, *Birds*, and the king of the hill, *Mammals*. How he loved these little paperbacks from the 1950s or so, found on the home shelf or picked up here and there in his early teens and studied like the books of the Bible. The front matter provided lots of good background information, and when you got to the individual critters, each page was a carefully arranged tableau. He reviewed these field guides now with the same relish as when he was but a lad with cheek of tan.

The first feline up opposite the Cat Family Tree page—with its badass sabertooth at the bottom—was the mountain lion, standing on a narrow ledge in browns on browns, with an arid, painted desert in the background. Three of its many alternate names are given. We learn they can grow up to eight feet long, reach two hundred pounds, and produce litters of two to five born in the spring that stay with mother for two years. Its footprints meander along the bottom of the page for identification, should you be so inclined. "Now very rare, these lithe beasts leap on prey from trees or rocky ledges."

Then there were the little habitat maps, most of which gave ranges, as with the three types of jackrabbits, but for the mountain lion it was "Originally" in blue and the shrunken "Now" in purple, reduced back east to a small strip of Florida panthers and a wider swath in the Northeast, though fifty years later the latter were thought to be truly absent. They were heading back quickly though, at least as far east as Michigan and Illinois in recent years, and the new Now of human habitation would speed things up even more. "In the early settlement of this state, this animal was believed to be a lion" read one old text on the natural history of New York. *The Catamount in Vermont*, slim, published in 1950, and reproducing photos of some famous final examples in that state, was dug out from among his father's titles for further reading on this topic.

The Zim *Fishes* was another favorite. The first individual member he highlights is the whale shark, largest of all true fishes, at close to fifty feet in length, shown dwarfing a poorly drawn boatload of pursuers (not *all* the background illustrations are well rendered, but they're fairly realistic and you get the idea). What kid wouldn't be intrigued by that, or by the weird gigantic swimming head known as the ocean sunfish (how he missed Google Images to check on that!), which was also taken for sport, the shame of killing such special animals as we understand it now notwithstanding? The circa-1955 depiction of a nighttime California grunion party was very evocative. He loved how the pier and mangrove habitat of the Florida snook was portrayed with such simple strokes in a tiny space above the sleek fish itself.

His favorite from this volume though was the trout treatment. A fly-fisherman fights a nice brookie clear across the tops of two pages, and the other three "native" species are laid out below their leaping cousin, with four nice tied flies on the bottom of the first page for balance. Although pumpkinseeds and crappies get as much respect as salmon and barracudas, Zim does diss the European brown trout, saying it can stand warmer water (a slap at any trout) and even omitting it in illustration.

Nature was stirring outside now and he could feel it right through the clammy walls. The prisoner had hacked at his hair and chopped back his beard toward the beginning, but he awoke one morning with an itchier scalp than usual and impulsively decided to take everything off, which he'd never done before. This was accomplished with scissors, a bucket of Svea-warmed water, scarce shaving cream from his travel wash kit (who was going to be putting such products into aerosol cans again any time soon?), two disposable razors, and a propped-up mirror. The process was ugly and laborious, but the end result was smooth and invigorating. His hair would come in natural now, and he would feel the new season and the new world on his face before too much longer.

"Impotent ice on April's changes / shuddering, grainy fingers strown." Something like that, about retreating winter, not too far off, from Goethe. Dar often had a photographic memory for such snippets, but not this time. So frustrating not to be able to look that up on the Net, and there was no *Faust* in the house. Even in a large research library though, you'd have to stumble upon that particular translation from the German. At least his *OED* said *strown* is an archaic form of *strewn*, so he probably had that word right. It must have been picked to rhyme with *grown*, or *flown*. *Snown*? Actually, *Half a Hundred Thralls to Faust was* in the house, from the 1940s if he recalled, but it was boxed upstairs with the other rejects. That may have shed some light, though it was really a study based on the translators, and not a line-by-line comparison of all their work. Skimming through the foreword earlier, however, Dar found the answer to a great question in his mind when it posited that nobody who knows two languages well could ever be fully satisfied with the translation of the one to the other.

He'd delved deeply into *Faust* once, on the suggestion that it so thoroughly addressed the enigma of existence, but whatever lessons it taught on that score had largely eluded him. The "Outside the City Gate" scene would always be Goethe's joyous ode to early spring though, mangled by forced rhyming in foreign tongues but always peasantly happy, redolent of moist earth on warming breezes, and emblematic of freedom from forced confinement and toil, the gaudy masses joyfully spilling out from squalid enclosures and churches dark with old night and mean cramping alleys and streets toward the hopeful advances of the new season into "the real heaven of the people," where they could dare to be human, or at least remind Faust that he was. Dar remembered bits from other translations that spoke of how the sun endureth no trace of white, snow fleeing feebly to nooks, and newly crown-less winter retreating back to the savage hills.

Looking out into his hills, it had snowed heavily over the winter, especially of late, and between that and the unusual cloud cover white was still everywhere to be seen, delaying his escape by several excruciatingly painful weeks. The road he stared at so often would probably have been brown and muddy by now with regular plowing, melting, and traffic, but it was still veiled in drifts that seemed impassable. He couldn't shovel himself all the way off this hill. He had no choice but to wait. There was no more snow up in the trees though, and water flowed freely off the roof on occasion, sending liquid suckers down to crack the foundation perimeter ice plate. Freshly cleansed sandy soil would be emerging in no time. Dar was more sick to death than ever of his unwashed cellar dirt, and would almost have put a match to the place on the way out just to set it free.

As he pined out the window one early evening, assessing the snow depth of the road in that different light, the shut-in caught some movement off to the far left. Of mammals, he'd seen quite a few deer, especially lately as they left their deep-winter yards, humped scurrying shapes one moonlit night that had to be a gaze of raccoons, to use the noun of assembly for that animal, and nothing else larger than a squirrel—not even his little pet chipmunk coming out of hibernation—but in the gathering gloom this was a lone person, probably male, the first he'd seen since the off-roaders last December! He was plodding along at a slow, steady pace, with an air of refugee resignation.

The ghostly emigrant did not look to either side and did not even hesitate at the intersection, continuing straight ahead on the seasonal road, though they were all seasonal now. Unless Dar recklessly pursued this man, his situation and purpose would probably remain a complete mystery. It struck him that there was little struggling or stumbling as there would be in deeper snow, and that the roads were probably better than he imagined, at least on the sunnier stretches. It also reminded him that scavenger types would soon be out and about too, in all likelihood.

And so the next morning Dar began to finalize preparations for departure and flight. The first thing he did was gently test the right-side steel door to see if it would budge against the weight of any remaining snow and ice. It seemed like it would do so freely, though he took care not to break the white wax seal above in spite of a strong desire to savor the full glory of fresh air and direct sunlight all at once right then in the final emergence he'd dwelt upon with such longing.

Now that he would be out of the damp tarpy pit in a matter of days, time moved very slowly. Dar made Go and Stay piles, pulled things he was taking along closer to the stairs, consolidated his food supplies, watched more snow melt, memorized the maps, and finalized his plans. He worked long hours, collapsing to sleep each night and often waking to bad dreams about what lay ahead. May Day was close now, and that became his target date. As things warmed up, the tomb stench was becoming unbearable, adding to his sense of urgency and anticipation.

ΩΩΩ

In the middle of these preparations, as he was using up leftovers and last dollops for lunch one day, two vehicles announced their approach from the same direction as before. This time, however, they parked at the *nearby* intersection, and rough-looking men bounded down and out. After a brief conversation they split into three groups, one heading up the road and out of sight, one toward Mel's, and one right down his own goddamn driveway. All that anxious waiting and wondering, and here they came.

Even though the tent was fairly well camouflaged and hard to spot through the low obscured windows, Dar hurriedly collapsed it down. Peeking from the edge of that window with one eye, he was just too late to see any faces, but their outfits spoke of crude survival, and a long gun barrel and sledgehammer rose up and down with their steps. There were three altogether. The smallest carried two dirty plastic gas cans. As they passed directly by, Dar wrapped himself in a portion of the tent far up in the corner, like a scared kid watching a horror movie, breathlessly peeling his eyes and bending his ears.

The group paused by the front door for a moment, clearly contemplating its big red X, and then they sledged and kicked it in. Dar could feel the force of these blows right down through the cinder-block walls. They issued some guttural remarks he couldn't make out and then seemed to turn their attention to the van just around back, facing nose out like a spaceship escape pod. He could hear the squeak and slam of the doors and hood as they were worked for the first time in a quarter of a year. He'd meant to lock it on that last day topside and must have forgotten.

The men continued around the rear of the house, as confirmed by the sounds of the shed door getting stoved in and items being tossed out on the lawn, but Dar didn't dare venture over to that window. As they exited the back yard from there and regained the driveway, ignoring or not noticing the cellar doors, he counted only two of them. Suddenly the missing man appeared just feet away on his side, and if he had been looking down at or in through the windows he probably would have spotted him. This was the one with the gas cans, and he must have been at that chore the whole time, as Dar should have realized. He noticed that the cans swung more slowly now, and a drab olive rubber siphon was looped through one of the handles. The raider placed them in the back of the truck and returned with two more to finish the job. "Remove nozzle, select grade." That act of thievery would be a serious blow to any escape plans.

This group joined the bunch at Mel's house, inside now, and an hour or so later the uphill contingent trudged past carrying bulky duffel and garbage bags. The fact that they drove in on the sunniest road and walked up the other indicated that the snowpack was probably still thick in some places. As they coalesced back outside and began to break open Mel's outbuildings, Dar got the impression they were mainly looking for food, gasoline, and whatever struck their fancy, like weapons or good clothing. As was the case with the previous gang, they did not seem to be especially concerned about meeting resistance. And none of them wore particle masks this time! A lone tracker who must have been following the forlorn man's footprints came back down the seasonal road empty-handed. In a close repeat of the last visit, they chatted out front and then drove away downhill.

Dar couldn't tell if some elements of this group had been there last time, but it seemed likely that this road would be frequented by such pillagers until it was fully exploited. Much of the hilliest stretch above would yield fresh pickings, and he could expect an increase in traffic. He got a better look at the vehicles this time, both off-roaders, including a neat-looking Land Rover painted flat green. They showed light streaks of mud, and he noted the ease with which they handled the road as they pulled away. Dar calculated that his van would probably make it out of the driveway and down the hill okay if he was careful about it. Just a mile or so, and then he would be on the blacktop road that saw more sun and melted more snow.

The next day rose mildly, complete with more blue sky than the recent norm. He'd planned on one more day of melting and prep time, but the events of the day before propelled him into action. Besides, in some ways it would be quicker to simply start loading the van than to continue working around all of the piles that were ready to go out. After a fortifying breakfast and more internal preparations, he suited up and got his head straight for what lay ahead.

Hunching at the top of the cellar steps and listening for sounds of human activity first, Dar finally pushed out. He could feel the snow slide off the doors in large slushy sheets, and he laid them down gently to avoid a big bang. The escapee was momentarily distracted by the rush of dank air funneling up past his bare arms and neck, beating him out, and then by a blast of unaccustomed bright light. He stumbled straight out into the back yard, in a semi-conscious effort to be completely free of that rotten chrysalis, before sensory overload stopped him in his tracks. The sights were not gauzy, and the sounds were unmuffled. Patches of grass he didn't have a good angle on from inside were poking up all over the place, baby leaves and vibrant red and green slivers of buds peeked out high and low, and the blooms of a hidden yellow forsythia bush were straining at the bit, no longer to be denied. A light breeze stirred, meltwater trickled everywhere, and then there was the sweet smell of it all and the sun's warmth on his cheek . . . all evidence of the sheer careless unfolding of whatever journey everything was on, rolling along for billions of years now— probably forward in time, probably predictably but somewhat haphazardly—completely heedless of human folly! Checking the roads quickly, which he'd meant to do first, Dar impulsively made a wet, grainy snowball and hurled it at a sapling on the edge of the lawn, surprised by how much it missed the mark. He noted with disapproval the violated shed and the litter of foreign footprints on his snow.

Glancing to the right toward the van, which would be his next order of business, there was the old metal bouncer chair, tipped against the house and happily waiting to provide more service. There wasn't any leafy privacy in the back yard yet, but Dar availed himself of it for a moment, calming down with deep breaths, adjusting to the light, and going over a mental checklist of things to do next and ways to stay alive. The biggest dilemma was age-old. What to do if you are detected and approached. How to gauge the intent of others. Those bearing weapons might be friendly, while putting trust in unarmed visitors might lead to captivity or death. It was far easier to guess how a wild animal would react.

A blue jay raised an alarm from the edge of the woods, and Dar was relieved to note that its scorn was directed at him. He'd often considered this one of the most underrated of local birds, appearance-wise, undoubtedly due to its commonness and rather raucous, bullying behavior. If the blue jay was as rare as the nearby Pine Bush Karner blue of Vladimir Nabokov fame was to butterflies, birders would flock from all corners just to catch a glimpse and sing its praises. Here was this fellow though, in such brilliant hues of blue, from sky to lavender, and with such bold bars of black and white, black-beaked, sharp-eyed, bristling its crest at him as it undoubtedly did to passing Native Americans on this same hill many moons ago, hopping around for a better look, and throwing cries to all four winds like a winged car alarm. Splendid!

That was enough nature appreciation. It was mid-morning now, and the question was should Dar leave that day or should it be early the next? The bigger, more immediate issue though was would the van start up? Everything hinged on that. His visitors had not harmed it in any way as far as he could tell, even taking care to close the gas tank door. The battery was eased in and hooked up, and *bam*, the sucker started right up after a couple of sputters, even though most of the gas had been siphoned out.

Over the intervening months Dar had gradually decided to head northwest to the Adirondack Mountains, as far away from big cities as possible, by hook or by crook. If everything went perfectly and he was unchallenged, the van would get him all or most of the way there quickly, and with lots of stuff. It was as simple as that. Walking might be safer in some ways, but he really wanted to put a couple hundred miles or so between his remnant woods and those truly deep forests right away, with his belongings, and you can't beat wheels or wings for that.

Next, Dar hogged the big van tire outside. The ground was already soft there under the snow and the job took longer than anticipated, but slate and sheets of plywood finally gave the jack enough stability. The gas tank was filled, leaving close to zero reserves. He shoveled off as much snow as possible and cleared the windows. Dar briefly toyed with the idea of removing the license plates but dismissed that as laughably pointless.

With the rear passenger seats down the van was really quite roomy. He momentarily imagined himself as the likable consumer in a post-apocalyptic Chrysler commercial, cheerfully touting the advantages of the Town & Country, including its combined wasteland mileage. Dar would have left the books for last but they had to be loaded in the middle of everything, as they would be abandoned first if necessary. He felt ridiculous doing this, and it made him doubt the wisdom of the entire plan. Different sections of the remaining space were devoted to categories such as camping, clothes, the chainsaw and gas cans, and food, with the most important items either on his person, like a compass, or near the front seat, like the guns and maps.

All this time the cellar doors were wide open. That black gash would have signaled activity from anywhere on that section of the road, but Dar just kept plugging away, hoping against hope that he could count on another day of solitude. The loading and other prep went slowly but things were finally the way he wanted them, and it was decision time again. Should he stay or should he go? When was the best time to be on the road? He should probably get past Albany in the dark but have daylight for the Adirondacks part, which was still very uncertain. If all went well, he *might* find an extremely isolated cabin where his presence would remain undetected. More likely though, roads would be impassible, or he would be waylaid, losing everything, or outright murdered. If this was easy, everyone would be doing it. On the other hand, how many were even left to try, or to try and stop him?

Just before dark Dar went out to the road to test the driving conditions, which seemed favorable enough. It was strange to be standing in the very location he'd been staring out at for so many months. This was followed by a most enjoyable dump back at the old notch, freed at last from bucket duty. With the greatest reluctance, he descended one last time into the befouled pit, bringing nothing down but a gun, a flashlight, and his sleeping bag. The young man fell quickly into a deep sleep. The mental urgency of a timely departure would be his alarm clock, but it went off a little later than planned, and he didn't wake up until close to two a.m.

Stumbling around in the dark, with only a few brief flashlight bursts for guidance, Dar started up the van and was reassured by the gentle hum of the engine. It felt like he was rising to catch an early flight, though there was also something of getting ready for the first day at a new job. He entered the spectral cabin through the front door for a last check, and noted with satisfaction that all his neatly labeled surplus boxes of books and LPs had survived the winter in fine shape. The records might never be played again, but the cover art and liner notes could still talk. Hopefully these collections would go to a good home before the roof gave way through wear, or perhaps a falling tree would hasten the process of reclamation. Would he ever come back? Probably not. Briefly contemplating if it might pay to haul the small wood stove out, he exited with nothing but the wall calendar. The front door was still hanging on by one hinge and he was able to wedge it shut reasonably well.

Dar put his van in low gear and tried to inch it around the house and onto the driveway. Two things happened. There was a significant cracking sound that he'd noticed before when moving a vehicle for the first time in months, and the tires were slipping on the snow and ice. He dug down in front of them, hitting dormant grass, but had to repeat the process several times before gaining the driveway, with its red shale purchase. Even then, it was touch and go, with some scary fishtailing toward the ditching on either side. He gunned it out at the top, countersteering to the left just in time. Less than a football field would get him to the top of the hill, where gravity would then assist, and only the off-roader ruts allowed him to reach that point in such a lousy winter vehicle.

From there down it was just a matter of maintaining the right speed. Fields opened up on the left, furrowed with retreating snow, and a few houses appeared. He began braking well before the hill bottomed out at the county road, making a left toward parts west. There were scattered patches of snow on the road where wind had deposited them or where shady trees crowded in, and his heart was pounding, but on the whole it was smooth sailing. The tires were still making a low thudding noise that was of some concern. He also realized that he'd wrenched his back digging the van out. Sometimes this pain passed right away, and on other occasions it incapacitated him for a few days, but for the time being adrenaline had come to the rescue.

Dar had finished up his last few dodgy meat strips the day before and had not eaten anything since waking up. Other than a still good supply of canned fruits and vegetables, he was down to his last regular store-bought goods, and he nibbled at some crackers while carefully working his way around natural fingers of snow across the road. Shivering, he had the brilliant idea to turn the heat on, and was blown away by the now-novel result.

As the thrill of driving again began to subside, Dar focused more intently on his surroundings. From what he could see in the headlights and under the scanty light of a near-new moon, most of the homes seemed to be in a natural state, though a couple had suffered fire damage, and one was in a flat black heap. A few front and side doors were open, and there were far fewer vehicles in driveways than there should have been, but things looked remarkably peaceful. A set of eyes close to the road reminded Dar to avoid common accidents. His thoughts jumped to the worst thing he'd ever hit, a cat, just outside of Catskill no less! He saw its final throes in the rearview mirror, considered stopping, and then remembered a friend who'd carried a beagle he clipped up to the nearest house on a desolate stretch and was badly beaten up on the doorstep for his effort.

After a while his hand automatically went to the radio. Nothing, all the way through. Not even more static on one station than another. He remembered AM radio, which seemed so prehistoric, recalling that it was the better place for emergency messages, though perhaps he was thinking of drive-in theaters or approaches to theme parks. That broadcast band was equally dead. He wondered if any genny-assisted ham radio folks were in contact with each other somewhere in the world, and felt sure they must be. An Australian communicating with a Zimbabwean or whatever. He popped the CD out and it was a bootleg of Radiohead live in Montreal. Sigur Rós fit the bill better, at low volume.

As he headed in a northwest direction that bypassed Chatham, wide striated fields presented themselves on either side. Although Dar's trusty JIMAPCO collection (named after a guy named Jim who started a map company) covered a good ten upstate counties, and he knew just where to turn, in prepping for this run he missed the ease and actuality of online aerial views. He remembered how a friend had flipped out when he viewed a red canoe up on sawhorses in his Google Maps back yard, as he'd parted with it several years earlier. Dar had never quite gotten into GPS, which old paper maps could now run rings around, but the overhead view would have helped with one uncertain part.

He reached the iconic Taconic Parkway in no time at all, however, psyched about the easy passage so far. He'd always loved this passenger cars–only highway. It was the perfect melding of FDR-type government (Roosevelt chaired the first committee on this project in the 1920s), engineering, and nature, ornamented with wonderful stonework and reaching one hundred miles south in gently curving lines that ran between the Hudson River Valley and the Massachusetts and Connecticut state lines. It was a natural conduit from New York City and the bedroom communities of Westchester County at its southern terminus, but there were no signs of mayhem or lines of abandoned cars, as Dar had envisioned.

The congealing plan was to catch Interstate 90 West a few miles up the Taconic, and then to swing northwest through the Albany area and clear up the Northway to the Adirondacks, heading west again somewhere below Lake Placid and the region of the early Great Camps. This was harsh country, but Dar had the temperament for it. Although he had taken *Walden* to heart at an early age, he'd enjoyed another classic about a family that braved the Maine woods with great success, though that was probably more doable in the 1930s, and was perhaps somewhat glorified in the telling. He couldn't remember the title for the life of him, but it was something like *We Moved to the Woods*, or *We Lived in the Woods*.

Mainly, though, he judged that his best chance was to get as far away from *people* as possible, at least until things sorted out one way or the other. No entangling alliances, and no demise at the hand of his own species. He liked the look of the water and the lay of the land better in the Catskills, with its milder climate and richer flora and fauna. The gentle Berkshires were also much closer, and for all he knew either region might be the Shangri-La survivors down toward the City were striving to reach, but the deepest woods beckoned loudest. This would be the best place to lie low, and his mind was completely bent toward that end.

The night sky wasn't bright but it was very clear. Dar didn't know how much this might help in avoiding detection, but when a long stretch in front of him appeared wide open, and what light there was illuminated the road surface just so, he switched the headlights off, slowing down to half speed. Stolen glances to either side revealed wide sections of countryside, quite peaceful under a field of stars, and largely devoid of snow. A fire twinkled far off to the north, but he had no idea if the blaze came from a single house or an entire city, or what had started it. He opened his window and drank in the cool night air, soon to be filled with mating cries and windshield splatters that had been somewhat delayed by the long winter. When tollbooths suddenly loomed ahead he chided himself for forgetting about such a potential roadblock, not to mention those damn license plate scanners, which until recently never slept. The way was clear, however, though he instinctively avoided the E-ZPass lane.

As his Town & Country approached the city the occasional wrecked car or piece of debris began to litter the highway, and Dar was forced to go back to full beams at this most dangerous juncture. He was crossing the Hudson River on the Patroon Island Bridge, about to skirt blacked-out Albany on the auxiliary interstate and break through toward the vast wilderness of the Great North Woods, when a sickening sight loomed large. Across the remainder of the span and down into the sprawling cloverleaf a vast roadblock of abandoned cars lay before him, cold celestial light reflecting off the countless curves of the automotive stylists' art. The logjam seemed to be the result of simple gridlock, rather than an intentional barrier, though he could not say for certain this far to the back of the pack, at night.

At that very moment his front right tire hit something sharp on the roadbed, issuing the unmistakable sound of a complete blowout. Dar killed the lights and jumped out, bitterly cursing himself for not paying better attention. He walked ahead to assess the situation, and to see if he could find a quality replacement tire in the bridge junkyard, eventually deciding in favor of the known compatibility of his somewhat chintzy spare. At first it was hard to say whether this jam happened all at the same time back when the virus news was just breaking, or in dribs and drabs over weeks or months, but a few rows in he could see where cars had unsuccessfully tried to turn around, trapping others in the process. A nearby gasoline tanker had smacked against the bridge railing and tipped over, blocking most of the span, its cab angling back like a broken neck. The number of open car doors and widely scattered belongings suggested great panic. Who knew exactly how it all went down? It didn't matter now.

Ω Ω Ω

The cockamamie but cultish 1970s movie *Damnation Alley* flickered up. Hackish actors travel all the way from their military base in California, from which they'd launched part of an all-out nuclear retaliation against the Russkies, to Albany, of all places, the source of a mysterious electronic emission. How original! The "Landmaster" vehicles they used were kind of cool, but the weak dialogue, weird tilted-axis sky, and mutant insects were laughable, as was the depiction of a fake, mountain-ringed Albany at the end, which had local moviegoers howling.

This in turn reminded him of *Rollover*, a somewhat muddy 1981 financial thriller with Arabs for bad guys in which the newly completed futuristic architecture of the Empire State Plaza, visible just downstream, was employed to better effect. Tepid sparks fell flat between Jane Fonda and Kris Kristofferson, and Dar even remembered the flaccid tagline: "The most erotic thing in their world was money." Another film had just been completed in Albany, a mindless CGI-laden actioner with a high SBU rating (based on a funny remark he and his college pals overheard once when some guy was complaining about a movie he'd just seen because "There wasn't enough shit blowing up"), complete with lots of physics-defying acrobatics on the nearby arterials, though they took great care not to ID the location city in that one. For movies that were supposed to take place in and around Albany, give him *The Last of the Mohicans* any day, even though it was mostly shot in North Carolina.

Crossing over the middle barrier to the south side of the bridge and dizzily peering down over the railing, Dar could see he was directly above the darkly glinting Hudson River, swollen with spring runoff and probably bright brown in the light of day. He could hear high waters rushing through grassy banks and the tips of greening willow branches far below, and the occasional tree limb or unmoored object shot past at incredible speed toward New York Harbor and the briny deep. Dar took the opportunity to add to the runoff, which reminded him of the old joke about two braggarts peeing off a high bridge. "Man, that water is cold." "Yeah, and deep too."

The river was not terribly wide here. A good swimmer could traverse it in the summer, and in olden times intrepid locals simply walked across during the hardest freezes, though one of Dar's special nightmares was breaking through river ice and getting whisked under to a swift ice-clawing, face-scraping death. It was near here, when Albany was known as Fort Orange, that Dutchfolk observed a "white whale" coming upriver, and not long before that in 1609 when Henry Hudson's *Halve Maen* made it this far up the tidal fiord, sending exploratory boats higher still. They named it the North River, a navigational term still recently in use on its lower reaches.

Dar had often imagined watching Hudson's comings and goings from the cover of shore. He'd read the journal of First Mate Robert Juet, which was scientific and somewhat commercial in nature but mingled important first-contact notes on natural history ("[Oozy] ground, and saw Salmons, and Mullets, and Rayes very great") with observations on the native population ("things of Copper they did weare about their neckes"). Currants, corn, oysters, and venison provided by the natives buoyed their spirits; the shores were lined with a "great store of goodly Oakes, and Wal-nut trees, and Chest-nut trees, Ewe trees, and trees of sweet wood in great abundance"; and fresh springwater for their barrels and "very sweet smells" emanated from the river's embankments. The inhabitants of this land were dressed in mantles of feathers and finely cured furs and were said to be a peaceful people, though there were skirmishes, and one John Colman perished from an arrow through the throat. And really, what early European visitation would have been complete without the usual shock-and-awe musket and cannon fire, trading cheap trinkets for hard-won commodities, some liquoring up, and, in this case, a good hand-lopping?

The actual source of the Hudson is at the high confluence of quaint brooks in the town of Newcomb—or perhaps it's where a piece of wet moss drips off the side of an even loftier rock, depending how you measure such things—but the poetic source is Lake Tear of the Clouds on the southwest slope of Mount Marcy, the state's highest lake on its tallest mountain. It dribbles down from there by way of Feldspar Brook, which empties into the Opalescent River, and continues to gather many other waters on its way down to the contender for greatest city in the world, created through four centuries of land grabbing, clear-cutting, earthmoving, draining, paving, and erecting. It's 315 miles long and gets to be two hundred feet deep and over three miles wide in places, with a drop in elevation of over 4,300 feet. A bona fide BFR. America's Rhine. Washington Irving wove tales of the valley's people, and the Hudson River School of painters practically founded conservationism.

If Dar could have had his choice of visits to the past, joining the Knickerbocker literati in the mid-1800s as a kindred spirit on the high veranda of the Catskill Mountain House, with its wide panorama of the Hudson River Valley, would be right up there. He was outbid at auction once on one of the salvaged columns of the Mountain House, finally burned down by the state in the early 1960s, only to be informed by a colleague after the fact that most old, white, wooden Corinthian columns auctioned off over the last fifty years for fifty miles in all directions were said to have graced the piazza of this famous resort hotel, including this much smaller imposter.

Dar did not call up these factoids, associations, and ruminations intentionally. They arrived on their own, often at odd and inopportune moments. They did so for everyone, of course, to one degree or another, but he suspected his had a different cast, perhaps more in service of the larger questions than about himself in particular. He learned to tolerate and even toy with these cogitations. They were allowed to stay in his mental system tray because this almost always had a steadying effect when things were tense or challenging.

The fact that a relative loser like him was alive and kicking, inhaling bracing air under the ancient stars and looking out over this big old city and river, at such a crossroads of humanity—the only soul around— was mind-blowing. He paid homage to those who came before, as was his wont, from coppery Indians to pasty powerbrokers, partly to put the scene in perspective. The vast majority of his attention, however, had been focused on what to do next, scanning the urban horizon for lights or activity of any sort, and looking back down the road he'd just come in on, which was dark and scary and could still convey vehicles. He judged the time to be three or so. Rising river fog began to obscure what little moonlight there was, and shifting shadows and reflections were playing tricks, but he felt relatively safe for the moment.

One of his unrealized flight check items was getting the spare tire out and ready to roll, for just such an emergency. This van was a "Stow 'n Go" model, where both rows of rear seats recede down out of sight, providing a flat cargo space with about 150 cubic feet of storage, but that dictated some monkey business with the spare. Dar actually had to consult the owner's manual to remind himself where the tools were and how to winch the tire down. You were supposed to assemble three pieces into a tire hook, but that was easier said than done under the circumstances, and he had to jack the van up, shimmy all the way underneath, and fight the spare off its cable instead. In the middle of this risky operation, his already strained back was wrenched anew, and this time the injury was deeper.

Cracking the old tire off and swapping it out was painful but manageable. His eyes were thoroughly adjusted to the dark, and there was just enough natural light to get the job done, with occasional brief help from his flashlight. Dar threw the blasted original in the rear, just in case. Stepping back for a better view, he became alarmed at the wimpiness of the donut replacement. Would that hold up at high speeds, and over obstacles? He'd noticed the manual warned against exceeding fifty miles per hour on it.

Dar stepped up to the north side of the bridge this time, wiping his dirty hands on his clothes and wishing for a little soap to do the job properly. He was more winded and shaky than he should have been. He patrolled the area behind the van where he would need to turn around, found the damaging hunk of fender that had farged up his tire, and heaved it far out over the dark roiling torrent, causing him to cry out in back pain. Think, fool! No room for more error.

Plan B had called for crossing the next bridge down, but rather than backtrack for miles, a quick look at the map indicated he could simply exit via the ramp he'd come in on, which would normally be ill-advised, and work his way over to the Dunn Memorial Bridge. He didn't know who Dunn was and why he was being memorialized, but this led directly to Western Avenue, the downtown Albany part of Route 20, New York State's answer to Route 66, which he was quite familiar with. The Great Western Turnpike was once lined with the kitschiest of tourist traps, including a last holdout giant teepee structure—complete with a life-size model buffalo out front in case that was not enough to get your attention—that still sold moccasins and stuff all those years later, but it was kind of a dead highway lately. Just a way to get to your low-wage job at a giant distribution center or regional convenience store or whatever.

This bridge was relatively free of automotive detritus, but another dead fleet of caught cars quickly came into view not far past its terminus. By making lefts and rights away from the Empire State Plaza, however, in all its governmental impassability, he was able to snake up through outlying neighborhoods. "Junk cars—up to $150 cash!" read a roadside sandwich board.

At one point he passed his beloved Spectrum on Delaware Avenue, an art-house movie theater once bursting with vitality, and still showing good memories. They ran home slides before the previews and served great coffee, cheesecake, and nut brownies. A decade earlier Dar had a light crush on a quietly edgy counter girl there, also in her late teens, a slip of a thing with spiky blonde hair. This ethereal creature seemed oblivious, but she once sat one seat away in a green-and-white-striped belly shirt for an under-attended but immersive afternoon showing of *Apocalypse Now Redux*. They chatted a bit, and laughed together when the leaping tiger startled her. He should have asked her out somewhere when it ended but figured she was already spoken for, or wouldn't be interested.

Dar pulled down an open side street to regroup, finding and parallel-parking into a good space, just like the old days when the theater lot was full. He contemplated the likelihood of more jams toward the closest approaches to I-90 West and the Northway. Most of the streets around this part of town were either gridlocked or down to a single lane. Cars were up on lawns at funny angles, presumably towed or pushed out of the way when there was still some semblance of order. He'd spotted serious barriers across a few streets, which would be a good way for cityscape survivors to keep wheeled troublemakers out. There was simply no way of predicting the best way to proceed. He felt like a sitting duck, and the darkest part of night was about to begin receding. A slight breeze shook a few pink cherry blossoms down onto his hood. Whoever lived there must have loved that tree in the spring.

Just then, well behind him in the rearview mirror, two vehicles passed by slowly, seemingly on the hunt. This was confirmed by the swinging of a mounted spotlight that smacked of predator or protector. Dar supposed there was a possibility they could be some type of police, but he didn't want to take that chance. He scrunched down in his seat behind the high headrest, relieved that he'd turned off the van and kept his foot away from the brakes. When they were safely out of sight, he pulled out with just his parking lights on at first, working slowly toward the nearby medical zone. Two large hospitals were located there, encircled and suckered by numerous health-industry remoras. He'd meant to bypass this area, as it had probably been a scene of panic toward the end, and was able to skirt around at the last minute.

Consulting his map, he worked his way back to Route 20, opting to go west awhile before picking up the Northway, but once again the ramp he needed was completely filled with abandoned vehicles as far up as he could see. Soon he passed the entrance to the area's largest mall. He knew there was a final chance to reach the Northway via the mall service road, but that was probably subject to the same jam, and this vast parking lot seemed imminently dangerous, the kind of place where new zombies go out of habit. Getting killed at Crossgates Mall would be a fate worse than death, so he continued west. Route 20 soon began its slow transition from city to country, and smaller businesses with broken doors and windows lined both sides of the avenue.

ΩΩΩ

The first faint rays of early dawn began to streak the sky. Dar had hoped to be on secondary or dirt roads in the Adirondacks by now, but that had always been the best-case scenario. As he headed toward the western border of Albany County, a new plan emerged. He would take Route 30, coming up very soon now, and hope to cross the Mohawk River into Amsterdam and parts north. This felt safer somehow. An old tune darted up. *"Here I go, swinging low, across that county line / The noose that was around my neck is far behind."* The biggest drawback was that bridges are always natural choke points. Dar knew he was lucky to get across the Hudson to begin with. If the Mohawk was blocked at Amsterdam, he could try farther upriver at half a dozen others, but that might be a bridge too far. The more time on open roads the greater the risks, and then there was the gas tank to consider.

As Dar mulled all of this over, reflective tape in the distance put him on alert, and he soon came upon a semi-official-looking roadblock at the northerly turn onto Route 30, with orange traffic barrels galore and the warning "Keep Out!!!" scrawled across one of the barrier slats. He got out for a moment to determine why this had been set up, and to see if there was any way around it, but whoever erected this thing had it buttoned up pretty tight. A deep, bouldered ditch and muddy fields before the turnoff were impassable. On the other side of the barrier, the farm operation on that corner might lead through, but why go through all the trouble of setting up this substantial bulwark if there was such an easy workaround? That might even have been a natural ambush spot back when there was more traffic.

Dar's lower back was somewhat stable in the generous van seat, but climbing down and walking around produced sharp pains. It was still fairly dark out, but in another half hour the headlights wouldn't be needed anymore. As he rounded the far side of the barrier a shadowy figure was standing right there! Dar jumped back, spewing out *"Fucker"* at the same time. He fumbled with the strap of his belt knife, admonishing himself for not bringing the gun. The son of a bitch just stood there, without moving a muscle. Dar could make out a cowboy hat, and his posture was weirdly relaxed, with a bent knee and one foot up against the barrier. And then it hit him like a carnival-bell hammer that this was just one of those stupid yard silhouettes, cut out from plywood and painted black, even lower on the good ol' boy and cutesy-poo evolutionary scale than bad chainsaw art or the Bent Over Lady Gardener lawn ornament. It had been spiked through the stomach and cabled around the neck to remain standing against the elements. Dar considered snapping it in half over his knee, thought how that would not agree with his back, and then had a little chuckle on behalf of whatever knucklehead put it there.

"Jesus Christ!" Dar muttered as he climbed back into the van. "Time to stop screwing around. What am I gonna do? *What's the plan, Stan?*" As he looked for the right map, faint but muscular engine sounds drifted in from straight ahead. He rolled his window down to confirm the unmistakable approach of multiple vehicles. Dar gunned his big van through the southern turn, which was not blocked off. He wanted to kill the lights but couldn't afford another mishap. No time to look at maps now. He knew nearby Route 7 would bring him west toward Cobleskill. Maybe these cars were heading toward Albany and wouldn't even know he was circling right past them. Maybe he could still take to the North Woods by dropping down and crossing the Mohawk through the town of Palatine Bridge or thereabouts. That route would actually go past his old house, the former but not future hop farm.

As these thoughts were racing through his mind Dar checked the gas gauge, only down a quarter but about to plummet after that hash mark the way many modern cars seemed to. He kept looking in his rearview mirror. Nothing yet, but those sounded like serious prowlers to him, unless things weren't so bad out west and somebody was filming *Damnation Alley 2*. He was hitting about eighty on the straightaways now, but it felt very risky on that tire. Just as quickly as he had entered the lowest corner of Schenectady County not much earlier, he now saw a sign for Schoharie County.

Dar mopped his brow and made sure a gun was close at hand. Even these simple movements caused bad back twinges. His most important portable supplies were in his trusty getaway knapsack on the front seat, and he felt his way to a bottle of painkillers with tire-greasy fingers, downing several. He stuffed a little strawberry jam into his mouth for energy, swigged some water down, and spit a portion back on his hands, wiping them on his shirt for a better grip on the wheel. Another physical need would be harder to address. His stomach had not been right since waking up, and he needed to stop soon before the shit hit the van. It was difficult to contain such internal pressures driving that fast, for your life, with a back that could not contort much.

Two sets of headlights were visible far behind him now, so the race was on. Interstate 88 ran parallel, built in the 1970s when infrastructure wasn't such a dirty word. It was a divided highway, great for truck traffic, and constructed in part as a safe alternative to the historically deadly road he was on now. The two routes ran close together, the interstate lanes high above and to his left. At the first entrance ramp he came to, Dar signaled left—an obviously ludicrous move, but double-stupid enough to perhaps throw them off—began the turn, switched his headlights off, and shot straight ahead. Both cars soon appeared on the upper highway heading west, probably aware of their mistake and suitably pissed off. If he could beat them past the next exit, he might gain the northern route and elude them.

The pursuit had the feel of a practiced routine, and Dar wondered if this was the end of the line. What had triggered the chase? Was there a trap ahead? Should he just pull over with the lights off over a rise and head back east when they passed? If escape was impossible and he was outnumbered by his assailants, he resolved to avoid a shootout, surrender whatever was demanded, and simply explain where he was going and why he ran, without any unnecessary details. Who wouldn't run? He still had a chance though. This wolf pack did not seem to be operating at full efficiency. Perhaps it was the B Team night crew.

The nice, somewhat sleepy agricultural-college city of Cobleskill was coming up rapidly now. There were all the new category-killer box stores and franchises that saved the locals from having to travel to Oneonta or Albany for the same goods and experiences. There was the rusty silver overhead railroad bridge that marked the east end of town. There was the bowling alley way up on the hill where he once had to go fetch his drunken father home at closing time. The main drag, thick with small businesses and fast-food joints, passed by in a flash, and before he knew it the more picturesque brick building part of town and his turn to the north were coming up. Things seemed dead, but it was still very early in the morning. Dar had to assume the high pursuers were about to drop down through the Cobleskill exit behind him or the Warnerville exit coming up just outside of town. They would be smart to split up for the final takedown.

Preparing for the sharp turn, a large white vehicle waiting in the middle of the intersection alarmed Dar, and he made a split-second decision to keep going straight, noticing too late that it was only an abandoned ice cream truck covered in obscene graffiti. The van did not take kindly to this weaving, and for a moment he thought it was going to roll over. Jamming on the brakes to avoid running up on a light pole, all hell broke loose inside, and the unsecured blown tire flew forward across the top of the book boxes with such force that it broke the spine of the passenger seat. Dar accelerated again. He knew that every move counted now but felt he was losing the battle, and losing control. For further confirmation of that, a squishy feeling in his baggy blue jeans meant that a certain amount of pent-up diarrhea had escaped at last. He cataloged another setback, a throbbing pinky, possibly broken.

Contemplating the probable prospect of getting his head broken, or fuller disembowelment, Dar got back to evasive maneuvers. Blasting out of the other side of town, the next cut-off he needed to pick up the northern route was blocked off with a triple row of junker cars. This was obviously to funnel incoming vehicles to the center of the spider web, but it also had the effect of pushing him toward the city of Oneonta and parts west. Calculating that the interceptors would be on him one way or another in mere moments, he made the first good left he could up a curving country lane, slowing down a bit as visible grit on the surface there might have slid him off the road.

He glanced to the rear in both directions just before rounding the first big turn and was relieved to find no one in sight. If nobody had seen him in the last ten or fifteen minutes there were a couple dozen residential streets or larger roads he could be on, and after just two or three curves he thought he might have shaken them.

Dar was heading south now, getting farther off course. He passed what looked like a proverbial one-room schoolhouse down by a creek. He spotted a glorious bluebird in a hedgerow, in brighter hues than ever somehow in the early morning light, and watched it flit out to a newish birdhouse in the fantastic Benton-meets-Wyeth field above. Fruit trees were in full flower here already, owing to the lower elevation and direct sunshine. The houses he passed were small but generally tidy, with a wonderful old farmstead a few miles in, and a small business or two, like the friendly-looking Pat's Place of Hair. A beautiful white church sat right on the road, and silent red barns dotted the hillsides, one with late-baled hay for the loft still on its conveyor belt.

Dar was sorely tempted to pull over for a while to get his bearings and lick his wounds, not to mention finishing his bathroom business, but those hunting him were not likely to give up easily, and he needed to be sure he was well rid of them. He continued on but was abruptly dumped out onto a county road that either led back toward Cobleskill, or farther south toward a couple of hill towns he was familiar with, Summit and Eminence. Suddenly vulnerable to rediscovery, Dar chose the high road away from trouble. Actually, he'd been trying to head away from trouble since he left, but things kept getting worse. This was really the only logical choice though. Maybe he could lie low for a couple days and then look for a safer passage to his Indies.

Summit was a back-of-beyond town, perched above two thousand feet with glorious views of the Schoharie Valley, and home to about a thousand residents before the virus. It had always had a Wild West feel to him. A buddy was drinking in a bar there once and got knocked unconscious from behind with a beer bottle. It turned out that the assailant thought he was dealing with the guy's older brother, and when he came to they had a laugh and a drink over that. Summit has a beautiful high lake, but the boarding house era had come and gone, the village band was long ago disbanded, and until it got closed down by the state, a shock incarceration facility there was probably its biggest ongoing claim to fame.

ΩΩΩ

Reaching the summit of Summit, the tiny town appeared completely deserted. The high-plains drifter dove down the more subdued-looking of two hollows, doubling back east now. This was a real road out, and not just a long shortcut like the last one. It went on for a good four or five miles, following a small meadow creek, and the terrain was very pleasing, being a mixture of open fields and dense woods. A few shady nooks held pockets of snow. Dar slowed down. He had a strong desire to pull over and take a nap. A pair of large clouds over the distant hills ahead looked just like big puffy sails. He rolled the window down, and pleasant birdsong and spring fragrances wafted in to lighten his mood and load even further. What a difference a little time and location can make, he thought. Homes popped up on occasion, some of which appeared to be seasonal bungalows.

A boxy purple insect trap hung from high up in a tree, on the lookout for deadly intruders such as the emerald ash borer. One couldn't blame politicians for not retrieving their lawn signs last November, since they barely did so under normal circumstances (he recoiled at the memory of a shooting range that accepted all leftovers for target practice but only used the ones they didn't support), or landowners for erecting signs of their own. "Dog Xing." "Boat for Sale." "No Pipeline!" "Looking for a Little Honey? Turn Just Ahead."

The road eventually came to a small, peaceful T intersection that Dar found most endearing for some reason. He turned the engine off and just took it in for a few minutes, trusting that some jumpy local didn't have a rifle trained on his skull. What a placid corner of the Earth! It was a humble crossroads where two farm lanes met, paved over now, a natural meeting place if there was anyone left to meet. What got him was the quietude. Nothing at all was moving.

It was like a photograph. It was in places and at times like this that the incredible fact the planet could rocket through hostile outer space without mussing a single hair really hit home.

Simple green and white metal signage told you what was in each direction. A newer house was just to the left. A strange vision of its residents in their driveway hastily preparing to vacate the premises came out of nowhere. A farm operation was visible farther up on the right, and that was about it. He turned left, which looked a little quieter, passed one other house, and finally pulled up opposite sunny fields that would have warmed the cockles of a French impressionist's heart. Dar stepped out in all his wincing, odiferous besplatterment, quite the spectacle. It seemed eminently tranquil and safe right there after such a wild ride and close escape. He examined the sand and gravel on the road and the grassy borders for any signs of fresh tire treads and then took a few steps into the woods to finish his business and clean up a bit.

Time to get his bearings. Dar could see from the county map that the road he came in on and the one he was on now both traveled downhill to the left of and relatively close to their respective streams, though in truth the streams had spawned the roads. These waters joined straight ahead of the intersection, just out of view, and then circled to the left behind the farm fields he now admired, natural recipients of centuries of rich runoff. High road and low stream traveled along together like irregular undulating wavelengths for another six miles or so, rubbing elbows here and there but mostly out of each other's sight. Map and sign said West Kill Road. As the road that he followed down to begin with had the same base name as its companion creek, it stood to reason that the commingled flows constituted the West Kill Creek, but his otherwise detailed map was silent on that subject. No matter. The important thing was that the road ran right down to the town of North Blenheim and the same Route 30 he'd been turned away from earlier that morning, though well south of that spot. And this looked like an ideal place to regroup, starting with a dip in the stream.

Proceeding down past a few nice houses and a couple of trailers on small lots, he appeared to be entering a wilder area. A Conservation

Department sign on the left announced something called the CCC Road that took right off into those woods like nobody's business. Not many steps farther was a pleasant stream that the map identified as Betty Brook, with its own companion road. Presumably these routes splayed apart farther in, as you wouldn't attempt to subdue a rough and rocky forest floor like that without good reason. He pulled over, brought the rifle out with him this time, and decided this little brook would be safer to wash up in than the much larger stream, which was usually far down a steep bank even at its closest juncture.

Stepping back out for a final check, Dar noticed something he hadn't seen at first. A rather large tree was lying across the road, just visible over a near rise. He decided to drive up and see what that was about first, as he would be trapped in the unlikely event that those road warriors showed up behind him. Luckily it was a pine tree, quite large but easy to cut. All he would need to do is make a space wide enough for the van to fit through, and that section would probably even roll out of the way for him in one chunk with a couple of good kicks. He judged how much noise such work would make, but was reassured by the fact that any holdouts in the area would probably have removed this blockage themselves some time ago. This was no intentional barricade. It had fallen over at the roots, probably in a big wind. The only real problem would be his bad back, as even the smallest movement brought sharp pain. His sore pinky was bothersome too. It was warming up good now, and the job would be sweaty and sappy, so he decided to get the chainsawing out of the way before bathing with Betty.

Dar donned his work gloves and primed his trusty orange Stihl, which started right up. This retrieved an old auction memory, when a full set of antique ice-harvesting tools came up once. Saws, breaking bars, axes, hooks, tongs, pike poles, and the like. Some newbie shouted out that they weren't worth as much as unaltered originals because most of the pieces had been painted orange, much like the pretty scenes inflicted on old saw blades and milk cans, and the ruination of cleaning or refinishing early weapons and pieces of furniture just to make them shinier. Before the world-weary auctioneer could reply, an old-timer did it for him. "You ever drop an iron bar in fifteen feet of pond water, sonny? That's why they painted 'em orange back then." Same with a Stihl on the forest floor. Outside labor again! Dar could tell if a chainsaw was being used properly from half a mile away by the sound and cadence of the work. He undercut the log first, taking care not to pinch the blade, and maul and spike were at the ready just in case.

Things were going smoothly at first, but ominous cracking noises called for a reevaluation. This enormous tree was tipped up by its roots on one side of the road and hung up by its crown on the other, bringing tremendous pressures to bear in the middle. Dar was plumb exhausted from the events of the last few days, he was weak from inactivity to begin with, and he knew he wasn't quite thinking straight. He needed a good sleep and some solid food. Nothing would please him more than setting up camp there and going down to the stream for a possible trout dinner after all those nights of sloppy tomatoes and stale scraps. That pleasant thought strengthened his resolve to get the chore over and done with.

Just to be on the safe side, he humped over the trunk, as it seemed less likely to explode out and impale him in that direction. He cut in as far as he could from top and bottom, widened the notch at the top, set his spike, and came down on it with the maul, swinging with as much force as his back would tolerate. The ringing of iron on iron up and down the valley was soon followed by the rifle-shot crack of the mighty tree split asunder. When both halves snapped back to where they wanted to be, he could see that the second cut would be much simpler and set to work on that. The chainsaw growled and the chips flew where they may.

Fairly fresh pine cuts a lot easier than dead elm or oak. The big middle section fell straight down as planned but was still pinned in at the top. Normally he might have urged this straight away by simply sitting down and pushing it with both legs, but he was spent and hurt. Instead, he made one quick clean cut down the middle, taking care not to dull his blade on the macadam underneath, and then the four-foot pieces were easily relocated. One rolled close to the van down below, which could have been incapacitated by such a blow, and for an instant he pictured the scene in a redneck segment of *America's Funniest Home Videos*, but the huge disc wobbled away at the last moment and plopped down off to the other side.

Dar shook some of the chips and sawdust off his person and returned the saw to its case, taking care to wipe the blade first with the short white cotton sock whose retirement job that had become. Feeling the need to catch his breath and rest his back for a moment, he slogged through a low wet patch of grass to the wooded border closest to the van and stretched out on the more elevated forest floor there.

It was gorgeous out, the first of May or very close to it by his reckoning. Whenever he had a regular job he'd almost always managed to take May Day off, calling in sick if all else failed. He took a couple of deep breaths and thought about how good it was to be out of the cellar, and off the mean streets. He didn't know all of his flowers, but several clumps of fringed polygala were nearby, with their underbrush-creeping stems, wintergreen-like leaves, and small delicate magenta blossoms. They looked like miniature orchids, which is why he'd looked them up once to begin with, having discovered a hillside colony in a grove of young birch trees, a composition of sheer perfection. He wished he could paint such things, but even his stick figures came out bad. This flower was said to increase milk production in nursing animals, and was also supposed to be an Iroquois remedy for inflammations of the skin.

Real hunger gnawed at his belly now. Still in recline on the forest floor, Dar turned over a rotten log looking for fishing worms and was delighted to discover a fine red-backed salamander there, though he always thought of them as russet-backed. This was a splendid specimen, angular, alert, pulsing with life, and seeming to stare back at him. His first instinct was to pick it up, but they were fast, he knew the tips of their tails detached pretty easily, wriggling around to distract pursuers intent on a meal, and he didn't really need the extra slime, though salamander slime was good slime. Maybe it burned or sickened you when it came from neon salamanders in steamy jungles on the other side of the planet or from certain parts of New Jersey, but not around here.

A large night crawler had instantly pulled itself down into a chamber of loose compost, and Dar was able to wholly extract him or her (they all have both male and female sex organs, if he recalled correctly, and could screw any worm they ran into, which would kind of make up a little for having to be a worm). Holding this primitive creature up to the light and admiring its simple features, Dar heard a small sucking sound just behind him toward the roadside. Turning around rapidly and grunting in pain from the effort, he saw a pair of serious-looking men, one with a large shotgun pointed directly at his gut. "Stay right where you are, mofo!"

"He korero taua ki Wharaurangi, he korero ta matau ki Otuawhaki."

The talk is all of war at Wharaurangi, but at Otuawhaki they speak of the making of fishhooks.

Wharaurangi is the hill above the famous rock Pohaturoa, while Otuawhaki was a pa [fortified village] where fishing canoes were kept at the riverside. A contrast is made between the interests and conversation of warriors and fishermen.

Reeds' Lilliput Maori Proverbs by Aileen E. Brougham and A. W. Reed (Wellington and Auckland: A. H. & A. W. Reed, 1976 reprint)

ΩΩΩ

Come, come with me my sunset kin
Down the Valley of Long Ago
Along babbling waters that flow
North and soon Mohawk's wed.

There, where Blenheim snugly lies
Between hills of birch and pine
Along this little river Rhine
Beneath the Valley's azure skies.

And farther down thru dorf and fort
As early Indian trails ran
Where the sturdy Dutch began
Their freer life to court.

Motor with me over trails away
Past crowded farms along the way
Marking paths of an early day
When Indians wild held full sway.

Come boys, off with me
Thru this Valley of Long Ago
Whose babbling waters still flow
Singing their way to the sea.

I'll take you first to Blenheim town
To the wooden bridge of great renown
And as we walk its mapled floor
You'll see the arch from shore to shore
That holds suspense this steeless crown.

Folks and Places Along the Schoharie 1888–1945: Highlights of Sight-Seeing Trip of the Author Thru the Schoharie Valley Accompanied by Frank J. Quincy and Stockton Quincy, Jr., His Grandsons by Frank Noxon James (Los Angeles, CA: the Author, 1945, with minor revisions from the 1946 second edition)

FIVE

"WHOA whoa whoa—*wait*," Dar blurted, thrusting his hands out palms down and waving them in a calming fashion. "I'm just passing through. I don't mean to trespass."

"*Trespass*? Hell! Who are ya, and what are ya doin' back here?" snarled the gun toter as he bent down for Dar's rifle. He was a buck in his prime, two or three inches taller than Dar, broad-shouldered and muscular, with a drooping dark brown mustache over a short black beard, impossibly white teeth, and heavily browed, angry eyes that drilled right through you—half Hollywood hunk and half caveman. He was quite agitated, but Dar calculated that if they wanted to indiscriminately kill him they probably would have done so already. He noticed a holstered Peacemaker under the big man's light slicker. His older companion seemed unarmed.

"Like I said, I'm just passing through. I drove over from Columbia County last night. I was chased by I don't know who and ended up here totally by accident. This is the—"

"Were you followed?" asked the other man in an urgent but calmer tone. Dar took a good look at him for the first time. Slightly shorter, balding, and with a little red still at the temples, he could have been a Lenin impersonator, with a healthy dose of Pete Seeger mixed in. Both men were wearing sturdy bush clothing and hiking boots.

"No. It happened hours ago," Dar replied, fibbing on the timeline so as to decrease their ire and anxiety. "They were chasing me toward Cobleskill, I snuck up to Summit on a side road, and I came right down here by pure chance. They have absolutely no idea where I went. I'm pretty familiar with the county. All I wanna do is get to North Blenheim and get back on a bigger road. I see on the map that it's straight ahead."

"There's plenty of ways to do that without—"

"Hold on," interrupted the senior partner. "Let's start over. What is your name?"

"Dar."

"What kinda name is that?" demanded Crazy Eyes.

"That's a first name."

Lenin suppressed a small chuckle, and Dar caught an intelligent, even kindly twinkle in his eyes. This obviously was the one he needed to work on. Just then a third figure came up the bank on the other side of the van, which answered the question of where they had materialized from. He carried a sleek rifle comfortably in the crook of his arm.

"Everything okay here?"

"Yes," replied the apparent leader. "We were asking this pilgrim a few questions. Apparently he was just passing through the county and got chased up here. He does not think he was followed, and I'm inclined to agree or we would have heard shooting instead of chainsawing." Damn, thought Dar, I *did* give myself away with that noise.

"I'm Bennie," said the new arrival.

"No names," growled the Cro-Magnon. "You know the rules."

"Whoops, my bad."

The leader wanted to get back to his questioning. "Where have you been living? Where are you headed to? What is your plan?"

"Well, to tell you the truth, I wintered in a lousy cellar, and I just want to get away from big towns and cities. This is my first day out."

"Your first day out?" repeated the older man incredulously.

"You sick?" asked the big man. "You don't look so good."

"I hurt my back bad. And I'm really beat. I was just hoping to stay here overnight and then be on my way."

"Well, ferget about that," said the brute, turning to his companions. "He's rollin' around in the dirt sweatin', it looks to me like he shit his own pants, and there's dark *blood* on his shirt. Fer all we know he has the sickness. We shouldn't even be this close to him. And he certainly don't look like no provider. We caught him eatin' a *worm* just now."

Provider of what? thought Dar to himself.

The kinder interrogator gave the antagonistic one something approaching a dirty look, but composed himself. "I don't see any of the symptoms," he responded.

"Look," said Dar, "I've been underground for four months and I'm weak from that. I've been driving all night, and my stomach's off because I ate something bad—spoiled meat I think. The guys chasing me didn't say anything about a restroom break, that's strawberry *jam* on my shirt, and I was getting worms to go *fishing*."

"Do you have any other weapons, Dar?" asked the leader. It was the first time anyone had addressed him by name in a long time.

"Yeah, some other guns in the van. And my belt knife." He slowly lifted up his shirt to show them the blade, and its surrender was neither offered nor requested.

"Do you mind if we look?"

"I guess not, but I need everything I brought with me."

"Okay. Why don't you two take a look and report back. I will chat with Dar for a few moments in the meantime."

"I know what I have. Why don't I just tell you?"

"You ain't really in a position to make demands, peckerhead," said Shotgun Man. "A minute ago you were beggin' fer yer life."

"Sorry, Dar, but let's do it this way. You guys get started. We need to get out of here as quickly as possible."

"All right," the still-seated detainee replied, "here's the keys." He fished them out of his pocket, opened the trunk and both sliding doors automatically, and tossed them to the latecomer.

"Hey, fancy. Thanks."

"No problem," replied Dar. "Just don't lose them. The replacement cost is something like two hundred and fifty bucks." Dave and Bennie laughed.

As soon as the men had their heads inside the van, the leader leaned in closer. "Sorry once again. My name is Dave, and that is Rick.

He does not take very kindly to strangers, as they used to say. He is usually manageable though, and a good man to have. We are a little protective here. We have to be."

"Well, where's here, Dave? What are you doing back here? What's your base of operations?"

"What we really have to talk about first are your plans," replied Dave. "You got a good taste of that road crew today. They will lie back and let larger convoys through if they look strong, but not singles. From what we hear, they do not like it when one gets away. I don't think you would have much of a chance heading back north from the bottom of this road. Maybe south, or due west back the way you just came, on smaller roads like this. But you would probably run out of gas or get caught, and if you don't get killed in the process somebody would probably torture our location out of you."

Rick returned with the guns and laid them out on the grass. He kept his hand on his holster while listing the inventory. "The pump-action Savage 30-30 he had. It's a Model 170. An okay deer rifle, but not that reliable. The lifter don't always center the right way, and the cartridge rim gets hung up or jammed in the chamber. Next—"

"I never had a problem with it," interrupted Dar.

"That's probably 'cause you only shot it at stumps or far-off tails once every few years. Next is a nice scoped Winchester Wildcat varmint model bolt-action .22 with two magazines, a five and a ten. Perfect plinker. Then there's a little Ithaca .410 bore shotgun, a *ladies* model." Dar bristled at that swipe. He'd received this from his grandparents at about ten years of age, used but very clean. It might be a junior model but it got the job done, and he loved the look of the blond checkered stock and the feel of it on his cheek to that day. Come to think of it, that was probably about the oldest personal item he still owned. "There seems to be lots of ammo fer all of these."

"Okay, thanks," said Dave. "Keep going. See what else." The search warrant had broadened, but Dar didn't protest.

About halfway back to the van Rick wheeled around. "Oh yeah," he sneered, fiercely staring Dar down, "and then there's a SIG Sauer P250 9 mm handgun tucked under the seat. That's a serious hunk of hardware.

It don't fit the rest of the group, and I don't see no extra bullets fer it. Is that one of the things you was goin' to tell us about by yerself?"

If Dave was perturbed by this development, he didn't show it. "Please finish up, boys."

"Anyway," continued Dave, once they were back out of earshot, "I am going to be blunt with you in the short time we have. We are somewhat divided on the topic of how to handle strangers, as you may have noticed, but it is a violent world out there now. It would be a shame for you to perish so soon after all that time holed up. Why don't you consider joining us, at least for a few months? We are trying to start something new here. Frankly, we could use some help, once you are up to it. Stay overnight, rest a spell, and let us give you some good warm meals. Let your back get better. See what you think. If you really need to leave, we will let things die down for a few days, and then escort you out on one of the routes I mentioned."

"I don't know. It doesn't sound like I have much choice. What's Rick's problem anyway?"

"Well, for one thing, he is upset about the tree. It took us a long time to set it there."

"What do you mean set it there? That's a blowdown."

"Actually, it was a leaner, and we spent a couple days digging down around the roots and cutting them free. Same at the bottom of the road, so you could not go out that way anyway, at least in your van."

"I guess I could have helped right there, with my chainsaw."

"We have our own chainsaw. We *wanted* it to look like a blowdown."

"I see," replied Dar, impressed by the thought that went into that, and increasingly intrigued by the general dynamics of this group. Rick was somewhere between ornery and hostile, and Bennie seemed okay, but he felt a kinship developing with Dave, and it seemed reciprocal. After all that time alone it was nice to talk to someone again.

"What about my stuff?"

"Basically, you could keep it, but we have a community approach to things, for the common good. Any donations would be a nice way to ease in. As for your guns, we would have to hold on to them for a little while, and then you would get them back. None of us has four of their own though."

Dar began to formulate more questions, but the other men were clomping back over. Dave raised his eyebrows inquisitively, and Dar nodded almost imperceptibly in the affirmative. This time Bennie did the talking. He was a little shorter than his companions and somewhat soft-looking, with rather close-set eyes that were eager but a little weaselly, or perhaps the whole face was chipmunky, right down to his slightly large front teeth and thinning light brown hair. He exuded an air of self-confidence, and Dar had a feeling that if Bennie was the swing vote in any decision regarding his immediate future it would be for leniency. The van sackers seemed to be in their early thirties, while Dave was probably more like fifty-five or sixty.

"Okay," began Bennie, who'd paid more attention to the van than the weapons it held, addressing Dave directly. "First of all, I'd say he *was* chased or had some kind of problems along the way. One tire is fully blown out, and he's riding on a temporary, so one more flat and that's that, and it's a little messy in there. As for supplies, he's pretty well stocked up on clothes and camping and fishing stuff, including a tent." Dave nodded appreciatively at that point. "There's a good amount of canned fruits and vegetables in boxes that look danged delicious. Four big gas cans, empty, a siphon, and some gas mix and bar oil for the chainsaw. A laptop. Tarps, tools, and a hardware chest. Some personal stuff—"

Rick cut in now. "And boxes of *books*." Dave brightened at that.

"They all books?" asked Bennie. "We only opened a couple."

"Yes," Dar responded, detesting this invasion of privacy but continuing to feel better about how things were unfolding.

"All right," said Dave, "here is what I propose. We drive the van through. I guess we should roll those two pieces up, wedge them back in somehow, and clean up the chips, on the soon side. It will raise suspicion up close, but that is probably better than leaving it the way it is now. That part sound okay, Rick?"

"Yeah, I guess."

"Sorry about the tree, man," offered Dar. "It just looked like it fell over by itself."

"Yeah, that was the idea."

"The other idea was that if the tree did not turn them back, a chainsaw would alert us to incursion, and that worked perfectly," Dave asserted. "Anyway, Dar is amenable to staying put for a while, and he will consider joining our little band. I think he would be a good fit. He will come back with us now, we'll put a home-cooked meal into him, and he can get a good night's sleep. We will park the van in the usual place for now. The guns can come over now, and the food too so it does not bake. We can take care of everything else tomorrow. Plan?"

"Works for me," said Bennie. "Welcome aboard, Dar."

"Thanks. Looks like I ended up in the right place," Dar responded, omitting any mention of leaving sooner rather than later at this delicate stage. He could see Rick suppressing a belligerent rejoinder, probably something like "We'll see if it's the right place," a sentiment Dar would be in total agreement with.

"I will drive," directed Dave. "Give your back a rest. You guys squeeze in where you can."

"You might want to throw somethin' over that seat first," needled Rick.

"Wheels! Hit the AC," Bennie bade, and off they went.

ΩΩΩ

Before long, just after a bend and dip in the road, Dave slowed down and Bennie hopped out, quietly closing the door and taking up a position in the woods that faced the route they had just traveled. "See you soon," was all he said.

Farther along, the streamside bank leveled off enough in one spot to allow for a small dirt road that snaked down and out of sight, ending in a grassy turnaround loop. Dave eased the van in slowly. "This is as close as we can get for the carry." Dar guessed that this was an old logging road, though it hadn't been swallowed back up by the woods as they usually are. They'd passed several state forest land signs, which was another possibility. Maybe this had been an access road for Department of Environmental Conservation workers, or for a rod and gun club. They unloaded what they needed and Dave locked the doors manually, pocketing the keys. Dave asked Dar to carry the ammo, and he and Rick transported the guns. The three men plunged downhill in single file. The undergrowth was thick but quickly gave way to a dark forest floor and easy hiking.

"All right," said Dar, "I guess I should ask where we're going."

"Off the grid," answered Dave.

"How far?"

"We will be there in less than half an hour, and we'll answer your questions when we arrive. There is a lot to fill you in on, but I will mention two things right now. We generally do not talk a lot or make much noise when we are out, especially this close to the road. And we try not to leave footprints or signs of any sort."

"I can do those two things," Dar whispered back, tiptoeing with minced steps, to the amusement of his new companions.

Before long the three men came out on the wide rocky banks of the West Kill Creek at the exit of a funneling canyonette. Dar blinked hard as he had when first emerging from the cellar. The young spring sun illuminated countless flat planes and bubbling plumes of the busy creek water, twinkling bars of clean sand and gravel, bleached driftwood up on the beaches, and the tender, shiny greenery of vines, shoots, and bough tips that were winding and reaching in toward the bright center from every direction in spite of the danger of washout. Sunshine glinted off fractured faces of calcite cleavage and bits of barite and other scattered sulfides, shot flares from clumps of white quartz, and laser-beamed off tiny star-strewn dots of mica in the broad, brown and gray alluvial fan of shale, sandstone, and limestone. Normally such creek water would be muddy this time of year, but the weather must have been on the dry side recently, as it now flowed dark and transparent over and around rock that ranged in size from smooth pebbles to huge, jagged slabs. The entire scene was one of unspoiled wildness and beauty.

Dar was surprised at the width of the creek, about thirty feet across in most places, and wherever it wasn't wide it looked deep enough to drown something in. This was clearly the main drainage basin in these parts. Distant craggy borders and undercut banks testified to the raging torrents it was capable of hosting. The footing was very good, as most of these stones rounded by centuries of stream spit and polish were half set into the mud and sand, with just the occasional ankle twister to watch out for. Barring drought conditions, it didn't appear that slimy algae or aquatic weeds would normally find a home in the main channel, even in the dog days of late summer.

"We cross here," advised Dave. "It is the best spot right now. Sorry about your boots. You can dry them later. Just go slow and watch your step."

"Actually," Dar interjected, "would you mind if I take a really quick dip and catch up in a minute? I'm filthy, and I've been dreaming about this for months now."

"We don't shit where we eat," said Rick. There was no particular hostility in his voice this time, and Dar didn't quite get how that aphorism applied, but Dave backed him up. "Sorry, but let's keep moving. Later for that."

Rick took his slicker off, carefully wrapped up the four long guns, held the bundle to his chest with one arm while using the other for balance, and crossed with relative ease against the not insubstantial flow. Back at the van, he'd emptied out Dar's rigid plastic cooler, storing all of the boxed ammo in that, and a rubberized canoe bag tamped down with a sweatshirt provided safer transport for all of the loose cartridges than the cardboard box they'd been in. Rick came back for the cooler and passed again without incident. Dar was impressed by the efficiency of all this, their military precision tempered by monk-like resolve and silences.

"Throw," Rick said to Dave, referring to the bag full of ammo.

"Here, Dar, you do it. I trust your arm better." Dar knew he was out of practice throwing things, but by swinging the bag a few times and timing the release properly, it would be an easy shot.

"Just make it good or we are all dead," Dave added mischievously at the last moment, adding a couple rotations to the lob, which arced perfectly into Rick's wildly tattooed arms.

Dar crossed without falling in as well in spite of his exhaustion, mainly because he could see the bottom and pick his steps. As Rick and Dave shouldered their weapons again and surveyed in all directions, silently and independently verifying each other's findings like hoofed prey on the lookout for big cats, sharp chattering drew Dar's attention downstream. It was a colorful bird, cavorting its merry way toward them in a series of aerial fits and starts. "Hey, a kingfisher," exclaimed Dar, "my spirit animal," feeling stupid the second that left his lips.

"Wonderful," said Dave. "You have a spirit animal! Mine is the red eft. You know, they start off as greenish aquatic spotted newts living in ponds for years, and then they come up on land and walk around as orange salamanders. Many of us have spirit animals, and I do not think the kingfisher is currently taken."

It took a moment for Dave's remark to sink in. Dar had assumed this was just three guys occupying a house, though now it looked like it might be a woodland camp of some sort.

"How about you, Rick?" asked Dave. "What is your spirit animal?"

"Me," came Rick's rather deadpan response.

"That's right," Dave responded, "of course. Nobody else had that one already either."

"*Many of us*? How many of you are there?"

"You will make a baker's dozen, if you stay," Dave gently responded, reading Dar's reaction with interest.

"Holy shit! How did you get—"

Just then Rick stopped dead in his tracks and crouched halfway down. Dave shot Dar a quick look and did the same. Rick had caught some movement up ahead, but he soon relaxed. Dar saw it now himself; two figures coming toward them on the same trail at a brisk pace. Rick put a finger to his lips and marginally concealed himself. Dave was a little further out of sight to begin with and seemed content to let Rick play out whatever game he was up to. Dar could see a long-faced youth with curly blond hair in the lead, in his late teens or barely out, wearing a tee shirt that looked ironic in design even though it was still too far away to assimilate. He was slight of build and had that untested look of a cocky college student. The lad was engaged in debate with a stocky, balding, slightly goggle-eyed fellow in his forties. He wore a gray flannel shirt and had a close dark beard that must have required frequent trimming and shaping.

"And when are you going to stop worshipping at the altar of John Maynard Keynes?" asked the bearded man with a certain amount of animosity as they came within earshot.

"There you go again," the youth sharply responded. "There's a difference between economic intervention and environmental regulation. I'm talking about three-eyed frogs, and you're hating on some dead scapegoat." Rick chose that moment to forcefully step out on the trail. Both men jumped back in surprise, nearly knocking one another down.

"You guys are just askin' to give us away, or to be jumped," Rick said sternly. "How many times do I have to tell ya to look around, and to keep yer voices down? Especially when there's been an alert."

"Sorry, Rick," said the lad, who spotted Dar just at that moment.

"You must be the chainsaw operator," said the other, avoiding Rick's scowl.

"Dar, meet Andrew and Cole," said Dave. The three men shook hands. "Dar will be staying with us for a while. He needs food and rest and then he can share any news of the outside that he wants to. Where are you headed?"

"Gwen thought we should check on you, at least up to the creek."

"Good," replied Dave. "Let's do this. Bennie is making sure we were not followed. Hang on this side until he shows up. Then the three of you can start bringing some things over from Dar's van. For today, get all the food. It is mostly canned fruits and vegetables in jars that are in flat boxes. Do not carry too much and do not break anything. Bring them over the water one box at a time. You might as well bring his tent and sleeping bag and clothes too."

"Will do," replied Cole. Rick stared him down. "No problem, Dave."

"Here are the keys then. Do not beep the horn when you lock up. And thanks, guys. See you soon."

As they started away, Rick asked Dar if he had an extra set of keys, which he did, in his knapsack. "Nice catch," said Dave.

"You ain't worried about Cole drivin' away, I guess," said Rick in a lower voice. Dar shot Dave a look of concern.

"Bennie should be back very shortly. It would be more likely that one of them would lose the keys in the stream, or lock them inside."

"Yep," replied Rick. "That kid's still out of it. I think he spent the first few months lookin' fer his controller, like this is all a big fantasy. But when it comes to Cole, good riddance I'd say."

Dave ignored Rick's remarks, which were clearly aired for the benefit of the newcomer, and they pressed on. Dar noticed they'd been climbing uphill since the creek, trending to the right around the base of a small but prominent hill that was probably a moraine, sifted down there in the dim past by a halting ocean liner of glacial ice. He could see the horizon ahead through an occasional break in the bright, liquid-green forest canopy, and it appeared that the long ridge on this side of the stream topped out less than a mile away and ran more uniformly than its somewhat choppier counterpart on the other side. This was a classic hanging valley of the Catskills, draining down into the broader basin. The trail they were on was narrow and probably followed a natural game path, but it was becoming plain to see that it had handled a good amount of recent activity, and human footprints were in evidence.

Rick cut away to the right about halfway past the odd hill on the slope, following an offshoot game trail. Within a few minutes they reached a broad level spot that did not pitch down toward the stream like most of this landscape. Dar was having some late second thoughts now. He knew he might be participating in a ritual that had transpired many times before, wherein cannibals dupe visitors into bringing the meat into camp under their own steam. They had not totally violated his right to bear arms by removing the last weapon at his disposal, but it would be child's play to subdue him. Dave had dropped to third place again, and for all he knew might administer the fatal blow himself from behind. Dar composed a rough chart of their travels in his head in case he had to bolt, finding it somewhat amusing that he'd drawn it like a parchment map from the endpapers of *The Hobbit*. He would probably have to run rather than fight, but he was physically spent, and they would know the area so much better.

Just at this dark juncture in his thoughts a tent came into view, followed shortly by many others. They seemed to be spread out over a fairly wide area, rather than organized in any regimented way. A few more steps revealed what appeared to be the central feature of this camp off to the bottom right, a large fire pit worked in stone and surrounded at the rear and sides by a rather tall split-rail fence affair that was completely chinked with mud and moss. Two pairs of long, white, plastic worktables were set up at ninety-degree angles on either side of the pit, their legs lashed together for stability. He could make out a large tent of old-school origin back behind that. Planks on sunken stumps were arrayed in an inverted V-shape running uphill from about ten feet in front of the fire pit. They formed three chevrons, not unlike sergeant stripes, giving this setting the overall appearance of part pagan amphitheater and part mess hall.

"Halloo," boomed Dave in a low shout. "We have a guest." At that, the door flap of the closest tent moved, but no one stepped out. "Susan, come," urged Dave. "Meet Dar. You will like him. He is nice."

"Damaged goods," Rick whispered into Dar's ear.

Dave extended his hand inside the tent, and a somewhat strange creature emerged on it. The main thing that struck Dar was how milk white she was, with a slightly indistinct face that looked like it had been taken out of the oven just a little too early. She had a faraway expression under poofed-up bangs reminiscent of Mormon women of the compound variety. Her bright red hair was very long and obviously much teased and brushed, and she wore what could only be called a frumpy housedress. Dar moved to shake hands with the young woman but she drew back upon his approach, and would not even make eye contact. "Nice to meet you, Susan," was met with silence, though she began humming to herself in a pleasant manner, twirling a long strand of her hair at the same time.

Another camp member approached now from the outer ring of tents, walking with a pronounced limp. She was probably about Dave's age, a bit roly-poly with a wonderful head of short salt-and-pepper hair, dark sparkling eyes, rosy cheeks, and a broad smile. She was wearing a parka, and Dar thought she looked rather like a white Eskimo. Any thoughts of being murdered on the spot and roasted on a spit dissipated by the time she reached them.

"Hi there. I'm Gwen. Pleased to meet you."

"Dar. The pleasure's mine."

"Gwen is our camp manager," said Dave by way of introduction. "She will get you all set up. Tonight you can sleep in what we call our stuff tent, because it is like a shed for extra stuff, with room to stretch out in the middle.

"I'll bring you a little something to eat, honey. Lunch will be on the fly today, but we'll have a nice dinner for you tonight. Is there anything I can do for you in the meantime?"

"Well, my deepest desire is to jump into a lake or something and clean up." Dar was streaked with grease and covered with wood chips and sawdust, and a light jacket he'd brought from the van and tied around his waist concealed the worst.

Before Dave could reiterate his earlier ruling, Gwen intervened. "Gee, Dave, I'd feel the same way, meeting new people and everything. The poor boy looks like something the cat drug in."

"Where is everyone?" asked Dave a bit sharply.

"The farm party won't be back for quite a while. The rest are watering. When we didn't hear any shots or anything, we thought it would be okay. Better to not all be in one place if trouble comes anyway, right? Cole and Andrew headed over to check up on things. Did you see them?"

"Yes, we did. We will review all of this later. Gwen, do you mind if I go back and see how they are doing? Rick will be around if you need anything. We are bringing some things of Dar's over from his van. He needs sleep more than anything, so perhaps he could catch a quick nap."

"By all means," replied Gwen. "Take care, and we'll see you soon."

Gwen removed a wheelbarrow and a few other items from the guest tent floor. Dar remembered taking his wet boots off, stretching out in the middle between an air mattress and a blue sheet, and looking up at the makeshift shelves, but that was all. He found a good position for his back and was instantly snatched into the arms of Morpheus.

ΩΩΩ

"Hey . . . hey . . . wake up." The new arrival tried to focus but nothing made sense. Then he could see the faint outline of the pre-dawn sky straight ahead through what must have been the tent door. Somebody was grabbing his foot and shaking it gently. "Dar. Wake up. You slept right through. Want something to eat?"

"I guess so now," came his disarranged response. As Dar slowly regained consciousness, he realized it was Gwen summoning him, and there was another figure beside her.

"Look, dear, it's up to you, but if you want, Dawn here will take you down to the crick for a washing. It's pretty warm out. We have a clean set of clothes from your belongings, including dry boots, and you could carry some warm corn bread with you."

"Corn bread?"

"Well, a cornmeal flatbread jonnycake. They're good, if I do say so myself."

"What about Dave?"

"Don't you mind about him. Everyone's still asleep."

Dar could vaguely make out Dawn now, her wide face peeking through the tent door. She smiled back at him. "I'm happy to take you. I want to wash some things out for myself. I can even bring shampoo. It would probably do you a world of good, and we'll be back in time for breakfast."

"You can have seconds," winked Gwen, "and meet everyone proper. Just don't dillydally."

"I don't know. I'm pretty grungy."

"That's the whole idea, silly," coaxed Dawn. "It isn't far. C'mon."

"Okay," replied Dar, more awake now and seeing the benefit of this plan. "Let me just put some boots on. And please accept this," he said, producing a near-full bottle of strawberry jam from his knapsack and handing it to Gwen. He gingerly tested his back and found that it was surprisingly better. Once in a while that happened, where he recovered the next day rather than later in the week. This was a good time for that to happen.

When Dar emerged, rubbing his eyes and yawning, Gwen was already busy at the fire pit. Dawn motioned for him to follow and carefully picked her way straight out through the top of the camp, where Dar had not been yet, and off to the left. She gave him a little shush as they cleared a final tent that looked especially survivalist in nature. This path too seemed to be part of the ancient game trail system, still climbing up the slope, and it was clearly in heavy use.

"Isn't the stream the other way?" whispered Dar once they were safely clear of the camp.

"Good question. See that hill? Camp is close to the right side of it, looking up from the stream. When we go *up* the valley to scout or forage or whatever, we go down from camp, like the path you first came in on, but when we wash our clothes or bathe, which we do more often, we go up around this hill and back down the other side to a spot on the stream farther *down* the valley that's safer for that."

Dar looked confused. "I didn't say that very well," apologized Dawn.

"No, I think I'm still waking up."

"It'll make more sense when you see it. Here," she said, opening her knapsack and unwrapping a crispy, deep-yellow hunk of still-warm corn bread from a clean rag. "Get something in your stomach."

Dar smelled it first and then took a big bite, savoring its texture and flavor. "God!" he blurted out with his mouth full, causing his guide to giggle.

Night's mantle was slipping off now, and as they rounded the top of the hill Dar could begin to make out Dawn's features better, as human beings will do. She was big-boned. He assumed she'd probably lost some weight in the last half year that would have been difficult to shed under normal circumstances, though maybe she never cared one way or the other back then. She seemed very comfortable in her own skin, and what skin it was! The young woman was wearing lime-green shorts and flower-pattern sneakers with no socks. Her alabaster legs were as solid and powerful as hinged booster rockets, with a little light dimpling behind the knees. They carried a generous caboose and wide hips toward the heavens above, and whenever the path turned he discerned commensurate breasts swinging freely over a reasonably flat, wide stomach. Long dark hair cascaded down over a loose powder-blue cotton print shirt. It had been almost half a year since Dar had seen any non-hostiles, let alone attractive, friendly females with kickin' curves, and it got the better of him for a moment. She seemed to pick up on this, as human beings will also do, and halted for a moment.

"Do you need to rest?"

"No, I'm good. I guess I conked out yesterday."

"You sure did. Most of us were away and we didn't even get to meet you. Dave filled us in a little though. Sounds like you had a rough time of it."

"Yeah. It went from thinking I was going to be killed in a car chase to country lanes with tweeting bluebirds, and now this camp, and you folks. And corn bread!"

"Before that, though, a rough time too, right? Dave said you were all by yourself the whole time. I don't think I could do that."

They stopped for a moment, face to face now, and Dar was somewhat taken aback. He knew he'd been out of circulation, in a major way, but she had the warmest brown eyes he'd ever seen. She was quite pretty in a plain way, with long waterfalls of lustrous dark brown hair, though there was something ever so slightly funny about her jawbone. It was just a little too big, like there were some extra teeth back there or something, and her chin was a little crinkled. But she had an adorable way of making it all work, and of biting her lip on occasion, and the entire effect was most charming. Everything seemed out in the open, with no artifice. If he had to guess he would have said country girl, and maybe even farmer's daughter, if there was still such a thing.

They continued to chat while descending the small trail that hugged the other side of the treed mound. Dar had thought she was underdressed at first, but the walk was warming, and he was thankfully able to keep his jacket tied about his waist. Before long a low rumbling sound could be heard, like an upcoming set of rapids on a canoe trip, and they came down to the stream at last. It appeared quite a bit different than the wide bright stretch Dar had crossed the day before, kind of jungly, though they were still under the lifting blanket of the break of day.

"When I was 'briefed' about this spot," Dawn explained, deploying the usually dreaded but in this case cutely executed air quotes, "they told me that the stream is farthest from the road here, before it makes a quick turn back, so we're less likely to be spotted or heard. There's a nice deep stretch right there with a good bottom where you don't have to worry about snags or water snakes or anything, near that rock that pokes up. I'm going to go down around the corner to our washing area to clean a few things, and to give you some privacy. Here's a bar of soap that you can't lose, so put it right back in this net bag, and a bottle of shampoo that you should use sparingly. I'll leave your towel up here with your dry clothes."

"Sounds good."

"Is it true that you haven't had a bath since the plague hit?"

"Not a proper bath, no."

"Then you'll enjoy this, even though it's cold. I'll need your clothes. Give them to me now and I'll do all the washing together."

"That's okay. I'll take care of them later."

"There is no later. And Gwen says your duds don't come back into camp if I don't get them right clean. I do this all the time. Don't worry about it. The only thing is we need to get back soon, and I don't have time to argue, okay?"

"I guess. How should I—"

"I'll turn around. Just undress and get in the water."

"Dawn, this is embarrassing, but . . ."

"I know, you soiled your pants a little. Rick told us. We've all done that. Heck, I used to do it *before* the plague. No biggie. Let's go."

"Okay. Just bury the underwear though. I have plenty. Gee, that was swell of Rick to share that. Maybe I can return the favor someday."

"We'd all love to see that. Give me your jacket first, and your belt, and I'll put them aside with your clean stuff."

The duds fell, Dar hobbled into the stream, and he found the perfect depth in which to anchor himself in some pebbly sand, facing downstream and looking up into the gray sky. Once the breathtaking shock of the frigid water wore off a little and Dawn was out of sight, he kneeled instead and began the fierce scrubbing he'd yearned for, from ear lobes and armpits to nether regions and toe interspaces and back again, followed by a blissful shampooing. He rinsed and repeated.

Just upstream it was deep enough to swim, and if it was warmer out and they didn't have to leave so soon, that would have been another checked item on his cellar wish list. One could just swim in place there every day, against the current, like in a fancy-schmancy exercise pool but without all the output, upkeep, and chlorine.

Although Dar was shivering violently upon regaining the shore, he checked who made the towel first before drying off, out of habit. Cannon, good and thirsty, with an indelible "D3" on the label. From his clothes that had been retrieved from the van, somebody had picked out a pair of faded blue jeans, fresh underthings, and a deep blue Irish knit sweater with a few wooden buttons under the neck, and it felt wonderful to be so freshly scrubbed and attired. Dawn showed up moments later carrying the dripping laundry bag, as if she had been waiting for him to finish.

"How was that then?"

"Incredible, incredible. I feel like a new man."

"Good. Let's get going. Just throw in the towel," she said.

"Can I carry that for you?"

"That's okay, I've got it."

"Here's the thing, though. I want to carry it for you, but we don't have time to argue about it, okay?"

"Ha. Okay, big guy. Thanks. I'll take it back though if it gets heavy. Just speak up."

At that very moment the first real rays of morning sunlight illuminated this Tarzan section of the basin, turning hundreds of wispy fog strands from dull gray to blazing white and bringing all the twisting greenery to light. Still shivering from the cold bath, Dar was suddenly swept by powerful emotions. He turned to his guide, slightly above him now on the trail, but he couldn't speak, and his eyes welled up ever so slightly. Dawn took a step forward and gathered him in for a warm hug, like a human furnace, guiding his head to the partially bare swell of her breast and softly rubbing his back until he regained his composure. He smelled deeply but silently of her thick, dangling hair and felt her heartbeat pinging along with his own. "I know," she whispered.

"That was very kind of you Dawn, to bring me here," Dar said, stepping back now, somewhat embarrassed by his verklemptitude. "Thanks so much."

"You got it. Now let's haul some beautacious butt or my ass is grass, and Dave and Gwen are the lawnmower. You lead this time."

In that part of New York where the Catskills break away on the north into rugged hills, there extends a bold and picturesque region through which the Schoharie has worn a narrow valley on its way to join the Mohawk in its course to the Hudson and the sea. Here, too, the Delaware takes its rise and the Charlotte runs westward into the Susquehanna. Though distinctively a highland, it is the beginning of that break in the Appalachian plateau through which a gateway opens to the west for the traffic of the continent. Though thus thrust out into the very center of the State's great thoroughfare, where the progress of more than three centuries has swept its base, it has been slow to take on the life flowing around it.

"Blenheim Hill" Series by Albert C. Mayham (Jefferson, NY: Jefferson Courier and Schoharie County Chronicle, 4/13/1905)

SIX

As DAR had observed over the years, the return journey from an unknown place usually seems much quicker over now-familiar territory. Before he knew it they were coming back into camp. Rick spotted them first, though he kept this news to himself. Moments later the murmurs of others alerted Dave, and he strolled out to meet them and to guide the newcomer in.

"Good morning, campers," he began, with a lilt. "I am pleased to introduce you to Dar, who as you know arrived yesterday, and whose jam you are enjoying this morning." This elicited a ripple of light laughter, hellos, and thank-yous. Dar gave a little left-to-right wave, searching out the faces of those he knew already. Bennie gave him a thumbs-up. Andrew flashed a peace sign. Cole tipped an imaginary cap. Most of them were arrayed on the benches, finishing their breakfast, though a few were clearly waiting their turn.

"You have yet to meet some of us," continued Dave. Having scanned the group, Dar was surprised to find that all of the remaining survivors were women, one of whom was just joining the assemblage herself, silently cooing "Oh" at the moment their eyes met. This many strangers in his face all at once was a little overwhelming. Dar momentarily thought of this new bunch as unnamed Sims, or the islanders on *Lost* that you never got to know, or even the redshirts on *Star Trek*, though that was a bit drastic. Dave proceeded, bringing Dar through the bench area for introductions and handshakes. When everyone else had been served by Gwen and her helper, who observed from afar with studied indifference, he sat down for another serving of corn bread and an astounding cup of wild mint tea. A couple of the breakfasters began drifting off, but most hung around and seemed eager to chat with the new recruit.

"From our never-ending search for the world's tastiest teas," warbled a middle-aged woman in pleasant tones as she sat down next to Dar with the remnants of her meal.

"I'm sorry. I'm never good with names the first time through."

"No problem. I'm Sadie, the head huntress here. *Forager* is probably a better word, as I don't do animals." Dar could see she had been a real beauty once. Everything had fallen along pleasant lines, however, and a pert nose and small flocks of cheek freckles still echoed the appearance of youth. Her billowy clothing was a little Earth Motherish, complete with big riding boots and a good amount of bangles and bling for the backwoods, including a few grouse feathers affixed to her curly reddish-brown hair.

"I know what you mean," replied Dar. "I'm kind of a reformed hunter, though I still fish. The thing about fishing is that you can let them go."

"They say the fishing isn't really too good around here. The stream is so small."

"Where did you learn to be a forager?" Dar asked.

"Some of it was on-the-job training. There's a few of us here into it and we share our knowledge. Dave especially. Nobody's been poisoned yet," she said hopefully, with a little titter.

"Good to know," replied Dar. "I brought quite a few books with me, Sadie. I know there's some on finding and preparing edible plants, the culinary side of survivalism, and things like that."

"No way!" she exclaimed, a broad smile coming over her face. Sadie stood up and squeezed her hands together, looking around for the right people to tell, but more of them had departed once they realized she'd nabbed him first.

As Dar followed her searching gaze, he witnessed an elderly gent gingerly exiting the tent that housed Susan, the wan redhead from the day before. He hadn't counted off the campers. That might be number thirteen, or there might be still others he hadn't met yet. He seemed to be heading down to the mess hall, as confirmed by a wave of the spatula from Gwen.

"Way!" Dar replied, getting back to Sadie. "I didn't have a chance to talk to Dave about the books yet though."

"Speaking of talking with Dave," said the good-natured leader who had returned from some other task, "let's take a walk, Dar, and I will show you the ropes a little. Are you all done with breakfast?"

"Yes, and sure thing. Nice meeting you Sadie," Dar said as he took his leave, shaking her hand, "and thanks for the tasty tea. What do I do with the dishes?"

"I'll bring them up for you. You'll probably get your own set later."

Dave was holding Dar's deer rifle and a handful of bullets, which he laid down on one of the benches. He then excused himself and approached the center tents to the side of the Commons—which is how they referred to the fire pit/kitchen/benches area—returning in short order with another camper in tow, who he introduced as BethAnne.

"Hello again," she said a bit coldly.

"I have asked BethAnne to come along, and she has kindly consented," explained Dave, "though with some reservations."

"Where are we going?" asked Dar, curious, but also desirous of attempting to break whatever ice had formed.

"Let's go out this way toward the creek," Dave replied, gesturing for Dar to take up the gun. They followed yet another path that headed directly behind the fire pit and out into the woods. Dar was getting his bearings now. He knew they were heading west and the stream was off to his right, about a third of a mile down. The trail angled that way and before long they came to a high, wooded bank overlooking the clear running waters. Dave took his fanny pack off and positioned himself on a small grassy shelf that afforded a good view upstream and down, gesturing for the pair to set themselves down opposite on a wide log there not far from the edge.

"Nice spot. I can picture Hiawatha holding a powwow here," quipped Dar. BethAnne glanced at him with mild amusement.

"Well, the wind up here keeps the insects off a little better. More importantly though, we can be alone to talk about things. I asked BethAnne to come along because I would like someone else to see how this is done now."

"I'll listen in because you've asked me to," the young woman responded, "but I don't see myself as the logical choice."

"Fair enough. Thanks for indulging me. So, Dar," Dave began, "you say you have been up around these parts before?"

"Pretty close to here. I lived on the other side of the county for a while, but I had some friends in Middleburgh, and I've fished the Schoharie from the covered bridge on down. And I know I was in Gilboa once years ago, to see the dam, so I must have driven through North Blenheim to get there."

"That makes you the only one with prior local experience. What do you know about the covered bridge?"

"Just that it's old, the longest of its kind in the world I think, and that it's the pride and joy of North Blenheim, as there wasn't much else going on. I noticed something in the paper not long ago about art shows held right on the bridge."

"Art shows. Interesting," Dave replied. "There *used* to be a lot going on in Blenheim, though. It was a thriving community for a long time. As for the bridge, which was finished in 1855, in addition to providing folks with the usual benefits of being able to conveniently and safely cross a wild river, the big bark tannery was on one side, the village side probably, and some of the hemlock trees they needed for that process were on the other. A company was formed. An expert carpenter from Vermont happened to be in the area repairing the covered bridge in Schoharie, one Nichols Powers, and he consented to take on the daunting task. It is a double-barrel model, with two lanes, constructed mostly of virgin pine, with a single central arch of mighty oak. The true overall length is about two hundred and twenty-six feet, if I recall. The longest surviving single-span wooden covered bridge in the world. The locals called it 'Powers' Folly.' When they were all done and ready to knock down into the river the falsework that was keeping it up during construction, the builder sat on top, vowing to go down with the bridge if that should be its fate."

"Like the chief engineers of Roman arches," Dar interjected, "who stood directly underneath when the braces were removed."

"Yes. True management accountability. I wonder if Powers knew about the Romans doing that. It held, to cheers, settling only a fraction of an inch, and has kept its perfect camber to this day. It operated as a toll bridge for many years, and has survived lightning strikes, floods, roof fires from when burning buildings in town sent embers, and various attempts to dismantle it. Legend has it that a jug of spirits was sealed over in an abutment by workers fearful of being caught by their Temperance Society overseer. Who knows about anecdotes like that though. I heard a good quote once that goes 'Just because something from the dim past sounds interesting doesn't mean it really happened.' The bridge was designated a National Historic Landmark, and Lady Bird Johnson sent a telegram about their 'cherished beauty spot.' I have visited it several times and it is a marvel to behold."

"How do you know all that?" Dar asked.

"A logical question. I have borrowed a good amount of historical material from the town archives. Mostly books, but also documents, and interesting copies of old newspaper and periodical articles."

"Yikes. That sounds risky or something."

"I know, but I am taking good care of everything. It is all in plastic bins. Actually, I was the town historian where I came from."

"No kidding! I have great respect for town historians. They're usually unsung heroes, with the occasional villain."

"Sometimes. Usually the villain is bad luck, though. Especially by fire. Also, you really need a good succession plan. I know about a local case where the town historian passed away and her son took almost everything. It all started showing up on eBay and other places. A concerned old-timer heard about a photo album from this collection for sale at the closest used-book store, loaded with historically priceless captioned images of early residents and scenes. When she tried to reclaim it for the town out of her own pocket, and enquired if the bookseller could do better than the asking price of three hundred dollars, all things considered, he said 'If you don't want it for three hundred, come back next week and you'll find it out on our sidewalk sale for five hundred.'"

"That sucks. There oughta be a law or something."

"Anyway," said Dave, "feel free to peruse what I have sometime. In the early 1700s, where we are now was the western frontier of New York. The things these people faced! Even after they had subdued the wilderness, survived armed conflict, and replaced their crude log homes with better abodes. They seem so brave and tireless to me, heroes in their own right. Every place has its history, of course, but it resonates more when you are in the same physical space they were. Just yesterday I was reading about an elderly local doctor who used to ride on horseback through the wilderness all night long, in winter, just to reach faraway homes where he was needed. Or the fearless, sturdy patriot who slowly turned old, got the shakes of some sort and a nickname to go with them, and drowned in the Schoharie Creek he used to charge across with musket and tomahawk, at Breakabeen, if I recall—from the German for the rushes that still grow near the water there, by the way—going down the bank for a drink, his whole life spun out in that one area. And there was another story about using ninety-six teams of oxen to move a nearby house! They even moved one-room schoolhouses around whenever necessary, to be near the largest families."

"I love that stuff too, Dave, but I have a feeling you didn't bring me out here to talk about bridge specs and oxen." BethAnne seemed to appreciate the reality check.

"Sorry. I get carried away by those things. Yes. So, Dar, now that you are more rested and relaxed, what are your thoughts about staying with us for a while?"

"I don't know. I thought I had a few days."

"Well, you appear to be a quick study to me. The truth be told, we are kind of living in dog years now. Everything happens quicker, or has more serious consequences at any rate. Every day is precious. It will be November before we know it, for example, and that will matter more than our past Novembers did. Like I was explaining yesterday, your chances of reaching some safe place are not very good. Life is relatively easy here."

"I'm very impressed with what I've seen," responded the reluctant inductee, "and thanks for all the hospitality, but I'm not all that comfortable committing right now. What if I want to take my van and my stuff and leave in July, for example? Would I be allowed to?"

"The short answer is yes, but we would want some input into how you leave."

"And into what I take with me?"

"What is yours is yours."

"I just don't know. In the long run, I think I'll have a better chance on my own. To be honest, I've grown weary of the affairs of men."

"Meaning men are the rulers, right?" fired off an annoyed BethAnne.

"Statistically, yes, but also I'm not as weary of the affairs of women."

"Har har," she responded.

"Can you commit to May, Dar? Try it out here for one month. Rehab yourself with our help, and if you want to you can leave after that, free and clear. You can go now too, but it would have to be sooner rather than later, like today."

"Jesus, why so quickly?"

"I told you already yesterday. We believe our presence here is undetected and unsuspected, but we do not want to take any unnecessary chances. The more you know, the more that can be gotten out of you. Consider this one factor alone. We do know something about what has been going on out in the world. It is survival of the fittest, and might makes right. Rape is right up there with pillaging and murder on the new hit parade, and we have a lot of women here. Probably far more than most surviving groups, in terms of percentage."

"What do *you* think, BethAnne?" Dar asked, turning to the stewing figure on the log next to him.

"What do you mean, what do I think?" she responded, her intense blue eyes flashing. "It's your decision!"

Dar stood up to stretch, scanning the leaping stream behind him. It looked very inviting down there. He was sure some of those pools were big enough to hold trout. And he'd noticed plenty of deer pellets on the way over. The ex-hunter hadn't tasted venison in over a decade, but the very idea of it had found him involuntarily salivating and smacking his lips when tracking deer from his cellar window. He also thought about the foraging skills he could pick up, Gwen's cooking, rejoining the human race—at least for a while—and dangling something other than participles.

"Alright, here's what *I* think," said BethAnne. Dave must have given her an imploring prompt when Dar's back was turned. "Most of us like it here well enough, though the realists understand it's probably only a brief reprieve. If I were you, I'd stay. We have a lot to offer. To be honest though, due to limited abilities and resources, you will be judged on whether you're a provider or just another mouth to feed. Some of us work very hard at what needs to be done, but there's some deadwood too, and we're at the point where we need to put some serious food on the table. It's all about avoiding detection—which would probably bring ruin—food, and surviving the elements. You would know better than me whether you're up for that or not."

"I guess I'd feel better about all of this if you'd just say what you mean, instead of beating around the bush like that." Dave cracked a grin at this, while BethAnne just waggled her comely bottom on the thick log and crossed her arms, though Dar sensed a slight softening.

"Dave, I really do appreciate everything you've done for me so far. I'd like to stay through May, and hopefully longer, but I reserve the right to leave later in the summer. As for the vitality of my wood, and helping to put meat on the table, I look forward to the challenge."

"Marvelous," said Dave, clapping him on the back. "Now that we have established that, I know you have a lot of questions, some of which I have put off answering thus far. I have found that if I can go through everything once first, most of them will be answered for you.

The only part I will leave out is the camp orientation that Gwen will give you, and Rick's ranger training. And anything that BethAnne may want to add at the end."

"Sounds good," Dar replied. "Do tell."

ΩΩΩ

Dave began with his own story. He owned a small landscaping business in the Pocono Mountains of northeastern Pennsylvania, a green one. His wife was already deceased, and his grown children were scattered. He was spared from the virus by strict isolation from others, and was getting by, but decided to try for a suburb above Boston on the extreme possibility that a daughter had survived there. He started by car on smaller roads and ended up stranded in Oneonta, the largest city to the immediate west of Albany, where he hooked up with an assortment of survivors. All the stores had been cleaned out weeks earlier, so they scavenged through cold, dark homes, bypassing those with dead bodies at first. Competing road crews made their lives even more miserable. At first they demanded tribute, then recruits— several of whom were happy to switch over—and then they began assaulting and kidnapping the women, making it risky for them to leave the ever-shifting home bases they'd set up.

When they got advance word that one of the crews was intent on a final deadly raid, they made a mad dash east, utilizing county highways rather than the interstate. The leaders had pored over local maps, looking for a suitable location far away from any population centers, and settled on Schoharie County in the general area of the Gilboa Dam, which was surrounded by green on the map. They occupied a large farmhouse toward the bottom of the road they'd found Dar on and wintered there successfully, heating with wood and hunting for meat. Facing starvation, they were fortunate enough to locate a nearby farm that specialized in feed grains, relieving it of many fifty-pound bags of whole and cracked corn and a lesser amount of barley, soybeans, and whole oats. There was unease, however, as most of them were still traumatized by their previous ordeal. Houses are close to roads, by definition, and roads brought trouble.

In late February several members conspired to steal one of the vehicles that had brought them there, making off with whatever guns and food supplies they could and heading out for parts unknown. This left a core group that became intent on examining all the options and coming up with a more tenable solution. They found themselves looking out the window all day long, as Dar had once done, even posting sentries, though that was boring duty that caused arguments. It was a paranoid existence, they felt like low-hanging fruit, and spring was just around the corner.

Dave was an admitted idealist, while Rick was more in the survivalist camp, but they agreed that relocating to the backwoods might be the answer they were searching for with regard to security and peace of mind. Looking over the maps again, they decided to explore the upper reaches of the very road they were living on, using snowmobiles stored in the barn to reconnoiter. Once they agreed on a site for the camp and the roads were passable, they used a pickup truck to bring supplies and people up. After that was accomplished, they did everything on foot and kept as far away from roads and houses as possible.

Dar found all of this fascinating, right up his alley really, and questions kept popping into his head, but he let Dave continue without interruption.

Rick had been doing specialized construction work on Long Island, lay low, and fallen short in his first bid to reach Alaska or Canada. He'd been the muscle behind this group's survival to date, including some mortal encounters back in Oneonta. Though Rick often butted heads with the senior leader, Dave had implicit trust in him, and Dar could see the respect Rick held for Dave. Gwen was also indispensable. She worked herself too hard, but had explained to everyone many times over that's how she wanted it. It helped her to get through, and to forget those she had lost.

There was a general feeling that the virus had burned itself out somehow, as there were no additional outbreaks in any of the groups they'd had more recent contact with. Most of the survivors had weathered the infectious storm through self-quarantine, which seemed to be the key. Andrew, however, was a local college student who never made it home in the turmoil of those first days. By the time he was desperate enough to steal a car, his family was no more. He'd been constantly exposed on campus as his companions died one by one, and was walking proof of natural immunity. Dave's public position was that Andrew was their most valuable member, in the hope that he could be studied for a possible cure some day.

Susan showed up in the city one day wandering aimlessly about, and they took her in as a charity case. Opinions were divided over whether she had some kind of developmental disability or was simply shell-shocked, or both. How she'd survived the virus and violence was a complete mystery.

Sadie was the offspring of West Coast counterculture types. She'd come east with plans to practice holistic health care and life coaching for a living. BethAnne interjected that she was stronger on the spiritual and referral side than she was with actual medical care, alternative or otherwise. Sadie was living with her sister's family a few counties away. As they began to succumb they barricaded themselves in the main house, sparing her the same fate. Gwen's husband had done something similar, leaving a note that he was taking his own life in a place where she would never find the body. Sadie survived in a trailer on the secluded property until finally making a break for it. There were quite a few farms not all that far from the camp. Sadie's specialty was extracting anything edible, from stored goods to perennials that were coming up all by themselves, in addition to foraging for wild foods. She was usually accompanied on these excursions by Dawn and Bennie and one or two others.

Dawn was described as "a good kid." She was a big help around camp and was a jack of all domestic trades. When Dave did not give any background for her, Dar enquired. "She hasn't wanted to talk about it much," was all he offered.

Of the original group, that left Liz, the one who was helping Gwen get the food out. All Dave said about her was that she had been some kind of management trainee, and was steady and hardworking. A bullet had just missed her in Oneonta, doing some ricochet damage.

"A wonk too," BethAnne added, "which will come in handy if we ever need wonks again." That was the Oneonta contingent.

Bennie was wintering in a small house near Route 30 close to where his truck broke down while passing through. He saw a thin trace of their smoke one day a mile or so away and simply walked up to the farmhouse and introduced himself. He was invited to join the group without much delay, as Dave and Rick were anxious to add more muscle to the mix after the desertion. Bennie was an admissions officer down toward the City. He came with his own rifle, though he hadn't proved to be much of a hunter.

The discussion over accepting Cole had apparently been more contentious. BethAnne chimed in when it looked like Dave was going to skip over the warts. Cole was always second-guessing their decisions, making crude remarks to and about the women—"like 'Got two nipples for a dime?' when it was chilly out, asking if we knew how to make penis bread out of dill dough, and wishing that he could wake up every morning 'at the crack of Dawn'"—and advancing tired political arguments that had little or no bearing on their current circumstances. It was getting to be such a problem that they were considering how to disinvite him, though they were probably past the point of no return there.

Cole had showed up out of nowhere. The foraging party was assessing a new farm beyond the fateful intersection where Dar turned left rather than right. He was passing by on the road, caught a glimpse of them, and asked for assistance. Sadie and Bennie weren't sure what to do and ended up bringing him back to the camp. Dave was dismayed, and Rick was fit to be tied. Cole was deliberately fuzzy about his general background, where he had been since the virus, and what he was doing on such a back road. He was paunchy too, unusual now. Dar surmised out loud that he may have been run out of some other community on a rail, and he could see them mulling that over. For Dar, this partially cleared up Rick's initial hostility and suspicion.

That was it for the survivors. There was one more Oneonta Group male who had simply vanished shortly after moving to the woods.

They had no idea if he'd just decided to go off on his own or what, but his disappearance made everyone jumpy.

ΩΩΩ

By this point in the briefing, it was apparent that BethAnne had been brought along partly to fill in the blanks on personnel issues Dave did not wish to address himself. She didn't appear to be part of the brain trust, seemingly composed of Dave, Gwen, and Rick, but perhaps Dave saw something there and was beginning to bring her into the fold. Dar asked BethAnne directly about her story. Dave told her to proceed, excusing himself for a walk down to the stream. She moved over to where he had been sitting in order to face Dar directly, and to keep an eye on the territory below as Dave had done before her.

BethAnne was an ivy leaguer and blossoming professional who'd simply decided to become a stay-at-home mom instead when the right marriage afforded that opportunity. She had rode the active virus period out much like Dar, in the suburbs of Binghamton, though she spent most of her time in a finished basement with a small, clever "safe space" behind the bar, retreating there the few times the house was ransacked. She didn't go into whether she'd had children yet or what had happened to her husband, and Dar did not ask.

When BethAnne finally ran out of food she made a break for Albany, in the hope that there might be more law and order in New York State's capital city. She traveled on the interstate at night but was waylaid just before Cobleskill and taken to the lair of her captors.

When the unrestrained and virtually inescapable nature of the virus had become apparent, a small contingent of workers at Howe Caverns and locals with connections (and no symptoms) established a safe haven there inside the sprawling underground complex. This was the king of subterranes among the 150 or so in cave-rich Schoharie County. A steady supply of clean water coursed through its limestone beds and galleries, the temperature stood at a constant fifty-two degrees winter or summer, and there was a good amount of food on site, including the contents of an underground cheese-aging room, so they just hunkered down at first. The general layout was highly defensible. There was only one way in by vehicle, on Discovery Drive, and if you were not welcome there you would quickly discover that. In the beginning, so she was told, things weren't too bad, and they somewhat jokingly referred to themselves as the Cave Clan.

Elevator service to the cavern floor, dim, sporadic, multicolored lighting, and ventilation by way of a huge fan were provided by a generator that needed diesel to stay fed, courtesy of the former local fuel companies. Underground living took its toll, however. Humidity was a constant 70 percent or so, elbow space was at a premium, with little privacy, and it was a stupefying and spooky existence. Once the "hot" virus period seemed over and armed incursions were on the wane, the huge topside main building was fitted up like a fort, complete with wood stove heat. The cafeteria and motel on the grounds were also put to good use. They even recreated on the new four-tower zip line there. Eventually the cave below came to be thought of more as a final refuge against attack and frostbite, and as a basement with as much storage room as you'd ever need.

Dar was quite familiar with this famous local landmark. Lester Howe had stumbled onto a cave system back in the early 1840s, noticing that in the summer his cows often preferred a certain small, brushy outcrop that blew a little cool air out onto an otherwise sweltering hillside. Howe *wow* blown cow. He and a neighbor explored the caves themselves, about 150 to 200 rope feet below, and over the years this had all been built up into quite a tourist attraction.

Basically, an animatronic Farmer Howe kicked things off in his study, you descended by elevator, and you were assured right off the bat that there are no bats in this part of the cave by your jocular, tan-jacketed tour guide, whose grandparent may have held the same job in his or her youth. Elevated brick walkways led past flowing sheets of calcite, long dramatic grottos, and incredible millions-of-years-old features with corny names like Titan's Temple and The Pipe Organ (guides hummed whatever that song from *The Phantom of the Opera* was and other tunes into its reverberating rock reeds to oohs and aahs). There was an atmospheric boat ride requiring adroit hand-maneuvered locomotion along the walls. On the way back you could kneel at the Bridal Altar, where hundreds of couples deeply in love had tied the knot, you wound your way through a long, high, tight serpentine passage called the Winding Way that for kids especially was the cat's pajamas, and your group rose up again at the conclusion of the tour like human lava. One of the guides went off script in answer to a question one time and related how the entire staff played hide-and-seek down there once a year, after-hours, including within the closed-off areas. They hosted a zombie weekend too.

At one point Dar had really wanted to write an over-the-top comedic screenplay about the rivalry between the staff at Howe Caverns and a nearby smaller, more naturally preserved attraction known as Secret Caverns, with its one-hundred-foot underground waterfall claim to fame, but it never got off the ground. The possibilities for small-town friction and hilarious mutual sabotage were endless. It could have had a happy ending, like one of the goofballs who was dating a counterpart from the other camp finds a spectacular connecting passage that allows them to merge, with a final argument over how to name the new combined attraction.

BethAnne continued her surprisingly detailed and candid narrative. This clan supported some ninety members at its peak in the very beginning, including a good number of precious children, but early on the virus penetrated the hive to its core, requiring extreme action to avert total annihilation. An era of oppression followed. Some fled, though such desertion was initially discouraged and finally prohibited. Food and supplies began to run low, and with so many members, they needed to establish a productive mergers-and-acquisitions program. At first road crews just systematically ransacked empty homes and buildings in ever-widening circles, but that evolved into recruitment, pursuit of passersby, and out-and-out borderland raiding. She knew they went as far west as Oneonta, and that they had formed an uneasy truce with other groups and confederations, particularly toward Albany. Daily life took on a military cast. A tribunal decided questions of law and the fate of anyone found lacking.

The leadership was decent enough at first, but events were always in great flux. At one point a dandified tyrant ran the show. Rather than attiring himself in a natty suit or military uniform, he walked around in Babe Ruth's jersey. Not just some reproduction—the real thing, liberated from the Baseball Hall of Fame in nearby Cooperstown—and not just his nameless Number 3 jersey, but his black, circa-1928 barnstorming tour shirt emblazoned with "Bustin' Babes" in big white letters across the front, a nice tie-in to his head-busting thug support. It was found in the possession of a "runner," as they referred to anyone who tried to pass through without halting on command. Apparently he'd been a warlord in his own right whose luck had run out, having barely escaped with his life.

This man was treated well at first, and tricked into thinking there might be a leadership role for him in the Cave Clan. He admitted to organizing the overthrow of a hopeful colony to the west that had set up shop at the Farmers' Museum in Cooperstown. It sounded like a valiant effort to Dar, but even though all the traditional tools and implements were still there, and scattered farm animals might have been rounded up and brought to a place like that, or imported from warmer climates someday, it's doubtful they could ever have gathered enough expertise to successfully revive all those old pre-industrial arts. That's what transmitted knowledge and apprenticeships are for. The colony's more immediate problem had been one of location. This collection of historic buildings was right on a big road, out in the open, and basically indefensible. They were easily overrun, and what livestock they had was slaughtered for fresh meat. A similar fate had befallen a peaceful community in the nearby town of Cherry Valley. Once this information had been obtained, the agitator was carted off to be put to death for fear that he would foment unrest there as well, and his considerable booty was added to the coffers, including some deadly weapons and a trunk full of the best baseball memorabilia in the world, for what it was worth.

Women in the Cave Clan were increasingly threatened and abused. Allying with a strong mate afforded some protection, and a new leadership initiative required pairing off. A close friend of BethAnne's had lost her man in a skirmish, under questionable circumstances, and was about to be "assigned" to somebody else. He was a real pig, and had probably paid a bribe to secure her. Tired of the struggle to begin with and now beyond remorse, she stole away in one of the underground guide boats to where the River Styx meets the inky Lake of Venus. It was terribly silent in most of the once again pitch-black caverns, the only sound coming from amplified plops of water that reverberated back up to the ceilings from which they'd dripped. The tour guides used to call these "cave kisses" if they hit you. She was going as far back as possible by boat, however, to the final waterfall, on a day when the entire system was surging with warm-spell meltwater and fresh rain, and the thundering din of this cataract guided her on as she steered the boat by pole against the bottom and by hand along the walls and ceiling. Once there, she lowered herself into the cold lake like a chalky apparition, tumbled over the edge, and slipped under a final rocky shelf where the black waters disappeared into the bowels of the earth. Her pursuers found her clothes in a pile on the bottom of the boat, a candle still burning on the seat. Her body was never recovered in the outlet stream. A legend arose that she was wandering around in the dark reaches on all fours, surviving on whatever she could find.

Hope was renewed when a female leader took office, but she turned out to be an aloof, dissembling opportunist who did nothing to stem the general slide into barbarism. BethAnne did not understand her motivation. In the previous life, career advancement at all costs often paid off, financially, but this had been a high turnover position so far, never ending well. A promising co-leader brought in to help right the ship turned out to be full of hot air, and rumors surfaced that the Albany group was secretly running things from afar now anyway. This was the end of hope for many of them, when they realized that independence and humane leadership was a thing of the past, and that resistance was futile.

This band of survivors gained new members at about the same rate it lost them, and it never again exceeded sixty or so in number during the remainder of her time there. Entire road crews disappeared on occasion, Bermuda Triangle-style, and it was not so apparent that they had simply run. Paranoia was in the air.

BethAnne and her man, whom she did not provide many details on other than his name, which was Dan, had been tasked to go through the McDonald's on the main drag in Cobleskill looking for anything edible that may have been missed before. Dar was quite familiar with that establishment. Mainly though, it had been his father's home away from home. He was more of a diner buff than a fast-food patron, but that was about the best this mini-metropolis had to offer at that time. Dar's father loved sitting there with friends or by himself, swirling his foam coffee cup and polishing off a Happy Meal while watching the world go by outside. Little did he know his youngest child would zoom past one day at the end of civilized humanity, running for his life. He was fascinated by how often the new businesses in a little building just across the street had their grand openings and then proceeded to go belly up within a matter of months. He would say things to Dar like "That cash register has to be ringing every sixty seconds," or "That door has to be hitting somebody on the ass on the way in and out all day long."

The couple pulled into McDonald's, disgruntled over such a boring and wasteful assignment, since this building had probably been turned a dozen times already for every last catsup pack the rats hadn't found yet. Smashed signage and yellowed receipts topped with "Now Hiring Smiley Faces/Management" littered the floor. Joking around, Dan cruised up to the drive-through, rolling down the window of the junky Grand Cherokee they were in. "Supersize me," he said, grinning lasciviously at BethAnne. He saw her merry eyes go wide with terror at the same instant he heard the server window slide open, and turned just in time to catch a rifle butt square in the face, breaking his nose and knocking several teeth out. He reeled back, sputtering and gasping for breath, and put his head down on the steering wheel for a moment before looking over at BethAnne in shock and bewilderment. Just as his assailant was trying to spin the gun around in close quarters and get in a fatal shot, Dan rallied and floored it past Window 2, turning out onto the main road back toward home base.

"*Go Go Go,*" she screamed as blood gushed down onto his shirt. He mouthed a few indecipherable words that probably amounted to

"What the fuck!" She didn't get a good look at the gunman, but two unfamiliar cars were hot on their trail already. They must have been parked across the street just out of sight. Outsiders would never try to pull off something like that right in town. All the main roads were under watch. The whole thing had been a setup! Dan was an excellent driver, and in spite of his injuries was putting on good speed. As they shot under the railroad bridge on the outskirts of town, she told him to get up on the interstate toward Albany rather than returning home, and he nodded in agreement. His face was swelling now, becoming unrecognizable, except for the eyes. She found a grimy towel on the floor of the backseat and held it under his nose to stem the flow of blood. He gestured for water and she got as much down as she could.

Once everyone was up on the eastbound lanes of the interstate, BethAnne could see there were no more variables, and that it would just be a matter of time before superior automotive muscle won out. The pursuers began to take shots at them, some of which were hitting their non-vital marks. One loud car was alongside now, wary of return fire or getting bumped downhill to the opposite lanes but bold enough to zoom up for a few seconds and shout profanity-laced demands to pull over. It seemed like they were toying with them now. This didn't make sense to her. Why lose a good ransacker and road worker like Dan, and how could they expect her not to raise hell about this back at the base? Then she recalled rumors of women being traded or paid out to other groups. Perhaps that was it.

Without warning, Dan stood on the brakes and steered right off the inside shoulder and through a shallow ditch, nearly bottoming out in the process. The pursuers slammed on their own brakes, burning rubber and causing one to fishtail into the outer guardrail. Both were able to back up though, and they began to do so at full speed. They'd all just passed a long stretch where tons of round rock had been deposited on the high hillside above for erosion control, and this terrain was just about to transition into a long rocky ridge that loomed above the highway. By coming in at just the right angle and speed, Dan was able to cut up the hillside following what appeared to be the vestiges of an old earthen construction ramp. It was the kind of feat that a professional stunt driver might have been able to pull off on every other attempt without getting stuck down low or rolling off on the way up, especially in an everyday vehicle. Tall sere grass stuck up in frizzy clumps, and small chunks of remnant snow were cut or spun out over the face of the ridge, cascading down in diminishing pieces as if they had been dislodged by a passing group of bighorn sheep. He proceeded along the top for fifteen feet or so before getting bogged down, though saplings began to dot the ledge and there was nowhere else to go anyway other than back the way they'd come.

Dar knew about this stretch of dramatic outcrops, not far from the town of Central Bridge. You could still see the long vertical dynamite-hole grooves from all the blasting necessary to trim it back. He'd passed vanloads of geology students that had pulled over to study them with their professors.

"What are you doing?" she screamed, but he was already pushing her out the passenger side.

"*Run*," he managed to say, pointing toward the wood line that was not very far away. "Don't make tracks."

BethAnne began to protest, but she'd gotten to know this man fairly well in the short amount of time they'd been together. He was a realist who thought that life was pretty cheap. She resented that, when so many she knew who thought it dear had been cut down by the virus or through savagery, but perhaps his come-what-may attitude had actually extended his lifespan. He knew he was a dead man now, though, and was going to take a few of these dickheads with him if he could. The utility of his plan became apparent to her. Dan had the high ground here, and it would not be easy to circle around him from either side. The biggest drawback was insufficient ammo, and that awful bludgeoning would be taking its toll.

In the few seconds it took for all this to go through her mind, Dan had retrieved his rifle from behind the seat and sprawled out at the rear of the vehicle, peeking out over the edge of the elevated shelf as best he could. A shotgun blast from his left shattered the back window, raining glass down on him. He jumped to his feet, spotted the shooter running zigzag up the old construction ramp in his tire tracks, led him

just right, and let him have it. BethAnne saw the man's throat explode
and watched him go head over heels right off the side of the rock face,
landing below somewhere with a dull thud. A swarm of bullets flew
up at them and struck the SUV or sang in the air overhead. Dan hit
the ground and got back into a prone sniper position, moaning loudly.
Either he was in pain from the jarring effect that had on his smashed
face, or he was trying to fool the men below into thinking he was
hit. He looked over his shoulder once and waved angrily toward the
woods. "Go," he ordered again through broken gritted teeth. That's
all she needed, besides her coat and knapsack from the backseat.

BethAnne headed straight into the woods, keeping to the high
ridge and "lining out" using landmarks that were directly ahead each
time so she didn't start making circles. Luckily it was late afternoon,
and she doubted they would pursue her very far into such darkening
hinterland. The snow they'd had that winter melted off the road fairly
quickly, but it still lined the ground up in these woods. It didn't impede
her progress too much, but it did leave tracks. She ran until she was
completely breathless, walked for a while, and then ran some more,
flinching whenever she heard exchanges of gunfire from behind.

As night fell, BethAnne dropped down into high fields for easier
passage, keeping Route 30 in sight to her left but regaining the woods
whenever side roads appeared that might put them onto her in an
instant. She could see a car far down below in the valley with its lights
off, cruising up and down the same long stretch, but proceeded along
the tree line and simply sat still whenever it came close. She knew
from her road crew–foraging experience that she needed to bypass
the village of Schoharie on its wilder eastern flank, and picked the
best spot she could find to cross the big road without leaving apparent
tracks, probably well after they'd given up for the day. She broke into
an ice-cold house, got right into bed under a pile of blankets, and fell
immediately into a deep sleep.

The Cave Clan fugitive continued this flight pattern for three
days, keeping off the roads, stretching out the very limited amount
of food she had with her, drinking from creeks, and breaking into
houses in the late afternoon as needed. The most dangerous part

was crossing the bridge over the Schoharie Creek at Middleburgh, which she accomplished at the deadest time of night, with nothing but moonlight to guide her.

BethAnne was running out of steam heading through North Blenheim, and her feet were nearly frozen. It was most fortunate that Rick had spotted her while scouting down below the house, before they'd relocated. He told her later that he thought she might be a "bait girl," a trick used in Oneonta that employed a seemingly terrified waif with running mascara who was tailed by road crews. A second variety employed little boys—fitted up with teddy bears or other props—called "screamers" for some reason, though the Good Samaritans flushed out in this manner were the ones who did the screaming.

"And so here we are," she concluded, with a half smile and tilt of her head. She stood up, brushed off her backside, and scanned below for Dave.

BethAnne had delivered much of her tale while looking down at her feet, or at bits of vegetation she plucked and twisted. This was obviously difficult to relate, and she seemed to rise out of herself in the telling of it. She'd dropped her guard, bared her soul, and transfixed her listener. Her narrative was highly informative, but Dar's biggest takeaway was that she was strong, deep, and nobody's fool.

He'd also had a chance to study her physical qualities more intently, and by the time she was done he realized how truly beautiful she was, in the less troublesome, non-drop-dead-gorgeous way he preferred. Needless to say, not all ravishing beauties and strikingly handsome guys were stuck-up, but he'd often thought being highly attractive must have been a curse in some ways—considering it in the past tense now, as with so many other things—though needless to say whatever they went through paled in comparison to the crueler side of lookism. Her face was perfectly oval, rendering the chin a little rounded, not unlike a pilchard's. Comparing her looks to a member of the sardine family would not exactly be well received, but it was a beautifully sculpted visage. She looked rather like an ancient princess of Britain, most fair, with light blue eyes under Grace Kelly brows, high regal cheekbones, inviting lips, and nicely styled, mid-length honey-blonde hair. She was clean of limb too (as far he could tell), shapely, with a little extra on the hips and bust, and of average height. Good teeth, he might add, if she were a horse, and she would think him a horse's ass for contemplating her in all those terms to begin with. A light sheen of perspiration gave her even more of a resplendent glow, sitting there on her little earthen throne on a sunny hillside amid all the biological splendor of early spring.

"Geez, I don't know what to say, BethAnne. That's an amazing story. When I was stuck in that cellar for months I imagined things like that going on, but wondered if people had pulled together somehow and I was down there for nothing. I'm sorry about the friends you lost."

"There's probably millions of stories out there like that," she replied, back in a standoffish mode now, complete with a little pout. "Things are ugly and brutal."

"I can see why you like it here. There's some hope for the future."

"Actually, I see this camp as the barest flickering flame. And I must ask you something. I haven't told that story to anyone else, other than a little bit to Dave about the logistics back in town. Especially the part about being on the road crew, though I was more of a scrounger than a soldier. I'd appreciate it if you'd keep all of that to yourself."

"Why share it with me?" Dar asked quizzically, shrugging his shoulders.

"I don't know," she answered a bit meekly, her mood changing yet again. "I guess I needed to talk about it all once. And you seem discreet to me. Are you discreet, Dar?"

"More than many, probably, but to tell you the truth, I'm still just getting used to being around people again after so much time by myself."

"Well, we'll just have to help you with that," BethAnne replied in a borderline-sultry manner, leaving Dar a bit nonplussed. She ran a little hot and cold, and seemed to enjoy this moment of dominion. He slowly retrieved his rifle from where it was leaning against the log, partially pumped it open to verify a round was chambered, snapped it shut again so vigorously that it gave her a little start, and hung it languidly at a slight angle off his thigh, the tiniest of smirks visible above his unshaven chin.

"Touché," she said, with the same little head tilt and smile.

ΩΩΩ

Dave returned in short order, probably because he'd heard the action of the rifle, and the trio prepared to leave.

"Questions?" asked Dave. "We will talk along the way."

"Yes. What about the older man I saw? Who's he?"

"Sorry. That is Herbert, our most senior member. He is in pretty good shape for his age, and highly interesting to talk to, but he's slipping mentally. He had come to visit a friend on this very road, not far from where we found you, close to the creek in a primitive log cabin with a stone fireplace. Rick and Bennie came upon him one day as they were completing a check of the most nearby homes. His host was dead of the virus, for quite a while we think, laid to rest by Herbert in a shallow grave. He had no heat or food, and no symptoms, so they thought it would be best to invite him back."

"Where did he come from?" asked Dar.

"He told Rick parts north, and he told Gwen from the Deep South. When I asked him once he said '*Sine loco, sine nomine, sine anno.*' You would probably get your own answer."

"He was telling me the other day that he piloted the very first automobile into the Adirondacks!" BethAnne added.

"What would you do if somebody showed symptoms of the virus?"

"We have discussed that," Dave replied. "Quarantine in one of the closest houses first, with support to the end."

"What do you know about it, and about the nuclear exchange? Did that really happen?" Dar picked up a foot-long stick and was going to throw it tomahawk-style at an upcoming tree, but sensed Dave would probably disapprove, and flipped it off to the side instead.

"We do not know much about the virus that you don't know yourself already, other than directly witnessing its effects on people, a fate you were spared. There are more questions than answers. How did it start? Was it zoonotic? How many have survived? Around these parts, I am thinking one in the mid-hundreds, or worse, and from the news reports it is not a stretch to say it is the same all over the world. Early on, there was a lot of suicide, and murder-suicide. Either folks had contracted it already, they knew it was coming, or they just got tired of the cold and hunger. The biggest question now is will it come back? Is it still active, or dormant, or did it burn itself out forever somehow?"

"One survivor in hundreds seems way too high for the mortality rate. One in ten would be phenomenal. That has to be wrong. Maybe there were mass migrations to safer places."

"I am just telling you my unscientific calculation. I hope I am wrong."

"Brief contact alone wouldn't kill that many though, would it? I mean, there would have to be fluid involved, like sneezing or something."

"All I can say is that many civilizations throughout history have been rapidly wiped out by contracting something they had no immunity from. This seems to have been some kind of super strain. Also, most people were out of food and water within days. They had to go out looking for it, which meant contact, and struggle. Each one of us has seen thousands of bodies."

"I lost power, and then I was incommunicado. I have a feeling I missed some news at the end there. Was there any hope of a breakthrough or anything?"

"Not that I heard on the news, or have heard about since. I would like to think that virologists are working that out somewhere, but this thing was so rampant and indiscriminate that it is unlikely enough specialists survived."

"What did the news cover toward the end?"

"Horrible events mainly, once it was clear help was not coming. For a while people were just posting their own reports, sending them someplace where somebody was able to put them up. I remember one from Florida. I'm sure some of the young tried to help the elderly in the very beginning, but you can imagine how things devolved. Recent hot-asphalt workers taking what they needed from retired doctors in ritzy condos, that kind of thing. There were also fresh water issues, all those guns, and the bottleneck at the top. Terrible prison stories too, from all over the country. They were often just abandoned there, behind bars. And the children. That was the worst part."

"What about the government?"

"Who knows? No word on that toward the end or since."

"And the nuclear exchange?"

"We never heard all the details, but it sounded real enough."

"Have you noticed worse weather, like clouds all the time?"

"Absolutely. We kept expecting some type of physical fallout. The weather seems better lately. As for radiation, who knows?"

"How did everyone do all that driving around? Where I was there were some big snowfalls."

"Over this way it was quite cold, but it was one of those winters where it did not snow too much. There were a couple of big ones at the end, but it melted off quickly."

"What about next winter? You can't stay out here, can you?"

"Well, that is the topic of much discussion. The majority favor moving back to the farmstead when the roads become impassable, and getting out again around March. Another possibility is picking out a house up here somewhere. We have time to work on that one. A way will open."

"Where should I set my tent up?"

"Why don't you work with Gwen on that? Another thing we have been discussing is limiting the number of tents. The footprint of our camp is getting too big. By the way, you should always feel free to bring up any issues directly with me, but we have meetings on Fridays, with an agenda and everything."

"You guys know what day of the week it is!"

"Sure," replied Dave. "Liz is our timekeeper. Today is Monday, the second of May."

"Well son of a gun," exclaimed Dar. "I had it right after all somehow."

As the trio fell into a hiking rhythm and the newcomer mulled all of this over, a pileated woodpecker, largest of all the local peckers, began deep drilling operations off to their right toward the top of the ridge. This and the beavertail slap were probably the loudest of common everyday animal noises one would hear in these woods over the last so many thousands of years, bested recently by chainsaws and gunshots if you wanted to count those, and not including anomalies like a runaway circus elephant that crashed and trumpeted through the Catskills back in the fifties once, as related in an old *Life* magazine article he'd read. How would you like to be a soft grub an inch or two away from that relentless hammering beak rocking your world?

Dar's thoughts flitted to the stately ivory-billed woodpecker, "definitely or probably extinct," and then to the Carolina parakeet, the only modern one we'd had, bright green with a yellow and orange head. He wondered if either had ever been as far north as New York State. There were some late sightings of this doomed parrot down south into the 1930s. They rallied to the cries of any wounded companion by the thousands, it was said, making the job that much easier for feather hunters. The last one, Incas, died in the same Cincinnati Zoo aviary cage as Martha the last passenger pigeon had some four years earlier.

The dusky seaside sparrow was another sad southern case. We knew more about this species because its extermination was more recent. It was the opposite of bright and moneymaking, so what happened? Pesticides and habitat destruction were the main culprits here, including "improvements" around the Kennedy Space Center. These little sparrows lived in a restricted and specialized environment to begin with, generally spending their entire lives within the same few miles, and were under the radar until too late. Down to six—all males—then down to four, with names like Green Band; old and blind-in-one-eye Orange Band heaving his last little breath on a particular day in June 1987. They lived out their days on Discovery Island in Disney World. How perfect was that?

A portion of Melville's memorized anti-paean to Anglo-Saxonism said it best:

These pirates of the sphere! grave looters—
Grave, canting, Mammonite freebooters,
Who in the name of Christ and Trade
(Oh, bucklered forehead of the brass!)
Deflower the world's last sylvan glade!

"We are almost back," announced drover Dave, breaking the newest member's avian fugue. "Any other questions?"

"Yes," replied Dar, his head bursting with too much heaviosity and new information. "Any way I can go trout fishing now?" Dave and BethAnne laughed at that.

"I would just like you to have your talk with Rick first. Then fish away!"

"Music to my ears. Thanks Dave . . . and *BethAnne*." This coaxed a sweet grin out of her, which in turn brought a satisfied smile to Dave's lips.

Old Blenheim Bridge
by Arthur Cobane (probably circa 1931)

The Schoharie Creek comes rolling down
From hills afar through Blenheim-town,
O'er gravely bed by rocky ridge,
To flow beneath a wooden bridge.

Two hundred thirty-two feet it stretches o'er;
A single span from shore to shore.
Though you search the world round and round,
No covered span as long is found.

Started in eighteen fifty-four,
It took to build a year or more,
Though not in use, it is standing still,
A triumph of the builder's skill.

In days long gone its vaulted roof
Resounded to the steel shod hoof,
In latter days the auto's glide
Scarce stirred an echo e'er it died.

The stories that this bridge could tell
Might easily a volume swell,
Of storms and floods and waters high,
At other times the stream near dry.

Emboldened by the darkened shade,
Some bashful swain here kissed a maid,
And this may have been perchance,
The beginning of a life's romance.

Its tragedy it too has seen,
In the dark waters that flow between;
Eternity and this earthly shore
A daring man dared dip his oar.

Old bridge, as seasons come and go
And newer structures near you grow,
We know you did your duty well,
Long may you stand your tales to tell.

History of the Town of Blenheim, Schoharie County, New York, 1797–1959 by Helen Patchin Bliss (North Blenheim, NY: printed for the author by the Middleburgh Publishing Co., 1959)

SEVEN

As THEY FILED back into camp, Dar felt all eyes on him again. He knew his novelty would wear off in a few days, but in the meantime this was a bit bothersome. He asked for Rick and was told he was off scouting. As he approached Gwen for the chat they needed to have, he saw her seek out and receive Dave's unspoken reassurance from afar. After that, word seemed to circulate among those interested that Dar would be staying on.

Gwen's briefing was simple and straightforward. Dar was already familiar with some of the details, but she barreled ahead so rapidly that there was no need to point those instances out.

Her job was to keep the camp in order, and to put out three meals a day. These were often light, but they would help keep you alive. If you didn't like what was on the menu, there was always the next meal. Any food that was in storage or being prepared was off-limits. To put that another way, there was no "help yourself" food lying around. Sizing up Gwen and her main helper, Liz, Dar suspected this did not apply quite as strictly to those who worked in the kitchen. A nibble here, a taste test there, all undoubtedly deserved.

The primary provider of wild and remnant produce was Sadie. She planned foraging expeditions and brought along various helpers, most often Dawn and/or BethAnne. They were always accompanied by an armed ranger, almost always Bennie. The main provider of game was Rick, who did not have much help in that endeavor since the breakaway group had departed late in the winter, taking the best guns in the process. He would fill Dar in on all of that. "Keeping Rick out of the woods is like trying to get a mule out of a cabbage patch." When in camp, everyone ate at the benches. This was to avoid leaving evidence out in the woods, and to discourage nighttime forest creatures after scattered morsels, most notably black bears. Any garbage was buried or composted. That was Andrew's job.

They used a variety of pots, pans, and utensils from the farmhouse. He was given his own mess kit. For plates and cups they preferred a good set of old picnic ware found in a big box labeled "Fresh Air Fund." They were made in the 1960s or so of some type of hard colorful plastic that probably wasn't toxic, but it wouldn't be eating off them that killed you nowadays anyway. Apparently there had been a little skirmish about this in the past, and Gwen had won. The plates were compartmentalized, light, and easy to clean. You did your own dishes, usually with a wet rag that you washed out later. There was a large supply of fresh rags if you needed any (he took a handful). You cleaned your own utensils too, though most just ate with their fingers whenever possible. Almost everyone had their own sharp knife, mostly of the folding variety, and they had a few whetstones. They used real mugs for their hot drinks. They had a few extras. Which one did Dar want? None tickled his fancy, but he chose the cleanest-looking, even though it advertised a bank. They took turns each day washing the pots and pans, in alphabetical order by first name, and you switched with others if you were going to be out of camp.

There was a small brook nearby that Dar had crossed over on his morning trek to the Powwow Spot (a name that soon took with the other campers). They liked the fact that its source was filtered groundwater from farther up the ridge rather than from a pond or something. Gwen called this "branch water." They hoped it would run all summer, but the prevailing opinion was that it would dry up, at which time they would weigh their options. So the drinking water came from *above* the game trail that crossed it, and if you needed to wash out rags or kitchenware you went *below* the game trail. Did Dar understand that part? Yes, he did. A large-volume, gravity-fed water filter bag you replenished after filling up your bottle hung on a tree near the brook. And he had his own portable filter, so Gwen knew he knew about "bad bugs" you might pick up, further identified at a later date by Dave as giardia, cryptosporidium, salmonella, E. coli, and the like. So far so good for the camp on that score, but warmer weather had arrived.

You did your own laundry whenever you wanted to, in the location and manner that Dawn had demonstrated earlier that morning. This was carried out strictly with "crick" water, and there was a stiff brush for stains. His pants had come out pretty nicely, by the way. "Thanks. Too bad there isn't a camp newspaper, though I imagine everyone has heard that important news already." Gwen cackled and pressed on. The only place to dry your laundry was on the clotheslines in camp or in your own tent. Bright colors like hot pink were strongly discouraged for outside use, which meant prohibited. If your footwear got wet you could leave it by the fire, or on a small card table that could be moved around with what little sun reached the forest floor there.

They had a very limited amount of medical supplies and personal hygiene products, and nobody with significant medical experience. It was your responsibility to try and stay in good health, and to report any problems to Dave or to her. If you suffered a serious injury you were probably done for, so be careful. Did Dar have his own toothbrush? He had several new in the box. Excellent. He saw her file that away mentally for future reference. Did he own glasses? Luckily, only Dave and Sadie needed them, and only for close reading. "What else?" she asked herself out loud. "Menstrual . . . no. Something else. I'll let you know when I think of it." That turned out to be dental floss. It was at the top of her wants list, in case he ever got into any new houses Rick hadn't checked yet, along with painkillers, antibiotics, and seasonings.

"Now for the fun part," Gwen continued, "the bathroom." After some trial and error, things were running pretty smoothly. They were lucky enough to own a portable "privacy shelter" camping tent, tall and narrow in shape, and complete with a sturdy plastic seat and hanging bucket. They'd even cut out and installed a plywood floor.

Rick had discovered this gear in a nearby bungalow, along with most of the other tents and camping supplies currently in use. The privy was located straight behind the central tents, off into the woods and uphill a bit. You did your business and then you carried the bucket a little farther back and dumped it down a deep pit that was ringed with flat stones and marked by the nearby pile of dirt which had been dug out of it. Stored water was used to swirl out the bucket, and woe to anyone who failed to return said bucket to the tent. Ropes on either side at waist level guided you toward the privy and pit at night, though several campers preferred improvised chamber pots. Rags were used for toilet paper, as Dar had done. You could rinse out your rag over the pit if you wanted to, or you could carry it away and rinse it out in the lower brook or the lower stream. Andrew was in charge of this operation. He dug new pits as necessary, refilled the water bottles, and kept the inside of the privacy shelter clean. He even hung pine boughs in there as natural air fresheners. "Dave says he's the most important one here because of his blood," Gwen opined, "but for the ladies it's because he does such a dandy job with the outhouse."

Gwen and Liz were in charge of the fire, period. The idea was to start it up only as needed and to keep it low. They preferred good dry sticks and thick bucksawed branches to using a chainsaw, though there were plans to fell and split some hardwoods in the middle of loud rainstorms and heavy snowfalls when the noise might be masked. They knew camp smoke was "the map tack of our demise," to use Dave's words, and were especially careful not to send any up on clear days. Light smoke when it was overcast was more permissible.

As for spying the flames from afar, especially at night, the fire pit had been oriented toward Little Round Top, as Gwen referred to the small nearby hill, and the surround they'd constructed hid the flames from behind and to the sides, though they might be spotted from the ridge above if anyone was ever up in such a desolate place after dark. The fire pit itself was "Dakota hole" in style, an underground chamber with air tunnels slanting in from two sides. It burned hotter with less fuel, which meant less smoke, the flames were lower, it was easier to cook over, and it could be extinguished more rapidly if necessary.

Cole had recently been given the task of stockpiling firewood, and Gwen was not very happy with the results. "If he snapped a fallen branch in two for every time he flapped his jaws, we'd have enough wood to run bonfires all day long."

Behavior was next. If there were any concerns or violations they would be addressed immediately, by the leaders or possibly by vote. Drugs and gambling were forbidden. These had not been a problem, nor would they be. The human race needed replenishing, but not just yet. If you were religious, as Gwen was, practice it but don't preach it too loudly. She did not appreciate cursing.

Batteries had been a bone of contention, as they powered devices that could reduce their alertness or give them away. Andrew made a case for listening to his music with earphones, even if only in his tent, but Dave had to put his foot down. They needed to look forward for now. Besides, for all they knew a single GPS signal or something could spell their doom. Rick was in charge of the battery box, and they were only provided for flashlights, which were only to be used in case of emergency. Dar could keep his solar lantern, but he was cautioned against making it too bright or using it more than necessary.

Camp clutter was to be kept to a minimum. If it didn't fit into your tent, it had to go. They made an exception for a miraculously unobnoxious, centrally located, antique garden gnome that everyone was quite fond of. He was heavily faded and paint-chipped in spots, and stood tilted to the side a little with his right leg forward. His right thumb was about to touch the top of his short, deeply furrowed beard, and his left hand held a small oval box at chest level. The broad face was realistic, he had blooming cheeks, his mouth was open in a weird but endearing smile, and his eyes followed you around. A thick forelock peeped out from under his wonderfully floppy, dark red conical hat, and a blue shirt, brown belted smock, and functional-looking sandals completed his wardrobe. Dar thought this had some real age onto it, as one auctioneer used to say, perhaps more than a century, time-traveling to this woodland camp in one piece from some Victorian garden.

It was time to talk tents. Where would Dar like his? She gave him some background first. There were eight tents set up around camp already, including the stuff tent and a big old canvas pole tent behind the fire pit that they called the stores tent. Dave and Gwen shared a small dome job next to that one "but there's no hanky-panky going on," she said with a giggle. Most of the women's quarters were situated in modern, matching double-walled tents toward the middle of the camp, to the right of the fire pit as you faced up toward the benches. Dawn and Sadie shared a four-person model with vertical walls and a divider curtain, which left room for their possessions, as did BethAnne and Liz. Susan and Herbert were in a smallish tunnel tent above the benches near where Dar had first entered the camp. They felt Susan needed some protection, and Dave was certain Herbert wouldn't hurt a fly. Bennie and Andrew shared a three-person affair farther afield with a vestibule for their belongings that made it roomy enough.

Rick's spacious camouflaged unit was beyond that still, up near where the trail circled Little Round Top. It had kind of an evil shape, like an elongated, stealth version of Darth Vader's helmet. Rick insisted on being by himself, but he did allow a substantial amount of camp valuables to be stored there in the extra space. This included what they called the cordage box, containing everything from string to rope and cable, and the fire box, which held all of the extra lighters and matches, as those types of items sometimes disappeared from the communal tents, and nobody would dare enter his. Cole was put up in the stores tent for now, but that was becoming unworkable, and they needed to make some adjustments. All of the personal tents were modern, with treated nylon and rain flies, but they were mostly three-season models, and some were brighter or in more unnatural colors than they should have been.

Gwen shared with Dar what she and Dave were about to propose. They didn't like the location of the first tent in camp, as it could be seen from much farther away than all the others due to the slight elevation there. Herbert was a big snorer and would disturb anyone he shared with other than Susan, who seemed oblivious. Rick had left one tent behind in the outdoorsman's bungalow where he found the others because it was only a single-person "tent cot" that suspended above the ground a bit on legs. Their plan involved relocating the exposed one down below the stores tent and giving that to Cole, setting up the new tent cot for Herbert not far from Dave and Gwen—which would be better for his ailing bones than the cold hard ground—and moving Susan into one of the big doubles in the middle as a third occupant.

The logical place for Dar's tent would be on the top outskirts, bumped out a bit in the large stretch between Rick on one side and Bennie and Andrew on the other, unless he didn't want to be that far out on the periphery. They didn't want to expand out beyond that. He was basically getting the last big lot in the development. They were in a nice little location, on fairly elevated level ground that did not seem prone to flooding, and further sprawl would reduce security and increase the chance of being discovered. It was nice having some space and privacy, but if anyone else joined them they would either have to set up in the middle somewhere, if they had their own tent, or share if they didn't.

The final item related to the food Dar had brought in with him. Gwen knew his mother had done all the canning, and she complimented her on it, one homemaker to another. Dar knew this would be coming up, and he had an answer ready. He wanted to keep one jar of each type for himself, in his tent. The rest would be his gift to the camp. Although Gwen was highly appreciative of this offer and made a big deal about it, Dar could tell that she thought this was about right—a reasonable price to pay for how they were saving his semi-sorry ass. It would pain him to see this group eat in one sitting a bottle of something that he would have stretched out for weeks, but that's how the cookie crumbles. He wouldn't miss the tomatoes too much, come to think of it. He did make one suggestion he knew was pure smarmalade. How about a Jam of the Week Club? Each Sunday pick one type, and polish it off with breakfast. Start off with something snazzy like razzleberry, or blueberry lime. "Oooh," Gwen exclaimed, pinching his cheek, "I can see you're gonna do just fine here."

ΩΩΩ

It was getting close to noon now, and Gwen bustled off to prepare lunch, advertised as a potato, carrot, and trout lily-bulb soup flavored with freshly picked wood sorrel. The rest of the afternoon was spent working with Dave at situating and setting up his new quarters, labor that was supervised by a small clutch of curious chickadees. All of the tents in camp were lightly ditched, and in Dar's case rainwater would be diverted out into the woods rather than toward the small centralized canal that ran down through the middle of camp between the Commons and most of the tents. "Nice color," Dave remarked when they were all done and had stepped back to admire it, eliciting a stored memory from the very day of the tent's purchase, when he went with loden green rather than electric ultramarine at the last second.

Once this was all set up, and everything of his had been relocated from the stuff tent, Dar lay down on his sleeping bag for a moment. He noticed some light streaks of tomato sauce from the exploding jar that were invisible down in the dark cellar. He could wash the whole thing out in the stream when it got warmer, but decided that a little spot cleaning and some rain and natural airing out would probably freshen it up best. Gentle shadows played on the walls, and a slight breeze carrying muted camp pleasantries wafted in through his air vents. A couple of hours later he woke up with a start, wondering at first if this was all a dream.

Dar joined the rest of the group, about half of whom were visible in camp, chatting, doing small chores, and even reading. Greetings were exchanged, along with compliments on the new tent. This was timeless human behavior, thought Dar. People are wary of change, and they like to see things settled in a way that is familiar and non-threatening. In spite of all the advancements and modernism, we are all peasants at heart, and he was no exception.

Cole was skulking down by the stores tent and had not bothered to come up and socialize. From what Dar had picked up on so far, there seemed to be a little dark cloud over his head, mostly self-seeded. The emergency weather alert system had kicked in and his every move was being tracked now, like a hurricane forming off the coast of Florida. This was another natural tribal trait. Identify "the other," ostracize, and expel. If Cole had a bug up his ass about his current housing situation, it sounded like that was about to be addressed, so maybe things would get better.

Dar had noticed Herbert on the upper side of camp minutes earlier and became aware that the elderly man had been zeroing in on him the entire time, like a torpedo on low batteries. He was a bit stooped over, his voice was a little wheezy, and his wool shirt smelled of mothballs, but he had aged gracefully, like an old board member or bishop from central casting. He had piercing blue eyes, well-groomed white hair, and was completely clean-shaven, unlike the other men in camp, whose whiskers ranged from Andrew's dirt beard to Rick's mountain-man look. "Hi there, young fellow. Welcome to paradise."

"Herbert, right?" said Dar, extending his hand and speaking a little louder at first than he found he needed to. "Sorry, I've been meaning to meet you. I've been busy learning how you do things here, and I just fell sound asleep in an afternoon nap without meaning to."

"Sleep's the best thing for you . . . I do it all the time," Herbert replied, laughing at his own private joke. "Say, I understand you've brought some books with you."

Ah yes, village gossip. The routes it takes. How it ripples through the human coral reef, informing opinions and shaping actions. It's something you don't see in cities or suburbs quite so much, and certainly not in single-occupancy dirt cellars.

"Twenty boxes' worth. They're still in the van I was driving. I'm not sure where they'll end up. What do you enjoy reading?"

"Anything good," he said with a wink. "The classics."

"I'll let you know. You can have first shot at them. I have some food and foraging books that Sadie is interested in too."

Dar's response did not seem to register with the elderly man. "Can you feel it today?" Herbert asked, looking up at the sky and then raising both arms and spinning around slowly one time.

"Yes," Dar answered, lowering his voice. "We sing the planet electric, with apologies to Whitman."

"No need to apologize . . . a nod is good enough. Good, good . . . I'm glad you're here." Herbert seemed to space out again for a few seconds. "There's a luna moth on my tent. You know, the quite big ones, with the long tapering hindwings. Luminous pale green, eau de nil. *Actius luna*. Sublime."

"Do you want me to move it to a safer place?"

"That's the ticket! When you get a chance. And don't bother with the World Wide Web. You'll get 'how to move a motherboard,' and 'moths move north due to global warming.'"

"Okay, I won't," Dar replied with a grin.

The young man knew this moth, and had seen them stay put for hours on end, often on screen doors and windows in the country. He checked a bit later, after Herbert had safely seated himself on a bench next to Susan. Dar didn't want to worry about him following and falling down, and he wanted to do this his own way, without any second-guessing. The gloriously improbable moth was there, as reported.

To scoop the fragile creature up in a rag might damage it, and to scoot it off to a nearby perch might leave it in jeopardy. He needed the right container, and went down to the kitchen to enquire after one. Gwen was not around, but Liz was busy getting an early start on dinner. Dar hadn't really spoken to her yet. She looked up at his approach, and he noticed what stunning, almost cartoonish, pure green nothing-hazel-about-them eyes she had.

"Hi Liz. I have an unusual request."

"What's that?" she replied expressionlessly in a shy, low voice.

Hmmm, what have we here? thought Dar. She was compact and top-heavy, with a heart-shaped face and extremely short dark brown hair. A lightly chipped front tooth and a small, newish-looking scalloped scar just under her chin line hinted at recent facial trauma and the new dearth of dental care and cosmetic surgery. He decided that she was probably the youngest of the women, in her early twenties.

"Well, I'm trying to relocate a big special moth for Herbert, and if you have a glass jar with a wide mouth I could borrow, that would work best."

"Let me look," was all she said, returning moments later. "Will this do?"

"Yes, nicely. I'll clean it out when I'm done. Thanks."

Dar placed the mouth over the moth, tapping the tent so it would unleash its bristly foothold, to no avail. Cole had noticed the proceedings and chose this moment to come up and chat.

"Hi there Cole. I'm in the middle of a delicate operation."

"Why don't you slide something underneath so it'll let go?" It never failed, in Dar's experience. If you do anything a little unusual out of doors, one or more men will make a suggestion about how to do it better.

"Because I don't have anything that would work, and because I don't want to damage it. Maybe you could go inside and flick the tent wall around where its feet are." That did the trick. Dar covered the jar with a handkerchief and thanked him.

"Glad I could help. Did you ever smell mothballs?" Cole asked as he exited the tent.

"Yes," Dar answered somewhat wearily, taking that as an observation on the mustiness of Herbert's clothes and living quarters.

"Really? How did you get the little legs apart?"

It actually took Dar a second to get that, and he laughed heartily. "You got me! Good one."

He sat down next to Herbert and held the jar up so he could see it. Susan took an interest in this, as did everyone else gathering for pre-dinner conversation.

"They only have about a week, you know," stated Herbert.

"I believe it. I'll walk it out a ways and let it go."

"That's your good deed for the day, young fellow. Well done. Now what can you do about these blasted mosquitoes?" he demanded loudly, playing to the crowd and pretending to slap one on his hoary upper neck. There were great guffaws all around. Susan even laughed, and Liz even smiled.

$$\Omega \Omega \Omega$$

After dinner, Rick invited Dar to his tent for his part of the briefing process. Although Rick's use of the language was a little on the primitive side, and he reminded him of a young, less mean and overdrawn Bluto, of *Popeye* fame, Dar thought he did an excellent job of bluntly and succinctly summing things up. Most of the campers seemed to be direct in that way, probably half out of necessity.

Basically, he and Bennie were the only "rangers" right now, as no one else had the aptitude or desire. Dar's main job in camp would be doing this type of work. He'd mentioned having hunted and fished, and he had the gear, so he qualified for the position. Rick didn't give any history prior to arriving on the West Kill, and there was no hint of philosophy or morality. He covered only two topics—surviving and providing.

The survival part was pretty simple. They had explained some of it to him already, and the rest was common sense. Most outsiders are probably out to get you or your possessions, especially when in groups. Outsiders are to be avoided at all costs. The longer they could go undetected in these woods, the better their chances. For the time being, buildings and roads spelled death and destruction.

If you see anybody anywhere and they have not seen you yet, don't let them. Don't initiate contact and certainly don't invite them into camp. Dar asked about how Rick had brought BethAnne in from the road, and he explained how that was different. He'd made sure she was by herself, and that was down at the house, and not in their current, secret location. He seemed sensitive on the topic of BethAnne, and they moved on.

Don't leave tracks. You can't help it in snow, but you usually can in mud. Those tracks can stay there for weeks, letting others know there are people nearby, or even leading them right into camp.

Walk through the woods like an Indian. Learn to keep your head up, take note of what is about to be underfoot, and let your feet feel their own way along when they get there. Don't snap big sticks, and don't even knock one rock into another by the stream. Those sounds carry a long way. Keep your eyes peeled in all directions, including behind. Needless to say, no trash, not even a seed or a thread. Dar understood all of this to begin with but continued nodding appreciatively.

Weapons. Rick was down to a 12-gauge shotgun, with a good amount of shot and slugs, as those who fled in such haste got most of the guns but did not have access to the recently relocated ammo cache. For personal protection he always wore "Mrs. Rick," his Colt .45. It was nickel plated, with the shorter barrel. In case Dar hadn't guessed yet, he was a gun buff, down now to only two specimens. Two shots in rapid succession near camp meant come quickly, three meant run for your life.

Bennie had a good deer rifle. He was cooperative about most things but funny about his gun, which he didn't like to loan out. Although Rick could respect that, Bennie wasn't putting meat on the table, and this had become an issue between them, and in camp. They'd only taken two deer since relocating. With one of them Rick took the shot from far away, the slug dropped too much, the kill was not clean, and too much meat was ruined. He'd missed a couple others, due to the short range, and had passed up on many long shots where a rifle would have gotten the job done.

Bennie had hit a deer once, grazing its brisket, but the wound was light and the trail went cold. He said he was used to hunt clubs, where you drove the deer toward each other's tree stands. A stand would be a dead giveaway now, and it was difficult driving deer with just two men. Bennie was a weekend warrior, too noisy and fidgety to "still hunt." Once Rick actually caught him smoking a cigarette that he got from God knows where, which a deer could smell a mile away. He was an ambusher more than a stalker, and you needed to be both.

The way they split the duties lately was that Bennie accompanied the women when they were foraging, and Rick did the long-range scouting, hunting at the same time. They sometimes checked out nearby houses together, often with Dave. That was what they'd been up to when they heard Dar's chainsaw. Cole he didn't trust with a gun or far from camp, and Andrew was a Bambi lover, though he did eat meat. As for the women, none in this particular group was into hunting, though Dawn and BethAnne showed some promise. So, two prime hunting directives. They needed meat, but they couldn't afford to go around wasting bullets and making loud noises that might bring the bad guys in. Did Dar want the job? Yes, he did.

It was helpful then to break the hunting down by gun type. The 30-30 should only be used for deer or bear. Rick had seen bear signs such as scat and flipped logs, and he caught a glimpse of a hind end just a couple weeks earlier, but bears usually made themselves scarce. Rick reminded him that this was the time of year they could be dangerous, protecting their cubs. Using a deer rifle on anything else would likely blast away too much meat. Rifles would be the best defensive weapon against invaders, though his 12-gauge would shine if the action was close. Rick had found and brought back 30-30 cartridges in the past, and he was likely to find more.

Dar's .22 with all that ammo would open up many more possibilities. For one thing, a well-placed .22 in the brainpan or heart would bring a deer down as well as a big rifle, with much less noise. It would also be good for rabbits, possums, woodchucks, and raccoons, all of which he had seen. Personally, Rick would not shoot a porcupine, as they were a bitch to process, or skunks, for obvious reasons. Predators like foxes and bobcats and exotics like martins and fishers would be meager and stringy, and he admired them too much. Coyotes, on the other hand, were their biggest competitors. They chased deer away, and they probably weren't even purebred. He'd seen them, but not close enough to get a shot off. Most anything smaller would not be worth the effort. You would have to shoot about twenty gray squirrels to make a decent stew, for example. "That's twenty bullets, twenty loud noises, and a lot of death fer not much meat." (So, maybe Rick did have a soft side.) The live traps Dar owned might be good for squirrels, however, if they hid them well. "We could drown 'em right in the traps and save the bullets." (Well, maybe not.)

The .22 would also be perfect for wild turkeys, which was the number two preferred game after venison. They'd got some down by the farmhouse but not up here. Dar mentioned that he had a turkey calling box made for him by his grandfather among his possessions, and Rick said he looked forward to seeing it. He also liked Dar's machinist's chest, and asked if he could look through that some day. The .410 shotgun would be suitable for ducks, which sometimes landed on the stream or in some standing water Rick would show him. Upland game birds like grouse and pheasant were a possibility, though he had not seen any of the latter, and chances were you would miss a grouse when it burst up in close cover, wasting ammo and making noise for nothing. Carrying two long guns was impractical, and you wouldn't want to be out there with a little shotgun when you suddenly needed a rifle.

Rick told him about finding a large beaver on the side of the stream a couple weeks earlier. At first he thought it was walking on the rocky shore, but there was no movement. He approached it slowly, trying to decide whether to waste a slug or not, but it remained motionless. He threw small stones at its head and determined the beaver was deceased, though it wasn't stiff yet or leaking out. He carried the heavy rodent back by a rear leg, half expecting it to curl up at any second and sink those big orange teeth deep into his arm. Back at camp the beaver freaked many of them out, as they imagined it was diseased, and he ended up burying it far out in the woods. Moral of the story: some of them didn't necessarily want to see where the meat was coming from, so make your decisions and do your rendering out in the field.

Don't drag deer back, as that would leave a long trail. They had to be processed where they fell the same day, alone or with help. The carcass would need to be buried that day if possible, or the next at the latest. He had a few shovels and picks stashed in the woods at select locations for that purpose. By the way, did Dar know how to field-dress a deer? Yes, but he wouldn't mind a refresher.

Next he talked terrain and territory. The site of their camp had been carefully chosen. It was in the middle of the middle of nowhere, with a good supply of relatively clean water. It was unlikely that anyone would use the country road parallel to the stream as a normal way to get from one place to another, and if they were just passing by once they probably wouldn't detect the survivors that far out in the woods. There was one forbidden stretch of water that could be seen from the road. The greatest chance of discovery lay in giving away their position somehow, or in being ratted out from the inside.

To make discovery even less likely, they had dropped the trees Dar knew about to form seemingly natural barriers. At the bottom of the road though, the last three-quarters of a mile was wide-open fields, and it met Route 30 there, which was probably within Cave Clan ransacking range. Rick didn't know how far out the house-by-house searching was conducted, but if they or anyone else ever cleared the barriers, or came by on foot, the hope was that they would pass through once and never return. He'd left some canned goods in the closest cupboards and some gasoline in vehicles to reinforce the appearance that no one survived back there. He even left a 1950s double-barreled Daisy BB gun in one house. "Hated to do it. A thing of beauty. Nobody bought 'em back then though, so they're rare. First one I ever saw. They were goin' fer over a thousand bucks mint like that."

The camp was in the middle of a sparsely populated region, surrounded by numerous state forest preserves. Much of these had been planted in the 1930s, and such mature reforestation tracts tended to be dark and lifeless. What the whole area needed was a few good lightning-induced forest fires, which would now be in the offing some dry late summer with no firefighters coming to the rescue. The Long Path that begins at the George Washington Bridge and heads toward the Adirondacks cut through not far below them. Best to stay off that, and off the paved road, even though both were decidedly convenient.

Tiny North Blenheim was the closest collection of buildings, sitting to the east at the bottom of their road, and most famous for its covered bridge. Dar informed Rick he had trodden its thick, dusty boards once and fished the Schoharie Creek below it often when he resided in the county, never imagining that he'd be living off the land on a little feeder stream above it some day. The widespread population of the town of Blenheim was not much over three hundred people before, apparently all gone now. He'd also investigated the tiny towns of Jefferson, Eminence, West Fulton, and Breakabeen in a west-to-east direction north of the camp, finding them plundered and lifeless, though in all small towns like this some of the pre-apocalyptic residents would have made the same assessment. Farther off in that direction, Summit, Middleburgh, and Schoharie, the county seat, were also depopulated. From all indications the Cave Clan near Cobleskill was like a big magnet, and within range of its pull you were either with them or against them.

Their camp was on the flank of a long wooded ridge, tucked in next to a small hill, as Dar knew. A firebreak ran along the top of this ridge, which he did not know. On its other side, to the south, there were scattered homes and farmsteads toward the high plateau known as Blenheim Hill, and Gilboa to the southeast seemed clear, but as you descended southwest toward the Delaware County line and the town of Stamford there were more roads, and the terrain was far too open for Rick's taste. He didn't know what if any human activity was going on over there, and he didn't want to give away their presence, so they strictly avoided that direction.

Rick doubted there were any holdouts nearby, though they had found Herbert, so you never knew. Farther out, in a twenty- or thirty-mile radius, he imagined a few survivors, probably holed up in remote cabins or farmhouses. If they were peaceable types, perhaps they could all rebuild society together someday, but he let on that Dave had higher hopes for that than he did.

Fishing. He thought Dar was overly optimistic. Rick admitted he was no great fisherman, but their stream was not very big, and it mainly carried brown trout, most of which were replenished every spring from nursery stock. Rick and Dave didn't like people wandering around the middle reaches of the stream. You had to give notice, and sometimes the answer was no. The only spot on the water you could visit at will was where they did their bathing and washing, referred to collectively as "watering," because it was on a secluded bend. Rangers, on the other hand, could go wherever they wanted, though they needed to be careful, of course, and to coordinate with each other. It might not be worth the risk of detection, however slight, for Dar to be lollygagging around on the stream all that much. That time would probably be better spent out hunting.

Dar said he appreciated those observations, but he still wanted to try. He was more interested in the upper reaches of the Schoharie Creek, however—which was actually a river and not a creek—into which the West Kill Creek drained. He had fished that extensively over the years, though mostly a little farther down than might be safely and easily reached now. He knew it held bass, walleyed pike, and numerous panfish. And there was a single spot down there where he once pulled out brown, brook, and rainbow trout on the same day! Also, Dar wondered, would it be possible to mount foot expeditions to the reservoirs not all that far away to the east, where gigantic fish were sure to be lurking? Rick was leery of any such plans but said he would consider it later in the summer.

When he seemed to be done with his spiel, Dar made a proposal on the guns. Rick could keep Dar's deer rifle for a while. He would hunt with the .22, and he would keep the small shotgun and handgun in his tent. The latter only had one clip of ammo, and it wasn't worth lugging around the woods on most excursions. This seemed like more than Rick had hoped for, and he was very pleased.

"Okay, that's about it. Thanks fer comin' over. I'll let Dave know we had our talk. And I'm sorry I busted yer balls a little yesterday."

"No problem. Good night, Ranger Rick. Thanks for filling me in."

"You got it, Ranger Darwood. See ya tomorrow."

"That reminds me," said Dar. "I'd like to try the fishing out early in the morning, to return around dinner. I know to stay away from that one stretch you can see from the road. Sound okay?"

"Go fer it, and good luck. And I'll take the rifle now, if that's all right. You fish, and I'll hunt, and we'll both keep an eye out fer the bad guys."

Traveling up and down the Schoharie Valley, north or south, we pass frequently the mouths of narrow side valleys which it is a delight to explore. Down some of them run cold trout streams. Following the course of these streams one may be out of sight or sound of human habitations for miles.

At Jefferson, eight miles from the farm, a new country road was finished the past summer, which carries one over to North Blenheim, in the Schoharie Valley. As beautiful a drive as I know, anywhere, is through Summit to Jefferson, and then to the Schoharie Valley this way. At Blenheim one can go south to Gilboa, Grand Gorge and the main road through the Catskills, and north through Breakabeen,

Middleburg and Schoharie, where one strikes the Albany–
Binghamton road, coming out over the Helderbergs. To most of
my readers, these names are but names. Let a person pass but once,
however, up or down the Schoharie Valley, and these names will
stand for something all of his days.

The Little Hill Farm, or, Cruisings in Old Schoharie by John Van
Schaick, Jr. (Boston, MA: Universalist Publishing House, 1930)

EIGHT

NORMALLY the former night owl would have just been punching in for his second shift now, but the downfall of civilization would knock almost anyone off their game a little. And that had been a tremendous amount of downloading and processing for one day. Returning to his tent, which now contained the remainder of his more portable belongings brought over from the van under Dave's direction, Dar spent some time prepping for the next day's expedition in order to get an early start, laying out clothes and the like. He'd set up a little dead electronics area in one corner, and wistfully contemplated the digital camera and emergency-use cell phone that would have normally been brought along, as well as the laptop that could not provide a weather forecast. Dar decided not to bring a gun, as he wanted to learn the lay of this stream first, and could probably expect to fall in once or twice in the process. Preparations complete, he hit the sack by nine, formerly unthinkable. Two in the morning was probably the old average.

His tent opened out to the woods, for more privacy, but it was oriented so he could peek through the rear air vent and see what was going on in camp. This morning, from his far corner of the site, he spied a few folks out and about. A thin line of rapidly dissipating smoke snaked up from the fire like, well, smoke snaking up from a fire. He guessed it was seven or so. Dar thought the privy setup was great, but he'd had enough of that kind of thing, not using a bucket anymore had been on his cellar bucket list, and he fully intended to spread the wealth, with the occasional in-house pit stop for show.

Dave and Gwen were both up, chatting amiably with Bennie, who was waiting for the foraging party to rise and shine. Dar stopped in to let them know what he was up to, only to learn that Rick had already done so on his way out. He took a quick mint tea with them. Gwen handed Dar a little cloth lunch bag. "You don't have to do that," he protested, but this appeared to be the normal procedure for anyone heading out on long trips. He checked a bit later, and the contents included something that looked like an oatmeal cookie, along with an apple, of all things, stored well enough over the winter somehow. Dave preferred for him to bring a gun but accepted Dar's reasoning "this time."

Gwen got in a final word. "What do you do when you catch one?"

"A fish? I cut the head off, gut it out, wash it off good, remove the skin and bones and fins with my fillet knife, wash it off again, and wrap it in ferns or plastic. If it gets too hot I sink that into the cold water once in a while. I know, hide the guts and stuff well, right?"

"Yes," she said, "but leave the heads on. I can do something with those. Don't fillet them. Just gut and wash them. I'll do the rest. Keep them as cool as possible, and keep the flies off." That sounded like extra weight in his bag, not to mention potentially yucky, but the upside was less work for him. He nodded and headed out.

"Your tennis socks are too bright," added Dave.

Yeesh, Dar thought, chill out. "I'll muddy them up first thing."

The other thing the new member did not share was how far upstream he first intended to go. The plan was to trek all the way up to the intersection of the two creeks or beyond. He calculated that it would take an hour and a half or so to get there, but had not factored in how weak he still was. And on second thought, he didn't want to violate protocol on his first day out, or possibly get lost in the dark on the way back. Finally, it occurred to Dar that Rick might be dogging him from afar with the aid of his own rifle scope, as a first test of sorts.

The freshly minted ranger traveled up the south side of the stream bank the entire way, keeping the water just within sight through the trees. He was easily winded and had to make frequent stops. The high road appeared on the opposite side at one point where the water looped close, and he could certainly see what they meant about possibly being spotted from above in that stretch. He knew roughly where that was in relation to other features and pushed on toward the general vicinity of where they first found him. Dar was wearing shorts for the first time since the previous summer, with running shoes that could get wet. He made it across the water without mishap and then through a flat stretch of thick brush, into fragrant mixed forest, and up the steep, wooded road bank, creeping carefully over its barren upper flank on shifting and vaguely malodorous flakes of slate that were already hot to the touch.

He could see Betty Brook and the faint outline of the felled pine far to his right, so he had overshot the mark a little, but all was peaceful and quiet on the dandelion-lined country lane. Finding his own bearings like that gave him a deep sense of accomplishment. A creature scurried across the road far down in that direction and paused on the shoulder, standing up for a look-see like a prairie dog. It was almost undoubtedly a woodchuck, *Marmota monax*, the only mammal he knew by its Latin name, probably because that was such a mellifluous moniker. It was on a list of potential punk/alt rock band names he used to make up for fun, along with The Telfer Copy (Dar and his bookselling buddies once played a drinking game based on every antiquarian book trade desecration in *The Ninth Gate*), and such non-pc examples as Charlemagne Was a Pussy. The naturalist/hunter made a mental note to bring his powerful little field binoculars next time. He retreated from the road the same way, taking care not to leave any obvious heel or hand marks on the upper bank.

When Dar reached the stream again, feeling a little like Adam in the Garden of Eden, he pushed on for a while and found a broad flat rock that would serve as a good rest stop and staging area. The tributary was not very wide there, but it was quite picturesque. He sat still for a while, listening to the laughter of the water and various bird calls, some of which he didn't recognize. He washed his face and wetted his short hair and beard, which were now in a neck-and-neck tie. Dar left his water filter in the tent on purpose, and his water bottle by accident. He took an unprotected drink and lay on his back, gazing up at small groups of cotton ball clouds drifting ever so slowly to the northeast. He then enjoyed the bland but satisfying pseudo-cookie that had been prepared for him. There was a small, indigo forget-me-not in the bottom of the bag. Nice touch!

Thoroughly refreshed, and on top of the world, Dar turned his attention to finding some bait worms. He left his gear on the rock and made small circles back up toward the road, finding all he would need under carefully replaced stones and logs in a matter of minutes. He drew on an old memory of how his father had performed this chore, bringing his little children out into the moist mysterious night with a strong flashlight, letting them take turns trying to nab worms by the head before they pulled down into their nocturnal holes like living rubber bands, and allowing the youngest to stand on his loafers and get walked backwards when he'd had enough. These were not all as huge as those dreamtime night crawlers, but they were very healthy wrigglers. He washed up good back at the stream, using bottom sand as an abrasive, and plunged his muddy sneakers into the cold water, pulling off burrs and tightening up the laces like a Greek warrior readying for battle.

Dar repeated a little spring fishing ritual now. He liked to go over every item of gear once, especially when he missed a season now and then, in order to remind himself what he had and where it was. Back at the tent were two tackle boxes filled with duplicate items, spools of line, and even some saltwater gear, but in the field he preferred a medium-sized black knapsack. At the very bottom sat plastic bags with which to wrap the potential harvest. When he went by boat or canoe, or was not far from the car, he relied on a small cooler with ice, but that wasn't something most would lug along in the backwoods, even back when you could get ice in warm weather. The knapsack also held his floppy bush hat to keep the sun off, and a light jacket in case a chill came on.

Everything else was in a smaller "shore bag" that had lots of pockets. In the long outer pocket, a sharp fillet knife in a hard plastic case, fishing pliers, a stringer, a clean rag, and three sizes of Eagle Claw snelled hooks in their original packaging. Dar read the text with interest this time, and enjoyed that old photo they still used of the guy in a hat with the long stringer of Montana-looking trout. There was a little flag on the back over "American Made Fishhooks," but two of the sizes also read "Hand Tied in Mexico," and the third said "Hand Assembled in China." What! We made these tiny little steel hooks here but still had to ship them out before they came back with a nylon leader in a package? That was just wrong.

Four items were in the middle section of the shore bag. A transparent plastic tackle box the size of his outstretched hand—with divided drawers of compartments that opened up from the top or the bottom—carried swivels, sinkers, and diminutive flies, spinners, poppers, and spoons. A soft plastic container of similar size carried larger examples of those lures. A rectangular flavored-coffee tin with a plastic lid held his fishing license, bobbers, and a small tube of natural sunscreen. And lastly, there was a lined bait holder, also a black nylon affair, made by the same company as the shore bag. It snapped around your waist, and it could hold a few other things besides bait, like a stringer and the pliers, thereby cutting down on trips back to shore.

He examined the tiny wear- and water-resistant fishing license, which was somewhat soulless compared to earlier incarnations, like most things. It showed the exact minute he dutifully purchased it last April. Actually, when he was a kid on his home surf he never bothered buying one, and had been chased but never pinched. As a more responsible young adult in less familiar waters, he did start laying out that steadily increasing hidden tax every year. Dar preferred securing his annual license from quaint town clerk offices rather than from chain store sporting goods departments. He always asked if there was a refund if he didn't catch anything that year, or if he could pay in fish later on, which drew eye rolls at best but never a laugh. They'd heard it all, like security screeners enduring jokes about the metal plate in your head.

When accosted by uniformed conservation officers—whom he supported and bridled against at the same time—which happened at least once a season, or used to anyway, he often began, "You know, I really meant to get my license this year . . ." waiting to see their reaction, and then he would whip it out, continuing, "and I did! Here it is." They were either amused, disappointed, or annoyed. One stammered out that he was going to give him a citation for "failure to give good account" before standing down.

Next, the almost complete angler considered his rod and reel. It was a Shakespeare outfit, dark brown with a maroon reel; nothing special but very reliable, light, and precise, as an osprey to the fish. With fresh line that was not arthritic with memory he could lay a worm or lure pretty close to wherever he wanted. And it was amazing how far one could cast with nothing but a tiny swivel, light snelled hook, and half a worm, which was all you needed for water like this. Sorry worm, but if anyone digs the circle of life, you do.

Dar baited up, put everything back in his knapsack except the bait belt, which hung snugly next to his survival knife, and headed downstream, glancing back at the wide rock to make sure he hadn't left any signs. This isn't bad, he thought. Look what he'd been through, in the cellar and on the road, and even in camp. They were pretty anal about a lot of things, and he didn't like some of the trade-offs of communal living, but all in all, not too shabby. *You did it*, though partly through dumb luck. So far, so good. Stay frosty!

On a small stream like this, the fish could really hear you coming. Tread very softly, don't knock or grind rocks, and wait a minute or so after you arrive. By May things will have settled out a bit. The larger fish have found pools and positions they like, and all kinds of good food was alighting or washing down now, often making them more indiscriminate. You look for a run or a pool that's deep enough and that provides some underwater cover, ideally rocky ledges or overhanging logs. Early morning and early evening were usually best.

Dar passed by a long set of riffles before he found the first pool, and it wasn't particularly promising. The small waterfall there made it too much of a roiling cauldron, it was guarded by piled logs and dead branches, and there wasn't much reach before the next set of shallow rapids, but the pool itself was deep, up to his chest. You measured hale hail by what size ball it was, and smaller bodies of water by how far up your body it would go. He dropped the worm in from mere feet away, saw it revolve down, and nothing. He tried a couple more times and moved on. As he picked his way along the bright bank he pulled up an old family story about his great-grandfather catching the biggest bass of his life rock-hopping down a stream, though that one was twice as big and supported more species. No bass here. Probably just trout, chubs, and minnows.

A more auspicious stretch soon appeared, where the Betty Brook joined in. He knew from his brief visit up there a couple days earlier that the brook had its own trout pools, though some were clearly the result of habitat improvement work, but he didn't want to scamper up the bank again, expose himself near the road, or, subconsciously, see anything man-made, to use that old term. The confluence of two streams usually meant colder, deeper water and more fish. He tried this section, once more without result. Perhaps the skeptics had been correct.

The morning sun was strong now, and he lingered again, not wanting to arrive back in camp too early. This was the day he'd been dreaming about, and he would have his way with it. Dar took off his tee shirt and sneaks and stretched out on another smooth rock. He'd developed prison pallor from all those months in confinement, and would never forget the chill, and the taste of that bad air, so this was heaven. Turning himself over like a hot dog on the grill amid the sizzling, splattering rapids, Dar's gaze fell upon a small cloud of tiny hovering insects against the shady side of a miniature Gibraltar. He wondered exactly what purpose that activity served, and where the energy involved went off to. All of this lulled the great camp provider to sleep.

ΩΩΩ

Staccato scolding awakened him with a start. It was another kingfisher passing by, or perhaps the same one, patrolling its stretch of water and noting a foreign presence. The sun was in a higher position. Dar jerked up and looked around, but order and harmony reigned supreme. He splashed cold water in his radiated face, slipped back into his shirt, and donned the bush hat.

Extending the riparian reverie, his thoughts waybacked to who would have passed through there before him. Natives, definitely. Streams were natural game areas and good pathways, though Indians greatly favored lowlands for habitation and hunting.

There was probably one local person who frequented this isolated vale fifty years ago more than anyone else, the alpha ranger in that little era—a name probably lost to recorded history even before the downfall—and a different one another fifty or a hundred years before that. Who else? Trappers, or men after timber, or bark for tanning, or flat river rocks for stone walls and foundations. Farm kids having fun. Pioneers in the field of geology—of which there was a famous local father-and-son team he'd read about in the paper once who roamed far, wide, and deep—maybe. Naturalists and poetic types, perhaps. Sportsmen, presumably, though this wasn't exactly a fishing hot spot, eh?

An episode of some classic TV show reran through Dar's head, though he couldn't remember which one. Something like *My Three Sons* or *Father Knows Best*. They book time at a failing hunting lodge that no longer holds any game. One of them discovers that the big lake on the property is chock full of trophy fish—as if the owner wouldn't have picked up on that!—and the business is saved. So simple. It was clear why they didn't do it the other way around, holding up a bloody, dead elk with its tongue hanging out to viewers at the very end instead of a big stringer of fish. He could picture the proud writer of that episode enjoying its first airing in his stylish circa-1960 living room, his aproned wife serving up pretzels and a tall, cold glass of Schaefer.

Dar and a couple of nerdy childhood friends really loved these old TV shows, first discovered on Nick at Nite and TV Land, and accessed of late through more flexible means. His father was an expert guide as well. This was an early warning sign of Dar's rather oddball fascination with and predilection for things that belonged to the past, and his later antiques and collectibles work sealed the deal. Some of these shows were simply funnier or more interesting than much of the newer stuff. Many were little preserved morality plays, from before we became so full of ourselves. Neil Young tipped his hat to the cornier ones in a song from his kick-ass rock opera *Greendale*, which Dar had seen live in Saratoga. He remembered the lyrics.

> *It ain't an honor to be on TV*
> *and it ain't a duty either*
> *The only good thing about TV*
> *is shows like* Leave It to Beaver

> *Shows with love and affection*
> *like Mama used to say*
> *'A little Mayberry livin'*
> *can go a long way'*

On the somewhat disparate note of water music for murderers, Dar blew a speaker once on Young's powerful "Powderfinger," toward the very end of the song at least, and "Cortez the Killer" was an awesome indictment of cutthroat colonialism. The truth will out sometimes, killers! Somebody wrote in an online comments section "I claim this song in the name of Spain."

Leave It to Beaver cracked him up, partially thanks to rascally Eddie Haskell, a minor character whose troublemaking and insincerity rose to archetypal status. It was a sweet show, though loaded with stereotypes and conformist baggage like almost all old TV. Years later a comedian did a bit in June Cleaver's whiny voice. "Ward, don't you think you were a little rough on the Beaver last night?" That in turn reminded him of some shockingly lurid Tijuana bibles he picked up once in an ephemera lot featuring Betty Boop, Dick Tracy, and even Little Orphan Annie! What price fictional fame?

Speaking of Andy Griffith, whose romantic adventures in Mayberry were only slightly more erotic and depraved than the dark underside exhibited by old maid *Hazel* or *The Flying Nun*, Dar traced a short, steamy scene in the excellent 1958 box office bomb *Onionhead*— stumbled upon accidentally in late-night repeat at an early age, and said to have driven Griffith into TV—to his first nascent stirrings over the mysterious allure of women. A temptress in heels and hose invites the reluctant World War II–era Coast Guard cook to her cramped Boston newlywed apartment after hours (buddy Walter Matthau is out to sea), folds a bed up into the wall and otherwise tidies up a bit, taps over to the kitchen to pour stiff drinks while he checks her out from behind (cue the salacious mood music), and begins to take her itchy sweater off back on the couch. "My skin's supersensitive," she purrs.

In earlier times, human sexuality would be going on all around you, like the waterhole scene from *Quest for Fire*, and farm kids got the idea from watching animals do it, naturally. In Dar's case this was more by accident, and a little embarrassing, like the time that future Cuban poet and novelist Reinaldo Arenas and his mother had to jump off their mare on a country lane when it was suddenly mounted by an aroused stallion, waiting together in silence until the "powerful and violent" business was complete. As a vacationing lad Dar crossed to the seaward side of a small wild island in the Gulf of Mexico and came upon hundreds of horseshoe crabs mating like mad at his feet in the foaming surf, returning to ask his grandparents why they were all riding each other. But in modern times everything was often behind closed doors, up until the underwear section of the old Sears catalog and newer easy Internet access anyway, when you were the one closing the door.

Maybe Dar felt this way because he was introduced to these retro TV shows at a young, horny age, but was the stock in trade of many of them straight-up sex or what? And in sort of a direct way that was never repeated, largely due to their rawish objectification of women. *I Dream of Jeannie* in that bottle just waiting to serve. Elly May Clampett down by the "seement" pond in her form-fitting bathing suit. (And what were we to make of Miss Jane Hathaway from that show, or Dr. Zachary Smith from *Lost in Space*?) "Lotsa curves, you bet. Even more when you get, to the junction, Petticoat Junction." Anne Francis as *Honey West*, with the sexiest mole of all time and that pet ocelot on her lap. Joan Blondell from *Here Come the Brides* (just kidding—he might have included her just to see if anyone knew their old stars and was following this screed; she was basically an aging madam in that, but it had the heartthrob boys the girls ate up at the time, Bobby Sherman and David Soul, and besides, he'd caught Blondell as a blonde flapper type in the interesting pre-Code *Union Depot* not that long ago, and *va-va-voom*). On the black leather front, the fetishistic Catwomen, and Diana Rigg from *The Avengers*. *Gilligan's Island*—bedroom Ginger or kitchen Mary Ann? He loved the bit in that one where millionaire Thurston Howell III had his wife preserve his first-ever drop of sweat in a bottle.

Speaking of skewering capitalism right up there on the screen, and not in somewhat ambivalent ways drier shows like *Dallas* did later on, money-worshipping banker Milburn Drysdale and his blueblood wife Margaret from *The Beverly Hillbillies* were just about Dar's favorite characters from TV Land. Mr. Haney, in the greatest sitcom of all from that era, *Green Acres*, also did a bang-up job of attempting to exploit others for profit, country-style, once hawking fake moon rocks off the back of his crappy truck. Oliver Wendell Douglas was a hoot as the single sane person in a surreal universe, dealing with one absurdity after another. When Haney claimed most of the rocks came from the dark side of the moon, Douglas asked how they were found. "With a flashlight." They did kind of the same thing with besieged Archie MacDonald in the first few seasons of the much more recent BBC show *Monarch of the Glen*. *Green Acres* was a victim of the "Rural Purge" that led to a dozen premature cancellations around 1970. The networks wanted a younger, more urban demographic. Westerns bit the dust a little before that, and variety shows got the hook as well. Mary Tyler Moore, Archie Bunker, and the diverse crew of *Star Trek* entered our living rooms instead, along with a *Mod Squad* of far lesser fare that worsened into the 1980s.

There *were* important advances, but for the most part TV lost a lot. Many of the new shows that were supposed to be more contemporary or sensitive or even sexy, like *Charlie's Angels*, were just plain dumb, as opposed to intentionally dumb. It was like the Sunday newspaper funnies he came across in his antiques work. They turned *modern* around the same time. They got some good work done, to be sure, but in general they just weren't as funny or thrilling as many of their predecessors. Maybe most such offerings always stunk though, and you just looked for the few you personally liked, or you got older and your tastes changed. There were proofs of this decline, however. Certain funnies from the twenties through the fifties were actually laugh-inducing, like *Louie* by Harry Hanan, drawn without words. Everyman Louie—short and bald, with a big nose, huge black mustache, and an expression that barely changes—is roused in the first panel by his wife from the couch, where he's staring up into space, to fix a leak in the basement pipes. He brings various tools down in a sweaty losing battle through the next seven panels, and in the ninth he's at the top of the stairs in a tiny black bathing suit. Early *Dick Tracy* was more hard-nosed, *Flash Gordon* more fantastic, *Prince Valiant* more heroic, and *Krazy Kat* kookier, though they generally had more panels to work with, large in dimension and rich in color. Some of these comic sections ran dozens of pages and included all kinds of interesting diversions, like costume cutouts and cereal premiums. Yes Aunt Jemima happily proclaimed "Whoo-ee! Dey's all shoutin' fo' my temptilatin' Down South Buckwheats," sports stars pitched tobacco, and there were more Dumb Doras than Brenda Starrs, but you could measure progress by the decade. Every Sunday comic section was an adventure. The modern funny pages were anemic by comparison, with maybe a mild yuk or two on the whole small sheet or two, and little or no pizzazz. In another proof, they tried to revive the prime-time variety show several years earlier and the result was embarrassingly lackluster. This huge failure was a mere shadow of the form at its height. The appetite was there, but the aptitude had been lost. He loved old radio the same way, though it stubbornly survived, and even showed signs of health. There were days when he was sick and tired of TV and went radio-only, and days on end when he did nothing but read, but he always slunk back for more.

It had been ever so fashionable to put TV down, or to do the whole PBS snob thing, but Dar was an unabashedly ardent admirer of the small screen, in spite of all its shortcomings. At least he usually did something else at the same time, like price books or wax boots. As an adult, he tended to watch either lowbrow or high, and not much in the middle. Just one or two regular network sitcoms if they happened to be on, and no medical dramas or police procedurals. Sports sometimes, but not all day long, and without excessive hooting and high-fiving. Very few series except for HBOish, where they were not beholden to advertisers and could get real. He couldn't tolerate most commercials for their naked lies, especially when it came to the energy industry. What if all advertisers were forced by law or morality to provide the same long recitation of possible side effects that Big Pharma sped through for whatever pills they were pushing? Most commercials were grating, or wastefully repetitive, and he worked his remote like a Stradivarius, though some did good work, or worked good, or were hilarious the first time.

Dar had a sudden hankering for an ice-cold beer and a mondo bag of cheese popcorn or something. Speaking of Schaefer (was that still even being made of late?), he'd read that there used to be a huge illuminated Schaefer Beer sign over the stands at Ebbets Field in Brooklyn. If you got a hit the *h* would light up, as would an *e* for error. Why not an *s* for stolen base—because that would use the capital letter? He'd seen a close game last year in which a stolen base leader was threatening, the drama heightened by an increasing downpour that was about to delay or even prematurely end the late-innings game. The visiting pitcher threw over to first base four times in a row, causing the crowd to boo and the runner to continually dive back into the muddy puddle near the bag, narrowly avoiding the tag each time. The sportscaster quipped that he was probably trying to get the guy's uniform so waterlogged that he'd never beat any throw to second. Funny.

You could learn a lot about an era by watching its boob tube beer commercials. Dar saw an interesting show once that traced their evolution. When simple black-and-white animation and cozy social settings with ever-present trays of frothy brew became kind of boring, those lightweight Miller Lite "Great Taste . . . Less Filling" ads from the 1970s got more into your face. And recently, dead serious, deep-voiced, with a little twangy guitar and the usual visuals: "The Rockies run down the length of America like a *back*bone, and for almost a hundred and forty years now, that's where we've brewed our Coors Banquet Beer, using only Rocky Mountain water, and the *best* high country barley. That's something we refooose to change, and that's what having a *back*bone . . . is all about. Coors . . . the Banquet Beer." The spineless coasts should have launched a boycott, but they were too busy ruining America. One online commenter on this commercial did take time out of his busy day though to observe "it̄s hard to say coors uses anything else besides water."

The lowbrow was mainly reality TV. Something to chill to during his lone dinners, or well past midnight when the work was done. Funniest or stupidest or wildest clips, unusual professions like tattooing, and antiquey stuff, from pickers and pawnshops to the *Roadshow* and the Barrett-Jackson vintage car auctions. His viewing habits were loaded with seemingly indefensible contradictions. Shows about cops and prisons assiduously avoided any consideration of economic and racial cause and effect, for example, yet he learned from them. The same with oft-baneful extraction industries like crabbing, mining, and logging. Half the time those shows were more of a study in economic desperation and organizational dysfunction. They could probably have made a post-virus program right there. *West Kill Shore. The Amazing Downhill Race. Pimp My Campsite.* The reality TV trend was putting scriptwriters and actors out of work, and much in this category was truly awful, or dishonestly staged, but a good deal of it was interesting and educational in its own way. And then there was *The Joe Schmo Show* from some years back, the ultimate send-up of reality TV, and perhaps of life itself. Everyone was in on the gag except for one contestant—*you.*

PBS was indeed the American gold standard of the highbrow, sullied as it was by creeping corporate co-option. And the sun never seemed to set on superior British fare like *Doc Martin*, and endless variations on the *Upstairs, Downstairs* theme. With cable, there was lots of great science, natural history, biography, and arts. Archeology and cosmology were his favorites. For a news and politics junkie like Dar, the fare had never been richer. The History Channel had sadly declined. One of his girlfriends used to call it the Hitler Channel, and then there was a Civil War–worship phase, but he had little use for it lately. Full days of *Ancient Aliens* repeats and other nonsense that had little to do with history, relieved only by infomercials. Same with the Travel Channel, which was rarely about true travel anymore. "Killer Beach Houses." "Jaw-Dropping Rentals." Still, with hundreds of channels, you could always find something, and could always learn more about life, cheaply and conveniently, or at least be entertained. And for learning about America when it was still great, though deeply flawed—when Detroit still cared, and was cared for—the unambiguous retro stuff ruled.

And then there was *cinema*, the other great screen communicator and entertainer, constantly evolving as TV was. It was of the arts— like dance, theater, live music, museum exhibits, etc.—and could be attended in public, of course, which was great fun, but unlike the others, you could easily enjoy movies in the comfort of your own home. And although most older film stock was inherently unstable, cinema was among the most permanent of the arts in a way, equal to recorded music and second only to the printed word, capturing something as forever as forever could be if we had just played our cards right. We can't watch a live play of a movie whenever we feel like it, on demand, but we can watch the canned movie version of a musical like *Singin' in the Rain* or a drama like *Death of a Salesman* or a filmed version of a live performance with the mere press of a button. Or words to that effect.

The Internet was something different. You could certainly be artistic through it, or watch art on it, but the Net was more of a platform than an art form. Its content was highly impermanent, and right now, totally inaccessible. Even in *A Boy and His Dog*, the seventies post-apocalyptic flick based on the novella by Harlan Ellison, a ragtag settlement enjoys old movies on film stock with the help of a generator-run projector. That was in the movie anyway, so it was probably in the book.

Movie lovers tended to have opinions about whether cinema was—had been—getting better or worse. It could be a little difficult to generalize about such things as censorship, as it came and went, in different forms. And although the technology was far superior now, and independent filmmakers had a better chance of following their muse and even breaking in, there's a certain mystique and patina to the older material. Some of his film buff friends maintained that they made roughly the same percentage of great or sucky movies in every era, and that was probably true. The very last one he saw at home was *The Naked Prey*, from 1966, about a hunting guide eluding African warriors. The arrogant Westerners he led got what they deserved, but it held out a little hope for racial harmony. The location shooting and minimal dialogue were very effective. The flesh-colored underwear he wore before scoring a *used* loincloth was ridiculous. What, Cornel Wilde didn't have an ass crack? He gave it an eight out of ten.

Surely, some prehistoric campfire storytelling must have been phenomenal, but it went up in smoke. Nowadays you could have caught a restored, uninterrupted film on Turner Classic Movies, as wonderfully introduced by Robert Osborne or Ben Mankiewicz, or from many other convenient sources, with the pause button and a stocked fridge and one of the Top Ten Bathrooms in the World (your own, no matter how bad it was) at the ready. Maybe the experience is the thing—and the sun would blink out in billions of years anyway if an asteroid or gamma-ray burst or pole reversal or galactic collision or blind greed and stupidity hadn't gotten us first—but *dagnabbit*, Dar thought it was good to preserve things. They come in handy.

He revisited certain older movies only once, for a fresh perspective, and viewed newer discoveries once only, as life was short. Of popular fare though, there was a small handful he could watch over and over again, whole or in bits and pieces. Mostly action films, like the first couple in the *Alien* and *Godfather* series, *The Fifth Element*, *Gladiator*, and the great *Rob Roy*; and he had some sentimental favorites, like *Ghost World*, *Vibes*, *Office Space*, and *Christmas Vacation*. There was so much to choose from though. Phenomenal directors like Chaplin, Buñuel, Hitchcock, Kurosawa, Hawks, Lean, Bergman, Kubrick, and the Coen Brothers. Classics like *The Wizard of Oz*, *Casablanca*, *Ben-Hur*, *The Graduate*, *Chinatown*, *Blade Runner*, and *Pulp Fiction*. Smashing and meditative modern fare like *Children of Men*, and *Spring, Summer, Fall, Winter . . . and Spring*. Silent cinema like *The General*. Fun foreign flicks like *Amélie*. Clever comedies like *Groundhog Day*. Clever comedies like *Kind Hearts and Coronets*. Magical musicals like *Once*. Bravura Best Pictures like *All About Eve*. Revealing romances like *Before Sunrise* (and *Sunset*). Cool caper films like *Charade*. How can you name just a few, though? The best way was by genre, where one could dig deep.

To take just one, which had been reinvented at least five times by his count, several involving Clint Eastwood, Dar didn't care for westerns growing up, dismissing them as too boring and simplistic, though his own generation had finally begun churning out the occasional good one again. But he'd gotten into them lately, coming off of a noir phase, and a World War II stint before that. He could do without the squeaky clean Roy Rogers and Gene Autry kind of stuff, and the goofy 1960s types with somebody like James Garner mugging for laughs, and the 1980s pretty boy ensembles. He detested super fake sets. A good peripheral yardstick for sci-fi movies was docking, and a good one for westerns was the signage in town, which was often portrayed in non-period words and ways. One store sign actually read "Antiques." The real gorilla in the room with old westerns, of course, in addition to abusing animals, was Native American stereotyping and genocide. That could be handled well once in a great while—and correctly correcting the record or simply depicting precontact times in a sweeping and popular way up on the big screen would have been a swell use of tribal income—but cowboy-on-cowboy action was usually better. Almost nothing is badder than a bad western, but one reason there were so many good ones is that they made so many thousands to begin with, so some were bound to work.

You had to see most of the John Wayne flicks once, as painful as certain scenes are, and inarguable classics like *Shane*, and the "adult westerns" which included some of Jimmy Stewart's best work, most notably *The Naked Spur*. *Butch Cassidy and the Sundance Kid* broke ground for the fun hip western. *The Missouri Breaks* with Marlon Brando and Jack Nicholson from 1976 was stellar. The critics were not impressed though. Dar looked it up in a movie guide once and it was the only one he found that earned the designation Bomb. Not even one star! Brando's other westerns were highly enjoyable too. *Ravenous* ruled in its extreme sub-genre. His favorite movie of all time in any category was a contemporary black-and-white western from 1962, *Lonely Are the Brave*, starring Kirk Douglas, who said it was his favorite role. Blacklisted Dalton Trumbo wrote the screenplay, which was based on an Edward Abbey novel. Surprisingly, a small film called *Will Penny* was the personal favorite of his fellow post-apocalypt, Charlton Heston. This is probably because westerns have to do with the great outdoors and base emotions and simply surviving, all of which are so real, which makes the performances more real.

Dar had stumbled upon a pure strain of western just a couple years earlier, and that was the output of director Budd Boetticher in his seven-film Ranown Cycle from the late 1950s, starring Randolph Scott toward the end of his career when he could call his own shots. *The Tall T, Ride Lonesome*—"the lone man seeking vengeance amidst a brutal and abstract landscape" said Wikipedia, when he looked there. These stripped-down B movies were the pinnacle of the art. For one thing, Boetticher was a horse guy in real life, and for another nobody could ride a horse like Scott. And then there was that fantastic location shooting, the casting, which usually included a baddie like Richard Boone and a bullet bra-ed bombshell, and the sharp, spare writing. Not perfect—what is?—especially the few times they got into town or ran into Indians, but great. These thrilled him, and he was glad he'd got to see six out of seven of them in time.

As for TV westerns, long-lived *Gunsmoke* was king, especially the half-hour black-and-white episodes. Dar caught a swell one about a year earlier where land-grabbers try to drive out a squatter. It was touching and unpredictable, though using the same little snippet of canned birdsong every time they were outside drove him nuts. In another, Marshall Dillon must escort a fiancé across hostile terrain, and it doesn't go or end well. He'd wondered if there was a "best of" list, and sure enough found one on a good fan website, complete with teasers like "Dillon finds an interesting use for a pitchfork." His two episodes hadn't made the top ten list, and he had never seen any of the ones that did, but it made him want to track them down. Looking at summaries of the worst ones, number six read "*Gunsmoke* is so good, we can't complete the ten worst list."

Sappy like *Little House on the Prairie* or *relevant* like *Dr. Quinn, Medicine Woman* or idiotic like *F Troop* or gritty and less hackneyed like *Have Gun—Will Travel* . . . to each their own. *Wagon Train* was often wobbly. They come across a smaller party of kilted wagoners in the opening shot, for example, and you know you're in for every unbearable Scottish cliché in the book before the happy ending. He'd caught a single episode of *Rawhide* not long ago, however—*Wagon Train*'s endless-journey-across-the-plains network competition at the time—which had always sounded like more of the same but was really quite good, and even kind of raw. He read some glowing reports online and had contemplated catching the other 216 entries in the 1959 to 1966 series, streamed hopefully, without commercial interruption—if it held up, that is (216 of almost anything is a stretch)—very gradually, like one a week, before he faded into his own sunset. *"Keep rollin', rollin', rollin' / Though the streams are swollen / Keep them dogies rollin' / Rawhide!"* Scratch that plan. He wondered why he never saw Eric Fleming (trail boss Gil Favor) in anything else until learning he drowned on the Huallaga River in Peru filming MGM's *High Jungle* at only forty-one years of age. Fleming should have stayed aboard Doris Day's more placid *Glass Bottom Boat* from his only other big film.

When rocker Warren Zevon knew he was dying of lung cancer, he said that he wanted to live long enough to see the next James Bond movie. (He also said "Enjoy every sandwich.") And back to TV for a moment, where was *Mad Men* going, and would *Game of Thrones* rule? Dar had never got around to seeing the classic 1945 French film *Children of Paradise*. Paradise lost, though he had caught *Cinema Paradiso*.

Anything that is recorded and preserved becomes historical evidence after a while, making it especially tragic, before the downfall anyway, that most movies made before 1950 had been lost forever, especially from the silent era. There are the societal mores—what they were saying about customs and conventions, intentionally or not— but there's also how things physically looked before they ceased to be. The trick is to differentiate between the fake stuff, like props and backlots, and reality. Dar woke up on the couch late one night in the middle of a silent film he never caught the name of. It had a nautical theme and a California feel. There was a lot of running around down by the waterfront. He was astonished by the multitude, size, and ferocity of all the steam-driven machinery of the day that happened to end up in the background shots. How well was all of that documented on film otherwise? That's why old photos and home movies are also so important, though most will not rise to Zapruder magnitude.

Heck, you can learn things from the interior and exterior incidentals in a 1930s *Three Stooges* short. Even in much slicker productions, like *Dr. No*, the first Bond movie, the filmmakers preserved great snapshots of 1962 Jamaica—exact roads, wharves, buildings, and shorelines, and a good look at faces, dress, speech patterns, race relations, transportation, and room settings—quickly fading memories that would have been important to document had we survived. Pictures told a thousand words. And then there is the footage that was *made* to educate, like a moving farewell from the final days of Linotype printing at a large newspaper, showing all the details of how that worked. Even avant-garde stuff, like Kenneth Anger's trippy, beatific 1949 short, *Puce Moment*, that Dar once found by accident online when trying to get a better idea of that color. Plenty there for the fashion or fabric historian.

Lately he'd been mining more recent and sophisticated fare. Using the most popular review site, he looked at the critics' top picks for each year, from the early 1990s to the present, with a cutoff of 80 percent favorable. He then took a quick look at the reviews—which weeded a few out, or reminded him that he'd seen them already—and ended up ordering or streaming most of those titles. The vast majority were documentaries or international films, opening up whole new worlds. The last of the former he'd seen was *Watermarks*, an ultimately uplifting 2004 documentary about an original Vienna poolside reunion of the 1930s Hakoah women's swim team, who came up through the rise of fascism there. And the films were all over the map; *The Devil's Backbone* one night, and *The Pope's Toilet* the next.

There was something else about movies—besides all the jobs they provided and supported, and the neat industry trivia, and so many other things—and that was the magic in the theater and up on the screen, all over the world. What they had done for us for over a century now. And blockbusters and franchises could be okay, but you were more likely to find special insights, surprises, and delights in smaller films. He couldn't get a scene out of his head from a John Turturro/Sam Rockwell flick about a man in midlife crisis looking for a lake he remembered from his childhood. They go swimming in a quarry pond and meet up with sisters named Floatie and Purlene Dupre, who jump in from high up. *Box of Moonlight*, from 1996. It just came on late one night, before the virus, out of the clear blue, and he was transported.

We sure stared at big and small screens a lot lately, the new opiate of the masses, and much of it was not real, or good, but it was still through the masks of tragedy and comedy, helping to propel us toward wherever we'd been going.

There was overwhelming lament for bigger lost things now, of course, and the focus must be on new challenges, but when it came to TV and movies, Dar missed them sorely, terribly. He thought about all of it sitting on racks in film vaults and in computer banks. These screen gems might never sparkle again before disintegrating.

He recalled "History Lesson," a short story by Arthur C. Clarke published in 1949. The first part concerns a band of primitive nomads trapped near the equator between the advancing glaciers of a futuristic ice age. They carry mysterious relics with them, including a frenetic Disney cartoon short, depositing them safely on a last remaining mountain peak. In the second part, the canister is discovered ages later by a visiting reptilian race that manages to project its contents back on Venus. The film provides long-sought-after clues about the beings that once lived on the third planet from the sun. They now knew that we were a crazy-ass race of weird-looking animals that crashed cars into each other and behaved in insane and incomprehensible ways. No wonder we never figured out how to survive the advancing ice.

"No, Your Honor," corrected Mickey Mouse in a nasty divorce court battle with Minnie Mouse. "I didn't say she was insane. I said she was fucking Goofy."

ΩΩΩ

Glaciology? Animals? Oh yeah—he was supposed to be learning about this stream, and catching fish; not daydreaming about water under the bridge and over the dam. It was probably midafternoon already. Dar got his stuff together and proceeded downstream. He knew he was approaching the "visible zone" now but wanted to go through it once looking for good pools. A couple presented themselves, and he cast in with no results.

Nearly halfway home now, Dar was getting a good feel for the West Kill Creek. There were some long straight stretches, but it meandered regularly within a well-defined stony bed. Although the stream narrowed to less than ten feet on occasion, it reached five times that width, charging in shallow columns through rocky bends one way and then the next like herds of wild horses. He ascertained the normal high-water mark by noting where debris was still hung up in the branches of young willow trees and other shore scrub. There were dual channels in a couple places and several sections where floodwaters took shortcuts, scouring the land there. The stream banks themselves were usually fairly low, though one or both rose straight up from the water on occasion to beetling bluffs far overhead. An inviting ledge at the top of one such precipice was the secret heart of the stream, with wide views in either direction. Proceeding down the channel, you needed to cross back and forth many times for clear passage. This was usually possible right in the stream, but sometimes required portaging yourself around due to deep water or large fallen trees that blocked the way, including a few massive logjams where a misstep would gobble you right up. There was a little human flotsam and jetsam from properties upstream, including a rusty iron strap that was taking its sweet time tumbling down to North Blenheim, but not much.

He came upon an interesting and rather enormous clay bank, grayish brown in color with notes of blue and yellow, imagining it to be loaded with clues to the ancient past. Even though it was May already, it still seemed frozen inside, and big chunks of cold greasy clay were plopping out and splashily rolling down into the stream under the hot sun. If you were unwise enough to traverse this stolid, towering bank, your shoes would be sucked into its slippery depths, or more likely your feet would fly out and you'd log-ride straight down into the water. He later encountered another exposed bank on the opposite shore, this one quite high. It was all unstable soil studded with rocks and littered with downed trees, and it appeared dangerous to be around, from top to bottom. Other than that, the terrain seemed peaceable, though it was plain to see any great rain would turn the entire basin into a muddy, roaring deathtrap.

As the stream lengthened it became more mature, and the surface structure began to look better for fishing. Dar started to get little bites now, though he was so sensitive to his line that even bold minnows nibbling at more than they could swallow registered. He came to a long deep pool whose best approach was over a sandy stretch currently above water. The angler snuck up, tossed his old worm in as an appetizer, put a fresh one on, and cast to the head of the pool about fifteen feet away, letting the bait drift down naturally. His custom was to hold the line, or when the lay and light were right, to just watch it out on the water, leaving the bail open. There was an instant hit. He cranked once and set the hook, felt the weight of a substantial fish, and saw its shining flank as it came toward the surface for a moment before diving down again. In unencumbered water he would have let the fish tire itself out more, but there was a big sunken log parallel to the far side and he didn't want to take a chance that his catch would break the line or dislodge the hook tangling up with that.

Dar stepped up to the shore of this proverbial limpid pool, reeled in a bit, and in one fluid motion slung the fish well up onto the beach behind him. He scanned in all directions and then went back to the flopping, gasping prey. It was a very healthy brown trout, measuring out against his rod at fifteen inches. That would be respectable anywhere, let alone on such a small stream. This was probably the king of the pool however, or even of the upper creek—a holdover from some previous stocking, though it would be nice to think these trout were propagating naturally as well. The pattern and colors of its shimmering scales were like the finest tile work in the world, an exquisite example of how we emulate nature. While most fish are quite handsome, the skin of a carp or catfish or eel is sort of unappealing, and even repulsive, at least to him. One could stare at the artwork on the back of a live trout for hours, however. Well, a minute or so, anyway.

He instinctively moved to cut the head off, relieving the fish of its discomfort, and remembered Gwen's request to leave it intact. What to do then? Severing it partway to still the body would be bloody, and smashing it in the head with a rock was too ignoble an end for such a magnificent fellow traveler. He plunged his pocketknife through its brain instead, and death came quickly, with a few final shakes and breaths and a subtle dulling of its golden eye.

Now Dar felt awful about this in a way, as he always did, but that was life. You crushed insects when you walked, and you destroyed the aspirations of lettuce when you picked it, or created the consumer demand that caused others to pick it. He got the whole thing about not eating anything with a face, though that seemed anthropomorphic. He understood what the animal rights group PETA was thinking at first when it launched a self-damaging campaign to rename the nearby town of Fishkill "Fishsave" some years ago, kind of neglecting the fact of life that "kill" meant creek. He was not a fish-feel-pain denier. But he had come to terms with all this before. It was sad, but natural, as it had been in the beginning (Big Fish Eat Little Fish), was now (especially now), and ever would be (at least between many living things), world without end (though both religion and science said it would end), amen. It all got back to evolution. Is eating things that were alive something we should be gravitating away from, or finding a good workaround for? In the meantime, Dar was like the Indians who took only what they needed, on a small scale. He had trouble imagining how anyone in good conscience could kill life-forms just for fun, harvest resources irresponsibly, or damage the environment for profit. And although he had given up hunting before this, and had been taking very few fish each year, and was trying to cut back on face food, those were the real sins—not his murdered meat or Sadie's slaughtered salads. The fish was gutted, rinsed out, and double-wrapped, and the knife cleaned and returned to his pocket.

Dar threw into the same pool and then tried its lower reaches, but either he'd shown his hand to the remaining denizens of the not so deep already or it was all played out. He devoured his apple, a bit mealy but retaining hints of robust harvest-time flavor, burying the core deep in the leaf litter of the nearby forest floor. Party time in Subterranea for lots of little critters!

He continued down and soon came upon the early stages of a beaver dam in a sunny spot off to the left, just where the stream veered away at an angle. It was probably the most logical location, the best site they could find on swiftly moving water like this, but he wondered how it would withstand the rains of Ranchipur. Dar began to step across the dam, only ten feet or so from the lodge, which is usually far out in the middle of the pond. Come to think of it, that was the plan, and someday the lodge *would* be more inaccessible. This reminded him of the early mountain man who hid in such a lodge overnight on a western river, escaping sure death at the hands of his pursuers. They used to say that a mature beaver dam was the only non-human, animal-created structure you could see from outer space, but that was before you could zoom in on gnat droppings with your own phone, or like one comedian joked, watch your distracted self crashing into a tree via live satellite. He cast into the still pondlet but it looked warm and stagnant compared to the frisky whitewater just behind him, a side dish of primordial soup. Larvae screwed up to the surface before slowly sinking down again, and pollywogs had found a good home there too, burrowing away through fine silt at his seismic approach. That meant frogs, and maybe frog legs for dinner later in the summer. There were no signs of the beavers in this precarious stage of their stream bend makeover. Maybe Rick's beaver was the solo builder, and it had died of loneliness, or self-doubt.

There were a few places where stranded water sat in dark mucky pools up on low shaded banks, but they were temporary in nature, soon to evaporate out. Dar had expected to find active feeders joining the stream, but the ridges on either side were not all that far away, or high in elevation. Numerous dry beds stood ready to accommodate freshets, but there had only been the one regular brook so far, though Rick said there was another farther down.

He passed the broad open spot where Dave and Rick brought him across on the first day. There were several nice pools below that, but as Dar neared the watering hole where they did their bathing and laundry he realized there weren't any long, deep stretches that would support fish as the waters receded to summer depths. It would all be about the pools. He'd tried perhaps twenty-five so far, but most of those would shrink down before long. There was enough light to proceed, and he knew from Rick that the stream ran for a mile or two more before emptying into the Schoharie. There were much larger pools down at the bottom—deep enough to have claimed lives, as he found out— below a picturesque waterfall where mills had once churned. He also learned from Dave at a later date that the Wests were early mill builders in this part of the county, and they wondered if the creek got its name from them or from its direction. Those pools probably supported larger trout coming up from the river, but it was too close to the roads down there. He could see that the West Kill alone would not exactly support a fisheries industry. He would have to go farther afield.

On one particularly wide stretch, a long, hairy spider appeared directly in front of his face, suspended on a single vertical gossamer strand that shone in the sun and did not seem to be connected to anything on either shore. If this was not surprising enough, it rapidly climbed up into a network of silken threads, scurried among them, gained much greater elevation in the breeze, and parasailed in this manner into the tall trees along the remote bank. What was up with that? What freedom, compared to his trapped cellar spiders!

Dar landed a couple more trout and one decent chub before quitting. It was still quite warm, and he grabbed his second bath in ages, in an unapproved pool, complete with a little of his own shampoo. He sat on the shore awhile in meditation, dismantled his rod, and stole quietly along the leafy bank until he found the trail that Dawn had brought him along on that first morning.

As Dar came into camp from above, past Rick's tent on the outskirts and down toward the Commons, everyone was eating or waiting for their dinner of pan-seared morel mushrooms, fiddlehead ferns, and wild ginger tea. The thirteenth member stopped to observe this scene for a few moments, almost not wishing to intrude.

"There he is," cried Dave. "I have been watching for you out this way," he added, nodding toward the trail he'd first been brought into camp on.

"How'd you make out," asked Gwen, "besides the sunburn?"

"Just four," replied Dar, "but I was trying to learn my way around, and apparently I'm still pretty much out of shape. It's a very nice stream though." Just as he finished those words he reached the worktable and pulled the wrapped fish out of his bag, handing the package to Gwen. Most of them gathered around for a better view. Gwen pulled out and held up the large trout, to gasps, congratulations, and even a group hooray. "You rock!" exclaimed Dawn. Rick gave him a big slap on the back. "Father and son," Cole needled when the second one came out, which earned a communal laugh. Gwen announced that they could expect some fish stew the next day, and everyone got back to the business of eating and chatting.

Normally fishing is associated with time off from work, recreation, or straight-up goofing off, but for the first time ever, at least for Dar, there was a more serious connotation. Yes, this had been a little unintentional ego trip just now, and he was glad to earn his keep a bit, but it touched on something much deeper. He knew that so many modern-day jobs, even "good" ones, did not produce good products or good results. Bad jobs provided little more than pay, which was mostly traded for food and shelter. Work could be great, but too often it was a stultifying waste of your life. At the dawn of humankind, most able-bodied members of the tribe participated in the struggle for survival, there was nothing abstract about it, and you had a real stake in the outcome. When we evolved away from that we often traded in our commitment, our connection to nature, and our independence, as surely as peasants gave up their own tools and means of production in the throes of the Industrial Revolution. Brute or rote labor in return for wages, and lately real wages were declining, and benefits (in places they were provided to begin with) were disappearing. So yeah, we lived longer and many were better off, especially at the tippy top, but many were worse off too, and we'd defiled and disrupted the planet while we were at it. It was nice to go back in time, drink in nature, and fish for his living that day. And fun!

Fish are said to have been very plenty formerly in most of the streams in Schoharie county. For many years after the Revolution, trout were numerous in Foxes creek, where now there are few, if any at all. From a combination of causes, fish are now becoming scarce throughout the county. In many small streams, they have been nearly or quite exterminated by throwing in lime. This cruel system of taking the larger, destroys with more certainty all the smaller fish. Such a mode of fishing cannot be too severely censured. The accumulation of dams on the larger streams, proves unfavorable to their multiplication. Fine pike are now occasionally caught in the Schoharie, as are also suckers and eels. Some eighty years ago, a mess of fish could have been taken, in any mill-stream in the county, in a few minutes.

History of Schoharie County, and Border Wars of New York by Jeptha R. Simms (Albany, NY: Munsell & Tanner, 1845)

NINE

THE DAYS were passing by with some regularity now, and the newbie began to feel like less of a spectacle. Rick asked Dar to accompany him on a couple of leisurely scouting strikes, familiarizing him with the local features and voicing opinions on various hunting prospects. From the highest vantage points he got a better feel for the woods in these parts. Large, dark stands of spruce, hemlock, and fir were surrounded by lighter, more deciduous swaths of maple, beech, ash, and birch, and mighty oaks, pines, and sycamores towered above the forest floor. There were small empty towns nearby, and a quiet road ran through, but they were in a big patch of relatively secluded woods, and there were no two ways about it.

The topic of Dar's first name came up at dinner one evening. "He doesn't like to talk about it," said Rick.

"No, I don't mind. My biological parents kind of imposed it on me. My father was from Dar es Salaam, and my mother belonged to the Daughters of the American Revolution. They imported Darjeeling tea for a living. When I was a baby they called me Darling, and when I grew up—"

"I think I like Rick's explanation better," said BethAnne.

An enticing rumor surfaced that coffee would be on the menu soon, dandelion coffee. The roots of the common weed were easiest to extract in the spring when the soil was looser, and they grew surprisingly large in sunny borders and non-compacted farm fields. They were big enough now, and the crop was in. The roots were thoroughly washed, chopped, ground, roasted, and steeped in boiling water. This brew wasn't caffeinated, of course, and there was no half-and-half to go around, but it tasted reasonably close to the real thing, dark and rich, and about half of them savored it every morning from then on. Not long thereafter, chicory root coffee was added to the menu. Dar mentioned to Dave that the next time he was trying to talk somebody into staying, he should remember to play the coffee card.

It rained constantly one day, not heavily but steadily, turning all of the surrounding leaves into keys on a woodland player piano that never came to the end of the song. The campers hung out in their tents and puttered about in their raincoats, completing what chores they could. Dar had been out early and caught a few small trout before the stream browned up, going directly to the productive pools this time. They had comforting fish soup for dinner, a rich base prepared with carrots, canned tomatoes, and wild parsnips. He was relieved to find no eyeballs staring up at him.

Stinging and biting insects were increasingly prevalent, especially when there was no breeze to push them off. Predacious mosquitoes and a small advance contingent of voracious black flies introduced themselves to the company, and with tenacious horseflies it was either fatally swat them or be bitten. The nylon head nets they had were a godsend, procured from the same providential bungalow where Rick found the tents. Lots of piercings got through though, particularly to arms and legs. Susan was especially beset due to her slow defenses and fair skin. Pants and long-sleeved shirts were advisable even though it was getting hotter out.

Sadie and Dawn brought fresh jewelweed into camp as a remedy. This tall plant grew in profusion close to the water, and as the summer progressed would be easily recognizable by its little orange trumpet-shaped flowers that hang down like jewels. You simply split the stalks down the middle and rub the juice on the affected area, or you crumple and rub the leaves on same. It was also said to be good for bee stings, poison ivy, and nettles. This most common variety of jewelweed was the spotted touch-me-not. As the plant matures, small, bright green, football-shaped seedpods appear. When touched or sufficiently ripe they explode out in all directions like the mishandled inner works of tiny pocket watches. Dar and his siblings were fascinated by these as children, touch-me-notting them near each other's faces to see if the tender fragments would score a hit. Anything up the nostrils brought the most laughter.

Camp assembly day arrived, pushed back from Friday to Sunday due to the wet weather. This regular event provided some structure, it was an efficient way to make announcements and discuss concerns, and it was good for morale. You were gently cajoled into listening in during the new business stage, and attendance after that was discretionary. This was held after dinner and accompanied by commercial stockpiled tea, weak of necessity but sweetened with local sorghum syrup from Gwen's magical backwoods pantry.

As the campers arrayed themselves on the amphitheater benches, Dave took center stage in front of the fire pit. He began by formally welcoming Dar to the community and thanking everyone who had helped him settle in. He then expressed appreciation for the significant contribution of canned goods, which would really liven up their menus, with special reference to the Jam of the Week Club. Next came a quick review of recent accomplishments, and some commonsense reminders about this or that. He asked Sadie to give a brief refresher on tick bite prevention, and on what poison ivy looks like. Dave followed that up with a few words on the telltale signs of animals with rabies, as such infection would now be a death sentence.

The first extra order of business was the new tent arrangements. Dave explained why they felt it desirable to relocate the one Herbert and Susan were using, and to set Herbert up more comfortably. While Dar calculated that these were the two most malleable members of the troop, and you could probably ask them to sleep in the privy without much complaint, he studied the others as this was unfolding. The group dynamics were interesting. In general, they seemed to accept the fact that this was not a true democracy. Dave, Gwen, and Rick called most of the shots. From what Dar could tell so far though, they were careful to make those shots reasonable.

Sadie, Dawn, and BethAnne looked a little taken aback when they learned that Susan would be tripling up in one of their tents.

Dave said that they should figure out among themselves how they wanted to do this within the next few days. He apologized for any inconvenience but didn't see any alternative right now. Perhaps they would be able to turn up another tent and make further adjustments. BethAnne asked why Herbert couldn't go in with Rick, who had the most extra room, leaving the tent cot for Susan. Dave explained as diplomatically as possible that Rick needed to sleep well, and that Susan should not be left alone. Liz didn't say a word. Either she was just taking this news in stride, or she knew about some or all of it ahead of time from Gwen and had a good poker face.

Cole, on the other hand, who looked dour at first, seemed very pleased about finally getting his own domicile. Being stuck in the stores tent like a sack of potatoes all that time was kind of like being on probation, which in truth it was. Dar knew he'd had a stormy beginning there, but he seemed adaptable, and had wisely decided to bide his time. Apparently that had paid off.

The next topic was the disposition of Dar's books, which shook him. He'd expected to simply observe these proceedings, but was now thrust into the limelight. More importantly, this was really something Dave should have brought up in private first. He had agreed earlier, with Rick's assistance, to relocate his van to an upstream property that they used for the purpose of hiding things in plain sight. It was rambling and dilapidated enough, for example, for Dar's tire and battery to coexist on the premises without being easily discovered. They used the same old OUT OF ORDER trick, but this time the flat was mounted and the spare concealed. His empty gas cans, machinist's chest, and miscellaneous other gear were also well secreted here and there about the property. The books had been left inside the van for now, disguised under a tarp with an open packet of floor tiles on top.

This was the first time that Dave or any of the others had really pissed him off, but he didn't want to make a scene right then and there. All Dar could say was that he hoped to make some of the books available soon but hadn't had a chance to make arrangements yet. Picking up on his consternation, Dave said that he was simply looking for suggestions. They could talk about it again soon.

"Anyone else?" asked Dave. This apparently was the portion of the meeting where anybody could speak up, part window dressing and part safety valve. He could tell Cole was biting his tongue, but there were no takers, and the campers drifted off to their tents. A triumvirate was better than a dictatorship, and people seemed fairly content, but Dar would withhold judgment until he saw how the high command faced more serious challenges.

$$\Omega\,\Omega\,\Omega$$

As he picked up his dried boots from near the fire and began to head in, Sadie sashayed up. "I don't think I can sleep yet. Care to invite me in for a nightcap? I haven't even seen your place yet."

"I don't know," he stumbled, "won't that cause tongues to wag?"

"Usually not on the first date, but we'll see how it goes," she quipped.

Dar let out a small laugh. "Sure, okay."

"Good. I'll be over in a few minutes."

As Sadie entered the premises she complimented him on how well things were set up, and then went to the rear to take a look out the air vent.

"I like your sparkly sandals. Very Princess Jasmine."

"Oh, they're just for camp," she said. "I should take them off. Sorry."

"No need."

Dar moved to the rear himself now. He hadn't entertained anyone inside yet and was unsure of the protocols. Once he was established there, Sadie sat down cross-legged in the middle, removing a diamond-knit shawl and her sandals. She was quite slim. He guessed she was pushing forty.

"Like the nail polish?" she asked, wriggling her toes for a better view in the fading light. As far as Dar had noticed, she was the only one in camp so adorned, with matching lipstick to boot.

"Gorgeous, and classic red too! Much better than metallic."

"I've been meaning to chat some more with you," Sadie began. "How's everything been going? How do you like it here?"

"Great. Very interesting, the way you do things."

"It's been a big adjustment, moving from the farmhouse. I guess we had to do it, but things were much easier there in some ways. A roof over your head, room for everything, and warm. There's a wood stove in the parlor for heat, and a beautiful, big old green and yellow Kalamazoo wood-burning range in the kitchen. And not all this mud, though things are finally drying out."

"What would you do differently?"

"I don't know. Not much, I guess."

"It seems like you've placed a lot of faith in your three leaders," Dar said, trying to get a feel for how much Sadie might be willing to spill some beans or dish some dirt.

"Three? We do all discuss most of the plans. We talked endlessly about whether to move out here or not. We're basically free to go, but most of us have been through a lot together, and we're thankful to have this much stability. There's some things we have no say in though, like whether to take new people in or not," her voice hardening at that.

"Like me?"

"More like Cole, or even Susan and Herbert. You were advertised as a provider, and besides, you're a cutie."

"It seems like you're the main person supplying the food."

"I coordinate things, but I have good help."

"I understand you're a vegetarian, still."

"Yes. I know it puts me at a certain disadvantage, but I'm trying to maintain it. A couple of the others were near vegetarian, but they've gone back over. I don't blame them, though. 'Hunger is an infidel,' as the saying goes."

"I was wondering if I could go out with you sometime. I'd love to see where you go and what you do."

"Sure, no problem. We'd be glad to have you."

"How does it work?" he asked. "How do you make your plans?"

"Well, there's two kinds of things we do, really. We forage for natural foods. Now that spring is here, that's getting to be fun. Then there's the farm part. There are about a dozen on this side of Route 30 that we visit regularly, some big and some small. There was food in some of the pantries, including spices and things, though we took all that out right away before somebody else did. Seeds too. It's all in the stores tent. Mostly though, there's one well-stocked root cellar at an isolated farm where the produce keeps better than it would here, so we bring it home as needed. The big three have been last year's potatoes and carrots from there, and feed corn in large bags from a commercial operation, which we keep here. And we're harvesting some perennials already. We picked chives when there was still snow on the ground! We've had rhubarb, and tender kale and radicchio, and baby bunch onions. One of the farms has the mother of all herb gardens too, nicely fenced in. I can't wait to see everything she had."

Dar briefly considered telling Sadie about the bag of marijuana seeds he had, hidden well enough that Rick and Bennie hadn't found it the day they searched his belongings, but decided against it. They were very old now, but there were so many that some would still be viable.

"What about when it doesn't rain for a while? Won't things have to be watered?"

"Yes. I am concerned about dry spells. Watering is hard work, and that means less time for gathering, and more exposure."

"I don't suppose you could plant anything around here."

"There isn't much sun in most of these woods, and the soil is weak, but mainly we don't want to give ourselves away. We're planting from seed in a good garden at the root cellar farm, but the trick is to do that without leaving obvious signs. We've laid long boards down between rows so we don't leave as many footprints. That keeps the weeds down a little too. Of course anyone halfway smart will see things like tomatoes and lettuce and realize they are new plantings, so that's taking a chance right there. We'd start new hidden gardens in sunny spots near water and away from houses that probably wouldn't be stumbled upon, but that means erecting fences, and if they aren't done properly, rabbits and woodchucks scoot under and deer jump over. Maybe next year for that kind of effort."

"Interesting. What about farm animals? Have you seen any?"

"Just a stray cat once, really. The livestock and pets must have been let go, or they wandered away. We don't see much evidence that farm animals were slaughtered for food. Everything happened so quick at the end, and it was so underpopulated up here to begin with. The thing we'd like most is milk, and eggs I guess, but even if we found some animals we couldn't really take care of them without living right on the farm."

"I see what you mean. Were they all empty of people?"

"It looks like most fled, but we did find some corpses. One old couple was in bed together . . . still are. I feel the ghosts, not just them, but all who kept these farms going over the decades and centuries. All those busy hands . . . all those hopes and dreams."

"And Bennie usually goes with you on these trips?"

"Yes. It's dangerous because they're usually right near the roads, and because when we're out in the fields we're highly exposed. He usually steps out first each time and we hang back awhile. These are also all pretty far away. We leave early, and often get home late. Lugging stuff is difficult too. You'd be surprised how heavy even a small sack of potatoes can get."

"Well that all sounds pretty neat to me. I'd be happy to come help some time."

"You got it. We'll pick a day."

"The food has been great. If there's some way I can return the favor, just let me know."

"It isn't a favor, it's just helping out. Actually, we've kind of fallen into traditional roles. The women are the sustainers, and the men still like to shoot things and shirk." Dar didn't want to tangle with Sadie, but this was out of left field, and a bit harsh, and it required a response.

"We come in pretty handy sometimes, though, don't we, like when a saber-toothed cat shows up, or when Hitler comes over the hill, or when you need a plumber?"

"I can't speak to the saber-toothed cat so much, but Hitler was a man, obviously, and it's men who make wars. And needless to say there were female plumbers, and there would have been more without all the usual suppression."

"I'll give the prehistoric pussycat a shot," said Dar. "Men could run faster and defend themselves better—for natural biological reasons unrelated to sexism—so you had to figure out ways to make us stay and protect you." He shot a quick glance at her well-turned ankle to press home that point. "And I get that Hitler's testicles are to blame, and how there would be zero tyranny in a world without males, but somebody still had to deal with him on the battlefield once he got going, right? As for plumbing, there were some women plumbers, but some of those rusty nuts were barely crackable by big strong men. And talk about a shitty job. Is that something you really wanted to be doing?"

"Are you kidding me?"

"Yes and no. I mean, women are more evolved, by far, so we're largely in agreement, but I like to play the devil's advocate sometimes, especially with overgeneralizations."

"Well, you play then, Dar, and we'll continue to work." Sadie put on her sandals and stood up. Their chat appeared to be over.

"I've offended you. I'm sorry. Most of my conversations over the last half year have been with small stoves."

"No . . . don't worry about it. Now I don't mean to pester you about this, but you said you have some books that would be of interest to Dawn and I. Dave said something about the books tonight, but I didn't quite follow it."

"Me neither, but I'll let you know as soon as I find out."

"Fair enough. Well, I should be going now. It was nice getting to know you."

"Same here. Any time. Say, you mentioned that one of the top three doesn't have much input?"

"No, I meant that Liz is usually in on the decisions too."

"Liz! She barely says a word."

"It's different the way she does it. She works directly with Dave. They have a little thing."

"A little thing?"

"Now now . . . I didn't come here to gossip."

Dar did not dislike Sadie, but it was obvious that they weren't hitting it off all that well. He felt a bit played, like maybe this was mostly about the books, or perhaps she just wanted to get a better line on him. Nothing wrong with that.

"Confucius say, 'Don't drop tantalizing half hints and then fail to follow up on them.' Seriously, though, I'm just trying to understand how things work here."

"Understood." Sadie stooped to depart.

"Not Tonight Deer!" Dar exclaimed.

"Excuse me?"

"That's the name of the animal repellant line I've been trying to remember since you mentioned your garden raiders. It's all-natural and non-toxic."

"Do you have some?"

"No, but I think the name is cute."

"Yeah, I guess."

"Maybe there's something natural you could use."

"I used to use pepper close to my house, for lilies and other flowers, but now pepper is more valuable as pepper. Okay. So I'll see you around. Good night."

"You too, Sadie. Thanks for coming over."

Dar stepped out and watched his visitor head back to her tent in the very last light of evening. He whizzed out in the woods and climbed into his sleeping bag to mull things over, lulled to sleep by the lively nocturne issuing from vast numbers of peepers and insects.

ΩΩΩ

The day dawned gray and chilly over the base camp like a mountain range of cold slate. After breakfast, Dar sought Dave out right away, wishing to clear the air about the books. The leader apologized for the manner in which this initiative had been raised at the meeting and asked Dar what *he* thought should happen.

"Well, clearly they can't all come here. They would be ruined, and there's no room anyway."

"Agreed. We should not leave them in the van either," replied Dave. "They could be discovered, and we cannot get at them easily."

"*Get at them* sounds to me like they are now community property. I was happy to donate food, and to let Rick use my rifle, but the books are different. Also, you're forgetting my proviso. I haven't committed to staying here permanently. Have you even told the others about that?"

"Some of them know. Let me ask you this though," said Dave, with a defusing smile. "Why did you bring these, if you did not intend for others to have access to them? Is it strictly a personal library?"

"That's not the point. Things are not settled here, for me or for you. If something happens quick and I need to leave, I don't want to have to worry about getting them back."

"If things happen that quickly, I do not think you will have time anyway. Either that, or you will roll your van over down some bank in a failed getaway where the books will rot, or go to relicts as fire starters."

"Well what do *you* suggest then?" Dar responded, making a mental note to look that unfamiliar word up in his dictionary later.

"In the same house where we left your van, there are loads of built-in bookshelves. Right now they are filled with bestsellers, tchotchkes, stuffed animals, picture frames, and other items. I suggest we clear and consolidate what is there and make room for your books, keeping them all together. We can stick the boxes upstairs somewhere. Then we could make a list, and people could borrow them one or two at a time. That way—"

"And who's going to do all that work, and keep track of who has what, and make sure nothing gets wet and ruined? Some of the older ones are on coated paper, which turns into cement when it gets wet."

"You would be the logical one to set it up. But we do not want just anyone running over there whenever they want. It would make more sense for just one or two of us to do that, maybe once a week, retrieving and returning books. Perhaps we could assign a librarian. We talked about this already for the superficial stuff there now but have not gotten around to it. Having a real library would be a big boost, Dar."

"It might make sense to put them on shelves and hope nothing happens to them, but I don't think I want to add librarian to my duties."

"Well, actually, we have a volunteer. Liz has expressed interest in this. Helping you set them up, making up a catalog, and keeping track of who has what."

"She can make it there and back by herself?"

"She probably should not go alone, but Liz is pretty good in the woods. She goes with the foragers sometimes. Actually, she is in the kitchen far too much, and this would be a good change of pace for her."

"I don't know," replied Dar. "That sounds like a lot of work for nothing if I leave in July or August. It also sounds like another way for you to get me to stay."

"Not to dump too much on you at once, Dar, but that is the other thing I have been meaning to talk to you about. Now that you have a small idea of all the turmoil out there, has it occurred to you that we might be your best bet? For one thing, you only have enough gas to go one hundred and fifty miles or so, tops, and you can't always depend on siphoning. Most vehicles you find will be emptied already. And there is a lot of ethanol gas around that goes bad in months rather than years. More importantly, though, what do you think you are going to find out there?"

Dar had avoided this topic so far, and was especially determined not to tip his hand about going north to Dave or anyone else. He'd made vague references to continuing west but had not stated a plausible plan or goal.

"One possibility would be the house my parents owned, on the other side of the county. I used to love it there."

"From what I understand, though," replied Dave, "that is only five or six miles away from Cobleskill. They would be on you right away."

"I like the deep woods up behind there too. Maybe there."

"By yourself, starting with next to nothing? That would be folly. With all due respect, the very best you could hope for would be freezing to death in your sleep in January. The worst would be starvation, or discovery."

Dar was seeing a new side to Dave. Perhaps he was a blunt realist after all, like him, playing the New Age eternal optimist to bolster and reassure everyone else. And Dar knew Dave had been through hell, far worse than he had.

"All right, all right, let's do this," offered the newcomer, somewhat sobered by the import of this last tack, which had equal bearing on his Adirondacks fantasy. "We'll put the books on the shelves, like you say, and I'll talk to Liz about what she has in mind, and we'll do more work on it later this month. I haven't been much of a ranger yet. Seven fish in seven days, and no meat."

"Thanks, Dar, I really appreciate it. Let's do the first part soon. And not to jump the gun, but Sadie is anxious—"

"I know she is."

"She is interested in the lore books, field guides to edible plants, anything like that."

"Okay. And do me a favor. If anything like this comes up again, please speak to me in person first rather than springing it on me in public, all right?"

"Certainly. My apologies for that. This will all work out fine."

ΩΩΩ

The two men had been having this conversation on the bench farthest away from the kitchen area, and the other campers gave wide berth, sensing not to disturb them. When they were finished, Dar went up to Rick's tent, happy to find him home for a change. Even though the weather was still overcast, he wanted to hunt down the road, up behind a swampy pond there. Rick was about to go out himself, in a different direction, and they wished each other well.

It didn't take Dar long to reach his professed destination. It was the only standing body of water visible from any part of the road, lying directly along the opposite side, long and low. There were a few small ponds and connecting rivulets up in these thick woods, but most would start to dry out soon. This would be the main watering hole in their immediate sphere, along with the two brooks and the home stream below. Pale dead trees stood guard over the dark surface, and a large piece of old bark hung stubbornly off one of them like a scruffy Golden Fleece. The dark pond's languorous liquid was deeply stained from the rotting vegetation on the bottom, and its outlet down the side of the road was more of a miasmal discharge than a bouncing brook.

Dar had to make a wide circle in order to bypass the adjacent marshland without bogging down, but it was still hard going. Cattails along the edge swayed with red-winged blackbirds in full throat, his personal first sign of true spring. He loved swamps, but this one had a particularly fetid odor. A sloggy recollection of conquistadors in the foreignness of Florida's ultimate swamps marched through his mind—men weighed down with armor but slashed by the sharp-edged prickly vegetation anyway, ill with malaria, their feet rotting, harried by angry natives, scared to death of cottonmouths and monster alligators, beat upon by the unrelenting sun and sucked down by the muck, finally falling, leaving nothing but a few blue trade beads and bits of silver. We drained swamps with the same relish as we depopulated indigenous lands, and with the same result, but thankfully some of each remained.

Rolling hills above this impoundment presented a better view, and Dar could now make out what were probably a couple of live muskrat dens toward the rear of the black bayou. It was hard to tell from so far away and without further observation, but he just didn't sense the energy and industry of an active beaver colony. Ten-foot-high rhododendrons were in full bloom all around him, their light pink flowers dispatching waves of fragrance on each gentle breeze past skunk cabbage ack-ack guns to do olfactory battle on the front lines of the stinky swamp below. He came upon a small, rocky trickle still burbling down through the evergreens and took position nearby. His seat was a bed of soft pine needles with a wide view in all directions. Red trilliums were a favorite deep woods flower, and they dotted the landscape below as if they had been ordered to take the hill he was sitting on. Tri . . . three garnet-maroon petals, three sepals, three leaflets. It was also called wake-robin, in a lovely reference to a fellow harbinger of spring; and birthroot, used by Native Americans to facilitate childbirth; and stinking Benjamin, for some mystery reason. The red trillium had no nectar that would attract bee pollinators, but between an odor of rotting meat and a color to match, it induced carrion flies to perform that chore. Dar had made a point never to sniff one, admiring the book-learnt cleverness of that adaptation but preferring the other associations.

He let his mind drift back a decade or two, back to his hunting days, and the Zen of that. A lapsed hunter was like a lapsed Catholic, or insert the religion of choice. You either grew out of it, or it had simply become too much of a hassle for the return on investment, or you rejected the practice now on philosophical or moral grounds. He was a smorgasbord Catholic on this point too, because he still fished, and he still ate meat.

In Dar's case, he knew just when the turning point was. He hunted because his extended family did. He'd done some bad things with guns growing up, crossing the line of hunting for sport. At age thirteen or so, a friend and he once shot at painted turtles in a pond, going for the head when they came up for air. This was more to practice marksmanship than just to kill something, but deep down he knew how utterly cruel it was. Another time he'd winged a downy woodpecker with a strong BB gun, and all it could do was hop around the lower girth of a huge barkless tree at about head level. He dizzily shot at it four or five times, at such close range that its feathers were billowing, until he finally realized that he was simply out of BBs.

Those things were awful enough, in addition to all of the more traditional game he'd slain, including gentle deer in those first seasons. One time though, he'd gone out with a .22 on the first nice day of the late winter, tracking a gray squirrel through the high, leafless canopy into very deep woods. It finally reached its nest, and was staying put. Dar took careful aim through the scope at quite a distance, squeezed the trigger, and watched it pop out and fall all the way straight down, dead on arrival amid a small shower of leaves, sticks, and stored nuts. It was a superlative shot, right through the head, blind, but it left him feeling incredibly empty. What did I just do that for? he asked himself. This creature, common but peaceable, wonderfully tinged with brown amid the gray, and splendidly built to do what it did, had endured the long bitter winter, and was just about to get his little rocks off (it was a male, upon examination). He kept his guns, and oiled them every few years, but this would probably have been the last living thing he ever shot.

Squirrels were all Dar was seeing from this vantage point, other than small birds. Not just grays, but slender, chattering red squirrels. He'd sometimes gone years without encountering these marvelous little Ewoks—minus the treacly sentimentality—deep in their coniferous forests. They were more territorial in nature. He'd once read that they did "an effective castration job" on grays. Even if they weren't totally *effective* though, that's gotta hurt, and mess your shit up. That was enough to put red squirrels on his varmint list back in the day, and he took as many as a dozen in one outing for stew meat.

The weather had cleared. After sitting perfectly still for an hour, taking the pulse of the deep woods and breathing in its ambrosial fragrance, Dar discerned dark motion far up on the other side of the little brook. He froze even more, not daring to blink, and turned his head imperceptibly in that direction. Not a person. Not a bear. Turkeys! A whole flock of them in all sizes, coming down from some feeding ground, perhaps to seek water and refuge in the upper reaches of the swamp. Low clucks and purrs reached him now. He looked for a bearded tom, but these were all hens and seemingly self-sufficient poults. He sighted in on a large one, waiting until it stepped out from behind some low shrubs about thirty yards away, and hit it right in the lower neck. The hen flew straight up and came down in a heap, followed by a few seesawing feathers, and the rest of the flock scattered in an instant.

Dar ejected and pocketed the shell, smoothed over any sign that he'd been sitting there, and went down to collect the bird. It was surprisingly heavy. He couldn't remember what Rick had said about field-dressing a turkey, but he'd read once that they had over five thousand feathers, and decided that would best be done back in camp. He plugged the hole in the neck with some moss, threw the turkey over one shoulder, and slung his rifle over the other. Dar rested once before crossing the road, laying the body down in a still life next to a small group of wildly striped O'Keeffean jack-in-the-pulpits. The trip back was mostly downhill, and in less than an hour after the shot he was back in camp with the prize. It caused a great stir, and the next night a dozen campers each had a big handful of steaming turkey for the first time in many weeks. Sated and lubricated, they drifted off into deep sleeps that night.

Just a few days later Rick got his third deer since moving up from the house, a nice button buck still in velvet. For the first time in camp, Gwen and Liz had more meat than they could use right away, so they began making venison jerky. They made good use of the heart and liver, and the company was even treated to small cuts of filet mignon one night, complete with baked potatoes and "asparagus" in the form of the tender shoots of great Solomon's seal, courtesy of Sadie and company. As an extra-special treat, they split a six of Dar's last beer, chilled as well as possible in the brook. Between spring being in the air and small satisfactions like this, the camp was in pretty high spirits.

ΩΩΩ

Dave, Dar, Liz, and Andrew spent one afternoon moving the books from the van onto shelves at the Ram House—their code name for this ramshackle property—throwing the curtains further aside to provide sufficient light, and employing the solar lantern for close work. Word had got out in camp that they'd arrived at this solution, and everyone who cared one way or the other was pleased. Once the bulk of the job was complete, Dar and Andrew wandered through the rooms, taking it all in. It felt odd to walk on floorboards again, and to contemplate walls. Looking through the kitchen cupboards, Dar found a vintage coffee mug of old restaurant variety, with faded green-and-red stripes around the top, and slipped it into his knapsack.

If Dar had been looking for a property to purchase he would have rejected this one, as he didn't like its prospect much. Everything was too hodgepodge, not much thought had gone into the additions and the placement of the outbuildings, and the house itself felt like it had cooties, though in truth most felt that way to him, then and now. Still, it was interesting to explore, and it had a few wonderful features, like an elegant center staircase. They brought an entire box of books back with them—the stuff Sadie wanted, and a good representative sampling of the rest, including some classics. They would reside in Liz's tent, and she would be responsible for them, from circulation records to adamant warnings about proper care and handling.

Cole was anxious to move into his own tent, and there had been some pressure on the four women to settle the Susan question. From what Dar could tell, there was no easy resolution in the offing. Dave and Gwen had been meeting with some of them separately, and it was probably on this topic.

One day BethAnne asked Dar if he would take her fishing. He had several extra rigs and was happy to accommodate her. They went upstream, slipping through the sun-dappled forest with youthful ease and coming out just above some of the better pools. They found worms together under gulch stones and rotten trunks on the flank above, and waded out to a friendly rock. Dar assembled the poles and began explaining hook size. It was hot out, and BethAnne was wearing faded salmon shorts and an airy peasant blouse. She sat down, took her sneakers off, and began waving her feet in the clear flow. While Dar enjoyed his aerial view of the glistening leg show, he debated whether to advise her on the importance of angling stealth, and decided that could wait until they approached the first pool.

"I like it here," BethAnne said. "I don't get up to this part much. They don't want us coming by ourselves."

"I know. I think you were all smart to pick this area. You could have found safer places in the deeper woods, but there's something about a stream that is alive and ever-changing."

"Not to mention who wants to lug water all day. Dar, there's something I'd like to talk to you about. I'll admit that I thought it would be easier to do so away from camp."

The would-be guide was just getting ready to bait up, but laid everything down and sat beside her, dangling his sneakers in the bubbly swirl next to her fair undulating feet. "What's up?"

"You know what they want to do with the tents, right? Well, I can see the rationale, and we all like Susan well enough, but she's kind of spooky. She basically just sits there and stares out into space or brushes her hair. All day long, with the hair. She won't even go to the latrine by herself. Somebody has to bring her. Herbert's pretty much out of it, and he doesn't care, but rooming with her would drive almost anyone else nuts. The other thing is we've all gotten used to the amount of space we have now. It's more than some people have, but we keep some community property in with us, most recently the *library* books, and we don't have anything of our own in the two storage tents like some others do. Sadie and Dawn are tight roomies. Liz is okay in some ways, but we don't get along that well. She could probably tell you what she doesn't like about me, but I think she's snooty and judgmental. Better and smarter than everyone else. It's sort of getting to me, all that silent disapproval. She's kind of a schemer too. I've tried to bring this up, but she's too emotionally constipated to deal with it. I see this new change as an opportunity."

"It didn't sound to me like there are a lot of options," said Dar.

"I'm getting to that. Just hear me out, okay? I can tell you for a fact that the plan was for Cole to move in with you, but they were afraid that would have scared you away, or caused a showdown. They feel they've given you fair warning for the next time, though. We do pick up new people, and it's probably going to be a guy. And he probably won't come with his own camping supplies, like you did."

"Your point?" Dar asked.

"It isn't a point as much as a proposition. What about the possibility of me moving in with you? That way, Susan could bunk with Liz, who would mind the least of us, and who might even prefer it that way, nobody would have to triple up, and you'd be protected from getting stuck with somebody who may be a jerk."

Dar was stunned at the boldness of this proposal. He didn't mind providing some counseling, which is where he thought this was going, but her plan would be a major threat to the little peace of mind he'd carved out for himself there.

"Okay, that's surprising. It sounds unworkable in more ways than one. The main thing though—and this isn't personal—is that I like living by myself. Then there's what the leaders would say, what everyone would think, losing space for my stuff . . . everything!" He paused in thought for a moment. "What about Rick? He seems to like you, and he's got a bigger place."

"Yeah, well that's part of the problem. Look, there are no rules against cohabiting. It simply hasn't happened yet, not including Dave and Gwen, which is just kind of practical. You'd think with a dozen people this would be going on already, but it just worked out that way. Rick is a throwback, Bennie leaves me cold, Andrew is a pup, and Cole's a dick. Dawn is basically asexual, Sadie takes her pleasures but she likes the setup she has now, and Liz is Liz."

"I don't really get it," Dar said. "What's the main reason you want to do this?"

"The main reason is that I want a change. It also solves this Susan problem, and it could help you out too in the long run."

"I hate to sound hardhearted, but what's in it for me, besides *maybe* not having to share my tent with a male jerk someday?"

"If you mean would I make it worth your while, the answer is yes," BethAnne brazenly answered, meeting his gaze directly, "within reason." They'd gotten down to the crux of it, and she had no other cards to play.

"Maybe we could draw up a contract," Dar responded after a pause. "Permissible acts, frequency, duration."

"Let me put this to you another way, Dar. I swear that I would be a good tent mate. I'll stay out of your way, I won't ask you to do anything for me, and I'm easy to get along with. I'll even get out whenever you want some alone time. I would keep everything but a change of clothes and my bag in the stuff tent. You can sleep late and snore and do anything else guys do and I couldn't care less. And if you want to talk about anything, I'd be there for you. I can tell you a lot about this camp too that you don't know yet. I've already confided in you more than anyone else. We could be allies. Also, for what it's worth, I really do like you, from the first moment I saw you."

"I'm sorry, BethAnne. You must be a little desperate to have to ask me this. You'll forgive my shock. I really like you too, and I can try to help you in other ways, but I think I'll have to say no to this."

The young woman pulled her knees up under her chin and

swiped the excess water off shiny shins with single slides of both hands. After a few moments she extended her legs straight out, closed her eyes, stretched her arms up in the air, twisted one way and then the next, shivered once throughout the length of her feline body, and pulled her knees up again. Only then did she face him directly, subdued but still strong. "I know you're an independent type, and you don't know me from Eve either. I don't blame you in the least. Do me a favor, though. Just consider it. This will be going down before much longer. All three things have to happen at the same time. Susan, then Herbert, then Cole."

"Okay, but I don't think so."

"Alright. Sorry again to spring this on you out here," she said, sweeping one arm with a flourish and looking around with a brave but slightly hurt smile. "Now let's go fishing!"

"Really? Are you sure you want to continue?"

"Definitely. I want to catch *something*."

Schoharie now soon found out that there was a new hand at the bellows. They were soon called upon [to] take leases and to pay rent, or to purchase. They refused all. The seven partners seeing they could gain nothing, tho't about trying the law: sent their Sheriff, by the name of Adams, to apprehend the most principal men and ringleaders of the whole, to bring them to terms of justice. But when the Sheriff began to meddle with the first man, a mob of women rose, of which Magdalene Zee was captain. He was knocked down, and dragged through every mud-pool in the street; then hung on a rail and carried four miles, thrown down on a bridge, where the captain took a stake out of the fence, and struck him in the side, that she broke two of his ribs, and lost one eye; then she pissed in his face, let him lie and went off.

Brief Sketch of the First Settlement of the County of Schoharie, by the Germans by John M. Brown (Schoharie, NY: printed for the author by L. Cuthbert, 1823)

TEN

DAR settled into his tent for the evening. He looked around at how well ordered everything was, drank in the solitude, and confirmed that he'd made the right decision about BethAnne. Now that there were good books in camp, he violated the no-lights rule by reading a little inside his sleeping bag, just like when he was a kid under the covers. Following the general rule that apologizing was easier than asking permission—with his own corollary that you don't get caught to begin with, and especially not the second time—he set up his dimly lit lantern inside the propped-open mouth of his sleeping bag as if he was still in it and walked around once to see if it shone through the tent wall, much the same test he'd wanted to perform outside the cellar prison. It did, ever so slightly, and he turned the lamp a bit lower.

Gwen sunnily announced one day that she wanted to give crayfish a try, if they could get enough of them. Cole immediately set himself up as an expert, correcting their pronunciation of the word, explaining how to devein them and how to pinch the tail and suck the head, and then proclaiming that they weren't big enough in the North anyway. He did a lip-snarling rendition of Elvis singing "Crawfish" from *King Creole*, however, that really brought the house down. Crayfish were known to inhabit the stream, and an expedition was organized. Apparently this was the first time all of the campers had been down to the West Kill at once. Sadie agreed to partake in the hunt but not of the eventual meal. Rick was too nervous about such tactical overexposure to join in, and he wasn't much of a water person anyway, so he scouted and hunted the perimeter toward the road and showed himself every hour or so.

Northern crayfish *are* smaller, so only the largest would do. The best method in a stream like this is searching off the main channel in water that is not too deep, turning over likely rocks, and pinning them down by the neck first thing, or immediately after one of their backward spurts. As there was no especially advantageous place to do this, they went to the closest point, the bright open stretch where Dar had first been baptized in these shimmering waters. Most of the party wore shorts or bathing suits. Gwen came down and found a good seat on the bank but did not go in. Herbert took his shoes off and rolled his pants and sleeves up but seemed more interested in observing than catching anything, willowing across the same twenty feet of bottom in a permanent stoop, his face inches above the crystal-clear water. Dawn helped Susan, who actually got into it a little, though she lacked the dexterity or final courage to pick one up.

They used a variety of containers for this, transferring the catch into a centrally located bucket that Dave periodically emptied into a larger sunken bait pail before rejoining Gwen. The two leaders took it all in, like proud ducks watching their downy newborns paddle around for the first time. They were spread all the way up and down this stretch of the stream before long, and the crayfishers really applied themselves, taking in over a hundred of the powerful little crustaceans within a couple of hours, and that was just the keepers. Some had big enough claws to warrant concern and be remindful of lobsters.

"Whaddya think now, Cole?" needled Sadie when they were gathering together and getting ready to troop back home.

"It ain't the best mudbug party I've ever been to, but it's one helluva wet tee-shirt contest!" he gleefully responded, prompting a few involuntary self-checks and pained groans.

"I see what you mean," Sadie saucily replied, looking him up and down with her hands on her hips like a pirate queen. "Your crawdaddy is looking pretty small there . . . but *nice tits*." Laughter ensued, and Cole reddened.

Rose-cheeked Gwen spoke up next. "If you wouldn't mind waiting a little longer for dinner, we should have these tonight so they don't go bad. Liz and I will take any help we can get. Cole's the expert, so I know we can count on him. And sorry we don't have any cocktail sauce or Cajun spices right now, but we'll make a nice gumbo or something." It turned out wonderfully, in with a couple jars of Dar's tomatoes and some scavenged cornstarch and spices, and they resolved to make this a weekly affair. During dinner, Dar informed the frontal brain trust that the Schoharie Creek not too many miles to the northeast was loaded with larger crayfish, which was one more reason to start thinking about going there.

ΩΩΩ

The timing of their outing had been good, because by late afternoon the next day they were visited by torrential rains. The small watering brook out past the Commons turned brown and swollen, as did the little canal system they'd constructed to drain the camp. Soon water began to flow in rippling sheets at disorienting angles across the entire site and underneath their tent groundsheets, coming down from the ridge above them as well as from the flanks of Little Round Top off to the side. A sense of panic swept through the camp. They shouted to each other through the din. Andrew went to check on the privy tent in his usually verboten neon-orange poncho, its radioactive glow fading away in mere seconds behind thick curtains of rain. Rick's tent was in the headwaters of this gully, unguarded by any drainage works, and he was concerned about losing the whole thing, including the ammo cache and fire box. Long plumes were shooting up off both sides of his big black rubber boots as if he were waterskiing.

As Dave was scurrying around, jumping over flumes and looking for potential snags and washouts, he slid down the scoured-out bank of the canal where it dumped into the woods, soaking himself and banging a knee. He was helped up, shivering, and had to retreat inside under Gwen's care. Some of the older tents began to soak through. The drips in the canvas stores tent in particular turned into continuous trickles, and Liz was fighting a losing bucket-brigade battle in there.

A handful of campers emerged now, driven out by the sensation
that they were about to be swept away, tent and all. Dar suggested
utilizing the many tarps he'd brought along. These were draped over
all of the airy structures, sometimes double, soon staunching most
of the internal leakage. The violent cold front next dropped hail on
the valley. It ricocheted off the trees and smacked their rain gear but
mostly slashed directly into the angry runoff like a meteorite shower
peppering an iced-coffee ocean.

When all seemed lost, the mad spring storm died down as
quickly as it had appeared. The campers stumbled around in shock.
They had chosen this site with some care, but another inch or two
of rain might have destroyed all they'd worked for. Rick and Dar
surveyed the damage and made mental notes about repairs that
would need to be made over the next few days. The widened ditches
could stay that way though, as they would carry off more water
earlier next time. Dave emerged, favoring one leg but seemingly
fine. He suggested a rare roaring fire, in order to dry things out and
pick spirits up, and before long the controlled conflagration was
crackling to life with a low lavender sunset behind it off to the west.

Everyone spent the next day cleaning up and drying off.
Rick's muddied tent had to be pulled up. They would wait until
the stream was running clear again, wash it off down there, and
let it dry out on the sunny rocks for a day or two. He would sleep
in the stuff tent in the meantime. The camp gnome had been
carried down into the woods, sadly losing his left arm and the
mysterious little oval box it held. "Dear Saint Anthony," Gwen
prayed, "please come around. Something is lost and can't be
found." They kept half an eye out for weeks but eventually gave
up. Andrew presided over a silly but heartfelt ceremony one
night, burying the fragment in absentia in what they called the
Grave of the Gnome Shoulder.

Rick wanted to scout out better places to weather such a storm
next time, and he made the short trek up Little Round Top to see
how it had fared. There was not much cover at the very top, and
you wouldn't feel safe in a lightning storm, but there was a raised

rocky area halfway up on their side that would keep them above any runoff next time. They all discussed this at dinner the following night, with tangents for dessert.

"I needed a one-credit course at college once," Dar related. "It was called Water As a Natural Resource. I thought it would be a drag, but the professor was great, and it was just about my favorite class ever. He said he wanted to call it something else, but had to use that title to get administrative approval. He started off by explaining that water is about the most powerful force on earth. It brings life and takes it away. It gives you the ability to go some places and it bars you from others. It goes wherever it wants to and you can't stop it. It's incredibly heavy. He gave the weight of how many pounds of water it takes to fill something the size of a refrigerator. I forget the number but it was really high, like half a ton or something."

"You probably shouldn't tell that anecdote unless you know the exact figure," Andrew said archly.

"Point taken," Dar answered with a broad smile. "Thanks for the guidance."

ΩΩΩ

Dave had delayed the final settlement of the housing situation, as the parties involved hadn't come to any agreement, and the flood event caused the cancellation of the last Friday meeting, though most still gathered out of habit. His fragility had been highlighted by the events of that day, and some of the campers harbored concerns about the viability of the leadership structure. Gwen and Rick alone would be a whole different vibe. All this was exacerbated by the looming uncertainty over what they should do when summer came to an end. Houses were unsafe, and wintering in the woods would mean long days huddled in the cold and dark, worrying about food and frostbite and the ultimate seasonal affective disorder—freezing to death. Winters in this climate would have been a relative cakewalk for early peoples, but *we* had become the naked ignorant ones. The flood reminded them all that this was not just summer camp, or some scouting adventure.

Cole sensed an opening here. From what Dar had learned, he'd come in like gangbusters. Dave had to give him an ultimatum about hijacking meetings and encouraging dissension. He'd been on good behavior for a few weeks, and had secured the promise of his own tent site. Cole began pressing his other agenda items again, individually, and at the next Friday assembly.

"All right," announced Dave after the normal preliminaries, "Friend Cole would like the floor now. I thank him for his patience, as we have had lots of other things going on recently, and then we had the big rain." Everyone was still in attendance except for Susan, who'd retired to her tent. Cole took his place in front of the fire and greeted the crowd.

"Thanks, Dave, and thanks everyone for the chance to address a few things. I know I'm one of the newer ones here, but in some ways that gives me a fresh perspective. We've done well"—causing Gwen to roll her eyes—"and May is a great time to smell the roses"— causing Sadie to do the same—"but there's something else in the air too, and that is danger. Danger from hostile outsiders, the danger of living out in the open like this, and the danger of next winter. I think we need to take a more active approach to staying vigilant, to securing our future, and to having a say in how we proceed. As far as how to restructure things, this is still America, and I don't think we need to look much farther for guidance than the Founding Fathers, and our own Constitution."

"Weren't *you* an outsider just a while ago?" asked Rick, who was too restless to stay seated, and had positioned himself just beyond the reach of the crackling campfire light.

"I'm referring to the Cave Clan, for one thing. I've certainly never been one of them," Cole responded, in a not-so-veiled swipe at BethAnne.

"What do the Founding Fathers have to do with this?" asked Gwen. "Lordy, there were more of them than there are of us. We're just a small group of folks trying to survive in the woods."

"It's not about numbers," responded Cole, "it's about the founding principles."

"Right," said Andrew, "like slavery."

"I know this isn't politically correct, and it's off topic, but do you think America could have become so great so fast without slavery at the beginning?"

"Yeah, America is doing real great right now," said Sadie.

"Actually, that gets back to how weakness will ruin a country."

"Oh really?" she continued. "Who ruined it, and how did that give rise to a worldwide virus?"

"I think we are getting offtrack here," said Dave. "What changes do you propose, Cole?"

"Well, for one thing, and nothing personal, but I think we should vote for our leaders."

"And how would that work?" asked Dave with a polite smile. "Would there be just one person at the top?"

"King Cole, right?" interjected BethAnne.

"Would that person make the decisions," continued Dave, "or would everything be put to a democratic vote, and if so, why would you even need a leader?"

"I'm thinking about more of a civil libertarian approach."

Dawn spoke up. "Things are civil now. You seem to want to make them less civil. And we have liberties too."

"You have the liberty to do what Dave, Rick, and Gwen tell you to." This caused some murmurs of discontent.

Dar wondered where Cole was going with this. Everyone was fairly happy with the progress they had made, and he didn't seem to have any natural allies. It was difficult to create a wedge under those circumstances. Perhaps he was just planting the seeds for future rabble-rousing. Dar had seen and heard enough over the last few weeks, however. He hadn't challenged Cole in person yet, because he didn't think it was his place to do so, but now was the time.

"If I may," said Dar, "making a distinction between civil liberties and what you mean when you refer to civil libertarians—many of whom hold a sincere and healthy regard for freedom but have become the half-unwitting shock troops of the rabid right—if America had nine lives, it would have been very instructive to let civil libertarians and neocons run the show one time. Just get together at the beginning and say, 'You're in charge now. Exactly what would you like to happen?' Roll right over. Don't—"

"Yeah, like that's gonna happen," interrupted Cole.

"I know, but I'm just trying to illustrate a point, so please be civil enough to let me finish," continued Dar. "That's a rude habit, and you do it a lot. As I was saying, don't fight them on a single thing—like no more taxes, or dismantling the Environmental Protection Agency and the Energy Department, or whatever—so they can't fearmonger and scapegoat their way into permanent governance. Let them break the social contract and violate basic Christian principles to their little hearts' content. That's a sweet scenario—minimal planning and services, or none at all, and when inevitable problems arise the collective mob of civil libertarian non-specialists can deal with them in their spare time, with nobody else to blame for the results but themselves."

"America *had* nine lives," Cole responded, taken aback but clearly eager to engage a new opponent, "and Big Government liberals like FDR and LBJ destroyed them all. Not to mention tax-and-spend career politicians on all levels, labor unions, atheists, the anti-gun crowd, the media elite—"

"Don't leave out witches and bitches," Sadie said.

"Or queers and uppity types," chimed in BethAnne.

"Yeah, so I guess it's okay for other people to interrupt. Do you think though that it's an accident how we went down under a president who was against God and guns?"

"Arghhh!" was all Dar could muster.

"Is that your best pointy-headed response? When a nation loses its faith and patriotism, it rots from within, and throws its gates open to the enemy."

"It seems late in the game to be debating things like this," responded Dar, "but you're taking that comment Obama once made about God and guns out of context. It's what you people do though. Anything goes. There was no limit to your depravity and lack of conversational integrity toward the end. Hypocritical swiftboaters, engaging in Big Lies at every turn and counting on an electorate gullible enough to swallow them almost every time. It was funny to watch members of Congress try to throw somebody in jail for something minor like lying to them about steroid use on a baseball team, or whatever, and then stand up there themselves and tell infinitely more devastating lies. Creating *true* security and prosperity would mean you'd be in power less, and the rich would not get to be as *filthy* rich, so you abandoned compromise for permanent gridlock and established the separate red country of Dumbfuckistan. You should all be forced to sit down with your eyes propped open like in *A Clockwork Orange* and made to read and reread Garrison Keillor's essay 'We're Not in Lake Wobegon Anymore.' It's about what happened to the once-more-noble Republican Party."

"Your true totalitarian nature is coming out."

"It was a torture image so I thought you'd like it."

Dar was sitting toward the back of the benches, off to one side. He could see that everyone was staying put, seemingly content to let things play out. Cole had harangued and even bullied many of them already, though Andrew was the only one who still actively debated him. He was a boil on the ass of the camp that needed lancing, but he had also tugged at some natural concerns. And then there was the post-TV entertainment aspect of sitting there and watching all this. Dave was probably the most perturbed spectator, but he had stopped trying to moderate things for now.

"Garrison Keillor," said Cole. "There's a real American hero. Right up there with Michael Moore. Maybe they should try getting real jobs."

"I'm sure you know a lot about both of them, from Fox News. And they had real jobs, even though they were in the, *gasp*, arts, so you wouldn't recognize them as such."

"They couldn't make it on their own with unpopular propagandist radio shows and bogus documentaries. They needed sensational headlines to rake in the money, the way Al Gore did. And I don't need a news show to tell me how the loony left is pairing up with the Democrat Party to divert attention away from its failures and its secret agenda by going on about so-called class warfare."

"*A*, I know the title is a little confusing, but Fox News was not a news show; *B*, it wasn't *so-called* class warfare, though that gets into statistics like the record rich–poor gap, and you don't really *do* numbers, or science; and *C*, you can't expect to wage economic war on the majority of the country and not have someone call you on it. And you know what? The agenda of the Democratic Party is not bad or evil. If you could secretly record private conversations about strategies and ultimate goals at the highest levels in both parties, what you people talk about would come out far worse in the eyes of the public."

"That's hogwash, and for your information, I'm not a registered Republican. You might say they're just the lesser of two evils."

"Yeah, you might, but you don't, because you were still parasitically feasting on what was left of the host carcass. I'm a registered Independent, by the way, and I even voted for a Republican twice in a row, for town highway department supervisor, because she did a great job."

"Good," said Cole. "There's hope for you yet."

"Here's how I see the difference. Locally, politicians need to get things done, and they are held to certain standards. In big cities that can mean something as basic as good snow removal. Your opponent won't forget to mention poor snow removal during the next election. In smaller places, you see them in the store, and can bug them about cutting services, or laying your brother-in-law off, or raising property taxes. Nationally, though, many *traditional* Democrats and progressives are stupid, and many *modern* Republicans and conservatives are mean and greedy. I don't really believe the first part, about being stupid, but it softens you up for the second part. Democrats can be naive, and certainly as corrupt— more so in certain cities and states, historically. But they don't walk in lemming lockstep, so it's far harder to impose order on them, and lately, they tended to show up for a knife fight with a peashooter."

"Like a growing majority of the country," said Cole, "I identify with the Tea Party. They were about to dance on your grave."

"So you want to revive that *here*?" exclaimed BethAnne. "I can't believe we're even having this discussion to begin with. Look around you, numbnuts!"

"Again, I'm talking about traditional American beliefs, and family values. Not politics."

"It's always very clear what that means," said Dar. "If we don't agree with you, we have immoral beliefs, or we are somehow *against* families. Just more diversionary culture wars, and fake wars, like the War on Christmas, and pseudo-scandals. And the ludicrously misleading names you dreamed up, like the Patriot Act, the Heritage Foundation, No Child Left Behind, the Committee to Save New York, and the Club for Growth. The Club for *Wealth* is more like it, for all of those, ultimately."

"It doesn't matter what you call things. People are just fed up with all the moral and fiscal irresponsibility of the left. That's why you're seeing a groundswell of opposition."

"You mean *were* seeing, right? And who knows how it would have ended. It was a groundswell generated by economic decline, right-wing think tank and talk radio propaganda, outrageous redistricting tricks, and phony populism. I went to a Tea Party rally in Albany last year, just to check it out. I understand the frustration with government, and I'm sure there were some good people there, but besides all the flag waving and simplistic sloganeering I saw two funny things. One was that black guy in the cowboy hat that kicked it off with a patriotic song. You were supposed to think he was local. I saw him on TV the very next night, in DC if I recall. He must ride the bus with the organizers, maybe even up front. He was about the only person of color there, other than lunching state worker onlookers, whose jobs you would destroy."

"You mean the bloated bureaucracy that's been immune from the hardships that the private sector has to face?"

"Yes, them, although progressives didn't cause those hardships. You and yours did. I sometimes think your message is that we shouldn't be happy until the entire working class is equally miserable. As for government workers, that resentment probably goes back to the first time some misguided hater spit on the first postman, but you've demonized them since Reagan—who was a government worker himself, by the way, and a union president before that when it suited him—on a whole new level."

"No, we're just calling a spade a spade. Big Government is completely out of control. What part of that do people like you not get?"

"I agree," spoke up Bennie. "Things used to run pretty well before government became so bloated and started interfering with our lives."

"When, though?" asked Dar. "When were things ever so great? If you're talking about the olden days, in small tribes, and later in small villages and towns, things were probably planned and executed fairly and well as often as they weren't. And when folks talk nostalgically about the *golden* days in their own lifetimes, as opposed to the olden days, they're often confusing the excitement and optimism of youth with what was really going on, or they are talking about an America that can't be the same in the modern world, or an America that never was to begin with. As populations grew and hundreds became millions, that had to be managed somehow. It's like coming into town on horseback, which would be pretty easy, compared to air traffic control over Heathrow or JFK, which is complicated, and requires organization and regulations. Do you still want to ride a horse to get from New York City to Iowa? And if not, what's your position on frequent midair collisions?"

"What was the other funny thing about the rally?" Andrew asked.

"Right. They had a raffle for a DVD, about 'taking back the country' or something along those lines. They announced the winner, and his name was extremely ethnic. Turkish I think. It caused a real undercurrent to run through the crowd. When he came up to claim the prize and he turned out to be swarthy, it doubled."

"That's the other lefty specialty, playing the race card," said Cole.

"What's the first?" Dar asked. "I forget."

"Class warfare," replied Cole.

"Because you guys would never dream of playing the race card, right? The Southern Strategy? Welfare queens? Willie Horton? Made-up stuff like buying a single grape for a penny just to cash in the food stamps for drugs and Cadillacs?"

"Exaggerated ancient history," responded Cole.

"What about birthers?" asked Andrew.

"We would rally around any person," said Cole, "as long as they have the right ideas. Liberals have made it difficult for conservatives of color. The whole Uncle Tom thing."

"The *right* person of color might have made it through the new Republican/Tea Party primary system if their otherness was non-threatening enough," said Dar, "but would they have gotten enough people up out of their La-Z-Boys on Election Day, not to mention the bigot bloc? When you do find one who will come over to the dark side, like Clarence Thomas, look how quick they are to play their own race card when they run into problems, after making a career out of pretending we had achieved color blindness."

"He was lynched by the liberal left, and officially exonerated. The Democrat Party takes blacks and Hispanics for granted. That was starting to change."

"I agree about taking them for granted, but for those groups it's the same lesser-of-two-evils thing you were talking about."

"And they wonder why they're at the bottom of the heap."

"Many of them know the real reason why. Besides prejudice and discrimination, they're part of the permanent underclass that makes possible the lifestyles of the rich and the superrich."

"Anybody can get ahead in America if they work hard enough. And a rising tide raises all boats. The problem with Democrats is that they don't understand the business community, and they handcuff job creators."

"It just gave the rich bigger boats," inserted Andrew.

"The moral and mathematical bankruptcy of the trickle-down fantasy was breathtaking," said Dar. "Back to the handcuffing fantasy, which ties into the uncertain business climate fantasy, let me guess how, okay? Ready? Here it comes. Taxes and overregulation, right?"

"Damn straight!"

"Taxes were highest under Eisenhower, a great, moderate, anti-imperialist Republican president who helped create prosperity. Taxes were lowest under Bush the Second, and look what happened there. You blindly worship Reagan, but he raised taxes I don't know how many times. I'm not sure he could have survived modern primaries, thanks to the Tea Party. I think most of you would fail a written test on what the Founding Fathers were all about too. When ultraconservatives control things, the fox is in the hen house, and it would be twice as bad under you modern Know Nothings. You talk about fiscal conservatism but take Democratic surpluses and turn them into record deficits through tax cuts for the rich and, more lately, unfunded, unjustified wars."

"Weak on defense. Your calling card."

"Well, two things there. Most of this country is not really capable of discussing the concept of pacifism, or the fact that all tyrannical governments foster blind, slogan-driven support for their own military adventurism. Putting that aside though, I'm sure you served in the military, just like your predecessors who dodged Vietnam and then had the gall to question the patriotism of those who were actually in harm's way. Shameless. Most of these new wars were only about oil anyway. I don't see us going into China to curb human rights abuses, or—"

"Did you serve?" asked Bennie.

"No, but you're missing my point, Bennie. Many who join up now do so mainly to get a job in this poor economy. They are strong and brave, they are making a tremendous sacrifice, and their patriotism is genuine, but that's just the icing on top of the need-a-job cake. These long wars have had an awful effect on the economy, on families, and in some cases on the very countries we were trying to help. I'd like to think most of these soldiers would rather be based at home, doing National Guard-type work like helping with disasters. Elite strike forces could take care of most of the rest."

"So you didn't mind Saddam Hussein?" said Cole. "Or what the Taliban was doing to women, and blowing up the biggest Buddha statues in the world, and the terrorist bases?"

"Yes, but it's all more complex than that, especially when it comes to who and where and why the terrorists are, and supporting secular dictators over religious dictators. And I doubt if you were losing any sleep over the women and the statues."

"And I doubt if you're losing sleep over the poor economy."

"Getting back to that, and the fanatical hatred of regulations, you reduced oversight and transparency on Wall Street and in the banking industry, and look what happened. Complex financial instruments like credit default swaps and flash trading that only created real value for a few. Toxic assets. Banks too big to fail. Home foreclosures. A great recession, close to a second Depression. As for environmental and health-related regulations, I'd love to see you down in a coal mine as the roof is collapsing, thinking about how uplifting it was to get rid of all those pesky regulations in order to free up businesses so they could keep more of the profits. Or maybe an asbestos worker who—"

"We're probably in agreement on banks too big to fail," said Cole.

"You say that, but your top one-percent overlords would not agree."

"And speaking of energy, we're sitting on a gold mine of safe natural gas as we speak, and you're blindly blocking that too."

"Funny you should put it that way," said Sadie. "There was a folder of newspaper clippings and documents down at the farmhouse about a gas pipeline explosion from back in March 1990 that happened right at the bottom of our road. I read the whole thing one night, in tears. I even remember the name, the Texas Eastern Products Pipeline Company, which went from Texas to Albany. They blew up a few other places as well. That gas is heavier than air, and when the pipe ruptured early one morning due to faulty repair work it flowed as a huge cloud of white fog right downhill, pooling up in North Blenheim where it meets Route 30 and the river. Something touched it off and there was an enormous fireball that went half a mile up West Kill Road right back to the source. The heart of the historic upper village was destroyed forever, something like fifteen structures. Two died, including the town's top go-to guy, who served as constable, highway superintendent, and high up in the fire department too I think. He helped others even after his clothes, hair, and skin were burned off, with nothing left on but a belt. The other man was just passing through town on the way to a temporary job. He told the ambulance crew how much he loved his family, naming them over and over, but took a moment to joke about the potholes they were hitting. The school bus had passed through only moments earlier. The children could see the fireball out the back—"

"Okay, okay, we get it," said Cole. "That sounds like a liquid propane vapor cloud though, not safe natural gas."

"The 1990 pocket calendars the company handed out back then said 'Texas Eastern pipelines are safe pipelines,'" replied Sadie. "Put that in your pipe and smoke it."

"Actually," said Dar, "fracking in New York State was probably just around the corner, though it's true it wouldn't have been as unregulated here as the industry wished. Still, think of all those millions of tons of corruptly exempted toxic chemicals hanging out underground ready to come back and haunt us, and all the defacement and upkeep on the surface, the lies about how many jobs fracking would create and where most of the money would flow, and the bust after the boom. It's the same old thing. Putting profits before human needs, and selling out for silver."

"I know much of the Pennsylvania experience has not been all that good," added Dave.

"You'd rather burn dirty coal then, or pay treasure to terrorists for oil?"

"You have a convenient point about coal, Cole," replied Dar, "but we're not the ones who played petropolitics all those years, fighting tooth and nail against clean energy, and putting vapid oil men in the White House to do their dirty work. And you're not counting the dirty *underground* aspect of fracking."

"It's always the same thing with you guys. The glass is half empty. The party of malaise."

"A Democrat looks at a glass of water and says it's half empty. A modern Republican looks at it and says, 'Hey, who the hell took half of my water!'" Most of the spectators laughed at that.

Dave spoke up again now. "If you will excuse me for a moment, I do not mind broad discourse, but I'm not sure our Friday assembly is the best place for extended political discussions about things that do not matter much in the here and now. Perhaps that should happen in a different setting. Before I retire for the evening, though, I would like to know if everyone feels we need another approach to how we make decisions here. I do not think we need elections, but I am open to suggestions. I ask you again, Cole. Exactly what do you want?"

"Elections would be a good place to start, with term limits. And I think we should all vote on important issues."

"Let's go around then and see who agrees with that," said Dave. He asked each person in the order they were sitting. Half said they wouldn't mind elections, and voting, but most of those added that they thought Dave and company were doing a fine job.

"That's hardly a good way to vote," complained Cole, "in public. There should be secret ballots so there's no pressure. And more discussion first."

"I think it's better in public," said Gwen. "Put your cards right on the table."

"I wouldn't mind voting on important issues," said Bennie, "and I'm all for term limits."

"Who decides what's important and what's routine?" asked Liz.

"That would usually be obvious," replied Cole. "I'd call what we decide to do about the winter important, for example."

"And what would you do?" quizzed Sadie.

"I wouldn't rule out moving to the big farmhouse for good, and eventually contacting the Cobleskill people with a proposal. They can only scavenge for so long before there's nothing left. They'll need fresh food at some point. We could provide that, in return for protection. We could settle in and even expand out into other homes and farms—just pick the one you like—and sleep in peace with roofs over our heads."

"We can barely feed *ourselves*," Dawn cried out.

"And what happens if they start makin' demands we don't like, or takin' our women?" asked Rick out on the edge. "Or if a whole different road crew hits us?"

"And what happens if the vote on something like that is split?" asked Dar. "If you lose, will you secede from the union? Or make your own deal with the Cave Clan?"

"I think you're abusin' our hospitality," said Rick. "Have from the start. Always startin' trouble instead of helpin' out."

"Why don't I run around the woods all day playing Daniel Boone then, getting first pick of the house spoils, and you can gather firewood? I'll take your tent too, while we're at it."

"Try it."

"Okay," said Dave, "let's tone it down. I am of course open to discussing larger issues. On the everyday stuff though, like camp life, which Gwen does a good job with, and security matters outside of camp, which is Rick's department, we need a framework. It is not a good time to change the game plan. I appreciate your suggestions, Cole, but I think it is too early to put any trust in other groups. We have time to make our winter plans. And as a reminder, nobody is being held here against their will either."

"What would happen if Cole leaves, though?" asked BethAnne. "Why should we trust him with our future? He could sell us out in a second. I've seen how they make and break deals over there."

The fire flared, illuminating Cole's round, perspiring head from behind, and licking hot orange up the sides of his close black beard. A memory of *Survivor* leapt up, the TV show where an assortment of people from all walks of North American life were thrust into wilderness settings, given idiotic challenges by God—who you got to see for a change in the human form of the hokey host—and drummed out one by one during the overwrought torch-lit tribal council, all subject to staging and heavy editing. The winner was usually the most manipulative contestant. He'd wisely stopped watching after the first handful of innumerable seasons. The biggest saving grace was that some of the settings and nature shots were fantastic. The time that a guy got stung by a sea urchin and had one of the women pee on his swelling hand to disinfect it was a TV milestone. Not exactly something you'd see on *The Lawrence Welk Show*. Quite an advancement from the fact that the 1970s bathroom shared by the six kids on *The Brady Bunch* didn't even have a toilet bowl, and from the shock of that first-ever offscreen flush on *All in the Family*. Wally and Beaver almost got a toilet on TV way back in 1957! They'd ordered a baby alligator for

$2.50 from the back pages of a "Robot Men of Mars" comic book— actually an issue of *Superboy*, with a fake cover—and needed a place to hide it. Rather than show the whole bowl, the censors finally agreed to a glimpse of the tank only, which Wally referred to as an "aquarium." Dar caught himself and refocused on the proceedings.

"I appreciate being taken into the camp," said Cole, regrouping, "but I should be allowed to express my opinions. And I don't mean to get overly political, but I see parallels here . . . how things go wrong when you put too much trust in the government, even the local government."

"You have a right to that opinion," said Dar, "and we must always be on guard against tyranny, but when the anti-government thing becomes kind of a mental illness, the solution is worse than the problem. And it's ridiculous in a group of thirteen."

"Here here," cheered Gwen.

"Here's the bottom line," said Dar, in a conciliatory tone. "Politics often brings out passion. And to Cole's point, that often goes double for local politics, because the results are so tangible. It's important for people to be informed and opinionated. It's good that we aren't just sitting around like those futuristic meek beings in *The Time Machine*, zoning out and getting picked off by those hairy brutes—"

"Morlocks," said Cole. "And the wimps were the Eloi."

"Right. Very good. So the trick is to have the discussion without the anger, and to be friendly afterwards, or at least cordial. Even Reagan and Tip O'Neill were able to do that."

"Hoover with a smile," said Herbert playfully from the front row, to everyone's total surprise, as most thought he'd been sleeping through all of this. They waited for him to clarify or follow up, but nothing came.

"These global hot spots and political movements and pressing issues come and go over time," offered Dave, filling the void. "Iraq, the Tea Party, the Patriot Act—those were just the headlines of the day. Long before that it was Barbary pirates, the Whig Party, and the Smoot–Hawley Act, none of which you hear much about now. But I will say one thing about President Reagan. The way he used the

word *utopian*, with that curling sneer, as if that would be a bad state
to reach. The first Bush had the same sneer when he talked about
northern spotted owls. I do not understand that mindset."

"Reagan just meant don't be naive," explained Cole, "and Bush
was talking about how jobs are more important than birds, even on
the left coast. Businessmen should be in charge, not politicians or tree
huggers."

"You know, it's funny," replied Dave. "Some of *that* also played
itself out right in this area, back in the 1840s, in the Anti-Rent War.
That system made some sense in the beginning, coming as it did from
European feudalism, with patroons acting as lords and renting land to
tenant farmers, but it didn't square with Jacksonian democracy. When
it became clear how unfair and unsustainable it all was, something
had to give."

"So they bit the hand that was feeding them," said Cole.

"You should learn about a topic before voicing opinions on
it, Cole. For one thing, the farmers were paying taxes on land they
did not even own. Do you support that? They had no rights either
when it came to disputes. Everything was weighted toward the rich.
It started in the hinterlands of Albany County and spread out, soon
involving thousands of disaffected farmers. Many of the younger
ones in particular donned Indian disguises and ran all through these
hills, holding secret meetings, blowing their tin horns when the
authorities came with eviction notices and posses of up-renters, and
gathering in great force, fifteen hundred strong at Summit once. It
was mostly nonviolent, though the tar and feathers sometimes flew,
and an undersheriff was killed one county over. There were three
tribes from this area, from what I have been reading. A Christopher
Decker of Blenheim Hill called himself Black Hawk. Red Jacket haled
from Eminence, and Tecumseh was from Gilboa. In 1845, a sheriff and
his assistant staying at Fink's tavern in North Blenheim were seized
late at night and driven up the West Kill Road to Baldwin's sawmill,
not far from where we're sitting now. They were brought to a remote
hilltop in the woods and further intimidated before being returned
to their lodgings. Soon all of this had an impact on statewide politics,

and most of the landlords gradually gave in, selling at a reasonable rate and enabling the farmers to stay on."

"Tarring and feathering and murdering—how law abiding," responded Cole.

"Political discourse has evolved greatly since then," said Dar. "Polished ideologues on both sides trotted out their talking points, playing to the camera, and the media was often more interested in gotcha moments than deep analysis. But when regular folks get together, they should be able to have rational discussions. People flame each other online in ways they would never do face to face, for example, or in a physical meeting, although some of those town hall meetings we saw on TV were pretty shameful."

"But not just from one side," said Cole. "What's happening now is concerned citizens have a more level playing field for the first time ever. They were suppressed before. You're just not used to hearing from them, and you don't like it."

"What's happening now is that almost everyone is *dead*," cried out BethAnne.

"I respectfully disagree, my dear sir," Dar responded, skipping over that observation. "One ironic dirty little secret of what you call the 'lamestream media' is that they were still polite and professional enough, or scared of low ratings or a boycott enough, not to call you out on the rampant disparity in vitriol and chicanery."

"That's where you pompous asses lose your larger audience, right there," said Cole.

"Well, unrelated to that remark, I am heading in for the night," said Dave. "Please feel free to continue if you like, but let us keep things civil, and maybe quieter too. See you at breakfast." Gwen, Dawn, and Sadie had also had their fill, and took the opportunity to depart. Herbert declined Dawn's offer to see him to his tent. Rick just disappeared.

"Shall we continue?" asked Cole.

"Continue what?" countered Dar. "Deciding the one true course for humankind, as defined by you?"

"It's called discussion, like you said."

"It's called harassment the way you do it sometimes," said BethAnne. "Especially with Andrew."

"I can handle it," said Andrew. "Know your enemy. I tell him when I've had enough."

"With Andrew, it's all academic," said Cole. "He hasn't been out in the cold, hard world yet. I'm just trying to save him some time and trouble."

"I basically stopped having these kinds of debates years ago," said Dar. "People's minds are usually made up already. Once in a while you find someone in the opposite camp that can handle it without rancor. It's kind of like with Boston Red Sox fans on the topic of the Yankees."

"Texas Rangers here," said Cole with a twinkle.

"Of course. One can't escape death or Texas. So just to clear the air, and to wrap this up, because I don't intend to debate you anymore, as the axes you like to grind don't have much place in these woods—"

"Gimme a break!"

"To continue, we'll never know how things would have ended up, but in my opinion your movement was leading the country to ruin. Usually third parties are doomed, but it was starting to shape up as the new Republican Party. Your primaries moved everyone so far to the right that moderates were exorcized. Your leaders were forced into signing juvenile, maniacal anti-tax pledges that committed them for life, compromise became a lost art, and you openly declared that your most important goal was defeating the president. Not jobs, or fixing roads and a hundred other broken things, or bringing the troops home, or protecting the environment, God forbid, but winning the next election. A permanent campaign. Prayers and probes but no progress. And the wealth disparity would have led to civil unrest sooner or later. That can't be sustained. You need a healthy middle class. We were seeing all the hallmarks of the decline of a great civilization. As far as losing manufacturing jobs, some of that couldn't be helped, but it was aided and abetted by millionaires who wanted to become billionaires, by a do-nothing, bought-and-paid-for Congress, and even by President Clinton. That's one reason he was reelected, that and because he came across as a back-yard burger flipper that common folks could relate to. The economy was doing well too, and—"

"He got lucky there," interrupted Cole. "He was in the right place at the right time."

"That's partially true, but it was all taken away and redistributed to the so-called job creators by the Bush tax cuts. We were losing more than seven hundred thousand jobs a month as that failed-businessman puppet president was leaving. Imagine how you'd be howling if it was the other way around."

"With President Al Gore, yes, I can imagine how we'd be howling."

"How could he have been worse? Forget about personalities, though. They were just the standard-bearers. We should have been taking the best and discarding the worst of both *systems*—capitalism and socialism—for decades now, fairly testing things to see what worked. A triple bottom line—people, planet, profit. But the radical right made that impossible, and we ended up with the worst of a single system."

"Wrong. We'll never know what would have happened if you hadn't stifled business and entrepreneurship so badly."

"I don't know, man," said Dar. "When you look at all the jobs created by the hottest start-up companies, that number pales in comparison to the total workforce of a single auto manufacturer back in the day."

"Oh, so now you're in favor of mindless jobs, and cars that pollute and depend on oil?"

"No, I'm just saying. To use another example, I came across a 1940s telephone directory from the Gloversville area once, which isn't far north of here. The variety and number of jobs in the leather industry there was just phenomenal. Page after page. There were two hundred and fifty different *glove* manufacturers listed."

"Buggy-whip makers too, I'll bet," said Cole. "Get with the program. Change is good."

"Yeah. I saw a tee shirt once that read 'Change is good . . . you go first.' We used to actually *make* things though," continued Dar, "things we still need today, and we farmed most of that out instead. And you can't blame it all on unions, which is where you always go next. It was more about higher profits. I don't think the outsourcers thought that through very well. What happens when the tinny toxic stuff comes back across the ocean or up from Mexico and the wage slaves here can't afford to buy it anymore?"

"It was time to transition, to increase efficiency, and to become energy independent at home."

"The transition to an information society was not a panacea after all. And I know your answer to everything else is Drill Baby Drill, but if we could have shifted to a greener economy, and avoided the devastating bubbles, we might have come through better. It's all just rearranging the Titanic deck chairs though when capitalism is so vitally based on greed. Bad things are going to happen. It simply finally caught up with us."

"Capitalism is the worst economic system," said Cole, "except for all the others."

"Good one, though I think that's from Churchill, and it was about democracy as a form of government. The other one I like is 'I never met a socialist who gave my father a job.' In one of the Scandinavian countries that were ahead of us in so many categories, however, that would be far less likely, as would be meeting someone who laid your father off. There's another one I heard about capitalism once, that there are only two people in the entire world who truly understand it—ancient clerks in the vault of the Bank of England—and they vehemently disagree with each other."

"Do you think Sweden could stand up to a new Hitler or Bin Laden?"

"No, but it didn't go around creating them either."

"Most true Americans know the difference between capitalism and socialism."

"They know capitalism every time they get screwed, deep down inside, but they don't know socialism at all, like the vast majority of Tea Partiers who don't want their entitlements touched, or the way rural communities feel about farm subsidies, or electrification back under FDR. They need to read the owner's manuals a little better."

"Unfettered capitalism is the key to recovery and success. That's unshakable."

"The funny thing about that is certain state-run economies are the most unfettered in the world. That's why countries like China could run rings around us. And with the gridlock in Washington, we couldn't adapt. It was all about quick fixes, and more recently, only about winning elections. Everyone knew we were on the way down, not that it's written in stone we always had to be on top to begin with."

"We were supposed to be on the ropes in the 1980s, when Japan was going to take over, and look what happened there."

"Good point, but this time it seemed much deeper and more irreversible, don't you think?"

"And that's another big difference right there," said Cole. "We *do* need to be on top. We were and are the greatest chance for world prosperity."

"You don't care one whit about world prosperity. You want narrow dominion. That's the screaming irony of capitalism. The perfect measure of success is monopoly. In the darkness of the confessional booth, we both know that. Destroying the competition, so you can eventually set prices where you want. With Amazon, for example, the competition was independent bookstores, and they were slaughtered by the thousands. Which big chain was it that used to send funeral flowers to nearby stores when it moved in? Those were people's jobs and lives they were ruining. Those were the unique local businesses that make places special, and they didn't have enough clout to blackmail state government for huge tax breaks. Not everyone can go and work for the last non-unionized big-box retailer or manufacturer left standing, Cole. There aren't enough non-automated McJobs there. The other great irony is that hiring new workers was a last resort, not a first resort, so you're full of it there too. We were heading toward a world run by ExxonMobil, Lockheed Martin, Walmart, and the biggest banks, financials, telecoms, techs, and online retailers, with a few leftover specialty companies, like Otis Elevator, and whoever made Elmer's Glue. The Apples and Googles had a chance to make a difference too, but they cashed in instead."

"You have an Apple, don't you?" asked Cole. "What about that? And did you want to pay twice as much for it because it was made here by slob workers?"

"Slob workers. Nice. I wouldn't mind paying a third or half again as much if the economy was good, and if I was paid well, but that would require your kind to care as much about the middle class, the third world, and the unfortunate as you do about the rich."

"You make your own fortune," replied Cole. "And market forces dictate how things come out, just like nature dictates what these woods are like."

"Google was supposed to be a good place to work," said Andrew.

"True," said Dar, "but Google had the same militant yen for global domination. It used its own page ranking to crush competition, played ball with the censorship requirements of oppressive regimes, violated intellectual property rights, and spied on us. Its informal motto was 'Don't Be Evil' but it should have been 'Hey, We Could Be Worse.' It even owned GoogleSucks dot-com, dot-net, and dot-org so you couldn't talk about them there. And let's not forget the massive unpatriotic tax avoidance all the big corporations like GE got so good at. As for Apple, it wouldn't have killed them to more humanely make their products over here. Outsourcers, heartless downsizers and dumbsizers who call themselves rightsizers and smartsizers, so-called right-to-work laws, the *follow the money* corporate 'reform' of our educational system . . . it all makes me sick. It's all code for the rich getting richer."

"And don't forget the role the IMF and the World Bank played in destroying the environment and actually fostering inequality," said Andrew.

Cole jumped back in. "Gee, they fit that whole thing on the bumper sticker where you learned it? God forbid that anybody should make money, or start a successful business. Dar wants all of us to work in a gray factory in Siberia, making bicycles out of cement."

"Always back to the commie thing, right? Where good old red-baiting Ronnie got his start, not to mention Tricky Dicky fingering pinkos like Helen Gahagan Douglas."

"Oh yeah, President Reagan, the guy who brought down communism. That sure was awful."

"Talk about being in the right place at the right time," said Dar. "Communism was about to tip over by itself. All he did was blow on it."

"There's a lot more to the greatest modern president than that."

"He was a B actor in his greatest role, and getting shot like that helped him get reelected. Four more years of damage, with a typical Republican deficit at the end."

"I'd take Reagan over Carter any day," said Bennie.

"Carter made some big mistakes," replied Dar, "like praying on his knees in the White House when he should have been out making his case, but he was a decent man. We were dispirited by Watergate and Ford's pardon, it was the Bicentennial, and we thought we'd give a goober a chance. Even with high inflation and everything, it might have worked out differently without the hostage crisis. Funny though how he's remembered for that, and Reagan got off scot-free for Iran–Contra."

"Carter was a disaster, but I'd take him over Obama any day," said Cole. "And I'd take four terms of Reagan over four of Roosevelt too."

"Reagan was quite likeable in some ways, and it was difficult and brave how he went out at the end, but it's sad and maddening and scary that so many people bought into the Reagan Revolution. I understand the hunger for security and prosperity, and his shining city upon a hill imagery, as fictional as Bush 41's bullshit thousand points of light, but yikes! I know it drove Republicans nuts that Clinton got two terms, but half the reason is because he sold out on NAFTA and things like that. He certainly reached some compromises though, which is a lost art thanks to the hard right. And then there was Florida's Shakespearian epic fail in 2000, with a strong assist from Ralph Nader and the Jeb Bush–directed state offices and the conservative Supreme Court. The Court advanced the cause of permanent Republican rule even further with *Citizens United*, ripping up the campaign finance laws so fat cats and neocon think tankers and political action committees could run the show more than ever, anonymously. Money became *free speech*, and corporations became *people*, just like the Founding Fathers wanted, right?"

"Your own ACLU supported *Citizens United*. You can spew revisionist history and twist things around all you want," said Cole, "but the fact of the matter is that you are out of touch with what most of the country really wants. When—"

"Oh, you mean like polls that show something like eighty percent of Americans think millionaires should pay more taxes? Read their lips!"

"If I can finish, when you say something like 'Dumbfuckistan,' that shows what you really think of average, hardworking people with traditional values, and of American exceptionalism. Those are just places you fly over on the way from Manhattan to San Francisco."

"You're right about that word. I apologize. It's just kind of an attention-getter, like hitting a bear on the snout with a piece of wood when all else fails, and I normally wouldn't use it, though it isn't far off from implying San Francisco is Sodom, like your side always does. I heard you say 'libtard' to Andrew the other day too."

"Because I'm for sane gun control," the youngster explained.

"Andrew on the Second Amendment!" scoffed Cole. "That's rich."

"He thinks the 'well regulated' part of a 'well regulated militia' only meant training and discipline," replied Andrew. "I don't think it rules out restrictions. It's an honest disagreement."

"Unfortunately," said Dar, "or maybe fortunately, the language is open to interpretation. Clearly they thought armed insurrection was a strong deterrent against oppression, but the struggle against Great Britain was so fresh on their minds. With deep rights comes deep responsibilities. The best test would be to bring the Founders here and give them demonstrations of everything, from assault weapons with extended clips to modern bombs. Let them read the newspapers and watch the nightly news for a few weeks too. Getting back to the other thing though, I'm part country boy myself. I don't mean dumb. To tell you the truth, I'd rather have most country folk for neighbors than punks or snobs or whatever. What I mean is that you used classic fear tactics and a low-information media campaign to herd them into your camp. You hold shiny hot-button objects like abortion and gay marriage up in the air with one hand while you concentrate on your true agenda with the other. Rolling back the New Deal and the Great Society, bankrupting the country as a backdoor way to destroy federal, state, and local government, union busting, austerity for all but the rich, and feeding the insatiable greed of those who keep you in power. You say you want to make government small enough so that you can drown it in a bathtub, but it's the masses you're drowning. You were up to dirty tricks at the ballot box too, blatantly restricting voter access. To me that's as un-American as you can get. It was all heading toward a bad resolution."

"Abortion is not shiny," Cole said. "It's bloody."

"Agreed it's not as cut and dried as some of the other diversions, but it seems like you only care about life before birth, and not after."

"Speeches like that don't play so pretty where I come from," Cole said.

"Well that's another big difference. People aren't going to figuratively or literally lynch you here for your beliefs."

"On that note, I'm going to hit the sack," said BethAnne. "I can take a debate like that *once*. It brings back too many painful memories. Cole, if you want to hear from the citizens, I'm one, and I think you're often way out of line. Most all of us do. You have no idea how much Dave and Rick and Gwen have gone through to help get us this far. Things were pretty peaceable before you came, and you should reflect on that. Good night!"

Cole met her glare but had no response other than wishing her good night in return.

"My apologies for indulging in all of this," said Dar to the few who remained. "I have to admit though that I just don't get you, Cole. I understand wanting to have all the marbles, but you bringing up God, and a responsible work ethic, and family values, and the oppression of women. Who do you think you're kidding? Was this your line of work somehow, or what?"

"As opposed to dropping out and contemplating your navel on somebody else's dime?"

"I'm through sparring, Cole. I think that's half the problem—you like that as much as you care about the ideology. What's that expression about don't wrestle with a pig because you both get dirty, but the pig enjoys getting dirty. I know the personal is the political, or however that goes, but most of the time politics has no bearing on how we interact with each other on an everyday basis. We're probably not in opposition on the vast majority of things, like how good crayfish gumbo is."

"Crawfish," teased Cole, "with a *w*."

"I'd rather discuss movies with you than politics," replied Dar.

"I'd be up for that. Did you know they'd finished *Atlas Shrugged*, and it was supposed to be released this past spring?"

"I didn't know that, but hopefully they stayed faithful to the original, so the movie would suck as much as the book."

"You wish," said Cole with a smile. The two men shook hands at the end, as reported by Andrew to other members of the Creek Clan the next morning. Bennie made sure Herbert got back to his tent okay. Liz had drifted away to batten down the hatches in the stores tent and lay the fire to rest. Dar headed back toward his own refuge, feeling mentally queasy but fairly satisfied with the results. The assembly debate had been somewhat petty and unpleasant, and he was taking out some of his larger frustrations on Cole—not that he didn't deserve it—but he'd probably done the camp a solid. As he ducked through the flaps under the mellow lambent light of a near-full moon, a pair of milky legs with pointed toes lay draped across the bottom of his sleeping bag. Dar jumped back, sharply sucking in his breath.

"May I stay with you for tonight?" asked BethAnne softly, shifting onto her elbow, looking up from under nightsilver tresses, and uncurling her moonglown legs a bit. "No strings."

"I'll have to think about that. I've thought about that. Yes."

The church has always been more or less in partnership with the aristocracy. The rich are good patrons. The clergy is conservative.

Reforms are not generally announced from the pulpit until they have been a long time working in the pews. In matters spiritual the minister may be a long ways in advance of his flock. In temporal affairs the congregation always draws the minister, a reluctant follower. When the anti-rent agitation began in 1839, the preachers, almost without exception, supported Van Rensselaer and denounced the tenants.

The Anti-Rent War on Blenheim Hill: An Episode of the 40's: A History of the Struggle Between Landlord and Tenant Growing Out of the Patroon System in the Eastern Part of New York by Albert Champlin Mayham (Jefferson, NY: Frederick L. Frazee, 1906)

ELEVEN

ACCORDING to the timekeeper it was June 15, and things had settled in nicely. Delicious new foods were coming to the table. Sadie had started some squash and beans from seed quite early in the remote farm field, and the first harvests were tender and tasty as could be. Although vast pieces of this territory were locked up in overgrown pine and spruce stands, the foragers began to identify certain open areas where natural food sources were more plentiful.

In some cases it is easiest to spot summer and fall crops by their spring flowers, and they noted these locations for future reference. In addition to dandelions they'd been incorporating into their diet since April, honewort, garlic mustard, and nettles grew in profusion and were quite delectable in salads or as boiled vegetables. Sadie and her crew devoured the reference books that had been secured for them. They provided excellent photos for identification, covered harvest times and techniques, and even included recipes. Wild lettuce had been a challenge, as it can look so weedy and taste so bitter. Wild strawberries in their miniature perfection, on the other hand, were a no-brainer, as they were easy to spot, had no dangerous look-alikes, and were scrumptious beyond words.

Encounters with wildlife made up an important part of their daily lives now, from finding a big June bug in your sleeping bag to the time several deer came running and leaping right through the camp, nearly mowing down Gwen. They used the smallest of the live traps to relocate mice far from the stores tent. Dar thumped on a nearby dead tree riddled with holes at the top one day to show everyone what normally nocturnal flying squirrels looked like as they scurried out to investigate. Raccoons often probed the perimeter at night, and were known to boldly walk through camp and poke about the fire pit. Prehistoric possums and prickly porcupines were revealed to an amazed Andrew for the first time. Dave logged the most exotic sighting on an early morning walk, a bobcat in full hunting mode. Dar remembered his grandfather remarking that you can go your whole life in the woods without seeing one.

The emergence of red efts rekindled a broader discussion of spirit animals. Some were dead serious on the subject, like Sadie, who transferred her association with the California mule deer to the eastern whitetail. Some were not so serious, like Cole, who said he felt deep kinship with the beaver. When Gwen the hen teased that the sloth would be more appropriate, Cole countered that it had to be a local animal, whereupon she volunteered the slug in substitution. Bennie said he didn't buy into the whole spirit animal thing, but that he was partial to woodchucks, though he could not answer Dawn's subsequent enquiry about how much wood they chucked. BethAnne declared "Make mine mink," but she had to convince some of them that she meant the live version rather than the fur, and did so with a barely sufficient explanation of the morphological and behavioral distinctions between wild minks, otters, and muskrats. Dawn picked bunny rabbits, as fawns were kind of taken. Liz didn't want to commit, but when forced she admitted a fondness for woolly bear caterpillars. Andrew chose badgers, based on some Internet phenomenon, and a spirited debate arose as to whether or not badgers lived in New York State. Zim was consulted. His zone map had them a few states away, but Dave said there had been rare sightings in Pennsylvania, and if they were there they could have made it to the western reaches of New York at some point in time. Cole beat Dar to "We don't need no stinking badgers" by milliseconds, and they left that habitat debate at NEWTCOT. Susan was as silent as a lamb, and Herbert was sleeping like an old bear in hibernation.

On the hunting front, Rick and Dar had added duck to the menu, as well as the occasional rabbit and woodchuck, along with more venison and turkey. Although Rick did not press Dar on the live trapping and drowning of gray squirrels, of which there seemed to be an infinite supply, he was insistent about going after a great blue heron they frequently saw on the middle stretch of the creek. It was extremely wary, but they'd noticed that it almost always flew to a particular branch far upstream when disturbed. The plan was for one of them to lay in wait for a head shot with the .410 while the other drove it there. Dar knew these large, tall birds were protected because they'd been so heavily hunted early on, the meat cooked as you would with a swan. They were somewhat territorial, like the kingfisher, so there was probably only the one on this expanse. He'd noticed another up on the swamp that probably reigned supreme in that area. Dar had always enjoyed herons, wading on stilts in the misty morning water, or lumbering off through saffron skies in the evening like the jumbo jets of local birdlife.

Rick made the point that it was either eating little fish that would otherwise grow up to be big fish, or scaring all the fish down into holes. This heron spent the entire day killing things, so why shouldn't it be killed? But Dar couldn't bring himself to do it. He'd observed this particular bird on his ranger forays so often that it seemed to have a personality. All animals did, no doubt, but he just couldn't comply. Bennie did the driving, and the meat was said to be good, though it didn't go all that far. Rick agreed to lay off herons as long as the camp wasn't starving to death. Dar wondered if another would move in to claim this territory, and if the busybody chatterbox kingfisher that patrolled the same stretch for the same minnows missed the more secretive and dignified heron as much as he did.

On one midday fishing excursion, a weirdly fat bat was flying around not far upstream. It was unusual to encounter a bat in the daytime, and Dar had never seen a stout one before, but perhaps it was a different species and that accounted for both oddities. More likely though it had rabies or something. Dar knew that the little brown bat in particular was falling victim by the millions to a mysterious malady called White-nose Syndrome, which had actually been first discovered in the caves of this very county, but that was a winter disease. The infectivity rate was quite high—above 99 percent in some locations—and there were grave concerns about local extinction. European bats seemed to have developed an immunity to this cold-loving fungus, which rouses them from winter hibernation and saps stored energy. The stricken creatures flew out in search of insects that were not yet available, or they clung near the cave mouth for a little pale sunshine where they could be picked right off the walls by raccoons and other predators. There was some thought that stowaways in cargo containers or the holds of ships may have brought the disease over. Dar knew how crucial bats were to the environment, but based on a bad childhood incident this was one of the few animals he wasn't too thrilled to be near. He didn't mind snakes and spiders and most other creepy-crawlies. He didn't particularly like rats, or a swarm of angry bees, not that anybody did, but bats really freaked him out. Inside of a house, forget it. He would probably push others out of the way to be first out the door, making his apologies later.

Dar needed to proceed upstream along this stretch, where the bed was easier going than the steep banks, and the odd flying rat was still making big, slow circles above the water. Bats are usually a blur, but he could actually see its scrunched face and count the beats of its wings. When it seemed to disappear for a while he made a beeline up the rocky shore, but halfway through the bat reappeared. He picked up his pace, but it began swooping closer and then started dive-bombing. Dar ran full speed toward the side now, wildly swinging his pole above his head in a circle without looking up. When he hit the bank he kept running until it was all thick tall brush before daring to scan the skies. He thought of that old joke where the cuckolded husband remarks to his wife that people seem to have their phone number mixed up with the National Weather Service, because guys kept calling to ask if the coast was clear.

There was another animal incident that caused quite a stir. Late one night when everyone was asleep, an eerie caterwaul arose from the woods. At first it sounded like a crying baby, then like someone moaning, and finally like the screams of a woman being brutally murdered. The noise was so loud that they couldn't tell how close it really was. Some of the campers emerged, but others were afraid to leave their tents and were shouting concerns through the walls. Dar thought he knew what it was, and Rick came down, rifle in hand, to confirm it. This was the contact call of a fox, usually a vixen looking for a mate. The fox screaming went on for some time, and turned from provoking sheer terror to becoming a source of pure annoyance. Nobody could get to sleep.

"Hell, I'm gonna go out there and fuck that thing myself in a minute just to shut it up," vowed Rick.

"I'll bet you would too, big boy," purred Sadie. It turned out that they were known for the occasional hookup, according to BethAnne—as unlikely as that sounded—and Sadie had been kind enough to school Andrew now and again as well. Go figure, thought Dar.

Another night the overpowering scent of skunk spray hung in the air, like mustard gas over the trenches. There was no wind, and it just wouldn't clear. Those who couldn't sleep sat out on the benches, some with watery eyes. They started a small fire, and Liz made mint tea with honey in the hope that it would clear their palates. The campers swapped skunk stories.

Cole had known a couple who couldn't get rid of a skunk under their big old front porch. It never sprayed them, but it was a source of constant concern, especially to the wife, who was of the opinion that they should hire a professional. The man of the house thought that would be a waste of money. He tried blocking off the entrance, but apparently there were several. One day he could see it under there through a hole in the latticework and was able to get a shot off, hoping to hook the body out, but the mortally wounded animal was able to crawl farther underneath first. Needless to say, the odor from its expelled and leaked-out anal scent glands and rotting carcass entered the house itself and lingered for weeks, nearly causing a divorce. A couple years later another skunk took up residence in the same place. This time they paid someone to live-trap it out, which caused a different kind of stink. The fee was $50 per animal, and to their dismay seven helpless pink newborns, small as could be, ended up on the tab, which led to a small claims court dispute.

Dar was down in his parents' basement once and heard the tiniest rustling of dead leaves behind the cistern wall. He assumed it was a mouse. When he heard it again a few days later he decided to investigate further by peering through the window from outside. To his surprise, this window had been left open in early spring by his father, in order to air out the basement. Anything could have gotten in, and did. Dar lowered a long barn plank down through the darkness until he could feel it reaching the floor. A minute or so later, a very bedraggled and emaciated skunk walked slowly up from the dark pit out into the bright sunlight of the side yard, swaying and blinking. The poor creature was clearly on its last legs. There were a couple of dog bowls on the ground right next to the house there. It seemed to smell the water and waddled over shakily, drinking down what was there in one sitting. It then proceeded to eat some of the dry dog food, slowly crunching away for a good ten minutes. Finally, the skunk turned around, looked directly at Dar and his parents, who were standing there in fascination—gratefully, it seemed—and walked slowly between them and the house out toward the closest windbreak up in back. Spraying them was the last thing on its mind. This was Dar's greatest animal rescue to date, and made up a little for the harm he had caused earlier in life and was precipitating again now.

Bennie wrestled a gigantic moss-backed snapping turtle in one day from a nearby marshy area, expecting a hero's welcome, but not a single member was in favor of killing it. It's one thing to order turtle soup, which none of them had ever consumed anyway, but quite another to do the deed, morally and physically. This was obviously a female out to lay her eggs. Dar had found an even bigger one once in the swampy woods behind a country auction hall, where he was taking a toot just before the first hammer. He excitedly told a couple of acquaintances about it, and one regular wanted to carry the she-beast right into the auction hall and sell it off. That idea was shot down too. Bennie complained to Rick, who gave wise counsel. "We might have eaten it a few months ago when we were hungrier, but remember, never bring live food into this camp, or it'll stay that way." Andrew volunteered to return it to the marsh but did not have the strength, so he and Dar carried it in a tarp stretcher, saving their backs and protecting their fingers. Gwen made mock turtle soup with crayfish the next night. When Bennie did not find this amusing, Cole quipped that he seemed to be suffering from a reptile dysfunction.

Fireflies were out in full flash now, bringing everyone back to their childhoods. What a combination of fairy and science they are, all around the world, and throughout history. Dar remembered a small item in an early London periodical he'd handled about a fancy ball in some exotic colony, where one of the attendees stole the show in a gown illuminated by hundreds of live fireflies secured in tiny muslin bags. "Rows of brilliants, which threw around her a light like that of the fabulous carbuncles of the *Arabian Nights*, glittered down her dress, and eclipsed all the jewels in the room." Did she copy this from ancient Japanese bioluminescent firefly lanterns, or was it her own bright idea? Whoever gathered them, servants perhaps, probably enjoyed the assignment, compared to the usual drudgery. Hopefully they got a firsthand report from a fellow lackey in attendance. To have been a firefly on the chest wall at that gay affair! The same insects had been winging around and blinking, in season, in these very woods, since the last ice age. He wondered what precontact peoples had made of fireflies, and if they were somehow comforting to the first Europeans in this new land of strange and exotic creatures. Must have been.

ΩΩΩ

What was the relatively recent human history of this place? Dar had a basic idea of the early settlement and tribulations of the "Schohary District" leading up to its formation as a county in 1795, but he began to delve deeply into Dave's collection of materials. Early local histories are usually referred to by the author's last name, and in the case of Schoharie County that meant Brown in 1823; Simms in 1845, along with his re-titled and expanded revision completed in 1883; Roscoe in 1882; and Warner's military history in 1891 (when the latter did poorly, its eccentric author buried most of the unsold copies, as he couldn't bring himself to burn them, even temporarily diverting a brook to ensure their destruction, but many were found in usable condition when dug up by the new property owner years later). These were typical first attempts at recording local history, crucial but flawed. There is hope, often in vain, for good corroboration and documentation, new primary sources coming to light, and robust reinterpretation.

After years of harassment by French forces and attendant misery and want, high taxes and tariffs, forced military conscription, and a particularly brutal winter, Queen Anne of England offered support to suffering Protestants in the Rhine region of what would later become Germany. Some thirteen thousand of these "Palatines" arrived in London in 1709, though in reality they came from many principalities in that general area, and from other countries such as Switzerland, and included a large contingent of Catholics at first. They soon found themselves worse off than before, in spite of the noble intentions of the Crown and the humanitarian concern of such luminaries as Daniel Defoe. Most of the emigrants had been lured in part by false rumors of free passage to America, and they eventually left England in disillusionment. Some three thousand sailed for New York in 1710, however, kicking off the largest migration of any one ethnic group to colonial America, with hundreds perishing in the process. They were quarantined in tents on what is now Governors Island until the bulk of the survivors was finally sent up the Hudson River to villages in the vicinity of Saugerties and Germantown called West Camp and East Camp. In order to pay for their passage and maintenance they were put to hard labor producing such British naval stores as tar and pitch. This proved a thorough failure, the monies ran out, and the contract was broken on both sides.

First Mayor of Albany and Commissioner of Indian Affairs Pieter Schuyler had journeyed to London around the same time in order to press for more protection from the French, and for an invasion of their Canadian strongholds. A group of Mohawks in his company, trotted over largely for show, was said to have taken pity on the displaced refugees, who had actually departed already, and a subsequent

Palatine claim that sachems in this party promised them land in what was then the western reaches of Albany County is even more fanciful. The Schoharie connection probably comes instead from an initial British Board of Trade suggestion that this might have been suitable territory for the naval stores project, but it lacked the large stands of pitch pine available in the area of the Camps, as well as easy access to the Hudson. The desperate Germans sent a delegation to visit the Schoharie Valley in 1712. They negotiated with the Indians, some of whom were instrumental in helping them through their first harsh trials there. One of their leaders, Johann Conrad Weiser, sent his teenage son to live with the natives, to learn their language and pave the way for friendly relations. Soon a reported fifty families made the trek through what was then a veritable howling wilderness— complete with bears, wolves, rattlers, and "painters"—where only indigenous Americans and French trappers had ventured before. The royal governor at the time considered this breakaway Schoharie group the most troublesome quarter of the Palatines, the opposite outlook being that they were the most adventurous, and the least tolerant of serfdom. It has been said that the French and English viewed New York as just another territory to conquer, the Dutch saw the region as a good opportunity for commerce, and this group of Germans imagined it as a Promised Land, where they might live in harmony with the similarly beleaguered natives.

These rich vales must have seemed like the lowlands of milk and honey to the skilled and hardworking refugees. Before long other Palatines followed, swelling the population into the hundreds, with thousands of acres under tillage. They established seven dorfs, or villages, along the Schoharie Creek, built mills, and were on the verge of great increase. The governor, however, conspired with a group of businessmen to usurp the Germans, declaring their titles defective and branding them as rebels, and the Dutch began to make their own inroads. When the elder Weiser was unsuccessfully dispatched to London to plead their case, his ship was robbed by pirates, and he spent time in a debtors' prison before finally making his way back to the valley years later. This was all naturally discouraging to the

Palatines, who were forced to rent or purchase land they had not properly secured to begin with, and waves of emigration to the west began. One group of families departed for the Tulpehocken settlement near Reading, Pennsylvania in 1723. Many others relocated to the Mohawk Valley. The Germans and Dutch eventually settled their differences, but they were gradually outnumbered by waves of New Englanders as the century progressed, in part because they were less averse to farming the rocky hills and highlands.

"Nine of them owned the first horse, which was a gray." That's all historian Brown had to say on that topic in 1823, about something that had happened over a century earlier. Simms added a couple of details about how it was an "old gray mare" purchased in Schenectady, which is where the Palatine settlers carried their grain on foot at first, rather than by beast to more local mills. A romanticized and highly embellished story by the future author of *Drums Along the Mohawk* appeared in a 1935 issue of the *Saturday Evening Post*, and was revised a bit for a 1962 children's book. Now, seventeen-year-old Jacob Borst and his even younger bride must sell their chair, the only one in the valley with a back to it, in order to pay their seventh of the investment (each partner could use the horse for one day each week, which would not have worked out as tidily with nine partners). They thought they were getting a fine black specimen with a white star on his head and one white hoof, but somebody else bought that one first, and they got stuck instead with "a flea-bitten gray, potbellied, hollow-flanked, with broken knees." (The written record was increasingly unkind to this simple gray horse.) They wondered if they'd made a big mistake, even at the discount price, as the struggling creature barely made it back, but when they checked in on her the next morning they found a "wet, brown mass at her side,"—a healthy colt—so two for the price of one! The official county seal once featured a light-colored horse trotting through the valley, but it turned brown (and a little friskier) around the time this fictional work came out. Dar once asked if even the original sentence could have been true, and a local historian replied, "Well, some horse had to be the first one," so that settled that. Jacob was the first Borst there in real life, however, and a Borst was mayor of the village of Schoharie when the virus hit just shy of three centuries later. And among the first small handful of settler newborns, the names of Bouck, Lawyer, and Mattice had also been borne down the river of local history and were still recently numerous.

The French and Indian War in the mid-1700s had a limited impact on the Schoharie Valley, but not so with the Revolutionary War. A local Committee of Safety was formed to address the growing concerns of the settlers, often meeting secretly in a cave. British forces sought to disrupt the huge shipments of Schoharie grain going to the Continental Army, and conquering New York State would split the rebel colonies in half as well. At first their principal agents were Tories loyal to the Crown, and their disaffected and swayed Indian allies. Soon, small outlying settlements were being harassed by hostile forces, and the buffer zone around the district was shrinking. Howe threatened from New York City, Burgoyne came down from Quebec, and St. Leger was advancing from the west. Kingston would be burned to the ground, and Albany was a prime target. Things looked bleak for the Patriots—also known as rebels by the Loyalists, who were in turn branded as traitors—and chilling tales reached their ears. An advance party fell upon three girls picking berries just outside the walls of Fort Schuyler to the west, only one of whom escaped, with two balls through her shoulder. The cause célèbre scalping of Jane McCrea to the north had a particularly galvanizing effect. The pivotal Battle of Oriskany in the Mohawk Valley turned St. Leger back, but hundreds of Patriots lost their lives in the effort.

Closer to home, Tories poised to take control of the Schoharie Valley in 1777 were thwarted by the first-ever U.S. Army cavalry charge in the Battle of the Flockey, which took place near North Blenheim in the neighboring town of Fulton. The hero of this swashbuckling episode, Colonel John Harper, had just made a narrow escape from his home in Harpersfield to the immediate southwest. From a pension application account of this flight by his young niece: "About two miles from the Fort night overtook us and it became so dark that we were compelled to encamp. Which we did near a small stream called West Kill. Some time in the night there came on a severe thunder shower and raised the water in the stream on which we were encamped and obliged us to leave."

In the Battle of Cobleskill the following year, a sizable force of regulars and militia was ambushed and routed. A small number of them took refuge in a house that was soon overrun. Historian Simms wrote of two who were incinerated ("The remains of Fester fell into a tub of soap in the cellar, and were known by his tobacco box, and those of Freemire were identified by his knee buckles and gun-barrel") and one who was butchered ("his body cut open and his intestines fastened around a tree several feet distant," with a roll of Continental bills stuffed into his hand to underscore the contempt of the Indians). The Cherry Valley Massacre saw close to fifty killed, including women and children, with many prisoners taken. This was followed by the Vrooman Family Massacre along the Schoharie Creek above Middleburgh. The war was suddenly up close and personal, and settlers felt unsafe working in the fields and laying their heads down at night.

Three substantial forts were constructed along the Schoharie Creek. The Continental Army finally sent extra companies to aid in the district's defense. Timothy Murphy of Morgan's Rifle Corps was among them, and he stayed on to become Schoharie County's most legendary figure. These troops calmed the citizenry, improved the fortifications, and launched sorties for about a year, but were soon called elsewhere. By order of George Washington in perhaps his blackest deed, the wide-ranging Sullivan-Clinton Expedition waged a horrific scorched-earth campaign against the home fronts of those Iroquois tribes that had sided with the enemy, causing great misery and starvation. Locally, the conflict peaked in 1780 when the British army itself joined Tory tormentors—and Indians under the skilled command of Joseph Brant and the brutal hand of Seth's Henry—in a devastating sweep through the county. Two of the forts were attacked, crops were destroyed, livestock was slaughtered, and scores of homes and barns were burned to the ground. Both George Washington and James Madison referred to the Schohary District in correspondence lamenting the amount of grain lost to the Patriot cause. This was preceded and followed by a series of smaller raids, murders, and abductions. When these border wars finally died down, Loyalist properties were confiscated, and Native Americans who had assisted them appeared at their own risk. According to Simms: "The fact was, several of them had been met in by-places by citizen hunters, and were mistaken for *bears*. A few disappeared, and the rest took the hint and left the country."

A story floats down about the fate of the notorious Loyalist Benjamin Beacraft, who returned to Blenheim after the conclusion of the conflict. It is said he was removed from his home and of his shirt and given fifty lashes with fresh rods near the foot of the future covered bridge. Ten strikes each for being a Tory; for waging war against his neighbors; for slitting the throat of a young Vrooman boy, harvesting his scalp (they were going for about $8 at the time), hanging the body over a fence, and bragging on this deed; for cruelly taunting captives as they were being transported toward a very uncertain future; and for having the audacity to reappear as if none of this had ever happened. Officially, he was grateful for being spared, returning to Canada with his tail between his legs, but descendants in one family could still point to the place alongside Bear Ladder Road where his body was secreted, in order to avoid repercussions, and one small later history does say "his bones are washed by the spring freshets along the Schoharie River above the Blenheim bridge."

These were the big events. So many little things, though, said to have happened. The Indian raider thrusting his deadly spear at a settler who parried it several times with babe in arms out in a cornfield, the child's laughter at this perceived game awakening "the sympathy of the savage" and eliciting mercy for both. The pastor who woke up one Sunday morning with restored sight after many years of blindness and said to his wife, "How old you look!" Historian Roscoe removing the remains of his much earlier predecessor Brown from a neglected enclosure that had been turned over to pigs, for reinterment elsewhere, and how the bones on his wagon gave off a phosphorescent glow that night.

BORING: DO NOT ENTER! That was the warning sign Dar thought should be hanging over such things as museums when he was quite young, before something clicked. Not totally over that by his mid-teens, he'd somewhat reluctantly visited the Old Stone Fort in Schoharie with his family on vacation years earlier—joined there by a relative from Albany—when they were first exploring different upstate counties with an eye toward resettling. This was the Lower Fort of three in the Revolutionary War, one of the finest such surviving edifices in the country according to Dave's materials, converted from an early German church and serving most recently as a splendid historical society museum for over a century. The names of those who built and supported the structure were still beautifully inscribed on its walls, minus those of certain Tories that had been chiseled off in the manner of ancient Egyptian defacement. Dar preferred to imagine this shrine to local history he hadn't appreciated properly back then as untouched by thieves and vandals, and didn't even ask Rick if he knew one way or the other. The mostly mute artifacts listed in Old Stone Fort printed catalogs from 1899 and 1933, along with later acquisitions on display, probably spoke more reliably than early tall tales and certain questionable or conflicting accounts in the first undocumented histories, not to mention the well-meaning fictionalized works that started popping up in the mid-1900s.

Once in the hands of the original inhabitants: "The arrow points are of the most beautiful workmanship—serrated, rotary, triangular, barbed, war, notched, stemmed, triple-notched base, level-base, etc., in flint, chert, jasper, chalcedony, obsidian, agate, quartz, etc., each material furnishing all the most brilliant colors.. . . The spear heads are also in all the rare shapes, materials and colors." These points took their place alongside axes, hammers, chisels, drills, gorgets, mortars and pestles, net sinkers, hammer and banner and smoothing stones, sinew dressers, scrapers, perforators, pendants, pipes, idols, an adz belonging to the supposed "last true blooded Mohawk in the valley of Schoharie," and beads "found" in old burial sites. From the earlier catalog: "First-class duplicates for exchange, none for sale."

Utilized by early settlers, hatchets, saws, post axes, planes and squares, plumb bobs, fireplace implements, candle molds and holders and reflectors and snuffers, lamps and lanterns, plows, yokes, horse bits and bridles and collars and saddlebags, scythes, flails, skipples used to measure wheat, "very old" hoes, hoisting forks, millstones, manure hooks, flax-swingling knives, hetchels, wool cards, a hop press, tools for making rope and dressing leather, tobacco boxes, an 1816 ballot box, haversacks, medicine bags, a leather fire bucket, imported tile, spectacles, compasses, pocket watches, looking glasses, inkwells, furniture, coaches, a much used funeral hack, early wooden business signs, and to call weary workers in from the fields, conch shells and dinner bells.

On the domestic front, corn brooms, butter churns and ladles, a batter pitcher, a shovel for a brick oven, a potato roaster, a sausage toaster, an egg boiler, broilers and warmers, a cheese press, a cutter for loaf sugar, a meat-cutting trough, rolling pins, a wooden tray and bowl "for mixing corn bread," pie boards, "ancient dishes" even then, pewter plates, silver utensils, a "recipe for making wine," buttons and buckles, combs and brushes, a bone-handled razor, spinning wheels, a loom, splint baskets, early chests, precious cradles, and the first baby carriage used in the valley.

On paper, in addition to important maps, grants, deeds and other documents, old books and pamphlets and newspapers, brought-over Latin texts, German catechisms, Dutch Bibles, and English readers, wills, bonds, bills of sale, slave papers, early money, papers of incorporation, legal and voting records, military orders and correspondence and lists of deserters, invitations and tickets to cotillion parties and Christmas balls, fair premium lists, psalm books, songbooks, sheet music, photos—including an early one of the Blenheim covered bridge—advertising calendars, circus and political posters, stage coach ephemera, a 1735 bounty receipt ascribed to the hand of the first Johannes Lawyer paying out sixteen shillings for twenty-four wolf heads, and a more sedate bank check from about a century later signed by James Fenimore Cooper.

In the fabric and clothes line, deerskin moccasins and wooden shoes and winter snowshoes and summer shoes made of straw, a Masonic apron from 1792, flags, needlework, a patchwork quilt, hats, children's suits, a soldier's blanket, military uniforms, dress coats, tassels and epaulettes, black satin and silver brocade vests, parasols, and baby bonnets.

In iron, a bear trap, ox shoes, bolts and knockers from important doors, jail locks and wrist persuaders, a "monster key" found on a battlefield, waffle irons, skillets, kettles, a coal carrier, skimmers and dippers, corn and spice mills, branding irons, bullet ladles, a cigar press, a wrench for tightening rope beds, and historic weathervanes that "high over all, witnessed the investment of the fort during the Revolution" and "breasted the storms" which frequented the valley.

For defense and destruction, tomahawks, bows and arrows, war clubs, swords and sabers and bayonets, flintlock pistols and muskets, many decorated powder horns, samples of grapeshot, cannon balls, cartridge boxes, holsters, a Navy revolver, a Sharps rifle from 1852, a Springfield from the Civil War, field canteens, and harder-than-ever hard-tack.

Things you don't know how they got there, like meteorites, alligator teeth, volcanic dust from Mount Pelée, gravel from the Dead Sea, Mexican spurs, a collection of horseshoe crabs, a "valve from engine that drew Gen. Grant's Funeral Train," and a Samoan girdle . . . or things you don't know what they are, like a "tailor's goose," "dove-gatt," "housewife," and "kuzzelbash". . . or oddities, like nails from the coffin of Timothy Murphy, a "Piece of Cloth made from Glass for the Princess Eulalie of Spain at the World's Fair," "$3000 worth of Macerated U.S. Greenbacks," the "Old Bouck Drum" played during the march of local convicted murderers to the gallows field, also known as "the death drum," and a "Shot Pouch of unusual and grotesque design."

Finally, artifacts directly connected to good German, Dutch, and Yankee surnames. "Tomahawk of Isaac Deitz." "Foot Stove of Daniel Hager." "Very Old Pipe, found in a tree by John I. Spateholts." "Indenture, binding John Feeck as apprentice to learn the trade of Carriage Building." "Ox Yoke. Made by Jonathan Stalker and presented by his great granddaughter Doris Stalker. It will be noticed that the draught staple of this yoke is a little off the center, and that it was made so to favor a weaker ox." "Trousers of Gen. Jacob Gebhard." "Garter Worn by Engelite Vrooman." "Saddle of Polly Sweetman made in 1795." "Earthen Coffee Pot, Heirloom of Schaeffer Family." "Sword, carried by Daniel Budd in 1815." "Beaded Vest, worn by S. Hoosic Mix." "Knife Carried by Berent Wayman in the Rebellion." "Cap Box, worn by Nathan Rickard, who was killed at Newburn, bullet passing through this box." Regarding a wooden hatchet donated by one David Willsey, who lived on Schoharie Hill: "His mental powers were very weak, while the work of carving wood at his hands was well nigh perfect." Who knows if these old catalog items had still been in the possession of the museum, or what had been added to the collections since.

A cannonball hole from the October 17, 1780 attack was still visible in the cornice molding at the rear of the building, which Dar thought was cool back then, and the manner in which the marauding force of eight hundred or so combined troops was detected and repulsed by all three forts on that day was thrilling to him now. Among the tens of thousands of artifacts that bespoke of aboriginal habitation, industry, conflict, and culture, an otherwise generally uninterested Dar did remember being particularly taken with two beautifully executed miniature German folk art chests—decorated with black, green, and white checkerboard squares on a red background—and he read about them in greater detail now. They had belonged to twin sisters Margaretha and Elisabeth Kniskern, inscribed with their names (spelled "Margreda" and "Elisabet") and the date 1778. Kniskern's Dorf was one of the seven original German villages along the Schoharie Creek. These little girls must have been among those who sought refuge in the fort during the attack, probably clutching these wonderfully painted receptacles filled with their most precious belongings to their chests on the way in. Their father Johannes Kniskern, a sharpshooter up in the tower during the attack, was probably the maker. Elisabeth was the great-great-grandmother of Perry Taylor, a mayor of Schoharie, and his wife Eleanor donated this family heirloom chest to the museum in 1940. Margaretha's chest was discovered in the tower of the museum in 1977, donor unknown. Both had made their way back inside the sheltering walls all those years later!

Lingering in the cemetery on the grounds that day while his parents made interminable small talk back at the front desk with that current generation of interpreters, Dar happened to overhear a conversation about a curious nearby monument. The family name of Civil War survivor Orson Spickerman was engraved on this large standing stone. It had been his favorite creek fishing rock, hauled up there by friends and family somehow upon his death. The young visitor thought that was pretty cool too.

Who were the custodians of all this knowledge, and all these artifacts? Three names seemed to stand out from the early days, according to the literature. Henry Cady, co-founder of the Schoharie County Historical Society, first librarian at the Old Stone Fort, and compiler of the 1899 catalog; Chauncey Rickard, chief guide in the reopened Howe Caverns, colorful master of wildly popular historical pageants, and compiler of the 1933 catalog; and Myron Vroman, a tireless, unassuming, seventh-generation descendant of the original Dutch settler Adam Vrooman, forced into mandatory Civil Service retirement in the 1960s after decades of Old Stone Fort service—along with numerous other devoted staffers, to be sure, from groundskeepers to office managers. One can imagine their feelings when they finally had to leave. Would the new caretakers show the same level of understanding and dedication? Would they keep the important collections and publications up, and respond in a timely and knowledgeable manner to enquiries? Would they strike the correct balance between respect for tradition and the need for change? Or would they turn out to be unqualified, unmotivated, or self-serving figureheads, or worse yet, active despoilers, and would the existing infrastructure be strong and deep enough to withstand that? Dar had absolutely no idea how this had all played out at the historical society over the last fifty years, which seemed well owned and operated from his limited exposure, but in general he knew this was a crucial issue for all cultural institutions, where show horses who credentialized and interviewed well or who had the right connections often beat out workhorses who were far less likely to drop the torch, and where a bad economy often led to culturecide by austerity.

As the decades and centuries progressed, the written record improved. Among Dave's history hoard was a folder on Ray Pollard, the Farm Bureau county agent who logged countless miles in service of local agriculture from 1916 to 1944. It cited his *Warm Chimneys* and *Along the Country Road*—two books Dar remembered leaving upstairs back at the cabin even though they were signed copies—as well as surviving radio scripts, and issues of the *Farm Bureau News* he edited. "We shall not talk about politics and religion," asserted the latter in an early number in the series. Another held Pollard's sweet but sad essay entitled "The Splashings of Betty Brook," about how eminent Eminence had once been. At one point his office was above a department store on Main Street in Cobleskill, with milk-testing equipment on one side, handouts and supplies on the other, and exhibits of early implements in an adjoining room. It is reported that his first five secretaries were named Lela, Lila, Lena, Lina, and Laura! Pollard introduced local farmers to the wonders of the tractor, crop rotation, and other radical agricultural improvements. He instituted large annual picnics, burying the corpse of "Poor Farming" in a mock ceremony at one such event and hosting principal speaker Governor Franklin D. Roosevelt at another, in 1930 at Howe Caverns. The entire county mourned his passing in a special issue of the *Farm Bureau News* that was brimming with brief testimonials from those who knew and worked with him. Dar usually paid little attention to such commemorative tributes, but these intrigued him.

"In the fall of 1911 as I was coming out of Goldwin Smith Hall, I noticed that some farm fertilizer had been spread on the lawn. I remarked to another freshman who happened to be going my way that it smelled natural. He agreed that it did. That is how I first met Ray Pollard."

"In April of 1916 there came to Cobleskill an eager, ambitious, delightful young man who less than a year earlier had been graduated from the College of Agriculture at Ithaca. Now he had been chosen as manager of the newly organized Schoharie County Farm Bureau and thus was established a connection that was destined to endure through almost twenty-eight crowded and fruitful years. And today, almost before his friends can comprehend it, his career has ended and the book is closed."

"We traveled the hills of the county together. We knew that first of all, if our missions were to succeed, we must come to know the people and they us. We spoke in barns and churches and Grange halls and orchards, telling men and women what the new Farm Bureau and the School of Agriculture hoped to accomplish. I recall that we stayed overnight with one family and that we both helped with the milking, eager I suppose, to show that we not only had a love of farm life in our hearts, but the know how in our fingers. It was early Spring. The mud lay deep in the roads, the wind was sharp and the snow banks fought a stubborn rear guard action for winter. But we were young, full of enthusiasm, we liked our people and life was good."

"Ray was an able planner and organizer, but he was impatient of the mechanics of organization. He wanted to work with people without so much fuss about it. He loved old things, the history of country communities, the long thoughts and the philosophy of farm people. He knew what he believed and he stood staunchly by his convictions. He accomplished great things in the practical sense, in the improvement of farming as a business, but he will be best remembered because of his understanding and interpretation of the true place and function of Agriculture, of the thoughts and the hopes and the aspirations of farm people. He built his life into their lives and thus for all time he lives on."

"Through the farm broadcasting of WGY, it has been our privilege to bring the philosophy and ideas of Ray Pollard to farm people far beyond the environs of Schoharie County. In the process, he acquired a tremendous circle of friends here in the northeast. To catch his viewpoint was to become an admirer and friend, and many a radio listener has been inspired and encouraged by Ray's radio essays."

"He was a man of outstanding ability in his profession and will be missed by a good many who had come to depend upon him. He was always ready to help anyone who was in trouble and quite a few owe their success on the farm to his help. We wish his successor, Mr.

Pendergast all possible success as he takes over the duties which Mr. Pollard so ably performed."

"The fields of alfalfa and other clovers, the better woodlots, the improved dairy herds and poultry flocks and the enduring memories of his friendship for us and ours for him are living monuments to our much loved agricultural leader."

"Much is written and said about the difficulties and troubles of farmers. Perhaps not too much as these things must be kept before the public if we are to get any consideration at all. Ray did not let us forget the pleasant side of farms and farming."

"The coming of war added untold duties and burdens to the already full program of the Farm Bureau Manager.... The members of the Draft Board always called upon him for advice in our troublesome farm cases and valued his opinion very highly. I have always felt that the extra burdens he carried as a result of the war emergency did much to hasten his death. I was never able to understand how he did all the things that he did."

"It is a perfectly safe statement that no other man in the world ever knew Schoharie County—its highways and byways and its farm people—as did Ray and it is most unlikely that circumstances will ever permit any other man to obtain the same intimate knowledge."

But by cracky, in the very same 1944 issue, the regular local reports showed everyone getting right back to work, the way Ray would have wanted it. Life goes on. Flat Creek: "Raymond Mabie bought a fine cow from Lewis Bailey." Cherry Valley Junction: "Farmers will have an incentive again this year to produce all the food that they can, knowing there will be a market because of the war." Carlisle: "Raymond Foster has sold his flock of pullets. He says the comparison between the price received for eggs and the price paid for feed is on the wrong side of the ledger." Rock District: "Our oldest brood sow must be slipping. She only had 15 pigs this time. When she was going strong she had 18 or 20." Fultonham: "It can still get down to zero although there are some signs of spring." Richmondville: "There have been two pairs of meadow larks around here all winter." Jefferson: "The sap is stirring and maple producers, help being available, will soon be hard at work." Hyndsville: "Mr. and Mrs. Elmer Rockwell and family of Howes Cave have purchased the former Orlo Foland farm and plan to take possession this spring." Charlotteville: "Ken Hillis is having his barn wired for electricity." Middleburgh: "We hope conditions improve in the poultry industry so that those buying chicks have not made a big mistake." Franklinton: "V. W. Lloyd has finished harvesting ice on Crystal Lake." West Fulton: "Luther Ingraham was unfortunate in losing a cow through a fall on the ice." Blenheim: "Dow Vroman has purchased a new milk cooler."

There was another printed artifact that caught Dar's eye in Dave's tent, something relatively modern, and he'd borrowed that as well. It was a complete 1959 issue of *The Lamp*, a periodical put out by the Standard Oil Company. The front cover featured a charming tempera painting of a highly stylized but instantly recognizable North Blenheim, a fall scene, in much happier days. The covered bridge is in the foreground, two hunters approach the woods, a school bus passes by, and there's an Esso service station sign in evidence. It's of the lower village, hard by the river, but you can see the farms toward the bottom of the West Kill Creek in the background, with Route 30 snaking away south through the brown foothills and out toward the looming, cerulean Catskill Mountains. If you applied some white paint over the title and date hovering in the clouds above them, you'd have a neat picture of the town, suitable for framing. It was probably the only national magazine cover this little burg ever got. The article it goes with is titled "The Empire State" and is filled with similarly wonderful illustrations by the same artist, Helen Federico; probably long gone by the downfall, Dar thought briefly. There's a nice stretch of dune road near Sag Harbor lined with signs for seafood, fishing, and the whaling museum; a soaring Presbyterian church in Bedford built in Carpenter Gothic-style; a stone dairy barn and silos in North Salem, also in Westchester County; a long stretch of colorful brick storefronts in Fishkill; a Kinderhook bandstand on a beautiful summer day; Doubleday Field and the baseball museum in Cooperstown; a Finger Lakes winery; the thundering Genesee Falls in the heart of Rochester's industrial district; a fantastic Gilded Age home in Saratoga; and finally, two inviting camp chairs overlooking an Adirondack lake and mountain range in all their pristine glory. The other articles in this issue were about who should pay for our highways (government should help, so citizens could afford to buy more gas . . . er, to travel more); an oil fungicide for Caribbean banana plantations (with a captioned photo that reads "Spray boy walks between the rows of plants with the sprayer strapped to his back"); how new oil will heat old Europe; and how oil will rid the Navajo of poverty. There were a couple of important Standard Oil Company internal promotions to announce too.

When the farmer unlocks the house door at five in the morning and steps out to see the barn and the outbuildings and the fields that lie close by, he must be sometimes thrilled with the joy of possession and grateful that his real estate and his chattels have remained secure through the hours of darkness.

Along the Country Road by Ray F. Pollard (Cobleskill, NY: printed for the author by the Cobleskill Press, 1941)

TWELVE

THE LATE but eager student of local history had read about the Brimstone Meeting House in one of Dave's books, and set out to locate it one morning. This early church, begun in 1815, was way up on Blenheim Hill. When it was completed, an emissary was dispatched to Catskill to buy pure white paint, but the price had gone up and he only had enough funds for cheap yellow ochre. One of the parishioners took exception to this color, refusing to pay his subscription. It was described in his lawsuit as "brimstone yellow," and the name took. It had been used as both a rallying point and a jail by both sides in the Anti-Rent troubles of the day, and was so abused and desecrated that it needed to be rebuilt in 1854.

About halfway there, going by woods rather than roads, Dar became hopelessly lost. This had been a great fear in camp, especially with someone like Susan, but it would not do for a ranger to go missing, though Bennie had spent two or three nights stuck in unfamiliar woods, and Dar wondered if Rick had gotten lost on occasion, as he was so often gone overnight. After several hours of crashing through bramble patches and thick brush, which disturbed and attracted untold numbers of crawling and flying insects, Dar came upon some remnant stone walls and then the nearly swallowed-up ruins of an old house, which he normally would have investigated further. His water gave out quickly, and wild blackberries alone did not slake a growing thirst. Gnats plagued his eyes, mosquitoes smelled their way to his sweat, ticks ascended his limbs, and cobwebs mummified his face.

Panic set in, but Dar resisted the urge to run. He looked down at all his bug bites and bloody scratches and wondered if a lifetime of such chemical infusions could have altered humans in the past somehow. He finally found a trickle of running water and followed it all the way down to the Schoharie, falling face first into its cool embrace.

Several of the campers had expressed an interest in switching up their duties a bit, emboldened to some degree by Cole's earlier challenge to the status quo. For Dar's part, he invited any of them to come along on rangering trips, though he was a little proprietary about the increasingly sensitive trout holes, as Sadie was about who did what on her farms. Dave made it clear that this was not an invitation to upset the applecart. It was merely a break from their customary roles and duties. Rick still did most of the pure reconnoitering, keeping an eye out for human activity of any sort. Nobody even bothered asking him to participate in this.

Gwen was not very mobile, and she declined an offer to get out of the kitchen more, though she enjoyed the weekly crayfish expedition. She'd shown an interest in bird watching, however, which was at its peak now, and Dar took her on slow, careful walks near camp, eventually including Herbert and Susan. Dave would have come if invited, and he was more of an expert, especially when it came to song authorship and LBBs—birder slang for little brown birds that are not easy to identify—but as much as Dar admired Dave, the wise-elder thing was wearing a little thin, and it was more enjoyable without him. Susan rarely spoke in complete or coherent sentences, and did not usually respond to normal conversation, but Herbert got fairly good results. Gwen and Dar thought she opened up on these walks more than anywhere else. Among other interesting finds, one day they spotted a cavity nest with a couple of shed snake skins carefully woven in. Dar assumed this was just a handy building material, but upon enquiry Dave said it sounded like the nest of a great crested flycatcher. They incorporated these intentionally, as a deterrent against predation.

Dar looked it up in his bird books. Flycatchers used cellophane as well, so maybe that was just an old anecdotal explanation that got misstated once and was repeated in error forever, as so often happens. Maybe they just liked shiny objects, as magpies did. Dave said no— they simply thought the cellophane was shed snake skin. Dar made the point that if flycatchers were supposed to be experts on the topic of the scariness of snake skins, and *they* couldn't tell the difference, how well would their use deter nest predation? And exactly which predators were they talking about? Something small enough to fit into the cavity, which meant other snakes, or small birds or mammals. It was unlikely that snakes were afraid of snake skins. Dave said he was certain that research had been done on this, and Dar wondered how you would validly set up such an experiment. They'd recently had a similar debate on whether skunks in dispute sprayed each other or not. Perhaps there was good scientific evidence one way or the other sleeping away in some soaring journal or monograph, but it was not accessible. Andrew had coined a term for this—NEWTCOT, for No Easy Way To Check On That—that the younger campers in particular found much use for.

Herbert asked if he could help with simple cooking chores like chopping roots and stirring soup and soon turned out to be of valuable assistance. Dawn and BethAnne helped in the kitchen more, and Liz, Cole, Andrew, and Dar got to do some of the farm work, which was sometimes tedious or strenuous but overall served as a nice change of pace. There were no forthcoming volunteers for privy duty, but Andrew was fine with that. He knew it bought him lots of praise, and the work was not all that bad or time-consuming. Dave continued to play the peaceful shepherd, often taking time out now for an afternoon nap.

ΩΩΩ

Although Liz hadn't said a word about BethAnne not returning to her own tent for several nights, an early morning bilge pumper spied her leaving his side, and the news spread like a flash fire. Dar had a decision to make. He'd found sharing his tent very comforting after all, not to mention a natural cure for chronic insomnia. They made their bed between two open sleeping bags. He'd forgotten just how much body heat another person could generate. If this came in that handy on chilly early-summer nights, imagine the winter! And then there was the abject emptiness of the previous winter, and his long stretch of solitude before that.

When it was time to go to sleep, BethAnne would turn her back to him, lying on her side with legs bent, and he fit in behind her like an adjoining piece of an idealized English countryside jigsaw puzzle. He ran his upper hand over those undulating hills, flat fertile fields, and voluptuous valleys for a long time, his face anchored in her fragrant golden hair near the slightly moist nape of her neck, their legs and feet as one. She always smelled clean and fresh, like a baby, but one that was big, bright, and bewitching. Her dreamy blue eyes animated the empty tent like the warm, low light that escaped snug thatched cottage windows in the wee hours, and her purrs of satisfaction and little sleeping noises filled the cold, still air like moonlit chimney smoke.

The allure of the female form was an incomprehensible mystery to Dar; especially the changing terrain and curvilinear swerves of the Middle Hebrides, twixt belly and thigh and back again around the Cape of Good Hope. The secrets of the universe might be held in mathematical formulas derived from them. This was anthropocentric, of course, as male horseshoe crabs must find the equally gnarly females they latch onto in shallow water pretty fetching themselves, for example, on some level, even though they are living fossils—and vice versa perhaps on the part of the greater female that lays ninety thousand eggs a year so that ten might survive—and this was only one planet of sentient procreators in who knows how many, *but still*. When the massaging and caressing was finished, he gently cupped a petite Teton, and they would often wake up locked in that embrace. On top of all that, she really did turn out to be easy to live with, and they seemed to be forming a deep friendship, though the eternally wounded man would probably never completely let his guard down again.

Dar asked to speak to Dave about this as soon as word got out. He was amenable, though he wanted to check with Liz first to see if she was willing to take in Susan as a tent mate, which she readily agreed to. Dave was also concerned about what would happen if they decided to part company but agreed they would try to work something out if it came to that. This was a real bombshell in the camp, but after several weeks everyone seemed quite used to it, though there was a bit more distance between Rick and Dar thereafter. Herbert was set up in style in his tent cot, which most everyone tried out once to see how it felt being suspended off the ground, and Susan seemed to settle in nicely with Liz.

Cole was delighted to finally get his own tent, and Dar congratulated him on it. The two men were getting along pretty well, all things considered, and they escalated the practice of always having a bad old joke ready for each other, or a category comeback joke. Cole's were raunchier, but he was a hopelessly chauvinistic horndog anyway, and it was all in private.

"Speaking of tents," Dar began, "an agitated man goes to his psychiatrist and says 'I'm a wigwam, I'm a teepee, I'm a wigwam, I'm a teepee.' 'Relax,' the psychiatrist says, 'you're two tents.'" "A man calls his psychiatrist and says he thinks his wife is dead. 'What makes you say that?' he asks. 'Well, the sex is about the same, but the dishes are really piling up in the sink.'" Ba-dump bump. On another occasion, "Did you hear about the lady who wanted to take a milk bath? The milkman asked 'Pasteurized?' and she said 'No thanks, just up to my tits will be fine.'" "Did you hear about the lady who got stuck on her toilet seat from suction? Just before the plumber came in she realized she needed to cover up, so she put a man's hat over her lap. The plumber said 'I should be able to get you out no problem, but that guy's a goner.'" "Hat jokes?" said Dar. "Very modern." "Oh, like *milkmen* are?" Sadie overheard one of these exchanges and served up a zinger of her own. "What do you call the useless piece of skin at the end of a man's penis? His body."

ΩΩΩ

Dar finally secured permission to lead an expedition to the Schoharie Creek. The headwaters of this river were on the wrong side of the Great Wall of Manitou, otherwise known as the Catskill Escarpment, so it had to make a huge detour from the western flank before gaining the

Hudson River. It flowed north for about ninety miles, emptying into the Mohawk River at Fort Hunter before quickly joining the larger river and descending south again to a point not far as the crow flies from where it started. It was impounded twice, at the Schoharie Reservoir by the Gilboa Dam, and a few miles farther down at the Blenheim-Gilboa Power Project. Dar had visited these before the virus but had never been in the waters above them. He was quite familiar with the Schoharie Creek below them, however, having fished and canoed its length down to Middleburgh, some thirteen miles away. Below that town it gets a little slower and muddier, and in general the more humans near a particular body of water the less he trusted or liked it.

Consulting the maps on the best way to reach the Schoharie, it was clear to the planners that proceeding down their small road to Route 30 and following that through nearby North Blenheim was not a good option. The road ran right next to the river, and one would be totally exposed. But by heading in an easterly direction through the forest, that was a surprisingly short journey of only two miles or so, and it would put them right out on the big water where it pulled away from the highway.

Although Rick had scouted this stretch of Route 30 often, he'd only seen vehicles a couple of times, well toward Middleburgh, assuming them to be Cave Clanners. And in a startling development on a long loop to the southeast a couple weeks earlier, he reported hearing and then seeing a small red and white airplane! The implications were enormous, and not merely as an omen of awakening technology. The most likely scenario was that somebody was making a life-or-death attempt to reach a better location. They could probably find a safe place to put down, like a wide road or even a small airport, but they couldn't possibly expect to find working pumps with aviation gas. In the worst-case scenario this was a spotter operating from a local strip, looking for signs of human activity or habitation. The plane was on a straight line though, and did not reappear. They threw green tarps over the brightest of the tents, were more careful with the fire, and suspended certain activities like the proposed Schoharie expedition, which was finally on again now.

Rick would lead them this first time, accompanied by Dar, BethAnne, Dawn, Cole, and Andrew. Cole claimed some fishing skill, and Dar had been working with BethAnne on the finer points of angling. Dawn was a good fish skinner from the previous life, and Andrew said he'd be willing to give that a try as long as he didn't have to end their lives. Dave had wanted to come along on this first trip, but he'd been under the weather lately and felt it wiser to stay put and not slow them down.

So they headed out one fine morning, with one gun, three poles, and lots of bait, crossing their road and climbing up through the deep forest on the opposite ridge above. Before long they descended again, this time through farm fields and across a small road. "Been there, done that," Rick said when a charming little house with lace curtains came into view. They were vulnerable here but stuck to windbreaks and patches of woods, and within minutes they were in another piece of deep cover. This came out onto an old shunpike road at nearly the exact spot where it and the large inviting river began to pull west away from Route 30. There was a wide gravel bank on the opposite shore, and they forded where it was only stomach deep on most of them. The rocky bottom was more slippery than on the high mountain stream, but all crossed safely.

From there it made sense to stay on that side of the river, opposite the bank with the small parallel road. There were no homes on this stretch, and it was doubtful anyone would use that road, but at least they'd have a chance to conceal themselves if they heard something coming, and the river would be a barrier if they were spotted and approached. Some surviving codger might be using the same fishing territory, so between all of that, high alert was in order. Route 30 to their backs receded, and they were quickly well away from it.

Having safely delivered the fishing party, Rick departed in security mode, and Dar took over the operation. They would start out with worms, always a good bet. Hooks were plentiful and could be replaced easier than lost lures. If you got hopelessly stuck, let Dar know and he would go out after the hook if possible. If you got a bite, set the hook well, keep tension on the rod tip, and take your time reeling in. They would stringer the fish to their belts for a while and stop for skinning whenever critical piscatorial mass was reached. Gwen would have to do without the heads this time. They would bring back pure sides, leaving the skin on to protect the flesh better. No yelping when you caught one. No screaming at water snakes. "No screaming if you see a bat either," added Dawn.

How many fruitless fishing trips had Dar been on where there was no action? Lots, especially on the smaller streams he preferred such as the West Kill, where you were less likely to run into others. He wasn't just avoiding human competition and the fish disturbation that came with it. He wanted to interact with nature on these increasingly rare outings, not people. From snooty fly-fishermen stage-whispering "wormer" to drunken college-kid canoeists racing their own feces downstream, which he actually witnessed once, he'd take the empty creel on the narrower stream any day. He didn't really enjoy gigantic lakes as much as moving water, or deep-sea or pier fishing, with all that diesel and testosterone in the air. The Schoharie Creek nearly always produced fish, though it didn't compare in beauty, wildness, and excitement to his ultimate river farther to the west, and it wasn't big enough for huge fish. As for solitude, on a typical lazy weekday in the past he might have seen a car or two pass by on the small rural lane across the way, usually pre-flight teens looking for a private place to smooch or swim or smoke a joint. A few kayaks or canoes may have passed by, though earliest spring was best for boating, before all the shoals and wannabe tombolos emerged. Chances were there would have been no one working the banks on foot as they were doing now.

The party proceeded downstream for ten minutes to a likely stretch where shallow rapids gave way to a long deep run. Cole crossed to the other side, and BethAnne threw in fifteen steps offshore. "Got one," shouted Cole a little too loudly almost right away. By the jerking bend of the rod Dar could see it was of decent size, and a minute later he was adding a nice smallmouth bass to his stringer. BethAnne hooked her own shortly after that, a large healthy crappie. She came toward shore to ask about keeping it, but Dar could tell she was afraid of losing it when taking the hook out. They'd practiced that with small trout, but fish this vigorous had game. It could wriggle and it could stab you with its fins. He pressed his dripping front to her wet back and, reaching around, showed her how to carefully put the point of the stringer through the mouth, out through the rear gill, and back through its metal ring before tying it to your belt loop and removing the hook, a fairly surefire way not to bobble the fish back into the babbling drink.

Once they were set up and getting regular bites, a good number of which produced results, and Dawn had enough catch of the day to start her skinning, Dar stuffed some worms into his bait belt and moved down to the next promising piece, just within sight of the others but almost out of earshot. He waded out into the slightly chilly water up to his thighs, found good footing on small rocks, and launched a full worm toward the far shore. As the long, loose line was pulled back toward the center by the current, the lively pink bait at its end swung naturally behind two large flat rocks that just breached the roof of the stream. He could see the clean sand and gravel behind them sloping down into dark greenish depths below the brief mirror surface afforded by this natural barrier. As the water erupted there he closed the bail and flexed the rod over his shoulder, hooking what was almost certainly a large bass. This was confirmed seconds later when it leapt clear out of the water in an attempt to throw the hook, the worm lashed to the lip of the great fish like Captain Ahab. "That's what I'm talkin' about," Dar said to himself as he began to reel it in. "First cast too."

The group continued slowly leapfrogging each other in various configurations until they reached a spot where the flow divided into separate channels and the small road receded out of sight. It was nice to be on a true river again. Large dark crayfish shot away in all directions. In one quieter section Dar came upon a series of sunfish nests. The small pebbly craters were spaced evenly apart, and were fiercely guarded by the brilliantly hued males who built them and spent most of their time fanning silt off the eggs under their care. These appeared to be redbreast sunnies, as opposed to bluegills or pumpkinseeds, distinguished by a brighter belly and a longer gill cover with a black spot on the end.

In Dar's longest absence, Andrew took charge of a separate stringer of chubs and suckers, some quite large, as they weren't sure if they should keep them. The lad towed them around the stream as if he were working for a big city dog-walking service, complete with waving tails, much to Cole's amusement. When Dar returned they formed a rough circle in the water and discussed this.

"Man," said Cole, "the round mouths and thick lips on those suckers are weird, so far down at the bottom of their face. I might date something like that, but I sure don't want to eat it." The women groaned at him, though this was a largely perfunctory reaction by now.

"They are kind of primitive," Dar explained. Necessary though, like all carrion eaters and bottom feeders, though they catch prey too. People used to think the mouth was how they held onto the bottom, but they hang low in the water column naturally, and the mouth is like that to cover more territory and to vacuum food in."

"What's this, fish school?" asked Cole.

"I get it," said Dar. "Like school of fish, but fish school."

"No, more like current events," said BethAnne. "Let him finish though. I for one am interested."

"Oh, but you can't expect to wield supreme executive power just because some *watery tart* throws a sword at you," Cole responded in a falsetto Monty Python voice that went right over everyone else's heads.

As the five of them stood waist-high in the river at slightly different angles to each other in order to scan for trouble or opportunity—something most of the clan did now without even thinking about it—engaged in this light banter, even as Cole waggishly claimed he had been peeing on them from just upstream the whole time, Dar had another emotional moment, like with Dawn on that first morning, better concealed but strong nonetheless. This all felt so *natural*! Vegetation swished and swayed above and below the water, sweet-smelling breezes escorted ephemeral seedpods all around them, the sun beat down through the bluest sky imaginable and soothed the deep cellar chill that might never truly leave his psychological bones, and birdsong drifted in from every direction.

The water had a hypnotic effect on him. There was the physical sensation, of course, but it was *going* somewhere. It wasn't static, like a parking lot or piece of woods or even a lake. How many younglings had stared longingly at meadow rivulets and major rivers throughout the ages, knowing they led to somewhere or something more exciting? "Those who go down to the sea in ships, who do business on great waters." The same with roads leading to the big town or city, and later, railroad tracks. Gathering food for the table, boon companionship, frolicking in and communing with a clean river, hope for the planet, a little sex in the air . . . this was almost more than Dar could have hoped for not all that long ago. It was his first big leadership initiative too, and it was going swimmingly.

"Suckers and chubs are bony, and kind of yecch to eat," he continued. "With all these tastier fish, let's let them go." Andrew was delighted with Dar's verdict and began carefully pulling the stringer out and releasing them one at a time.

"They're kind of a nuisance," said BethAnne. "You think you've got a good one on, but a bass half their size fights harder. They swallow the bait right down, it's hard to get the hook out, and you have to put a new worm on all over again. And I don't know what I'd do if I caught an eel in here."

Cole was clearly contemplating a lewd remark when Andrew spoke up. "Catfish are even worse. My dad took me once. They can stick you bad with those venomous spines, and their whiskers are kind of creepy too."

"I still say suckers are the weirdest," said Cole.

"All God's creatures though," ventured Dawn.

"The sucker wouldn't be his first mistake," replied Cole.

"Bet you don't know why there's so many of them," Dar asked the group.

"Okay," said Cole, "I'll bite. Why?"

"Because there's a sucker born every minute."

A few homes came into view. They stayed closer together now, and when they reached the stretch where Route 30 reappeared they decided to call it quits. Vast, weedy fields lined the county road now where tall, bright corn once flourished. They were not all that far from Bouck's Island, where Dar had done the majority of his fishing before. This was the home territory of an early farmer who had worked his way up from local office to Erie Canal commissioner to governor of New York State, the only son of the soil to do so. Governor William Bouck's Palatine grandfather, said to be the valley's first-born white male, was abducted from the same piece of land by a Revolutionary War raiding party, when according to one account he "was as harmless as his age was imbecile." He was spirited toward Jefferson until his dramatic rescue along the "Westbrook," which sounded like their West Kill. Still farther down this heavily agricultural section of the valley was the breathtaking Vroman's Nose, which Dar had climbed numerous times. This lofty sentinel was the most iconic natural feature in the county, looking down on the broad, rich vale and undulating river from its stone dance floor, and inspiring onlookers from human time immemorial. The Indian name was Onistagrawa, or Corn Mountain. There was a book in Dave's collection with the evocative title of *Vroomans Nose, Sky Island of the Schoharie Valley.*

Rick had divided his time between staying abreast of the group and looping out to the big road to look for signs of activity. They'd hiked along perhaps two miles of shoreline and bagged about thirty keepers. The catch included bass, the largest of which was over three pounds, sunnies, scrappy crappies, two brown trout, and some brilliant yellow perch. No rainbows or brookies, and no dominant walleyed pike, but maybe next time. They cut directly back toward the camp, which was only a few miles away in a straight line. Gwen and company did their magic and the meals went over big in camp.

Apparently Rick had reported directly to Dave about the expedition. He thought the results were positive, but agreed with Rick that the risks seemed high. Although they were fairly well concealed during much of the trip, there was significant danger of detection. Rick recommended quick-working teams of two or three instead, and sticking to the more isolated parts of the river. Dar and BethAnne would form one base unit, and Cole and Dawn the other. Liz and Andrew would come along on occasion as skinners and crayfishers.

Bennie stated a preference against joining in on these trips, as he had no love of fishing and less of skinning. Sadie wanted no part of it. Dar would bring or loan out his handgun, protected in multiple ziplock bags. This was more practical than lugging a rifle along, and it would free Rick up from escort duty. Dar thought all of this sounded reasonable, though he was concerned about losing or breaking gear. His favorite rod and reel would not be loaned out.

ΩΩΩ

It was the high tide of summer now. Everything was going full blast, and significant numbers of plants and animals had nearly or completely accomplished what they needed to do in order to survive as a species for another year, though many others were still in the thick of it. Some robins were on their second brood already, and bits of baby-blue eggshell were in evidence on the ground. Bright new leaves had unfurled, and every living tree and bush was under full sail. Berries, seeds, and nuts were coming along nicely. The grasses were getting higher, buttercups, daisies, and supple young black-eyed Susans dotted the meadows, numerous butterflies including the monarch, cabbage white, and swallowtail flitted about on their important business, bees were making honey, and fawns and fox kits were learning the ropes. As temperatures warmed, treetop cicadas clicked out their constant ear-splitting come-hithers from so many directions at once that they served as a hypnotically buzzy background score for the drama of all that bustling biology down below.

The campers made their own music by staging get-togethers once or twice a week in the evening, depending mostly on the weather, their schedules, and their mood. Dave and Sadie played a little guitar, and Rick had found them a nice one. Sadie had managed to hold on to her fiddle through thick and thin, and she was possessed of a sweet voice. They also had a couple of harmonicas and a bodhrán. Needless to say, all of the instruments were played as quietly as possible.

Among some sheet music found in a piano bench at the Ram House was the songbook for John Denver's *Aerie*, an earnest album Dave remembered fondly from the early 1970s. This was played straight through one night, minus a few of the schmaltzier selections, in a concert they had rehearsed. Dave and Sadie sang a lovely rendition of "Casey's Last Ride," and Dave belted out a strident "Readjustment Blues." Sadie shone on the stage. The fire illuminated her chestnut hair and glowed off the rings on her fingers, long silver-and-turquoise earrings, and a Flintstonesque necklace of large half-moon-shaped art glass in red, green, and brown.

The entire group was particularly affected by her version of "All of My Memories," with Dave on harmonica.

All of my memories lay in the life of the highway,
All of my nights in old motels asleepin' alone,
All of my days on the road with no one beside me,
All of my dreams of a place that I can call home.

Somewhere in the shade near the sound of a sweet singin' river,
Somewhere in the sun where the mountains make love to the sky,
Somewhere to build me a faith, a farm and a fam'ly,
Somewhere to grow older, somewhere a reason to try.

'Cause I'm tired of big cities and so tired of big city ways,
The scratchin' of sunset and walkin' around in the maze,
Some sweet taxi dancer try'n to save me from bein' alone,
Ah, it's much worse than lonely, there's no place I really belong,
Awhere I belong.

I'm leavin' the city life, in my mind, not flyin' away,
I'm leavin' tomorrow and all of the old yesterday.
I'm leavin' the trash cans, the bright lights and telephone lines,
I'm leavin' my sorrow and all of my mem'ries behind
To see what I'll find.

Somewhere in the shade near the sound of a sweet singin' river,
Somewhere in the sun where the mountains make love to the sky,
Somewhere to build me a faith, a farm and a fam'ly,

Somewhere to grow older, somewhere a reason to try.
Somewhere to grow older,
Somewhere to lay down and die.

Most of the campers had used the Internet, some more heavily than others, but it was safe to say that Andrew missed it the most, and that went double for his smartphone. Visiting with Dar in his tent one day, he spied the thirteen-inch Apple MacBook Pro in the corner and asked if he could just hold it on his lap for a while. After he opened it up he draped the power cord over his left shoulder, held the cord with his right hand so there was slack above and below, gripped the little, perfectly designed clip with his other hand, and slid the cord back and forth through it. Then he gripped the cord below the clip with his left hand and slid the clip up and down with his right hand, alternating back and forth every ten seconds or so.

"Wow . . . that comes right back to me. I did most of my work in my bed or on the couch," he explained, "plugged in from behind. Playing with the cord always helped me to concentrate. It feels weird doing it again."

"You can hold my laptop any time. Call me right away though if you connect."

Andrew shut the top and ran his hand over the cool finish of the aluminum unibody, its progress slightly impeded by the plastic logo on each pass. "And this always felt like something sticky on the skin of an otherwise perfectly smooth alien spaceship."

"Or the midsection of a Cherry 2000," remarked Dar.

"What's a Cherry 2000?"

"Look it up. Whoops . . . forgot. Maybe I'll tell you some day when you get a little older."

"I feel a little older, so whenever you're ready," said Andrew. "You know," he continued, "there's a bird or an amphibian or something out in the woods that makes a noise like an electronic notification sound. Do you ever hear that, or is it just me? It's exactly the same every time, perfectly uniform, like when the microwave is done or something. Some bird songs sound kind of metallic, or computery. I hear other device alerts too, and even ringtones sometimes."

"I'd say you should get out more, but in and out aren't what they used to be."

"I remember the last thing I ever looked up before the Web went down for good on campus," said Andrew. "Those of us who hadn't managed to get home were trying to figure out the difference between a dust or particle mask, and a respirator. The masks just made people *feel* safer. They provided some protection against blood droplets and fluids, or touching your own nose and mouth, but that's about it. Even correctly fitted surgical N95 respirators wouldn't stop tiny flu particles for sure."

"I didn't realize you were such a prepper."

"I wasn't, but this was on our minds. In the middle of that I found an older page from the swine flu scare with examples of designs people had made on their masks, like a beautiful butterfly, and animal and skeleton faces. At the bottom there was a photo of a toddler giving a big pig a full-on kiss through a fence, and the caption was something like 'You little bastard, you killed us all.' It's weird though. You got so perturbed when a lookup took five seconds longer than it should have, and look at us now."

"I don't remember my last lookup," said Dar. "I always wanted to go through and clean everything up, files and photos, etc., but I never did. I used to shoot myself in the foot with passwords too. I would pick pet names and then forget which was which. I finally started using 'Deaddog15' for everything—fifteen years being about how long regular mutts live—and that solved the problem."

Dar did not have Internet access in the cabin and didn't use his laptop there for much of anything else. He was caught with his batteries down when the power went off for good. He turned it on once in a while just to glow up a screen, for a last gander at what personal images he had, and to browse his files, looking for anything useful, but he knew it was almost dead and decided to get it over with, like putting down a faithful pet. There was very little chance that somebody would show up in his neck of the woods at the last moment with a planet-saving flash drive or something. If power and maybe even the Internet were ever restored, he'd still have his laptop. Until then, however, it would be as useless as an ejection seat on a helicopter.

He retrieved a time capsule David Bowie clip when still upstairs at the cabin, and went out on that. It was a live version of "Moonage Daydream" he'd found once from the surprise final performance of Ziggy Stardust at London's Hammersmith Odeon on July 3, 1973. The shaky, rather raw clip was about six minutes long. It had everything. The glam, the hair, joyful hedonism, clever stagecraft, sitting right out there with those ecstatic bobbing girls a few times, and the otherworldly Bowie himself, in a short kimono, flirting with his flamboyantly dressed yet macho lead guitarist. You couldn't take your eyes off him. And then he exits abruptly in the middle of the song for a wardrobe change, and Mick Ronson takes over with a soaring, strutting Les Paul Custom solo. You lose him in a yellow-orange spotlight once during the farthest far-out Echoplex swing of his martial tour of the stage and realize the crowd is pulling him down, but he breaks free with the help of a roadie and comes back for a guitar-shredding finale. His mascaraed eyes are black pits above the dark maw of his silent Munchian Scream. The camera happens to catch a single drop of perspiration falling off his chin in close-up—one drop of human sweat preserved for every unrecorded ocean spilled. He wondered if ancient rulers demanding the greatest entertainment in the land would have worshipped this band as gods or put them to death on the spot after a performance like that.

Although Dar appreciated classic rock, he mostly enjoyed the random streamed offerings of good college radio when he could get it. Even though he hadn't been into Bowie all that much, he also happened to have the more staid "Five Years" from a 1972 BBC studio performance. He watched that one too, but only once. "*News guy wept when he told us, Earth was really dying / Cried so much that his face was wet, then I knew he was not lying.*" Then he went back to "Moonage Daydream" and watched it over and over again at full blast until it blinked off. It was so in the moment, everyone was having so much fun, and maybe it all still could have been saved in 1973, though some would look at this video and say that's where we went wrong.

ΩΩΩ

The fun but constant and painful topic of foods they missed the most came up after dinner one night under a Rose Moon. They went around in the order in which they sat, choosing the perfect meal.

Andrew: "Probably my mother's lasagna, with the whole family there. And not to complain, but a salad with real Italian dressing. And warm bread, with a cold beer. Beers, plural. And bubble tea doesn't go too well with that, so I get to have one of those the next day out with friends for lunch."

Sadie: "One meal only? I don't know. What about a fresh tomato, basil, and mozzarella salad with balsamic vinegar and olive oil, wild mushroom ravioli in vodka sauce, fresh bread, and a nice pinot noir?"

Bennie: "Nobody shoot me, but a Big Mac at McDonald's. Two all-beef patties special sauce lettuce cheese pickles onions on a sesame seed bun. With the big fries and a garbage can full of Coke. To go, in my truck."

Herbert: "My favorite flavor is 'What the heck was that!?'"

Dave: "Probably pretty much anything at a favorite Thai restaurant near us. I would just go in with my family and enjoy seeing what was available that night."

Gwen: "My husband and I only got out of the country together once, to Montreal, trucking. It was winter but not too cold. We wandered around off the beaten path and found a fancy French place with live violin music that cost too much money, and I don't even know exactly what we ordered, because we just pointed at the menu and shared what came, but I would have whatever that was all over again in a heartbeat, and that day and night too."

Dar: "Tough one. Maybe a Reuben on rye, fries, a pickle, and a cold craft draft in a small Lower East Side deli. Also, I was always hoping they would perfect a gigantic pistachio nut. And on my headstone, I'd like a nice carving of a fresh sesame bagel with cream cheese next to a steaming cup of coffee, or poppy or onion if they're all out."

BethAnne: "'Thank you, waiter. We'll start off with the jumbo shrimp cocktail. Oh, what's that, you've had trouble getting that in since the virus? Or anything else?' Seriously, though, it was fish for me until recently, but now it's chicken. Something simple, roasted maybe, or even barbequed, with a nice rice dish, and a big salad with blue cheese dressing. And wine for me as well."

Liz: "I don't know if I could pick one thing. If it was a restaurant, I'd have to see what's on the menu."

Rick: "I'll play. Steak and mashed potatoes with gravy fer me, with a big mess of Brussels sprouts the way Ma used to make 'em, boiled and then cut in half and sautéed with shallots. Washed down with black cherry soda. And homemade chocolate chip cookies with real coffee fer dessert."

Cole: "Steak for me too. Also, pizza, lobster, hot wings, collard greens, tacos, and cheesecake. Just put the rest in a doggie bag."

Dawn: "Probably the Thanksgiving Day meal, with all the usual extras, including stuffing and pearled onions and pumpkin pie."

Dave: "And I will take the liberty of ordering for Susan. She'll—"

Susan: "Macaroni and cheese please."

Hired men on Blenheim Hill twenty-five years ago worked by the season, ate with the family, and put their wages at interest. In the winter they taught school, cut cord-wood or attended Stamford Seminary. Those who had settled down to working out as a life occupation were often employed by the year. Day help was migratory, hands drifting in from the river country after the corn was planted and the hops tied, returning to the low lands in time for the wheat harvest and hop-picking. They seldom came back in winter to cut wood for the cold was greater than in the valley and the lack of the tavern with its social cheer was a hardship.

One hand, a resident and householder and father of a family, probably worked on every acre of the five thousand during his long life. He always rented a house and garden, kept a cow and a horse, and raised his own pork and poultry. He lived to be seventy-five

and his period of service covered sixty years. His pace was slow, but sixteen hours is a long working day. When weariness rested heaviest, in the middle of the week, he would say: "I wish it was Saturday afternoon and the supper dishes on the table." He knew the full history of every person in the community. He could give complete details concerning every event of local note from time immemorial. His was the best version of the cold spring tragedy when a pair of stags went down and were never recovered. He was authority on the great snow storm when the little gray mare Nance walked the stone walls. He remembered all the horses raised since the Mexican war, oxen that bore the yoke in Filmore's time, and cows long since gone beyond the milky way.

Another farm hand who worked on Blenheim Hill at intervals for many years, came from somewhere about the Head-the-river. He was a bachelor, middle-aged, honest, steady, industrious, temperate, frugal. He saved his money and had a snug sum in the bank. He was clean in habit, particularly in dress, and always wore a good hat, in summer a Panama. The only time he was heard to swear was once when training a fractious calf in the art of drinking milk from a pail. His hat fell off and the calf stepped into it.

Among the many good men who worked for the farmers on Blenheim Hill back in the golden age, one in the eyes of the inhabitants was a veritable Marco Polo. He was a sailor, a native of New England, who had been all over the world. He made port but once a year and remained only through haying. He was past fifty, of wiry build and equal to his lot row at all times. Turning grind-stone when a boy for two men to bear on at a time was the reason he assigned for becoming a sailor. He was a ready talker and never tired in describing the lands which he had visited. Every Sunday he bathed and washed his clothes, going to the nearest pond for the purpose.

On the eastern verge of Blenheim Hill where the road drops suddenly 600 feet to the mile, there stood in by-gone days two log houses tenanted by families with a numerous progeny. Here dwelt a man of unique personality, long a familiar figure. He was nominally a shingle shaver but could turn his hand at anything. Intemperance was his besetting sin and profanity his accomplishment. He talked incessantly, was possessed of great native wit, and would have made a successful pleader had he been educated to the law. He was given to changing his habitation and occupied at different times several tenements, working for nearly every farmer in the community. In his latter days he was converted during a revival held in the brimstone church and his ready tongue now stood him in ready service for his prayers and testimonies were loud and long.

The memory of these hired men, and many others, is linked inseparably with the history of the days when farmhands were afield at sunrise on the longest days in June.

"Blenheim Hill" Series by Albert C. Mayham (Jefferson, NY: Jefferson Courier and Schoharie County Chronicle, 6/1/1905)

THIRTEEN

SEVERAL smaller fishing expeditions to the Schoharie Creek went off without a hitch, though on one occasion Cole was wading through a slight backwater and came upon a submerged human skeleton that was sort of seated on the bottom and seemed to smile and wave at him. It was early July now. Warmer water forced the increasingly lethargic fish deeper, and they were not biting as well in the high heat of midday, which is when the party tended to be there. The West Kill itself was fairly played out, due in part no doubt to the spring deluge washing some of the bigger trout down. It was still easy enough to pull four-inch chubs out, with the smallest of hooks, and thirty of those went a fairly long way when the flesh was cooked well enough to pull right off the tiny bones, but this was tedious for all concerned, including the chubs.

Dar had been lobbying to visit the large impoundments in the other direction, southeast toward the town of Gilboa, and finally got the green light to do so. Looking at the state map, these were the largest bodies of water anywhere around, the next closest being the Hudson River to the east, and the Catskill, Delaware, and Croton System reservoirs to the south and southwest. By this time the young man was back in excellent hiking shape. This would be a three-day trip. Normally Rick would have accompanied him, but that was too long for both men to be gone, and more time than either of them wanted to spend that close together. Although Rick was fairly certain there were no holdouts and little if any road crew activity in that area, it was a dangerous journey, and Dar preferred to go it alone in spite of BethAnne's protestations.

So the day arrived and off he went, fitted up with an old pack frame that contained his fishing kit, the camp stove, a bolt cutter, and other necessities, including a small amount of food that would travel. His sleeping bag was securely tied to the top, with a little pup tent Rick used for overnights and his disassembled rod similarly bound along the sides. Dar borrowed his 30-30 back for this trip, for reach and stopping power.

Looking at the county map, the Blenheim-Gilboa Pumped Storage Power Project was much closer than the Schoharie Reservoir, only a few miles away in a straight line, but it did not seem all that safe for what he wanted to do. This rather ingenious New York Power Authority hydroelectric facility, created in the early 1970s through eminent domain, employed two five-billion-gallon reservoirs, one above the other. To generate electricity during peak statewide demand, or to serve as a backup if another plant failed, water cascaded down a long underground shaft from the upper to the lower reservoir and was pumped back up into storage using cheap surplus power, usually at night. So a part of this process was by way of good old gravity, but he wondered how the whole thing was holding up with no overseers. They must have been loath to abandon it.

Dar had looked into using this site some years ago, but there were too many rules and restrictions. The main problem was that you needed a permit to boat on it, only so many were issued, and they went fast. You had to call ahead of time to say you were coming, and your boat and property were inspected on the way in. Even if you were just shore fishing, parking was in designated areas only, and you were equally subject to scrutiny by security personnel all day long. So there was a post-9/11 vibe, and they allowed motorboats on the lower artificial lake, which often meant noise, wakes, and oil rainbows on the water. Dar understood the reasons for such rules, especially when it came to controlling invasive species like zebra mussels and terrorists, but it was all a bit much for a nature outing. The more current issue was that these reservoirs were out in the open, with long rocky shorelines. There was a clear view of the lower one from Route 30, and access roads ran immediately adjacent to both of them. With such full exposure, it would be like shooting fish in a barrel for anyone patrolling this area. Finally, you were not permitted to leave your boats, and he wanted one.

The Schoharie Reservoir some six miles from camp was operated by the New York City Department of Environmental Protection. It provided remarkably clean drinking water for downstate rather than electricity for the entire state, so things were done a little differently. You needed an access permit to be on the property, a year earlier anyway, but it was free and relatively easy to obtain. Lately, you had to get your boat steam-cleaned by an approved vendor to safeguard against harmful stowaways, and you usually left it there for the season, most often chained to a tree. Only rowboats were allowed, and no engines, though when he looked into it once the scuttlebutt was that this might be broadened to include canoes, kayaks, and even small sailboats someday. Low sheep fencing ran around the perimeter way out by the access roads, more to delineate than restrict, and there were periodic gates that admitted people but not vehicles. This body of water was far larger than the hydro facility, it was wilder, and utilizing it was much mellower. Roads did not run as close, and boats would probably be available. All this justified the greater effort in reaching it.

The Schoharie Reservoir was created in the late teens and twenties as the northernmost outpost of the nineteen-reservoir water supply system for New York City that was spawned in part by a sanitation craze. Dar had read much about it when he lived in the county. The impounded waters of the Schoharie Creek flowed south through the Shandaken Tunnel, the Esopus Creek, other reservoirs, and the phenomenal Catskill Aqueduct on its way down to the Big Apple. The Gilboa Dam held it all back on the other end—right where the town once sat—close to 2,000 feet across and about 130 feet high, next stop if it broke, North Blenheim. The price for all of this was one irreversible old crime, one fixable current sin, and one great big worry.

The happy, picturesque, progressive town of Gilboa, New York, first settled in the 1760s, was in the way. It had to be sacrificed back in the construction phase, following the usual procedure. Condemn the land, seize the property, remove the trees, raze the buildings—over four hundred in this case—and relocate the residents, dead and alive. Many drowned towns, violated villages, and hapless hamlets were reservoired to death in upstate New York in this manner, some twenty-four or so in all, not to mention numerous outlying farms and isolated homes. Tight-knit valley communities with names like Lackawack, Arena, Olive Bridge, Rock Royal, and Neversink were sunk and nevered. In many cases, including Gilboa, faint outlines and remnants reappeared when the water level got low enough.

To add more injury to insult and injury, the practical effect of damming a once naturally flowing river some thirty-five miles from its headwaters is that it must start from scratch at that point. With sufficient strategic flow this might be biologically viable, but too much of the water went out at the opposite end down to New York City, or was diverted for summertime recreational purposes south to the Esopus River Valley. When the drop was relatively sudden and the flow got cut off, creek creatures below the dam—before feeder streams farther down finally began to replenish the waylaid waters—had little time to wriggle to safety. They suffered, in part so that tourist-dollar tubers and kayakers could play. And that wasn't just at the *top* of the Schoharie Creek Part Two. Inadequate and unnaturally fluctuating flow led to unstable conditions for fish and other wildlife along the remaining fifty-plus miles of this river. The effects were felt by *people* who depended on the Schoharie Creek back then as well, right away. Mills could not generate the same level of power, there was not enough water for ice harvesting in the winter, it was often too low for irrigation and too dirty for bathing in the summer, and the fishing turned lousy. That's how we were treating this historic valley, and that's how New York City treated Schoharie County, especially then but even now. Hiring more locals to keep it all running would have eased bad feelings, but that didn't seem to be a priority either.

The worry part had to do with the dam itself. It was old. The catchment basin was huge relative to the size of the reservoir. It filled fast and it spilled fast. The dam's performance was one contributing factor in the spring 1987 New York State Thruway bridge collapse down at the bottom of the river. Ten lost their lives. Some went down with the bridge, and others drove into the gap. The last body was recovered over two years later. If the old dam ever let loose, it would create another Johnstown Flood top to bottom. Dar knew they had been addressing these engineering and environmental concerns, strengthening the massive stone-and-concrete structure and allowing for better emergency releases and colder steadier flow, but he didn't know if the work had been finished in time, though it would all come undone either way now in deeper time.

Dar had stood on the side of this dam in solitude at dusk years earlier, having driven there that day from his parents' home forty miles away. This day he would hike to it through the woods from six miles away. He left camp early, heading due south by compass. This took him over the ridge and firebreak above camp and down the other side through patches of state forest land. He crossed several small roads and skirted one large farm operation, veering southeast until Route 30 showed up to his left. From there the compass would not be necessary. Dar shadowed the road from just inside the woods. When the bottom of the reservoir came into view he made a risky crossing through a large field with nothing but a thin shelterbelt for cover, followed by a mad dash across the highway and down into the safety of thick woods again. He knew that was one of the more dangerous stages of his odyssey and was glad to have it behind him.

The shape of the impoundment right there was rather odd. From the air and on the map, the section he was passing looked like the head of an enormous mollusk with two large antennae that was just about to hit the dam but had turned left at the last second. As he suspected, these were actually brooks leading to large pointed inlets. He followed the first antenna as it curled out into the woods, cutting right across to its companion feeler before hugging the sticky neck directly down toward the main body of water. He knew Road Seven was well in back of him. This was the dirt access road that ran the length of the reservoir on that side, sometimes to dramatic heights. Were there six concentric construction roads before that, underwater now?

Dar wanted to put some distance between himself and the dam, so he took the first good game trail he found going in the right direction. Gliding quietly along, he eventually startled a small mammal that he couldn't classify at first. It was quite dark in color, with a bushy tail. He finally decided it was a melanistic fox squirrel, larger than the common gray squirrel and relatively rare this far east in any color. His grandfather used to tell him about an old colony of black fox squirrels deep in his woods. There was also an encounter with an albino buck that had turned into myth among local hunters over the years. Some time later Dar alarmed a doe that wasn't quite sure what to make of him. The information exchange began, but the intruder didn't participate at first. The deer tilted her head for a better look, took a few steps forward, stamped her foot a couple of times, and flashed her bright white tail. When he finally unfroze in order to proceed, she hightailed it out of there with loud snorts to warn others danger was nearby. I *knew* that was one, she thought. Haven't seen them around as much lately.

Shortly thereafter Dar left the trail, headed straight downhill, and strode out onto the stony shore, drinking in all that open sky and water. It was a forceful reminder of how closed-in their little forest home was, and how the firmament was so narrowly circumscribed now, dictated by the width of a streambed or defunct road and the height of the ever-reaching trees closing in from both sides. Scanning for trouble first, as always, Dar began skipping stones. There were perfect ones to be had everywhere, the mark of an untrammeled rocky beach. He'd been to lakesides in more populated areas where the last good skipper was probably chucked sometime in the 1960s. It was nice to just throw something again without having to worry about the noise or mark it made. This was one thing he excelled at, bending low and sailing them out there fifteen skips or more, a skill Dar had always looked forward to passing on to his children. Hopefully the rock didn't mind going from sunny shore to deep dark bottom.

The dam structure was to his left, somewhere around one or more bends, and to his right there was aqua as far as he could see. Dar trained his binoculars on an interesting treed island way over on the other side.

It wasn't exactly Madagascar, but it would have been fun to paddle over by canoe and see how this somewhat isolated ecosystem was doing. A little farther on he could make out the Manor Kill emptying directly into the reservoir. He knew from Rick that there was a fun-looking biker bar called Nick's Waterfall House just up that creek a bit, off the county road that ran along the opposite side of the basin.

From his reference books he knew the reservoir was just short of six miles long, and half a mile wide on average, with a general depth of fifty feet but hitting nearly three times that in certain spots. He'd heard about herds of deer crossing the ice in the dead of winter, five-hundred-pound black bears swimming from one side to the other during heat waves, and beavers circling in confusion over the intake chamber and the human version of a dam. Gazing down to the far end of this expanse, it occurred to him that this was probably as close to seeing an ocean again as he would ever get. It was a sunny day but there was a good wind, and small whitecaps foamed across the bock-black sea.

This was as good a place as any to start fishing. The shoreline was rocky all around. Dar could picture saplings establishing a beachhead in the years to come, and the dam itself failing sometime in the next century or two. It reminded him of those *Life After People* episodes on TV. Half of that content was preposterous, and they didn't even explain why everyone had instantly disappeared to begin with, but it could be informative and chilling, like footage of a once-barren sports stadium near Chernobyl that was filled with surprisingly large trees a mere twenty-five years later. Surveying left and right on his side of the reserve, it looked and felt safe. He wouldn't have been that easy to spot from the opposite shore unless someone was camped up on the heights with good optics.

Dar chose a large, classic red and white Dardevle, throwing it far along either side, working his way out toward the middle with each cast, and pulling down at the last moment sometimes to slap the water. Lures like this were for predators such as walleyed pike and bass. Reservoir fishing had always felt a little strange to him, partly because they often lacked the natural features that fish like. On famous trout streams like the Batten Kill, fisheries folks were beginning to realize that if a tree fell into the water and it was not directly impeding the best paddling route, it was better to leave it there for cover. They were even creating this cover by dropping clusters of trees in along the banks, and constructing shelters on the bottom with large flat stones. He looked for natural vegetation such as water lilies and grasses but there was none to be seen along this stretch.

Within twenty minutes Dar had a nice bass. He took a break and poached it up on the Svea in a small lightweight pan. The fish went well with one of Gwen's journey cakes, which is what some of them jokingly called jonnycakes on long trips, and a few swigs of honey-sweetened pink-sumac lemonade from a small thermos. He took this meal where the shore rocks met the woods, watching for movement, and found himself daydreaming about the merriment and scenery at public beaches.

Planning time. Dar knew just where he was, but he pulled out the county map anyway to help him focus. His original idea was to circumnavigate the entire reservoir and pass through the town of Gilboa, not far from the dam, on his way back to the camp. Rick and Dave strongly advised against this, as it would entail far too much exposure. Rick had not been to Prattsville yet, where the Schoharie Creek came in at the top of the reservoir, and there might be survivors there. And why travel all that extra distance looping back around, so close to paved roads? Dar could hike all along the western shore for six miles or so and turn around before Prattsville, but about halfway there Road Seven began to swing back toward the water. He was on the most remote quarter of the shoreline, and the fishing was not likely to be very different anywhere else, with the exception of the larger feeder streams that were too risky to reach. Now that he had a better picture of the situation, he saw the wisdom of their counsel. He would not press his luck on this trip, but he still wanted to find a boat.

It was early afternoon now. Dar had planned on hiking just inside the tree line to avoid possible detection, but the ground was steep there as it pitched down into the reservoir, and snags and downed trees abounded. Coming down a few steps from the top of the stony shore, he could see right away that staying upright would expend too much energy, and tons of wave-tossed driftwood and nail-ridden lumber blanketing the middle of the short beach invited injury. His clearest path was right down by the water. It felt relatively safe, and he could steal away quickly if necessary.

The first boatyard on his side finally appeared. Sixty or so flipped-over watercraft were scattered about helter-skelter amid the vegetation, mostly flat-bottom aluminum jon boats, along with a few wooden rowboats. At first glance he didn't see any oars, but somebody always leaves them, and he finally located a good set belonging to a good boat. He was going to establish camp a little farther along the shoreline, away from the disheveled civilization of the motley marina, but upon reflection thought it might be better to have a waterborne escape route at the ready in case he was hassled by bears or bad guys.

The golden overlay of late afternoon was giving way, and long shadows cast by even the lowest rocks were flowing into the common pool of dusk. There was still time for a little fishing before dark. He switched from the big flashy spoon to a giant night crawler on a big hook. As the light wind died down and the surface calmed, he could see soft dimples and sharp swirls where fish were feeding. Throwing toward the largest of these, his bait was immediately sucked down, and moments later a decent brown trout lay at his feet. He filleted it and flung the head and entrails far out into the water. Dar also landed a crappie and a rock bass. He let the latter off his stringer and had the other two for dinner, the trout winning out as expected.

The Thunder Moon of July soon rose through long, eerie clouds. Mercifully, it did not live up to its name on this trek. He knew Rick relied on this little tent when far afield but did not see how it offered him much protection from the elements. In lieu of fulminating bolts, lightning bugs shot over the vast, glimmering expanse of carbon-black water like slow-motion tracer bullets. Crickets and tree frogs led a merry nighttime chorus, and all the scene lacked was a spiritized Indian lass with long raven hair and a red buckskin miniskirt rowing her birchbark canoe in from the mist. Gadzooks, where did that come from? Circa 1920s and '30s Indian Maiden calendar art by Eggleston or Goddard, no doubt, which always sold well at the antique centers, remoisturized more recently by Land O'Lakes Butter.

It had gotten too dark to prep the boat as planned. Tired now, Dar brewed some tea, crawled into his tent, and read a little by shielded candlelight from a worn Ace paperback copy of *Big Planet* by Jack Vance, a late Golden Age sci-fi favorite from his youth. This was his first night alone since joining the camp. It would have been a little spooky here even with some company. He cradled his rifle and began to drift off. A cacophony of strange animal noises reverberated through the thin nylon barrier. Some were clearly amphibious in nature, but fur and feather were represented as well, including the distant yips of a coyote, and the vast body of water just outside had a sounding-board effect that magnified all those croaks, cries, and coos. He wondered if animals ever made noises they weren't *supposed* to, as humans did—deranged mutterings, for example—where others of the same species wondered what the hell is that all about? Even famous mimickers like the mockingbird probably stuck to the script. Humans are so very extracurricular. We are unique in killing each other for ideological differences too, rather than just for nourishment or to secure territory. Was all this a symptom of our waywardness or of our advanced nature? He slipped into dreamland, choosing not to dwell on all the bedlam just outside, including rustled leaves and snapped twigs.

The modern-day explorer slept later than planned. He treated himself to a leisurely breakfast of dandelion coffee and corn bread, enjoying the panorama of this small inland sea before breaking the tent down and preparing his pack. Dar flipped over the dewy jon boat of choice, scooted a few large spiders out, and severed the cable that ran to an adjacent boat and then to a small tree. He considered leaving his pack in the woods, but this was the most stable of watercraft, and he decided they should stay together. He kept his boots dry by poling away from the shore, and he rowed out to the middle and slowed to a stop. It felt very odd being on big water again. He just sat there for a while, drifting along with no sound save the lap of small waves against his hull and the cries of distant seagulls. He had a flashback to the night on the bridge leading into Albany when he got the flat tire—why just me?—but it passed quickly. On a regular deep-freshwater fishing trip he would have laid some bait on the bottom with one pole and cast around with another, but this was just the dry run.

The reservoir held pretty much the same species as the creek below and above, but with much larger specimens, including huge carp, walleye, bass, and trout. Dar didn't know exactly how big they got, but the state record carp from a warmer-water reservoir a couple counties away weighed in at over fifty pounds. This was a mixed blessing, because unless you were talking about an ocean fish such as the striped bass that returned up big rivers like the Hudson to spawn in the spring, which meant less exposure, all of these eastern lakes and rivers were subject to their own localized pollution, in addition to untold tons of airborne defilement from upwind industrial states like Illinois, Indiana, Ohio, and Pennsylvania. They had all become adept at raising their stacks over the years so they could pass the PCBs and other toxins to the east. Mercury in particular is found in greater concentrations in older fish. To borrow a thought from Gwen though, it probably wasn't traces of bad stuff in fish that was going to kill you first these days.

He tried casting, near the surface at first and then letting the lure sink deep before jerking it along. This produced one good hit but no captures. Then he spent another half hour bumping a jig along the bottom, also with no result. Finally he put a small sinker on and let a big worm drift down. The morning sun was hat-hot already, and the aluminum boat was beginning to roast his nutmeats from below as well. Dar had a great urge to jump in, but he was not sure he could hoist himself back on successfully without flipping the boat, which rode pretty high. It looked easy but probably wasn't. That was the difference between being almost twenty and almost thirty. From down in the water it would be difficult to propel the craft toward the shore, not to mention silly-looking. And then there was that horrible, old irrational fear that something in the twenty-plus fathoms below would grab you by the feet and pull you right down. Not a known predator, or some leftover prehistoric creature—as the reservoir was only filled for the first time in 1927—but something like getting surrealistically snagged by the spire of a deep bobbing church, or more mundane entanglement with submerged branches or a rope or cable of some sort. A more primitive part of his mind imagined the poltergeist of a pissed-off Gilboan out (and up) for revenge. There were local legends about glowing ghosts ringing the reservoir at night, and one who crossed the road all the time. Impossible things, yes, but so what in the half minute of terror you'd have to ponder it?

This paranoia gave way to a more realistic concern. He was highly exposed to rifle fire or motorboat interception out there. And his shiny boat must have been reflecting the sunlight like a mirror. He resolved to use a darker one next time, in blue or green, as there was a wide selection to choose from. A V-hull would be less rowing work than a flat-bottom too. Most importantly, the boating part of trips to this reservoir would be safer with some armed backup. You can't row and shoot at the same time too easily.

Dar didn't want to give up on the bigger-fish-in-deeper-water test, but with all that in mind he decided to call it quits for the day. He rested the rod against his leg and began to wheel around toward shore, intending to troll back to the boatyard. In the middle of this slow swing the rod suddenly ran down his thigh, smacked into the side of the boat hard enough to issue echoes, and somersaulted right over the edge. Its very upward flight was curtailed by a fierce pull from below. Dar was completely flabbergasted but knew he only had a second to react. He dropped the oars, threw himself to the gunwale, and grabbed the buoyant handle of his favorite rod just before it was pulled down into the dark depths, nearly capsizing the jon boat after all in the process. Line was racing out of the reel and shooting drinking water back into his face as he struggled to get it under control. Drifting down a river, this might happen if you got stuck on the bottom, but sitting in still, deep water it could only mean a monster fish. His mind briefly sunk back to all those boyhood times when he asked his father or grandfather how he would know if he got a bite, or if it was just something else, or nothing at all. "You'll know." If only they could see him now.

Dar tightened the drag a little and checked his reel to find that much of the remaining line was played out already. He tried cranking in, but the best he could manage was an occasional standoff before it started whizzing out again. Normally this was one of his favorite sounds, but it looked like this might be a long fight, and he was still most anxious to get off the water. His thoughts ran to cutting the trip a day short and getting right back to camp with this prize trophy before it spoiled. It dawned on him that the fish was making a run toward the dam, and it was actually moving the boat in that direction. What was next—lashing it to the side and fighting off sharks?

Through the rod he eventually felt a turning point in the struggle. The tighter drag was probably wearing the quarry down. He began to reel it in. Then there were three very sharp tugs, almost like somebody was tapping him on the shoulder—even though they came from so far down below and were only transmitted through a thin length of monofilament—and *snap*, it was off. The rod tip shot up, and some of the line lay limp on the surface. Dar performed his usual instantaneous assessment. The biggest regret was not knowing what kind of fish it was. The line was eight-pound test, and the leviathan felt like a ten- or twenty-pounder, but pounds of what? Did he fail to *carpe carpio*, or was it more of a game fish? Secondly, if the lure was still in, he hoped it would fall out soon so the animal would continue to thrive. Thirdly, he hated to lose that classic piece of fishing hardware, with its goateed devil logo. And finally, *Good*, because he could get off the open water now.

Dar dragged the jon boat back to its original position and arranged the cable in a way that hid the cut he'd made. There was an old red wooden rowboat way up on the periphery, left no doubt as an unsalvageable junker, its metal DEP ID tag pried off so as to avoid any responsibility for it. Dar kicked the bottom in some more and tucked the oars well underneath it. It was only midday, but he had learned enough already. Unless there were some grassy pickerel beds or other cover, and with the exception of the fish-friendly convergence of the mother and feeder streams on the other end and the Manor Kill on the other side, the fishing would probably be about the same on the remaining three-quarters of the reservoir. He didn't feel like spending another night alone out there either. He would head home now, with a detour through the town of Gilboa if things looked safe.

ΩΩΩ

The hike back to the dam went quickly. There were huge cranes and tons of equipment around, and extensive safety and security measures were in evidence, so they must have still been shoring things up. What a difference from a decade or so earlier, when anyone could walk right up to it. It was like one of those old color postcards of people just spreading a picnic blanket out near Old Faithful. These things needed protection, but police-state mentalities often took on a life of their own. Dar strode out to the end of the huge earthen embankment on that side of the dam and stood over the straight drop and low level outlet works there. He briefly considered making his way across to the less dizzying portion of the overflow spillway, where excess water was directed down a stair-stepped facade into an energy-dissipating side channel and training walls, but decided against such exposure. Instead, he continued down around the massive works to the west side of the creek, hopping the embankment where it was low enough and making his way back up to the spillway channel floor. He could see fish trapped in the plunge pool there. They would need a big rain to wash them out into what was left of the natural creek bed below, replenishing those dribbling channels and emaciated pools at the same time. He wondered how the water-to-New York City part of this at the other end was working, if at all. If the cyclopean wall above him gave way right then, he could have dead-body-surfed the leading edge of a fifty-mile flood surge so strong that it would act as a solid barrier when it hit the Mohawk and Hudson Rivers, backing them up as well, like dams made out of water.

Dar entered the woods down by the creek, crossing at a low point just before the old quarry molestations and angling uphill toward the Gilboa town hall, in the same building as the local post office. He knew something of this town from his time in the county, and from his recent readings. Gilboa, which meant "bubbling spring" or "fountain of ebullition," among other translations, was named after Mount

Gilboa in the Jezreel Valley of northern Israel. King Saul was said to have lost three sons battling the Philistines there, falling on his own sword to avoid capture. Ironically, considering the newer Gilboa's fate, a unique purple iris grows around this biblical site, coloring the landscape and drawing many visitors in the spring, and concern over habitat destruction led to the successful blocking of additional development there.

The destruction of the early riverine settlement had been terribly complete. The new central school, old by now, was farther along the road that began to run around the opposite side of the reservoir, and the twelve hundred or so remaining citizens had been widely spread about on outlying roads and hillsides. They did their shopping in nearby towns, Prattsville being the handiest for basic food. There were no stores and few places of business. The closest eatery was Clark's Restaurant and Bar, right above the reservoir, which had "the best dam burgers" around. Rick had busted in, with as little damage as possible, and took its unbreached status as a clear sign that this was an especially remote, lifeless area, because what starving person wouldn't have tried to enter before him looking for stale rolls and such? He reported on its rustic furnishings, including a musty two-headed baby goat taxidermy mount. Rick had been very taken, for him, by all of the old framed photos on the walls depicting the construction of the dam and reservoir, almost like cave paintings now. If you liked this place and the old-timer owner, this may have been the spiritual center of town, but for most it was probably the town hall building back closer to the dam. Those were the only two choices in post-reservoir Gilboa. There was no there there.

The modest building came into view on a small rise, and Dar boldly crossed the road and approached the front door. It was closed but surprisingly unlocked, as if one of those nice, proficient postal workers would be right at the counter ready to help. He took time to read some of the emergency messages and expressions of love and loss that were tacked and taped to the walls—mostly to departed youths, should they return—as well as an events calendar for the previous fall, and then looked in on the adjacent town-meeting room, with its blackboards and neat rows of wooden chairs. He could imagine the anxiety level of some of the gatherings in there, and how trifling that would all seem to the same folks now, if any of them were even alive somewhere. There were some shelved local histories in the room that were not represented in Dave's collection, and he helped himself to some of them.

Exiting the building, Dar investigated a small row of curious objects set back toward the dam in a slim rectangle of light brown gravel. Educational kiosks explained that these were some of the famous Gilboa Fossil Forest tree stumps. These particular specimens were first unearthed in the 1920s right near the Schoharie Creek bridge he'd just skirted, in a quarry that produced facing stone for the construction of the Gilboa Dam. The stumps themselves are actually natural casts of the hole that was left when the original material decayed and sediment was swept in during flooding, resulting in detailed sandstone likenesses not dissimilar in concept to the anguished plaster-cast bodies of Pompeii. They had bulbous bases and rapidly narrowing trunks. The then New York City Board of Water Supply decreed that the Riverside Quarry be filled in after construction was complete, for practical and aesthetic purposes, much to the dismay of Winifred Goldring and her fellow paleontologists of the day, who had so much more work to do.

This little metaphorical valley that included his home creek seemed especially susceptible to the ravages of flooding, then and now. The trees in question were thought to have flourished in a cataclysm-prone delta plain along the coast of a huge inland sea in the Middle Devonian Period, some 385 million years earlier. Although ancient stumps in Gilboa had been noted as early as the 1850s, a devastating flood in 1869 led to major finds. Since these trees first sprouted, continents broke apart and drifted, seas turned into forests, and the moon something like doubled its distance from Earth, but most of these stumps had been found *in situ*. That is to say, these were casts of the lower structures of trees that had grown up right there, in that very spot on the land mass, before it had wheeled up from south of the equator. If you could put your arms in a circle around the stumps in their life position and travel back millions of years to the right place in time, you would be hugging that very live tree! If you went back a mere ten thousand years, however, you'd be pretty cold, underneath a solid mile of glacial ice rather than on the steamy edge of the ancient Catskill Sea. Such are the changes that wash over our planet.

The evocative kiosk artwork provided a good idea of what the immediate environment would have looked like, thanks to the geologic and fossil record. Snowcapped peaks rose in the distant background as a tetrapod crawled up out of the watery home of its lobe-finned ancestors, drawn toward the vital young forest. You'd probably know it if you got a bite casting your Devonian Dardevle from the shoreline of *that* body of water in the Age of Fishes, where you would be carrying out an interesting test of oxygen levels at the same time.

Typically, past imaginers of the past would have thrown a few dinosaurs or cavepersons into such artwork, in spite of the fact that they came much later, though Answers-in-Genesis creationists were busy reinterpreting their own time-compression theories. The planet was baked up in six days six thousand years ago, like before—and animals changed a little, but not into other animals—along with all the other literal Young Earth interpretations, and with the same disturbing gender and racial theories, but now dinosaurs had gotten a ride on Noah's Ark after all (babies, to save space), saddled stegosaurus returned the favor by driving us around after things dried out, etc. Half of America *said* they believed in all this stuff, even if many of them did not practice what they preached. The Creation Museum blog may have been a good place to debate these things and test one's beliefs, but it was heavily censored. No Dead Sea scrolling for illuminating historical, scientific, secular, biblical, or extra-biblical points of view. Still, there had been many great floods, maybe even global ones, and life survived and adapted in both probable and incredible ways.

There was a spectacular find in 2007 at a Conservation Department road-shale quarry not far away, on the slopes of South Mountain. A research team had serendipitously unearthed the fossilized remains of a trunk *and* first-ever intact *crown* from the same ancient species. The tree in question, *Eospermatopteris*, was more like a tree fern—a link between smaller vascular plants and the types of trees that populate modern forests. It shed whole frond-like branches rather than leaves, and there is evidence that it set down roots of equal depth in this steamy wetland environment, rather than an anchoring taproot. Yet it was relatively wide, and probably well over twenty-five feet in height. This early forest pioneer differed from later seed plants in that it was geared toward getting a leg up over surrounding plants by simply rising higher. The relatively meager crown of this tree was not optimal for photosynthesis, but it reached the sunlight best, and that was good enough. Several years later the fossil remains of a smaller lycopsid-like tree and a low, woody rhizomatous plant were discovered in the original Riverside Quarry site, demonstrating that the planet's first forests were far more multistoried and complex than previously thought.

As early plants like these dropped detritus and died of old age in boundless numbers over millions of years, they performed the important function of sending carbon into the atmosphere above and building up a forest floor below, where only rock or water sat before, providing suitable habitat for insects, arachnids, crustaceans, and other arthropods that together make up 90 percent of the animal kingdom. And the still, hot, oxygen-depleted inland Devonian seas gave rise to fish developing strong lungs, jaws, and, finally, feet. The immediate area was famous for land fauna fossils as well, making little Gilboa the planet's best source of information about its earliest life-forms. Coming of Age in Gilboa! These sites had been discovered so randomly that it made one wonder what other startling revelations lay beneath, probably forever now.

Of the stump finds from when the reservoir was under construction, samples were shipped out to all corners of the world, many by the contractor, Hugh Nawn, a brawny hewer who knew how to get this dirty job done. We lost track of where many of the Nixon administration's hundreds of Goodwill Moon Rock presentations ended up (one dusty sample rose from an obscure file cabinet not long ago)—and they were much more spectacular in the common imagination, and unearthed, or de-mooned, much more recently—so it was no surprise that whatever Gilboa stump list must have once existed was in hiding, or more likely no longer extant. Some of the 1920s stumps went to the New York State Museum in Albany, which was so instrumental in their interpretation and preservation. The 1869-era stumps that had been displayed at something called the Geological Hall in downtown Albany were eventually intermingled with those specimens, and the distinction between the two groups was lost with time.

You would think these were probably the best-preserved examples, but they had been used in a re-creation of the ancient forest in the old State Museum, before it moved from the State Education Building to more modern quarters in the 1970s. This long-term exhibit utilized constantly running water, which reacted with the iron pyrite in the stumps and formed sulfuric acid and other destructive residues. The ones that remained outside in Schoharie County all those years benefited from the more occasional rain, which washed through the porous sandstone and removed harmful residues.

The ten stumps in front of him were these same hardy survivors. They had sat out in the open in their original 1926 exhibit space near the Riverside Quarry just down the road until they found themselves underwater again in a 1996 flood, which could easily have washed them back down into the enfolding arms of Mother Earth. They looked pretty pathetic sitting where they were now, but not if you knew what they represented. He wondered if they'd ever been pranked by local teens somehow, but civic pride and this town's history of deep loss may have intervened. There was the biggest and best, the money stump they used in all the photos, as it showed the bark pattern so clearly. He ran his hands over them. Time to say goodbye now. There was that moment at Yeats' grave in the empty Sligo cemetery on his one and now only overseas trip when he couldn't tear himself away, needing to do something meaningful yet relatively unobtrusive before passing by. It had rained heavily, which was one reason why nobody else was there, but the sun had burst forth again, and he left a wet handprint on the headstone and took a picture of that. For these stumps, after a 360-degree turn, he impulsively touched his full tongue to the top of the largest. This wasn't that weird, considering the Blarney Stone, and no Gilboa hooligans or dogs could have peed that high.

It was high time to move on now. Dar would have stopped at the nearby Gilboa Museum to look for useful artifacts, but Rick reported that it had been ransacked already, with the exception of heavy fossil slabs and early farm equipment. More likely, its modest historical treasures had been relocated for safekeeping before the very end. That reminded him of the late-night comedy-show joke about the looting of the National Museum of Iraq in Baghdad, because of course U.S. troops guarded the Oil Ministry but left that unprotected. Something about the unfortunate coincidence that the big exhibit there at the time was Handcarts Throughout the Ages. Funny, sort of.

The fantastic, newly discovered crown of *Eospermatopteris* sat in the now-dark bowels of the Cultural Education Center in Albany, along with the older fossil stumps, and if that huge modernistic edifice literally collapsed someday they would be buried all over again. From what Dar understood from a frustrated aunt who'd just retired from there, the New York State Education Department institutions in that building had been on their knees anyway, to varying degrees, underfunded, depopulated, and demoralized by the steady loss of expertise and the gradual dumbing down of crucial aspects of their statewide missions. The out-of-favor State Research Library had been perfect-stormed more than its sister program areas, in part because it relied so heavily on purchases and subscriptions rather than donations and deposits. There would have been great outcries when it came to the demise of such jewels in the crown downstate over, say, the Starbucksification of the New York Public Library, or turning the Guggenheim Museum into a skateboard park, but this was only jerkwater Albany, and besides, can't you get all that stuff online now anyway? He could picture modern slaves down in the sprawling subterranean stacks scraping gold leaf off the older book bindings and page ends into little yellow balls by candlelight for the rest of their post-apocalyptic lives, like that old tender in the belly of the oil tanker in *Waterworld*, praying for an end to the darkness.

Dar crossed back over the stream and road and was surging through the deep forest toward familiar territory in no time, feeling safer with every step. He found a particularly rich red-raspberry patch, stopping to eat his fill, and made up a bit for his fishlessness by harvesting a good supply and noting the location for future reference. He paused at the firebreak to see if the camp was at all visible from above, but by July it was thoroughly shrouded in the leafy depths of the hillside. He descended for a happy reunion, a thorough debriefing, and warm embraces from BethAnne, who was happy to have him home a day early. It was agreed to make this trip on a regular basis, staying longer and perhaps even sending alternating runners back with the catch of the day.

ΩΩΩ

At the next assembly, Sadie asked the campers to be on the lookout for mayapples. "This is what the plant looks like," she said, handing one by the stem to Rick first. "The leaves are kind of umbrella-shaped, large and light green. You'll find them in colonies. They're pretty common, but many colonies don't bear fruit every year. If you find any, remember the spot for our harvest notes, and pick as many as you can. The fruit will be about the size of eggs, sort of yellowish. You suck out the insides, and it tastes tropical. If they're still green, let them ripen, but go back soon because animals like deer will be after them. They must be truly ripe—mottled—or they'll make you sick. And don't swallow the seeds either. They prefer open sky, so look for them in clearings. For tonight, I have two each for you, the first we've found."

This was a small but pleasant surprise, like a lollypop from Grandma on distant summer days. She pulled them out of a long bag at her side, which reminded Dar that women often invent useful things like pouches, and men hard pointy indiscriminately deadly things like drone missiles.

"Mayapples in July?" asked Cole.

"They look a little iffy," said Andrew.

"Hey, somebody had to eat the first oyster," BethAnne observed.

Back in their tent under soft diffused moonlight, Dar drizzled some of the mayapple juice down onto his mate's own full and halved passion fruits, lapping it up with slow abandon. "Somebody had to do that for the first time too," he said. "I believe it may have been one of my ancestors."

Dar had taken to the habit of reciting passages from works such as William Roscoe's 1882 *History of Schoharie County, New York* during the Friday assembly, when all the regular business was done, both as an object of interest and as a continuing token of his mixed regret for getting so political on that one occasion. Some of them were rather amusing, like an old fishing story from nearby Summit.

> *Our earliest recollection of this resort, is, when but a youth, we sat beside the late "Squire" Boughton, and vainly tried to force the obstinate "bullheads" to bite after our patience was exhausted in coaxing, while he, with ease and grace swung out and lured the largest to his well-filled basket. The Squire's inward chuckle occasionally found vent, and upon one of those (to us) mortifying times, his boast rang out long and loud, that his basket would hold no more. But not content, he swung out again and his successful hook, fearful, perhaps, it could do no better, caught the handle of the basket, and to the joy of our crushed feelings, basket and fish were thrown rods from the shore and disappeared to the bottom, while the Squire, without a word, sought his home.*

He chanced upon a description of "sloughters" from this old book, a term unique to Schoharie County, and shared that as well.

> *The average number of paupers, for the last five years, has been sixty-two, many of whom were once energetic business men with ample means, and well bred and affable women by whom fate has dealt harshly. While the majority of the remainder are those who belong to a class, to use the parlance of the people, known as "Sloughters," whose morality was lost long years ago, and not inheriting any principle, they have failed to find it, and instead, are content to eke out a miserable existence in licentious habits, until the winter returns, or their physical condition is such as to make them objects of care.*

Dar knew something of this derogatory term. Although sloughter was spelled various ways, and its "them's fightin' words" meaning had morphed into fairly harmless usage—standing for local old-timer, for example—the term had most often been applied pejoratively to an easily identifiable group of supposedly ignorant, lazy, crossbred ne'er-do-wells, and was once strongly associated with certain surnames. The epicenters had been a particular hill near Schoharie and a certain hollow near Middleburgh, though sloughters and subgroups with names like honies and clappers were once fairly widespread in the southern half of the county. Sloughters were not quite as distinct as the Jackson Whites of the Ramapo Mountains to the south, or the isolated remnants of hill people still found of late in the Appalachians and all over the world, but in general they were considered to be a mix of lower class whites, Indian blood, and escaped slaves and "negro wenches," with anything rolling around loose, like Civil War deserter and bog Irish, thrown in for good measure. "Tri-racial isolate" was a more scientific term for some such groups. The more they were ostracized over the years, the more tight-knit they became.

You thought twice before entering deep sloughter territory back in the day. They were known to shoot at World War I military recruiters, and to appear in the backwoods like a scene out of *Deliverance*, though more for your downed deer than your rear. Dar had a friend who grew up in this area and who shared some transmitted tales from the mid-1900s. There was one about a sloughter who couldn't afford any bullets and deliberately confronted a bear in its den with nothing but a big knife, though that may have been bullshit. Their earlier habitations were said to include chicken coops and tarpaper shacks. Dar had occasion to visit someone in a low sloughter house once that was built back around "the war"—which one he did not know. It was explained that they ran out of materials to raise the roof high enough, so families spent their whole lives bending down when walking around inside. Favorite pastimes used to include cockfighting, drinking, and raiding crops. A sensationalized *New York Times* piece on sloughters from the early 1990s raised quite a ruckus in the county, as it inaccurately portrayed folks living in Polly Hollow as they had been generations earlier.

After the local-history recitations, Herbert spoke up. "Art was telling me about the military camp in these parts."

"What military camp?" asked Rick, perking up.

"It was out here in the woods somewhere. Top secret. Maybe CIA."

"That sounds pretty farfetched," said Cole. "It's hard to keep secrets like that, even in an empty county like this."

"Maybe your friend was thinking of the Watervliet Arsenal," said Bennie, "or the Air National Guard unit in Scotia. Those aren't very far away."

"No sir. He said it wasn't too well known until the State Department came out with a tit-for-tat list of places the Soviets couldn't go, after they did that to us. November, 1983. It reduced the total amount of restricted area in both nations from twenty-four percent down to twenty, but it updated everything. At first Schoharie County wasn't on the list, and then a large block in the deep woods was, not far from here. At first one of the local newspapers talked about it, and then they clammed up."

"Where near here?" asked Rick. "Eminence? Towards Gilboa?"

"Near here."

Silence came over the group, as most were too polite to say what they were thinking about Herbert's faculties. Rick, however, did not seem to shake the story off that easily. Dar knew he would be approaching Dave on the subject soon, but what could he say? No easy way to check on stuff like that anymore.

The Passing of "Old Gilboa" by a Former Resident

In the old Schoharie valley,
Up among my native hills,
With its water-falls and bridges,
And its quaint old-fashion'd mills.
It was there I used to wander,
Many, many years ago,
Up and down the dusty roadway,
To and from the town below.

Gloomy thoughts surge in upon me,
And my heart it now grows sick,
At the painful sight that greets me,
'Long the old Schoharie creek.
Oft I ask myself the question—
Yes, I ask it o'er and o'er;
"Is it true, or but a rumor,
That Gilboa's to be no more?"

Motor trucks and huge steam shovels,
With their gangs of brawny men,
Sure are tearing things to pieces,
On Clay Hill and in the Glen.
And the village, it's deserted,
All the natives, they have fled;
Some have gone to other quarters,
Some are sleeping with the dead.

Dear old town, 'twill soon be flooded,
Not a vestige left, or scrap,
And that once proud little hamlet,
Will be stricken from the map.
Slow, but sure, the work's progressing,
Soon—yes, at an early date.
'Twill be said, "Gilboa's surrender'd
To the iron hand of fate."

In the hallow'd ground just yonder,
Where our precious dead were borne,
There to rest beneath the daisies
'Till the resurrection morn.
Oh, the scene it is appalling—
They are taking them away,
Hear the click of spade and shovel;
Yes, we hear it, day by day.

Many damage claims are pending—
Some are large and some are small;
There should be this stipulation:
"A 'square deal' for one and all."
It's a case a sheer compulsion—
Taking what another owns;
Surely, it's no trifling matter,
Forcing people from their homes.

"Home, sweet home" the poor man's castle,
Love and friendship, joy and mirth.
Mingle here, and intermingle,
"HOME" most sacred spot on earth.
There are sentimental reasons,
Not a few, when all are told;
(Money values count but little)
More enduring they, than gold.

Charming spot, where children revel,
And the place where they were born;
There's the little chamber window,
Where the sun peeps in at morn.
Many pleasant recollections,
Cluster round that long-lov'd spot;
Recollections fondly cherish'd,
That can never be forgot.

As I turn and look about me,
Where the schoolhouse used to stand,
Where I went each week day morning,
Holding fast to brother's hand.
And the church where once I worship'd—
They are gone with all the rest.
Oh, the tears, I can't suppress them,
Strange emotions fill my breast.

Of the Buckinghams, Mattices,
Strykers, Baldwins, Cronks, and Weeds
Of the Frisbies, Shalers, Southards,
Beckers, Mackeys, Potters, Reeds.
Of the Warners, Hazzards, Haydocks,
Just a remnant now is left,
And our home town, once so pretty,
Of its beauty is bereft.

There are doctors, lawyers, teachers,
Preachers, printers, not a few;
Unpretentious, conscientious,
Brave and noble, tried and true.
It's "Old Home Week," I can see them,
And the tears that trickle down,
As they gaze in breathless silence,
At the devastated town.

New York City needs more water,
So the noted experts say;
Ashokan is not sufficient,
With its million barrels a day.
Thirsty Yorkers must have water—
Yes, they need a large supply;
More than ever, now they need it,
Since the country's gone bone dry.

Old Gilboa, you sure are going,
And the thought disturbs my sleep;
You'll be buried 'neath the waters,
Swallow'd in the angry deep.
Dear Old Town, we'll not forget you,
Not as long as life shall last,
At thy bier we pay this tribute—
"Thou Hast Had An Honor'd Past."

by Varner D. Mattice (Stamford, NY: Stamford Mirror-Recorder, circa 9/1921)

FOURTEEN

THE HOPE and freshness of April and May were of a day, the plump prime time of June slipped all too soon, the lazy hazy heat of July simmered away on the sly, and now august August, the bonus month of summer under the Maize Moon, with a first tiny taste of fall at the very end. Cicadas were still broadcasting at fifty thousand watts, but there was less birdsong. Goldenrod and purple asters were in full bloom. Clumps of stiff black-eyed Susans and the sinewy girders of lavender and violet New York ironweed were as stubbornly established as machine-gun nests. Queen Anne's lace began to tatter.

When Dave joined foraging trips, he often led brief wildflower walks through the farm fields, concentrating on a single plant or two each time. Azure-blue chicory flowers were out now, unmistakable for how close they grew to the tall stalk, with their square-tipped, frayed petal ends. The Roman poet Horace consumed and commented on this plant, and it was used by numerous cultures as a food source and to cure ailments, from the Egyptians—and undoubtedly earlier by those who had no writing—right on through to modern times. Each flower only blossoms for a single day, but there are so many that some will always be out. They track the sun, closing forever around noon when it is hottest. In one tale of its origin, a beautiful maiden who'd resisted the advances of the sun was transformed and forced to stare up at her scorned suitor each day, wilting at the apex of his might.

The muggy, temperamental air still hosted floating seeds, though nothing like the particulate haze of spring. They considered milkweed on another walk. This common plant can be consumed through the seasons. In the spring its young shoots look and taste like asparagus (asparagus being the "tastes like chicken" of wild edible plants); in early summer unopened flower buds are remindful of broccoli; in midsummer unripe seedpods can be eaten as vegetables, boiled or thrown into a stew; and the pink flowers of later summer can be dipped in batter and fried as fritters. Gwen had even sprinkled fresh pod silk on one hot dish to give it the appearance of melted mozzarella cheese. The same silk had been used for everything from lining Indian papooses and buffalo robes to stuffing World War II lifejackets, and it was a better insulator than goose down. Milkweed foliage is the main food source for monarch butterfly larvae. Not only are they able to ingest the milky leaves, but the sap they contain gives them a bitter taste for the rest of their lives, making monarchs unpalatable and even poisonous to predators. Dave demonstrated how the hairy understructure laden with toxins kept most ground insects from ascending toward the lofty pollen prize. If ants made it that far, their sharp feet soon pierced more tender sections that released the sticky, latex-like milk that dried on contact with the air. Unless they jumped off in time, they were immobilized and doomed.

If Dar was going to leave this woodland band and strike north, now was the time to do so. If he had to abandon his van in the process food would still be available along the way, and most importantly, he would have time to set up before winter, hopefully in an abandoned cabin with a wood stove. Now that August was here he reflected on the pros and cons.

Clearly, these people had the right idea. They were going back to the land, though many of their strategies were necessarily defensive-minded. He'd had interesting conversations with some of them about the nature of survivalism and the future of humankind. Everyone still alive had immediate memories of what passed for civilization. They were not fading yet, even as the light continued to dim, though for most survivors these memories were increasingly tinged with melancholy and even deep remorse. Unless civilization could be reclaimed soon—presumably by some central organizing force like local or federal government, with some level of police or military assistance at first—it would fade away in just a generation or two, replaced entirely by armed enclaves and endless anarchy.

The world would be awash in remnant everyday items for decades to come, but at some point people would have to learn how to make things again, from hoes to shoes. In the meantime, attrition was undoubtedly thinning the ranks one person and settlement at a time. Staying alive was becoming a young person's game, especially tailored for strength and agility, with bonus points for brutality. It might take centuries to reverse the slide, and humankind would probably repeat all the same military, religious, economic, and environmental mistakes anyway. Dar had grown to cherish many aspects of this mode of living, with this set of people, but couldn't escape the feeling that he'd be better off tending his own garden, perhaps with BethAnne for company.

Early one morning Dar left her side for a day of deep contemplation, under the guise of a fishing trip. He woke up hungry, savored a few of his mother's canned beets, and planned on a camp-stove trout or two for lunch, selfish as that was. Liz was up and about, however, and she offered to make him a cup of ersatz coffee and some hash browns and onions. He watched her form a little paper and kindling mound and put a match to it.

"What's cooking today?"

"I'm in the middle of a big bunch of bills now, including from the utility company, which is kind of funny."

Regarding the making of fire, which was so in vogue again, Dar had learned that they planned to go through their matches first, then a few magnesium fire sticks, and finally the scavenged lighters, of which they had hundreds. The flint and steel method was somewhat difficult, though they were all encouraged to practice, for the future. Not even Rick or Dave pretended that bow drill friction should be part of their repertoire. The same with char cloth. Why fuss around making that when they had a ton of scrap paper from various homes to start fires with? They often got a kick out of the content—how pressing and important it had all been then, and how insignificant yet deep felt on a different level now.

Liz made a little "save" pile each day that Dar enjoyed poking through. He picked up an uncaptioned 1930s black-and-white snapshot of a toddler in a field with his curly blond head pressed against the side of a big black Ford, crying his eyes out. It looked like a picnic outing. His hair and all-white clothing glowed off the photographic paper against the rich dark automobile and thick wavy grass. The parents probably thought this was funny or cute or they wouldn't have taken the picture. There was also a little hand-colored Victorian-era Reward of Merit, presented to a name he couldn't quite make out by one "Wm. L. Cottrell, Instructor." A young woman in a pink dress on a pale green hummock reads to a little boy holding a small bat of some sort and a girl with a long thin doll stretched across her lap. There's a cradle on the ground, and fancy scrolls along the side in pink. As they generally went through these tinder hauls in site order, this slip of paper may have been saved by the grandmother of the bawling picnic tyke from her own childhood. If there was a connection though, it was lost forever, even before probably.

Dar remembered a funny chat he had once with somebody trying to sell him some old family photos along with a load of books. "We hate to part with them, but we have absolutely no way of knowing who they were. If only somebody had bothered to caption them." When Dar asked if he captioned his own photos, the man replied "No, but that's different. These are a hundred years old!"

He looked out over the campsite. Light steam rose from a couple of the tents, and some of the nylon walls showed slight movements within. He could hear Herbert snoring. He made eye contact with the cryptic gnome, who seemed happy to see the morning fire capering up.

Dar wanted to get very far away, and made good time along the usual bank farthest from the road. Exploring a sandy bone-dry side channel separated from the active creek by a dense stand of willow, he encountered a somewhat widespread colony of ten or so interesting plants with single columnar stalks that towered above his head, like something you might expect to find in the Sonoran Desert or toward the top of African mountains, and he wondered to what extent these neighbors knew one another. This turned out to be common mullein, which grows up to six feet tall in poor fields and "waste places," though these were two feet higher still. Maybe it was *uncommon* mullein, or the soil was extra poor. He intercepted six deer heading toward the flank of the ridge, the most he'd seen at once in these woods. A century earlier, if a single deer had been taken anywhere in the county it might have made the newspapers, but they had more than bounced back. The water volume above the intersection of the two creeks was now quite low, and he felt vulnerable near the farm up there, or less in the wild at any rate, so he halted just short of it and began to gather some worms. They did not come as easily due to the generally drier conditions.

ΩΩΩ

The driftwood along this stretch reminded Dar that Schoharie County was named after a corruption of the local Native American word for that, which went something like *To-wos-scho-hor*. It was said that this "flood-wood" was tangled and piled up so high at one confluence in the Schoharie Creek, like a "mausoleum of the forest sugar-tree, gnarled oak, and lofty pine," that the natives who used the span as a bridge couldn't even see the water down through it. He'd found an interesting piece along the shore on an earlier trek. It looked like a fantastic wizard's staff from a Hollywood prop department; tall, gray, dense, fully tapered, and complete with an appendage—set with a small root-held stone—that doubled back down from the knobby, crazily grained top in the vague shape of a leaping wolf. It rested in his tent now next to a forged steel golf wedge, both at the ready as last-ditch defensive weapons.

Though one early historical account put the number of Indians living in the valley when permanent settlers first arrived in the 1700s at several hundred, it was probably far lower. They were reduced to mere dozens by the outbreak of the Revolutionary War. As usual, precontact facts and figures were sketchy. Dave's borrowed copy of

Folklore from the Schoharie Hills, New York, published in 1937—which focuses more on the tall tales of Revolutionary War hero Timothy Murphy, the Anti-Rent War, sloughters, and the European origins of local witch and ghost stories than on the original inhabitants—repeats the tale that an old chief bestowed this rich land, basically uninhabited at the time, upon his son-in-law, Karigh Ondonte (also subject to many spellings). The footnote is weak. "Beatrice Snyder had been given a clipping containing this passage to prepare for some school exercises, but neither she nor her teacher knew the source of it."

One of Dave's folders was labeled "Schoharie Indians." It included a 1945 article from the quarterly bulletin of the Schoharie County Historical Society that began as follows: "Although so much is known and has been written about the geology of Schoharie, there are scarcely any scientific records of the aboriginal occupation of our Valley. The State Museum confronts us as we enter with a reconstruction of that ancient Devonian swamp in what is now Gilboa where the oldest tree stumps of the world once grew on our soil. Throughout these museum halls is exhibited the prolific marine life once embedded in our rocky cliffs. But the sections on archeology are very meager in Schoharie exhibits. In the state publication, 'Archeological History of New York,' there is only one page out of the 750 devoted to Schoharie County and in the state publication 'History of the Iroquois' it is not even mentioned."

Dar had read up on this when he lived in the county, and now learned more. The oldest site discovered, near Cobleskill, went back about nine thousand years. Some sources suggest that the valley was most heavily populated from about 1000 CE up into the 1500s. Based on the archeological record, it may have turned into a relatively empty buffer zone between warring Mahicans and Mohawks after that. More recently, it hosted an assortment of wanderers and refugees from multiple Indian nations. These Schoharie Indians were tolerated by Mohawks to the north, before finally being driven out by the winds of foreign disease, war, and change. There were known settlements, of course, and early stories of support and conflict, from feasts and footraces to subterfuge and scalpings, but how little we know of everyday things. Dar would rather have walked invisibly among a precontact settlement in the Archaic or Woodland Period for several days than to have made the same observations for weeks on end among those heavily exposed to early European stock. He'd watched archaeologists at work farther down the Schoharie Creek, at the Pethick site, hunted for arrowheads and net sinkers in cornfields near the river with his father, and visited the nearby Iroquois Indian Museum, but artifacts only told so much. A comprehensive survey was required, pulling together everything old and new on the history of Native Americans in this rich valley. Too little, and now, too late.

As for the lower West Kill Creek, what had happened nearby, within a few miles of where he was now, over the last five or ten thousand years, in all areas of study? Surely the survivors' camp he belonged to must be a notable entry in the lost history of local events.

ΩΩΩ

Dar had always been respectful of private property, but the POSTED signs he saw along this section now meant nothing. He stepped into the empowering water like a Piscean Antaeus, which also cleaned his shoes and cooled his feet. What comes to mind when you encounter something like a stretch of stream—or anything, for that matter—and have time to contemplate it without distraction? Part of the equation is often what can I get from this? Fish, for example, or a cool drink, or a good place to build a mill or dump toxins. But one should also ask, scientifically and spiritually, what is this? And then there are those who think can I help in some way? Habitat-improvement volunteerism, for example, or simply scooping out an otherwise doomed group of tiny puddle-locked minnows, some of which were already turned on their sides, gasping for air.

As he squatted to wash his hands and face after this small act of mercy, a pair of American black ducks came weaving up the bed, splashing down in one of the deeper pools below. They were more of a pond or river duck, and he was surprised to see them there, though it was not uncommon for mallards to puddle-jump in on their way to larger bodies of water. The black duck is dark brown and fairly nondescript to a novice birdwatcher, save for the distinctive black-bordered purple section on its wing. He'd seen a spiffy hooded merganser on the reservoir, and both ducks were added to his New World birding list.

John Burroughs' observation about birding came to mind. Book learning was all right, but you needed to have "original experience" with birds, and by extension, with all of nature. Dar knew this to be true. He had all but given up on wrens, for example, when a Carolina wren built a nest in a hanging plant immediately outside his back door once. He was right there for the building and birthing. His field guide said that wrens are all "small energetic brown birds; stumpy, with slender, slightly decurved bills; tails often cocked." But the Carolina was the reddest and largest, as big as a small sparrow, with a conspicuous white stripe over the eye. Now two of the others have that stripe, but the long-billed marsh wren is also striped on its back, and the Bewick's wren also has white tail-corners. He never failed to recognize the Carolina wren after that. Wren schmen . . . who cares? The other species of wrens did, for one, and Burroughs too, and he three.

"Though there remain not another new species to describe, any young person with health and enthusiasm has open to him or her the whole field anew, and is eligible to experience all the thrill and delight of the original discoverers.. . . First find your bird; observe its ways, its song, its calls, its flight, its haunts; then shoot it (not ogle it with a glass), and compare with Audubon." This is from the first edition of his *Wake-Robin*. In an interesting, rare footnote to a subsequent set of collected writings Burroughs adds: "My later experiences have led me to prefer a small field-glass to a gun." Indeed.

In the late spring, on a return trip to the dark, swampy pond, Dar spent some time watching a pair of nesting wood ducks. The male of the species was generally thought to have the most striking plumage of all local birds. It's so spectacular in color and pattern that unless you're an ornithologist or serious birder you don't even know how to begin describing it. In Dar's layman's terms, working from the iridescent top to bottom, there's the sleek, swept-back green-purple-and-black-crested head lined in streaks of pure white; its bill, which is red, black, and white with a notch of orange at the top; the brilliant and sort of freaky red iris; the proud chestnut breast speckled with white like some royal robe, flowing down to a white stomach; the buff yellow sides; and a confusing trail of shiny blue, purple, and blue-green color swatches along the back amid black and white borders running down to orange feet.

In a world without wood ducks, only someone on acid might fill in a blank outline of a duck that way. How on earth did something like that evolve? Everything else too, of course, from pygmy shrews to sequoias, but sticking to beauteous birds, just in the last few months he'd seen multitudinous types of multicolored spring warblers, a creamy rose-breasted grosbeak, a deep cyan-blue indigo bunting, and a fiery orange and black Baltimore oriole whose yellow-orange mate had fabricated a fantastic high-hanging sack nest right along this very streambed, making sure it was all just so. This was not to take anything away from plainer creatures, most of which he admired just as dearly, though he had to admit he'd make a black duck a dead duck before a wood duck. But again, it was all such a miracle! Existence, energy, laws, diversity, purpose, and end result, if the result mattered, or if there even was an end.

Dar rose up and reconsidered. There are four classical elements you can sense on our planet, as our ancient forebears themselves could, and did. They are earth, air, water, and fire, not to be confused with the long-lived R&B group Earth, Wind & Fire, who had perhaps defied the odds even further and were still doing concerts somewhere. Modern science prefers to consider these elements as four states of matter in solid, gaseous, liquid, and plasma form, though he hadn't looked into this recently and maybe that had changed. By any name, these elements were all around him out there on the creek, as opposed to in some office space, or in outer space. In his favorite childhood cartoon show, *Captain Planet and the Planeteers*, there was a fifth element, Heart, which was used to help vanquish such "eco-villains" as Hoggish Greedly, Duke Nukem, Mame Slaughter (the only one Dar the young hunter felt guilty about), and Looten Plunder. In even *more* classical times, there was also a fifth element. It went by many names, including "ether," and "the quintessence." This was thought of as the unchanging heavens above in some cultures, and as that beyond the material world but which could affect the material world in others. So those old white-robed philosophers had their finger on it. At that relatively primitive stage in our comprehension of life—or in the broader sense, in all of existence—they were pondering physical laws and metaphysics, as we do today. Or maybe their robes were off-white. Who's to say?

Admittedly, all of this was kind of over Dar's head. Especially air, the most common and comforting element to humans, though it's nice to have earth to stand on while you breathe it. Fire is a very weird thing, when you think about it. It's generally the most temporary element, unless you work in an incinerator plant or steel mill, or end up burning in hell for all eternity. Fire used to occur naturally, and sporadically. More often in recent times we created fire and summoned it at will, though it often got away and ran out of control. Where did fantastic *light* fit in? Was that a combination of air and fire, like some kind of elemental mixed-colors crayon? What happened when one ship carrying lots of red paint and a smaller ship carrying some blue and a little black paint crashed into each other at sea? Both crews got marooned. A long voyage for such a dumb joke.

Water was the element that engaged Dar and blew his mind the most. Especially clean, clear creeks where you could see everything. Swamps and deep rivers and lakes were fascinating, and even permanently muddy or caustic waters have their place in the ecosystem, but give him a clear mountain stream and a day off to enjoy it in! And then there were the oceans, which we crawled from, and which felt like the womb when the water was warm, often signifying for many that they were finally, at long last, on vacation. With all of these bodies you could rest your hand on that plane between the two worlds of air and water, with its interesting surface tension, or when it was deep enough you could just sink down to eye level and do it that way. Most creatures lived in the water, equipped against drowning in it or being crushed by its pressure; on it, like a water strider; or out of the water but generally needful of it, like us.

McElligot's Pool by Dr. Seuss was responsible for some of this. It seized him by the ear as a child with a hard tug. A kid goes fishing in a tiny farm pond filled with junk, the farmer scoffs at him, and the lad goes on to imagine how it hooks up with the rest of the world, and all the exotic fish one could catch, and how you never really know what goes on down below, or how big things really are, and whatever else the good doctor was prescribing.

Much later, there was a single panel in an issue of *Heavy Metal* that also had some impact. He'd picked up an early ten-year run of this science fiction and fantasy periodical on a house call and kept it for himself, back in the mind-expanding days. He left it upstairs at the cabin in two boxes because it was heavy, and because the common post-apocalyptic themes were too heavy, and because a lot of it was stupid, as illustrated by so many front covers featuring robots with tits bearing weapons. But much of the content was fantastic, and one panel in some obscure story that very cleverly depicted the thin gulf between water dweller and land lodger had really grabbed him. It did more than a whole book on that topic might do. He'd meant to reread the batch, looking for that, but never got around to it.

On a more traditional note, history—and natural history, including the wonder of water, and the mysteries of life, the universe, and everything—had all been pondered and tackled and treated by countless others before him. Lots of that output was sitting around in big research libraries, or on the Net. He once heard a learned man lamenting the fact that if he devoted the rest of his life to even a single topic of interest, he could never read all there was, as he might have been able to do just a century or two earlier. The scholar accepted this but was saddened by it.

When it came to something like water, measurements were important, but so were *impressions* in good prose and poetry, of which he had sampled only the tiniest draught. "Prosaic" was one of those fugitive words Dar had been using incorrectly, until he had recent occasion to reconsider it. He thought it simply meant in prose form, rather than in verse, and not "lacking poetic beauty or fantasy, dull, unimaginative, tiresome, plain and ordinary," as dictionaries had it. Prose writing could be just the opposite, so where did that disparaging derivation come from? Google would have steered him toward Prozac. He would ask his big dictionary, though the why was always more elusive than the who, what, where, and when. And to complicate matters, "prosody" was the study of poetic meters and versification. Probably not too much of that still going on, he thought.

Dar had only recently gotten over a vague disdain for poetry. It could be just as bad as regular writing, though at least the wordsmiths had reserved a special one for that—"poetaster". . . why not "proseaster" for an inferior author?—but it usually didn't half kill you as he imagined creating a book could. He thought poetic success—if that still even existed so long after Shelley said that poets were the unacknowledged legislators of the world—could be bought much more cheaply. He'd finally come around on this, though, and knew poems were often ideally suited to get the job done. Poetry actually had to be better than prose, in a way—polished stones where tons of raw rock wouldn't do—*because* it was shorter. It sure didn't seem to pay better, however, though perhaps lyricists were the modern poetic legislators. "Writing a book of poetry is like dropping a rose petal down the Grand Canyon and waiting for the echo," wrote a poet more famous for that quote than for his poems. Did Rainer Maria Rilke ever compose any poems about water? Why did Rilke pop into his head? Because his very name sounded so poetic? Because rills ran down from Mount Rainier? He knew next to nothing about Rilke— except for a book about his private letters he'd started—other than that Salinger liked his work. Maybe Rilke was stilted, or off-kilter. "Do not say anything against rhyme!" he once corresponded. "It is a mighty goddess indeed, the deity of very secret and very ancient coincidences, and one must never let the fires on its altars burn out."

He understood the immortal American naturalists better. John Burroughs, whom he always kept close, and who grew up just one county away, wrote: "There is ever a lurking suspicion that the beginning of things is in some way associated with water, and one may notice that in his private walks he is led by a curious attraction to fetch all the springs and ponds in his route, as if by them was the place for wonders and miracles to happen." And Edwin Way Teale said something about how a stream was only concerned with one thing—gravity. That was true in a way, but there was so much more, though who was he to tell Teale that, or to disagree with any naturalists or historians or scientists on anything for that matter? We all have our own original experiences though.

Dar had spent youthful summers catching bait on his favorite water of all time, the pure and mighty Upper Delaware River to the southwest, which also began its journey one county away. You faced upstream with an old rectangular wooden-framed screen of thick stainless steel mesh wire held against your legs by the strong current, flipping over and returning to their original position rocks the flatter the better in order to dislodge the bounty, hellgrammites, the shiny-black-on-flat-black larval stage of the dobsonfly. Half the time they let loose, forming themselves into a protective ball and stretching out again after the screen caught and held them a second or two later, and half the time they tried to crawl around to the other side of the underwater rock and you picked them off by the hard collar. The only other gear involved was his grandfather's faded green tin can that hung around his neck on a thick string, thirties-looking, tall and oval in shape, with a fitted mesh top. As bait, these critters sold for good money in town to visiting fishers of bass. They were a special treat for fish because they were meaty and normally inaccessible, and they stayed on the hook well for anglers. They required clean water and were good indicators of the absence of systemic pollution.

Hellgrammites got pretty big, up to three inches long. They were powerful little buggers, able to fight strong currents and catch prey, and they looked nightmarish. One showed up in an old Indian rock pictograph. Nobody knew for sure where the name came from. Dar made quite a study of them at the time. The shiny black "collar" over the thoracic segments was actually composed of hardened dorsal plates. The abdominal segments were covered in hairy microspines, carried pairs of tracheal gills, in addition to onboard spiracles that allowed them to breathe out of water, and had protective lateral filaments that resembled legs. A pair of prolegs at the rear with their own sets of hooks did all the heavy grabbing. If you didn't pick them up by the collar, these aquatic predators would turn around and give you a nice bite with their curved serrated pincers. They were ugly as sin and beautiful as an angel at the same time.

Once in a while Dar had held one by the head and put the whole body in his mouth, kind of like with a laid-out, peeled shrimp. Its hooks would immediately grab the back of his tongue, all those legs started pumping away, and it was soon pulled out safely, to their mutual relief. The hellgies in this river were washed clean all day long. They spent a few years underwater, pierced the interface when they crawled out to hibernate in rock-side cocoons that protectively resembled bird droppings, and eventually emerged for a brief span of winged mating and egg laying in a new form he would not care to have anywhere near his person, let alone in his mouth, thus magically living underwater, on land, and in the air before the end. Adult males got three days, females ten.

The river bottom itself was sparkling clean. Bending over to do the work, you were looking through this window to another world for hours on end. You got used to how the shiny, perfect specks of mountain sand swirled around in the current. You took note of all the little fishes and insects and plants down there. There was nothing scary about this process, though he didn't lift the heaviest rocks, because an eel or catfish would sometimes shoot out and slither across his leg. Once when Dar had been intently focusing in on this subaqueous diorama a startlingly large, armor-plated blimp of a wood turtle swam underwater right in front of him on its brave, angled journey from Pennsylvania to New York. The intricate carving of its deep concentric growth rings, delicate yellow carapace streaking, and brightness of its orange underparts were brought home in a way that would have been impossible in its usual dusty haunts.

He had the West Kill Creek now. It was not as panoramic or diverse, but it was special, and private. Even before humankind created so much unnatural wasteland, there were parts of the planet that were uninviting, and this was certainly not one of them. A small cluster of cardinal flowers grew nearby, the brilliant red petals set out brighter than ever against a background of hot gray and beige rocks. A large piece of bleached driftwood ending in flared, boney roots up on the bank completed the composition. Nearby daisies were very busy with bees and butterflies, but the tubular shape of the cardinal flower made insect navigation difficult. Enter the shimmering ruby-throated hummingbird, which one did during this contemplation, effortlessly maneuvering between and dipping into the awaiting blossoms. Nectar of the gods. This garden universe *does* vibrate complete, thought the healthy man still in the middle of it all.

Would the Adirondacks be this copasetic? They were colder, wetter, snaggier, and darker, the insects were more fierce, and there were more bears. Nature lovers were not always loved back. He thought of Teddy Roosevelt's terrible Brazilian expedition—outdoorsmen far tougher and more skilled than he starving in a jungle that did not even freeze up but still wasn't ripe for the picking. Of the fifty-plus mammals in the Adirondacks, about half were mice, moles, voles, shrews, and bats. He could expect fewer types of edible plants, and acid precipitation had hurt the fish and fowl populations there more than it did in the better-buffered Catskills. In weak moments Dar was sometimes supremely bored by the woods, even actively hating their implacability, and he just wanted things to be back the way they were, with stores and screens and cars and couches. And that was *with* the comforts of home back in camp, a steady supply of food, and the symbiotic relationship with a dozen other people. For the most part they pulled together as a team, and they had your back. Perhaps he should stay with them for now, and put his final decision off for one more month.

ΩΩΩ

In one of their little nighttime conversations in the tent, BethAnne wondered if Dave's health was failing. He was looking gaunt, was low on energy, and slept more than before. Dar speculated that the hard living conditions might have been catching up with him, but BethAnne discerned some wasting away, and she picked up on how Gwen and Liz were reacting as well. Perhaps Dave knew he was on the way out. There was a certain resignation lately. The two men spoke a lot, but as for getting close, Dave was a little on the formal side in speech and manners, and a tough nut to crack. They had veered toward the topic of mortality once in a private chat some time earlier, however, before there were any obvious health concerns.

They'd been walking the isolated Betty Brook road together, Dave after early blueberries and Dar on the lookout for game. A trail of small blue plastic ribbons affixed to saplings and bushes caught Dave's eye instead, and they followed it out of curiosity, thinking it might be an easier route down to the brook, or even to a good fishing hole there. It led instead to a solemn family cemetery in the midst of overgrown woods, enclosed within a rectangular stone wall and accessed through a surprisingly narrow entranceway. The space was filled with moss, ferns, high weeds, and several fully grown trees. There were only three headstones, with room for quite a few more. Dar always expected to find musical first names like Eliphalet and startling ones like Obedience in such old cemeteries.

In this case, Maria, wife of Jacob as so stated, had died December 20, 1871, at forty-eight. Her carved marker was of weathered marble, its rounded, cracked-off top properly lying faceup and behind the base rather than facedown or directly on the grave. The others were of simple fieldstone, without decoration. Daughter Mary E.'s date was July 24, 1855, "aged 2 years 4 mos 2 d's," and daughter Neoma A.'s September 30, 1862, "aged 4 years 11 months." The girls had small footstones inscribed with their initials. Dave pointed out that most footstones disappeared over the years, often removed by those who had to cut the grass and were tired of dealing with them. For graves surrounded by stone walls, that is often where they ended up. Chances were they'd had other children who had lived longer, and perhaps their descendants had stayed in the area. Jacob was absent. Presumably he'd remarried and was buried somewhere else. Dar wondered aloud how often Jacob might have visited this site afterwards, if ever. They walked back in silence until they regained the road. Dave surmised there was an old foundation or cellar impression nearby, to go with the family cemetery, probably out of sight or on the opposite side somewhere so the ghosts weren't right in the back yard.

"I have a copy of a nice old periodical article about Schoharie County gravestone inscriptions that was in with all the history files," said Dave. "One large obelisk with the names of the young children on each of four sides read 'So fades the lovely flowers.' Sometimes they gave the cause of death, like 'He was killed by the fall of a tree.' And dire warnings, like 'Be ye also ready!' There was one where the husband ordered 'Forever Thine' for his wife, but the engraver ran out of room so it reads 'Forever Thin.' Another humorous one went something like 'Here lies the father of twenty-nine. There would have been more, but he ran out of time.' And there is a special one I have committed to memory, from the Lutheran Cemetery in Schoharie. Gwen recognized it as coming from Job. 'There is hope of a tree, if it be cut down, that it will sprout again, and that the tender branch thereof will not cease.'"

"Why cut the tree down to begin with if you don't have to?" asked Dar.

"Sometimes there is no choice with trees, and never with people."

"But it said *if*, not *when*." After a pause, Dar continued. "I'm reading another one of Anne Rice's vampire novels now, the one where they can switch into other bodies. Not something I brought along. They were at the house already, in with all the paperback bodice rippers, but they're really well written. The immortality part is what's most interesting. The fascination we have with extending life, and neat things like certain vampires just getting tired of all the changes and simply stepping out into the sun after two or three centuries."

"I can't say that I have ever read them," Dave responded. "I have never really understood that, though. You have your time, and that is that. You are thrust out onto the stage and you do what you can for yourself, and hopefully for those you love, and for the world. You have your moment in the sun, you take your small pleasures, and then others get a turn. For one thing, what would we do with all the extra people? Limit families? Kill to make room? Send them off on spaceships? It would probably come down to wealth too. Who could afford extension and who could not."

"Well, there would've been those little details to iron out, yes. I used to joke with my friends though that I would get in the news as the last person to die of natural causes. I was about to get my first printed, grown, or built fix, or I was reaching out for the fetal cocktail, or whatever they come up with to reverse the aging process—as that's probably the only way that would work, slowly, back toward sweet youth—and I croaked right there."

"That would be tinkering with the perfection of the way it works now. And life might not seem so special if it was elongated or eternal. I think we need to be challenged too."

"We've already doubled our life-spans in the blink of an eye though," responded Dar. "Maybe that would have been part of our natural evolution."

"You still have the organic optimism of relative youth, and you do not believe in an afterlife. You can't assume everyone would feel the same as you about extending life."

"True. Even with the vampires, some wanted to keep going, but others grew weary."

"Maybe that is not the best example, as that meant they had to keep killing others to survive. Back to the real world, though, whatever happens happens. You can extend your life by paying attention to the laws of physics, and by practicing good health, and you can spend the time you do have *carefully*. That goes from big life decisions right down to your choice of reading material."

"No vampire books for you . . . got it. I don't know though," continued Dar. "Putting where humankind is now aside for a moment, I don't like, 'You can't do that anymore.' And I love it all too much, like a movie or book that you don't want to end. I think of baby sea turtles. Some get picked off by seabirds in that first mad instinctive dash toward the surf, and most of the rest die before reaching maturity. But a few make it all the way, well past a hundred. I read once about a British family where its members kept dying in the normal way, and a Galapagos tortoise brought back generations earlier that kept outliving them was in the will each time. Or a surfer. Most wipe out or peter out. Only a very few ride the perfect wave to the top of the beach and land right on the blanket where all the good stuff is. In recent times, that meant over ninety, in good health, happy, without too much strife and undue loss earlier in life, and maintaining as much independence as you desire until the end. But why not twice that age? This may be made up, but I heard once about a surfer in a remote area of South America who got caught in some kind of small tsunami and was able to ride it all the way to the hilltops. That's what I want to do. If it didn't involve getting frozen, which seems unworkable, or becoming too robotic, or through some other questionable means, I would be happy to stick around. I'd take it a century at a time and see how I liked it."

"Let's save humankind first," responded Dave. "That is really what the tender branch inscription is about now."

I Saw From the Beach
by Thomas Moore

I SAW from the beach, when the morning was shining,
A bark o'er the waters move gloriously on;
I came, when the sun o'er that beach was declining,—
The bark was still there, but the waters were gone!

Ah! such is the fate of our life's early promise,
So passing the spring-tide of joy we have known;
Each wave, that we danc'd on at morning, ebbs from us,
And leaves us, at eve, on the bleak shore alone.

Ne'er tell me of glories, serenely adorning
The close of our day, the calm eve of our night;—
Give me back, give me back the wild freshness of Morning,
Her clouds and her tears are worth Evening's best light.

Oh, who would not welcome that moment's returning,
When passion first wak'd a new life thro' his frame,

And his soul—like the wood, that grows precious in burning—
Gave out all its sweets to love's exquisite flame!

The Portable Irish Reader edited by Diarmuid Russell (NY: Viking Press, 1956 third printing, with handwritten corrections and restorations according to *The Works of Thomas Moore, Esq., Accurately Printed from the Last Original Editions* (Leipzig: printed for Ernest Fleischer, 1933 new edition), based on the original poem and air ("Miss Molly") as it appeared in *A Selection of Irish Melodies, 6th Number* (Dublin and London: Power, 1815)

FiFTEEN

DAR was back on pretty good terms with Rick. He had an old tee shirt that read "Deer Herd Reduction Specialist," but he was more into guns and self-protection than hunting per se, though he was a regular-season deer hunter who used all the meat he took. What Rick was *really* into was freedom and self-sufficiency. The weeks he'd spent scouting out the best place for the camp had been about his happiest ever, on some level. He said as much to Dar. It was like the opening up of the early West, when you could pick your plot. No money, no lawyers, no government. He said he read something once about a homesteader back then who pulled up stakes when another family moved in twenty miles away! *Jeremiah Johnson* was his favorite movie. Rick had a lot more brains and heart than Dar thought at first, and he seemed more content these days.

Bennie was affable enough, but there was something there that Dar couldn't quite put his finger on. BethAnne was of the opinion that he might be a closet case, with no outlet. It would have been natural for him to make a play for one of the eligible females, but they never saw any attempts to do so. Just as this group was as white as could be, it also seemed super straight. BethAnne divulged some bi-curious tendencies to Dar one steamy night, but that's about as close as the camp came, as far as they could tell. Little cliques formed though, and Bennie was well liked by the foraging crew he spent so much time escorting, so that was a good sign. By now everyone had been pretty much up into each other's business in such close quarters. They basically knew and generally accepted the habits and moods and even the smells of their companions. One of Bennie's claims to fame was the stinkiest feet award. His tent mate Andrew was probably best prepared to deal with that, coming directly from a quad of college boys, and they got along well themselves. Perhaps Bennie was like BethAnne's Dan, just rolling along with the punches. Sometimes the simplest people were the happiest. Not everyone analyzed things to death or had a particular raison d'être, and not everything was an obvious or clever metaphor for something else. Dar always had to remind himself of that.

Andrew was everyone's favorite in a way. He had a pleasant manner, and it was clear from how polite and respectful he was that he'd had a good upbringing, but it had a lot to do with his unbridled youth. Andrew's recent main goals in life had been having fun, getting laid, and passing his classes. He still had that glow, in spite of the hardships and deep personal loss, and it reminded everyone of their own tender years. Also, Andrew was an open receptacle, and those who had a natural inclination to pass on wisdom—like Dave, Gwen, and Cole—found him willing to listen. For Sadie's part, she did this more by deed than through words. Dar gave him some advice on practical progressivism once, as Andrew leaned that way. Think twice before you discard old rules, because they are often there for a good reason. Try to figure out why the other side thinks something is important, and if they might be in the right. Don't take your eyes off the prize as you get older. Be on good behavior, be as a black hole unto narcissism, and be of good courage and cheer in the quest for heaven on earth. The other thing Andrew brought out in the group was the longing for children. They would be a burden right now, especially an infant, but it would be great to have a few kids around to remind them of the wonder and hope of life.

Cole continued to come along in the eyes of almost everyone. He was still somewhat annoying, and lazy, but he began to lay off the doctrinaire political diatribes. In retrospect, Dave was glad this had all come to a head at that one assembly and privately thanked Dar for his part in it, as did several others. Dar and Andrew still sparred with Cole a little, but they generally did so in private, and without as much bile. Cole was happy to have his own tent, and pleased to be in charge of small fishing trips down to the Schoharie. Dar enjoyed talking movies with him. Cole had lost a good amount of weight, which made one wonder again where he'd been before. He was put in the uncomfortable position of having to ask Rick to be on the lookout for some size 36 pants in his travels.

Susan was an object of pity and affection for most of them. Liz and Dawn pitched in the most. She tended to follow Herbert around in camp. When he read a book or something, she would sit nearby. Early on, Rick lobbied for the women to dress more like the men, and to cut their hair short; especially redheaded Susan, who stood out the most and might give them away. Herbert got wind of this and made the point that Susan would have the best concealment of all during the peak fall foliage season. On another occasion Herbert asked him if they could cut up his camouflaged tent and make hats and clothes for the women out of it. Rick dropped the request.

Gwen was the cheerful rock. Dar unsuccessfully enquired about her previous life once, but she was usually about the here and now, and being the keeper of the hearth. He tried to remember that saying about "Happy are the hands that help others," but "Happy is the country that has no history" from his phrase dictionary was probably more apropos in her case. She'd admonished him a couple of times for using curse words—a bad old habit that had been hard to break. In partial defense, Dar said he was largely reformed, and he told her the story he'd heard once about a father vowing to put big money in a swear jar every time he cursed, because the children had been copying him, "but it doesn't count when Daddy is driving."

Sensing a void, or disquietude, Gwen began to pitch religion at Dar now and then, in a gentle way. She usually kept her beliefs to herself, but had developed something of a fixation on Judgment Day lately. Eventually, in response, he asked her why we can't argue with the Bible, as it argues with itself so often, and he brought up his own example of the "good" Hawaiian—substitute anyone here—someone who was as decent as could be their whole life. Because they died before the magical date when the first missionaries arrived, in 1820 or whenever, that good person would cool their heels in purgatory or burn in hell forever. Meanwhile, many of the Christians who despoiled that culture or the world in general would ascend to heaven, and even the worst murderous offenders could do so through deathbed repentance as long as they were baptized. In *Good* We Trust would be better. She gave the standard response about how the workings of the church were different than the true glory of God. He pointed out that the God you believe in is nearly always dependent on the place you were born and the religion of your parents. She said to check back with her the next time he was in a foxhole, where he assured her he would feel more spiritual but irreligious than ever. She asked why he used the name Jesus so often if he never wanted to meet the fellow, and they left it at that, with no hard feelings.

Dawn was a lot like Gwen—stalwart, and basically content, but she seemed mournful deep down inside. Was it their present state of affairs, had something bad happened well before that, or was she pining for something? Everyone was kind of shocked when they first heard BethAnne would be moving in with Dar, but he found Dawn's reaction the hardest to read. He wondered if she might have opened up to him had they ended up together instead. He was certainly attracted to her. Talk about an office romance though! You couldn't get much closer than these campers were. The logistics would be difficult and the price of discovery steep, not that she was discernibly interested to begin with. Beyond that though, he greatly enjoyed her company. It wasn't as simple as BethAnne was too intellectual and agenda-driven, and Dawn wasn't the sharpest tool in the shed but she was warm and simple and selfless, but there was a scintilla of that. Dawn was the only one who had seriously followed up on Dar's offer to come along on hunting trips. She wasn't sure she could pull the trigger on a deer, but she might try. She was sitting next to him when he got his second turkey and was fine with those proceedings. Sadie did not approve, but she was not the boss of the world, as Dawn put it. When she accompanied Cole on expeditions to the Schoharie Creek, Dar was always anxious for her safe return.

Sadie was admirable, and did lots of hard important work, but she and Dar were not especially close. It may have been chemical or it may have been something else, but neither lost sleep over it. He accompanied the foragers on some farm trips, but she seemed touchy when he did so, guarding against any intrusion on her sovereignty. It got to the point where he just asked what grunt work she needed and performed it without making any comments or observations, not unlike an old day at the office. Once he learned where all of the locations were, he sometimes volunteered to come toward the end of the work session in order to serve as a pack mule, which she appreciated. Dawn felt a little bad about some of this, and Bennie seemed to enjoy it a little. Cole stopped helping out for the same reason. Dar made a point to visit all of these farms on his own, however, in his rangering capacity. They were comforting somehow. One sported a row of tiger lilies along the front, as if nothing was wrong. In a couple of cases Sadie had keys and the doors were locked, but he could gain access by ladder through upper windows, taking care to leave no signs. These houses had been picked pretty clean, but he enjoyed exploring them anyway, except for the one with the desiccated bedmates.

Dar had grown very fond of Herbert. They were all used to his eccentricities by now and generally accorded him the respect for one's elders that was often lacking in modern American society, but you never knew what to expect. He would withdraw from conversation for days on end, going through the motions of the daily struggle without comment, and then he'd turn around and animate some proceeding, speak with authority on some obscure topic, or issue arcane and inane remarks that left them scratching their heads. He always referred to their camp as "The Happy Valley." One day on a bird walk with Susan, he entrusted the care of a set of keys to Dar. Herbert explained that they were to his Robinson Crusoe house, and that he was not to divulge that to anyone, "even your lady friend." He was doing very well for his age, however, which he once calculated at 150 years, though he was no longer able to trim his own toenails, imposing on Dar to perform that task every month or so "the next time you have your chainsaw out."

That left Liz, who was pretty enigmatic in her own way. She was a hard worker, but he knew she harbored lots of opinions, including a high one of herself. Liz was definitely a smarty-pants, though philosophical or abstract thoughts did not interest her in the least. He'd made several attempts to break through, but she was guarded, to put it mildly. Dar remembered seeing a "golden cat" in a big zoo out west once. The other cage signage was highly detailed, but all this one said was that it was from Mongolia, and something like "Not much is known about this animal." That's how he viewed Liz. BethAnne and Cole seemed to be at the top of her enemies list. Dar could be too for all he knew.

Things were good with BethAnne. He was quite in love with her by now, enjoying all of the fringe benefits that came with that, though there were closed doors to the soul there as well. Within a week the sum of her possessions had made its way back over from the stuff tent after all, but the manner in which she asked for this contractual revision was sweet and funny, and it was mostly contained within two large duffel bags that sat one on the other and fit in well enough. It was nice to have someone to care for and download to. She changed his behavior in little ways, like no more using the pee bottle when it was raining out, and she harshed his mellow a bit here and there, and vice versa no doubt, but all in all it was a happy union. They made a point not to flaunt that out in the open. They brewed wild tea late at night right in the tent, read by low light under the covers, and did other forbidden things.

Once when fishing the West Kill together under the influence of the last of Dar's red wine and under siege from the stings and arrows of outrageous insects, BethAnne covered all of her exposed skin with slick primeval clay from the large bank he had discovered. This provided immediate relief, and she said she loved how it felt. She took her top off and asked him to do her back while she slathered the last white with the dark ooze. When the rocky shore gave way to a sandy bank downstream, she kicked her sneakers off and gave him the look. Her blue eyes blazed from behind the mud mask that was beginning to cake in the sun, and her lissome body was streaked with multiple shades of clay. They embraced, she pushed both their shorts off and pulled him down to the lapping shoreline, and within seconds he was inside her, deeply satisfying the Mud Tribe female before pulling out at the perfect moment.

They lay panting awhile, and then he gently carried her out into the middle of the stream, where the clay completed its unlikely escape from the viscous monolith of its origin by slipping off her ivory and pink skin in cascading veils. "I have a surprise, my little pilchard," he said, returning with a sample-size shampoo bottle he'd liberated from a farmhouse, and they threw even more caution to the wind by skinny-dipping out in the open. He sat behind BethAnne with his legs alongside hers, shampooed her hair, and sudsed over every curve looking for clinging clay. Enchanneled bubbles curled around her knees and toes and headed down to the more traditional bathing area far below.

"Heavenly," she said when it was all over. He dried her off with his own shirt and watched her wriggle back into everything. "Pilchard?"

"That's just a little term of endearment, dear," he responded.

"Sounds fishy to me."

Dar began to smooth over the sand where they had lain with his foot. "Hey," he said, "I didn't mean to be such a big stick in the mud a while ago."

"Okay," BethAnne replied, with her smart, winning smile, "that might be the worst one yet, and that's saying a lot."

When the women bathed they usually went down together in small groups, without a male escort. Dar had been loaning his handgun out for that purpose, where Bennie's reluctant rifle had earlier served. BethAnne provided some pillow talk color commentary on that. Gwen, a once-a-weeker who got a half-hour head start on the trail so they didn't have to wait for her, let it all hang out like she was in a ladies' Turkish bath, but without the towels. Sadie was efficient, with overtones of the goddess thing. Dawn was natural but a bit demure. Liz declined to join, probably taking care of this when she did her laundry, or on those occasions when she helped Susan bathe. Most of them made an attempt to shave their legs and underarms once in a while, though with decreasing frequency. They picked times when they knew Rick was far from camp, and asked the other men to give them some privacy just before they went.

$$\Omega\,\Omega\,\Omega$$

Most of August was far wetter than usual, shortening the summer to some extent and giving them even more pause about the upcoming winter. They began laying in a good supply of chicory and dandelion roots and mint leaves for coffee and tea, with Herbert doing most of the processing at his own pace. Hazelnuts came into season, plucked from large thickety shrubs identified by their smooth, gray bark and thin, hairy, tooth-edged leaves. The nuts themselves were encased in leafy husks, with one end poking out. They were very good just roasted, but the kitchen crew was excited for their first chance to make flour from nuts, as laborious as that process was.

Wild black cherries had appeared in late June, the locations of these trees with their beautifully distinctive bark having been noted over the previous months. The giants had been removed decades and even centuries earlier for their desirable wood, which now sat as fine furniture in countless mute rooms. Their more slender descendants still produced delicious fruit, though for those on the tart side the problem would always be the new difficulty of obtaining sweeteners. Making maple syrup was a lot of work and smoke. Maybe someday.

One of the big farms had some beehives stacked in the barn, but they hadn't got them out quickly enough. That left wild hives, and a couple of reachable ones had been located by the rangers. Dave had some experience with bees. Rick would swing his mighty axe, and Dawn and Sadie would help with the harvesting. Protected by gloves, ponchos, and head nets, they started a smoky fire at the base of these trees in the ancient way to calm the swarm, breached the inner sanctum, and hurriedly scooped the dripping honeycombs into buckets, transferring the golden prize into empty canning jars back at camp. Dar watched the first time, when they raided a windbreak hive, from as far away as humanly possible.

As the company fell deeper into these rural rhythms, Dar began to wonder again about the physical area they were in, and its human history. He'd stored the small bundle of books lifted from the Gilboa meeting room in a corner of the tent, and consulted them now as if they were the ancient writings of a bygone civilization. The most promising title was *History of the Town of Blenheim, Schoharie County, New York, 1797–1959*, authored by Town Historian Helen Patchin Bliss, and oddly enough not in with the local archives material in Dave's possession. Somebody probably borrowed it out years ago and never returned it. As the upper village of North Blenheim was also known as *Patchin* Hollow, Helen Patchin Bliss was probably qualified to write this, and imbued by the responsibility. It was a signed copy, with a newspaper review neatly pasted onto the front inside cover. The clipping featured a nice photo of the smiling school teacher/postmistress/historian in all her local DAR regent properness. It said five hundred copies had been printed, and that one could be yours at the Old Stone Fort in Schoharie for $1.50. It had probably been worth $100 lately, especially signed.

One of the neatest things about handling old books is the items that fall out of them upon inspection, and there were two of interest in this volume. The first was a printed notice for a revised and expanded 1994 update to the town history by one Fanchon Dewell Cornell, Helen's young helper on the 1959 edition, according to the credits. This would also have a limitation of five hundred copies, the proceeds going to the Blenheim Bridge Historical Association. The second piece was a clipping from the 125th anniversary celebration of the covered bridge, dated 1980, with Helen's successor, Fanchon, standing next to the newest town historian, Josephine Fuller, who is wearing what is hopefully a period dress and holding a small flag. A nicely hand-lettered sign behind them reads "Blenheim—the best place to be from. We (heart symbol) Our Bridge." As for the physical book, it was a standard, modest local history from that era, in softcover, with light green wrappers and an illustration of the town seal—the covered bridge over the creek—centered between the title and subtitle. Helen spells "Foreword" with an *a*, bless her heart, and that is followed by a nice dedication, a clear table of contents, a little map, and a brief word about the seal. There was a 1908 motion for the town clerk, an earlier Patchin, to "purchase same as cheap as he can," and Helen's parenthetical: "This seal was bought from A. C. Gibson at the price of $8.64, and was audited and paid for on Nov. 5, 1908."

"The writer presents this historical sketch to its readers; to all those who love this little Town of Blenheim and whose memories are closely entwined about its early settlement, its later development, its achievements and successes; to those who are justly proud of the part that its citizens have displayed, in adversity as well as in prosperity, in war as well as in peace, in the past as well as in the present."

Their home creek received a mention in the very first paragraph! "The surface is a hilly upland, broken by the deep ravines of the streams. Schoharie Creek flows north through the east part, receiving Westkill and several smaller streams from the west. These streams often rise very rapidly, sometimes doing great damage. They are bordered by steep hills, rising to a height of 300 to 500 feet." He was surprised to see West Kill spelled as one word, but found it like that in some of the other works as well and wondered which was correct.

All Dar knew about the little upper village of North Blenheim down the road from their camp was that it contained a handful of structures that had survived the pipeline explosion on the periphery or were built afterwards, in addition to a fairly characterless modern town hall and garage. Sadie related from her discovered clippings how the town had accepted a lump-sum payment of around $160,000 from Texas Eastern Products in lieu of spreading nearly three times that amount out over decades and applying it to the lost tax base on an annual basis, spending the entire payment and then some on this one building. There were pros and cons to that course of action, according to discussion at the time, but where they really may have dropped the ball was in failing to file a decent class action lawsuit. One interesting relic from the center of the blast zone survived, though it had probably required repainting. It was an old blue and orange historic marker from the 1930s that read "Indian Trail: Westkill to Delaware River and south to Susquehanna

River and west. One of the many trails giving Iroquois control of large areas," as pictured in Helen's book. She proceeded to bring the town back to life for him.

North Blenheim is separated into two parts by a steep hill that nearly reaches the river and only allows enough room for the road. The upper village is situated where the West Kill Creek meets Route 30, and the lower village just to the north is farther downhill where the same road meets and crosses the Schoharie Creek, at one time over the old covered bridge, and now across a more modern span just downriver. By 1872 North Blenheim contained "two churches (Methodist and Reformed), two school houses, two hotels, two stores, two wagon shops, two blacksmith shops, a harness shop, a shoemaker shop, a tailor shop, a paint shop, a grist mill, two saw mills and about fifty dwellings. There was a fine water power, and a steam sash and blind factory nearby." It was on the Middleburgh and Gilboa stage line. By the time of Helen's book, in 1959, most of the fine Greek Revival houses remained, but the Reformed church had been replaced by a Presbyterian church, many of the rustic trades had vanished, and there were five gas stations. Fifty years after that, not a single storefront business remained, save for a small packaging company at the top of the upper village on Creamery Road (there's always a road by that name in these towns) and a colorful service station at the bottom of the lower village down by the covered bridge.

Going back, the Blenheim Patent—named after a battle on the Continent, like the last place Dar had lived, on the upper Danube in this case—was granted by the British in colonial times, the name perhaps suggested by the pioneers themselves. In one of the bibliographies he found *The Captivity and Sufferings of Gen. Freegift Patchin of Blenheim, Schoharie County, Among the Indians, Under Brant, the Noted Chief, During the Border Warfare in the Time of the American Revolution*, published in 1833, so great-great-great-granddaughter Helen certainly had deep local roots.

She includes a brief section titled "Creeks and Roads—Interesting Names," describing nine creeks, twenty-nine roads and settlements, and some of the old mills and businesses associated with them.

"Devil's Run—runs down Dave Brown Mountain—very treacherous—enters the Schoharie Creek, a little below the covered bridge."

"Blue Rock—a rock resembling a nose which protrudes above the water—when old-timers could see this rock, it was safe for them to ford the stream—below the old covered bridge."

"Nudabark—the very steep part on the old George Souer place (Everett Dewell farm)—derives its name from the fact that bark from trees on this steep hill was stripped off, and the 'nude' logs were left to rot, leaving bare spots on the hillside."

"Blenheim Hill Road—Cider Barrel Hill—between North Road and Welch's Corners; jokingly called Cider Barrel Hill because a resident had the misfortune to have the end-board of a wagon come loose while going up the hill with a load of cider, causing the barrels to roll back down the hill."

"Betty Brook—on a turnoff the Westkill Road—built by C. C. C. workers—now a wood trail leading into Eminence."

Helen then goes on to cover some of the local cemeteries, many of which are private (and one of which held her remains—as discovered by Dave and Dar at a later date—peacefully overlooking the village and river); the postmasters (the first, in 1820, was a Lewis Patchin, back when they ran it out of their homes, and the author herself had the job from 1938 to "still serving"), along with anecdotes about early mail delivery; the churches ("But how disappointed the choir must have been to have the proceeds from the first concert which they gave go towards repairs on the parsonage instead of books for their use, as expected"); and the teachers ("Teachers boarded around at different homes, free of charge, usually getting the coldest 'guest' bedroom!") and their one-room schoolhouses (Westkill No. 2 was up above them toward Jefferson, Betty Brook No. 8 was not far away, and Upper Village No. 7, where Helen began teaching in the 1920s, was down by the bottom of their road until it burned in 1955). Local organizations included the Blenheim Lodge No. 651 of the Independent Order of Odd Fellows, Woman's Christian Temperance Union, Epworth League, Ladies' Aid, Young People's Society, Grange, Willing Workers,

Christian Endeavor, Farm Bureau, Just for Fun (which perhaps wasn't too much fun as it only lasted for a few years around 1926), Rod and Gun Club, Daily Vacation Bible School, 4-H, Youth Fellowship, Home Bureau, Union Christian Society (formed to unite two dwindling churches), Eastern Milk Producers, Boy Scouts Troop 102, and the Westminster Youth Group, organized in 1958 by the Presbyterian churches in North Blenheim and Breakabeen and attended by little Gail Shaffer among others. It also gave the names of those involved in industries and trades as taken from old directories (Abram Loucks was a bark peeler, Foster Jump made shingles, and they even had a cigar maker, one Maxson Kenyon), and a list of all the town clerks and supervisors.

There is a section on "Floods, Hurricanes, and Fires" that global-warming deniers would have enjoyed. There were major floods in 1869, 1874, 1903, 1936, 1938, and three in the 1950s. From 1874:

It seemed as if the very "floodgates of Heaven" were open upon us, and the "vials of wrath" were being poured down in all their fury. The upper village sustained the entire damage done, the "big creek" doing no injury. The heavy rains of Sunday afternoon raised the Westkill much higher than ever before, and the third one, at night, converted the stream into a second rate Niagara. It first carried away H. Shafer's mill dam—the bridge below—then followed Josiah Dudley's shoe shop. Another stream from the Jefferson way carried away William Snyder's saw mill. Then the stream, mingling with the Westkill, changed the current of the latter, throwing it against the rear of the buildings along the main street. It took away the house and barn of Frederick Becker, barely giving the family time to get out of the house, with no time to save anything whatever. This was followed by the fine residence of Jackson Mann, together with his barn and cooper shop, and a quantity of stock and tools. Mr. Mann succeeded in saving a goodly portion of his furniture, but lost eighty-six hives of bees, the result of much labor, and time. John Shafer's house still stands partly undermined, barn gone; also the barn of Mrs. Pierce, in which Mr. Parslow had about $100 worth of goods. James Baldwin's barn was also carried away. Another stream, emanating from springs on the hill above the village which was

dry Sunday morning, also did heavy damage. Lewis Ellerson's barn was
partially undermined; also the shop of George Sours. The stream came down
directly in front of the house occupied by Dr. J. D. Havens, and so sudden
was the onslaught that the house was surrounded with water before the
family was aware of any danger, the blinds being closed and the thunder
so incessant. The doctor immediately took his wife out of the window, and
on again reaching the house found it impossible to get out with his two
boys. He remained in the house for one hour and a half, no one being able
to get to them, the current being so strong. By almost superhuman efforts
he finally succeeded in getting out of the window, with one boy on his back
and dragging the other, hanging on the garden fence, upturned trees, etc.
Richard Shafer also suffered considerable by the same stream. His fence was
carried away, and garden completely ruined. An avalanche of clay soil came
down back of Andrew Martin's house and completely filled an ante-room.
Lorenzo Morehouse's residence, like a "city set on a hill," furnished shelter
to the drenched people, who were driven from house to house. The creek side
of the street is almost an entire wreck. No one has any heart to undertake to
tell their loss, as the creek now runs directly in the rear of their village lots.
In many cases large portions of the lots are washed away.

In an 1847 fire: "Hezekiah Holdridge home in the lower Blenheim village burned. His wife, Catherine, sons George G., Charles A., Munson, daughters Rhoda L., and Delia M. all perished." From 1883: "Jane Carley, a Negro woman, burned in her home, across the creek opposite the village." And during a 1955 flood: "The water came within six inches of the floor of the old covered bridge!"

It seemed there were several parts to the town of Blenheim, and it was a little confusing at first. What used to be thought of as Blenheim, or the Ridge, was taken off by Gilboa in 1848 and renamed South Gilboa. Then there was something called Blenheim Hill, known in the olden days as the Hill or the Backbone (so New York did have a backbone after all!). To reach this two-thousand-foot plateau, you continued a little south on Route 30, took North Road to the right, which ran parallel to West Kill Road, and then made a left up Blenheim Hill Road, in the area where Dar had gotten lost some weeks earlier. Eminence rose up on the other side of the creek, toward Summit, and the old name for that once-thriving, now largely vanished highland village was Dutch Hill.

Settlers first came to the Backbone in 1795, and by 1850 its five thousand acres were divided into thirty or so happy farms. Dairying was the main pursuit, and crops included hay, oats, rye, wheat, buckwheat, potatoes, and peas. "One of the never failing crops was the crop of stones. It has not yet failed, though the harvesting of this crop is now sadly neglected." What they paid to live so high up was often compensated for by relative immunity from all the flooding problems and worldliness down below. By the late 1800s, however, the exodus began. It was too elevated for maximum farming, the thin soil weakened, the markets were difficult to reach, and the young felt too isolated, especially after the Civil War. Helen quotes one local as remarking "People left to better themselves and the world as there wasn't room or opportunity on the Hill for both betterments." Down in town, which serviced all those farm families, small businesses dwindled as well due to fewer customers, and the availability of more cheaply manufactured goods produced elsewhere, so it was a dual death spiral. The population went from 2,725 in 1840 to 427 in 1940, and it probably got even smaller and older after that. Still, there were a few recent families left that were into the tenth generation or so.

The town historian closes out with sections on the Anti-Rent War and the covered bridge, and a list of local veterans from the Revolutionary War through Korea, sprinkled with little vignettes. The original Blenheim House with its small theater burned down in 1938, but on August 15, 1927, for example, eleven of fourteen actors in a local presentation of *Peg o' My Heart* were from the Cottone family, renowned for their Sicilian cheese-making skills and business.

"Time marches on!" concluded Helen Patchin Bliss. "And although Blenheim today is not nearly so populated as it was in days gone by, residents will continue to rejoice in their heritage as long as there remains some to tell of the glorious history of this little town."

Dar also reviewed what was probably the most definitive modern countywide history, from 1994, with the provocative title of *The*

Sloughters' History of Schoharie County: From the Arrival of the Wisconsin Glacier to the Devastation of North Blenheim. Did little Blenheim really deserve a mention in the sweeping title due to its relatively recent pipeline explosion? Dar recalled the preeminent Catskills historian Alf Evers once remarking that his publisher advised against the subtitle of his seminal 1972 work, *The Catskills: From Wilderness to Woodstock,* because "who's going to remember Woodstock a few years from now?" The county history was very useful, with an interesting section on sloughters, and an extensive and selectively annotated bibliography. One of the works it listed was by a Beatrice Mattice—whose surname is one of those that went all the way back—with the lovely title *They Walked These Hills Before Me,* from 1980. Dar wondered if there was a copy of that snoozing away in the Middleburgh Library, or on a nearby home bookshelf. Last-gasp local histories like that were about as late as you could reach where the author still had some deep personal connection to the olden days of blood and dirt, stone and wood, leather and iron, and horse and buggy, complete with passed-down family stories about settling the wilderness, defending the county during the Revolutionary War, and sending sons to the Civil War.

There *was* still room for the real deal, however. *Time Wearing Out Memory,* a phrase taken from the first, brief history of Schoharie County in 1823, was the title of a large-format architectural photography book published in 2008. Its chemical black-and-white images of decrepit yet proud structures in "the oldest continually farmed county in New York" were poignant beyond words. It featured abandoned farmhouses, tenant houses, smokehouses, sap houses, outhouses (including a two-seater), and one-room schoolhouses; carriage, dairy, and hop barns; old stores, hotels, and churches; defunct Odd Fellows, Masonic, and Grange halls; corncribs and wagon sheds and chicken coops; early autos out in the weeds and woods; the very church he'd sped past in his flight toward Summit; a thirteen-sided barn in nearby Jefferson; an upstairs theater in a former feed store in nearby West Fulton; a country store continuously operated from the mid-1800s in nearby Breakabeen; and the most marvelous doghouse on the old Peaslee farm up on Blenheim Hill, sided and shingled in hundreds of big old license plates. Where did they get that many?

There were quite a few local photos, but most of the county was represented, all the way over to the old Western Turnpike roadside Commodore Cabins (if only those walls could talk!) on the other side of his old digs. Most of these structures had suffered from neglect, but they'd survived, in part due to the mixed blessing of economic underdevelopment. Still, the authors noted those that had disappeared in the few short years since they were captured on film. Dar and BethAnne savored this book in the candlelit tent one night, and fantasized about having made a home together somewhere in this Brigadoon county before all the troubles had descended. BethAnne even talked about reopening the Chapman House down in North Blenheim—which went back to the 1840s or so, and was still chock full of antiques, as pictured in the book—renting out rooms, serving up fresh local food, including trout, and dressing in period clothing ("on occasion, and with modern underwear"). Dar could see several of the other women in camp doing something like that before BethAnne, but it was a nice thought.

At a later date Dar found an interesting 1945 historical quarterly article titled "This County of Schoharie," by the other great local evangelical agriculturalist, Jared Van Wagenen, Jr., that shed even more light.

Just how many inhabitants the county had in 1795—one hundred and fifty years ago—we can never know but the census of 1800 counted 9,808. Ten years later this population had increased to 18,945—a phenomenal increase of more than 93% in ten years. There is a two-fold explanation of this teeming increase. One explanation is that the New Englanders were literally swarming into the rough and heretofore unoccupied lands in the southern part of the county. The other factor was what now seems a well nigh incredible birth-rate. The census of 1845 contains the first vital statistics in our history and it reveals the fact that every time the county filled a coffin, it filled two and one half cradles. By 1820 we counted 23,154 inhabitants which is a greater number than we have had at any time during the last thirty five years. This census of 1845—just one hundred years ago—enumerated 32,488 inhabitants and so far as population is concerned, Schoharie County might have been declared grown up. During the next twenty years the population

*gain was a scant two thousand reaching in 1860 the all time high of 34,469—
more people than we are ever likely to have again in any foreseeable future.
Then began a slow, relentless decline which continued for seventy years,
culminating in 1930 when the census enumerator could find only 19,667
inhabitants—less than sixty per cent of the number in the year preceding the
breaking out of the Civil War. At the present time the decline seems to have
come to an end and once again there appear indications that we may expect
a slow increase in population. In some ways that year 1860 was the Golden
Age of the county. The open country everywhere was full of people. Every
farm and every farm house was occupied. The typical family was much larger
than now and the cross-roads school houses overflowed with pupils. It was an
era of buoyant hopes and every tiny hamlet felt sure of itself and its future.
Nowhere had there arisen a prophet of evil to speak of a day when there would
be rural decadence and empty churches and abandoned farms. Hope was not
yet alloyed with doubt. Even on the thin, windswept hilltops of Huckleberry
Kingdom, there were men walking between their plow handles and planning
for the morrow.. . .*

*Judged by population or wealth or industrial life, Schoharie must be
reckoned as one of the three or four least important counties in the state.
Nonetheless, there are some of us who like to believe that it possesses
characteristics which give it a certain uniqueness—perhaps distinction. It
is probably the most agricultural county in the state, meaning thereby that
in no other county does so large a percentage of all the people live from the
soil.. . . Its predominantly rural character is evidenced by the fact that save
for the one county of Hamilton which is really very little except a summer
playground in the Adirondack wilderness, there is no other county whose
largest village is as small as Cobleskill.. . .*

*Schoharie County was settled in the first place by pitifully poor German
Palatines and it would seem that as a people we have preserved a measure
of that democratic simplicity. In the entire county there are only one or two
farm estates that can in any way be called pretentious and probably there is
no man whom Theodore Roosevelt would feel called upon to denounce as a
"malefactor of great wealth."*

*Agriculturally Schoharie County, while relatively small in area, presents
a singular diversity of soil types and topography. The fertility of the ribbon
of chocolate-colored stone-free illuvium known as the "Schoharie Flats"
has been a legend for more than two hundred years. Less well known are
the rolling limestone hills which make up the alfalfa belt of the county.
Nonetheless, these two deserve to be reckoned among the most valuable farm
soils in our state. On the other hand, the county has too much land as steep
and stony and generally difficult as any region from which men ever tried
to wring a living. Salute to those brave men and women who with perhaps
mistaken courage climbed to those hilltops and cleared the forests and built
homesteads and laid stone walls, and reared school houses and churches and
made what they believed would be an enduring agricultural civilization.
In a general way, it is something more than a hundred years since these
first settlers came and in most cases their great grandchildren have looked
around them and fled. Another century will see these one-time farms almost
completely returned to the forest from which they came.*

*The political history of our county must remain an unsolved riddle. What
was it that through long years made Schoharie County (more especially
the northern part of the county) overwhelmingly Democratic when all
the counties around it faced the other way? In the presidential campaign
of 1896 when Bryan ran the first time, it was the only county east of the
Mississippi and north of Mason and Dixon's Line to vote for the Great
Commoner. No wonder somebody coined the happy phrase "The Gibraltar
of the Democracy." There is a story that a waggish assemblyman on the
floor of the Chamber once characterized Schoharie as "the County with
one railroad and two thousand Democratic majority." It hardly needs to
be added that the present generation of voters have failed to keep the faith.
All of which is a proper subject for inquiry and mediation on the part of the
political philosopher.*

*So it comes to pass that Schoharie County has arrived at the somewhat
mature age of one hundred and fifty years and there is surely no indication
that the end draws near.*

Some of us who have the honor to hold birthright citizenship in the county may paraphrase the famous pronouncement of Daniel Webster concerning the New England college from which he was graduated, "Dartmouth is but a little place, yet there be those who love her."

So, Schoharie is but an obscure county, yet there are some of us who hold it dear.

The campers rounded out August in fairly good cheer, in spite of the wet weather. They continued to catch fish in the Schoharie Creek, and were sending along a third or fourth person now to concentrate on large crayfish. Dar brought BethAnne with him on the next reservoir trip, spending two nights. Everything was as he'd left it, and they caught and came home with some lunkers, including a walleye that was bony but delicious, in addition to a slew of large bass and the biggest brown trout of his life. They stood on the starry shore one night serenaded by an owl, and Dar added an osprey and a bald eagle from that trip to his bird list as well. He tried to picture how ice fishing might work, but tracks in the snow would be a problem. Somebody could follow them back for miles.

The rangers had reported finding bear scat in far-flung locations over the last couple months, and now it was turning up rich with berry seeds. Rick brought one enormous turd in for show and tell, giving rise to much woodsy toilet humor, from Cole in particular. They'd seen tracks as well. It was disconcerting to know they were sharing the forest with such a powerful creature, but there had only been that one brief sighting. When Andrew beheld the behemoth bruin bowel movement he exclaimed "Damn, Nature, you scary!"

Rick had been in every nearby house at least twice, and he began to push farther out, bringing back some interesting finds. Gwen's top request now was a tall order—some type of small, manual cooking oil press for use with nuts, corn, and sunflower seeds. He found a mother lode of batteries in one house, where he left hundreds of stockpiled incandescent light bulbs behind. No more airplanes or drifters passed through, but they once heard a faint rifle shot, coming from miles away but of great concern. A minor earthquake hit one afternoon, of all things, swaying the trees and unnerving Gwen.

Dar and Cole passed each other using the privy one morning.

"A termite walks into a bar and asks 'Is the bartender here?'"

"A skeleton goes into a bar and says 'Give me a beer and a mop.'"

We came to a resting place and breathed our horses, and slaked thirst at the stream, when we perceived our Indian looking for a stone, which having found, he cast to a heap, which for ages had been accumulating by passengers like him, who was our guide. We enquired why he observed that rite. His answer was that his father practiced it and enjoined it on him.. . . This custom or rite is an acknowledgement of an invisible being; we may style him the Unknown God, whom this people worship.

History of Schoharie County, New York, with Illustrations and Biographical Sketches of Some of Its Prominent Men and Pioneers by William E. Roscoe (Syracuse, NY: D. Mason & Co., 1882)

SIXTEEN

SUNDAYS in camp were not extremely different from other days, with the exception of some private prayerful moments and football fantasies, but they all still remembered what they once meant, and there was usually a certain amount of restfulness in evidence. The last Sunday in August loomed like any other, but overnight and early morning rains intensified, and before long it became apparent that the camp was under threat from flooding again. Opinions differed, as the traditional rainy season was basically over, and most thought it would pass, but Rick asked for help moving his belongings to the stuff tent and relocating his own shelter up to Little Round Top at first light, and soon his caution was justified.

Tarps were thrown over the more porous tents earlier this time, and when heavy winds began to tear at them they were staked to the ground. Dawn relocated the ceramic gnome to one of the worktables, and everyone did a double take when they noticed him up there in the middle of all that turmoil. When there was no letup, Herbert was carried by Rick over his shoulder to the higher shelter up the hill, and Susan was soon led there, but Gwen refused to go. She would not be carried, the footing was slippery, and her slow pace in such heavy rain would have been too chilling. She huddled in place, frantically searching a soggy Bible for a desired passage that she uttered over and over. "Oh mountains of Gilboa, let there be no dew nor rain upon you." Dar suppressed a momentary urge to rip it out of her hands and throw it into the biblical deluge they were enduring. *"Good night!"* was Dave's exclamation of choice as the rain intensified.

Cole's tent was about to fall into the rapidly expanding drainage canal, and it was quickly struck and removed along with its contents. Everyone carried most of their belongings to the stuff tent, which seemed to be highest and driest, and it was soon transformed into a proverbial exploding closet.

The rain may not have come down as fast as the last time, but it was steady and heavy, lasting for hours on end. All of the campers were soaked to the skin and shivering. They gathered in the old canvas tent because it had the most floor space, huddling together under quilts and blankets and hoping or praying for an end to the tempest. Two of the worktables were unlashed and brought inside for a dry place to take turns resting, and candlelight made a brave stand under the sodden canvas.

The scariest part was the endless freight-train commotion of the West Kill down below them. Rick, Bennie, and Dar went down to take a look and were astounded by the sheer volume and force of it. Once the creek came within view they instinctively held on to strong trees, far from the obviously unstable banks, as any slide into that raging maelstrom would mean instant death. It had been one of the rainiest Augusts in memory. The ground was supersaturated to begin with, and the water had nowhere else to go. The furious brown autobahn carried bobbing trees and other objects along at breakneck speeds, and large rocks and boulders could be heard grinding and banging into each other far underwater. They reported back to camp, and Rick brought Sadie and Dawn up to the safer location to help with the others, and just in case.

By afternoon the storm had subsided, but the creek was still roaring below. The fire pit was destroyed. They started another on its ruins. After making coffee and tea, Liz gamely began preparing the planned supper of supawn, roasted potatoes, and wild leeks. They all dipped their spoons into a jar of grape jelly for a quick pick-me-up while they were waiting. Clean water was in short supply, and they rationed it until the feeder stream eventually ran clear again. This source had nearly played out over the summer but was salvaged by the construction of a small dam above the trail crossing that would now need to be rebuilt. A bucket on the periphery had kept its footing somehow, and they measured eleven inches of water in the bottom before using it. Dave surmised this had been a tropical storm, rare for New York, and perhaps even a hurricane—unnamed, of course, unless they wanted to pick one themselves—with even heavier localized torrential downspouts higher up on the mountainsides. It was almost certainly a widespread, multi-state event.

Rick had an urgent meeting with Dave and Dar the following morning. He wanted to reconnoiter, to assess the impact, but they needed food more than anything and were low on meat. Dar agreed to hunt full-time. The woods were very quiet with no dry leaves to rustle, and he was able to down a plump whitetail the very next day. This raised most everyone's spirits. Some of the others made an expedition to the root cellar to replenish their stocks. All of the benches had been swept downhill, and Dar helped to reassemble the little amphitheater that had impressed him so much that first day in camp. The immediate cleanup took days, and the long-term a couple of weeks. And heavy rain returned less than two weeks later, inflicting more damage.

Rick was gone more often than not through the month of September. Crossing the West Kill had been impossible, so he'd followed it down to North Blenheim, which had been hit hard by scouring. Rick had good news and bad, depending on how you felt about "the rebound." The two creekside country roads that came down from Jefferson and Summit to the west were impassable. No vehicle would cross them again without major mechanized reconstruction. Route 30 was wrecked on the Cave Clan side of their outlet, more than once, for long stretches in some spots. It took Rick twice as long as it should have to reach muddy Middleburgh, which he was surprised to find still standing. He went as far north as Schoharie, much of which looked as if it had been deeply submerged. Whole blocks of homes and businesses were ruined forever by the flooding, with nobody left to effect repairs. Some of the high-water marks measured out at ten feet. Inside, insidious fields of black mold ran up the walls and met on the ceilings. What a stark contrast from its glory days as the most successful of the seven Palatine settlements along the river—Brunnen Dorf then, meaning the village of springs, later Fountain Town—sprouting so many elegant buildings, assuming the role of county seat, and even appearing as the star of an all-Schoharie *Late Show with David Letterman* some years earlier (the host poked good-natured fun at the town, which later renamed the road to the village sewer plant Letterman Lane). The plague scattered and killed its people, and the flood most of its structures.

Rick went as far south as Prattsville, at the far end of the Schoharie Reservoir. It had been devastated by the engorged and enraged Batavia Kill as it joined the larger creek, appearing more like a war zone than a flood zone. Entire sections of road were missing. Houses pitched down toward the street into gaping, muddy moats where front yards used to lie, or back toward the creek, scoured out from behind. Some rested perfectly next to their foundations, like Lego pieces, while others were twisted partially off. Horse trailers, mobile homes, and school buses had tumbled along for miles on their final journey. Piles of debris, sheets of building material, escaped furniture, incongruously relocated sheds, and flipped and deformed vehicles dotted the landscape. Every skinny tree, bush, guardrail, side view mirror, and traffic sign post was horseshoe-wrapped with vegetation, fabric, plastic, and strands of dirty pink insulation. Uprooted and blasted trees barred routes and obscured views. Mud made toxic from fuel and hazardous chemicals filled basements and sat high on church pews. Heavy bluestone sidewalk slabs were thrown around like dominoes, and white and yellow road lines on disjointed chunks of asphalt pointed in every direction possible. Covering much of this was a layer of fine silt that had set like cement, raising little clouds as you walked across it.

Miraculously, the reservoirs and bridges he passed had held, all except for the wonderful old covered bridge in North Blenheim, gone without a trace save for the abutments on either side. Was there no end to this town's sense of loss, even with no one left to mourn it? Rick was not normally given to sentimentality, but he remarked that it was almost good nobody was alive to see the widespread destruction and have to deal with its aftermath. This was all made more sad somehow by the crystal blue skies and calm weather often associated with late summer—like September 11 a decade earlier—which almost served as proof that this shouldn't have happened.

Andrew made an innocent enough remark about global warming during dinner a couple of days later, which Dave interpreted as global "weirding" instead, but Bennie, who seemed to be losing it a little lately, got up on a soapbox about how that was all a conspiracy between "the-sky-is-falling types" and biased scientists who wanted more grant money. Even Cole was taken aback, as nerves had been rubbed raw enough already, although he did chime in with an opinion that "poor people" who can't afford to rebuild after flooding needed to relocate. This hadn't been your average flood though. It reached numerous previously safe sites. Humankind had been starting to get the idea that one-hundred-year floods might be coming five or ten times more frequently due to all of our overdevelopment and carbon crimes, and after you've been in the middle of one it isn't just actuarial or academic anymore.

Bennie also wondered out loud how they could compare the loss of "nothing" towns none of them were even tied to with the wider devastation wrought by tornadoes, earthquakes, and hurricanes like Katrina. Dar considered responding but couldn't put how he felt into words at the time, and did not want to start a big argument either. Contemplating this later, he thought it had to do with the "slow time" of centuries-old villages. A time traveler from 1850s Cleveland would be in culture shock a century and a half later over how much everything had changed, and the older residents of any rust belt city had witnessed steady decline over the decades, but to see an entire, once-cohesive, still largely recognizable town go down all at once was heartbreaking. Also, Gilboa and North Blenheim had already been sorely mistreated by bad governmental and business neighbors, as opposed to being ravaged by acts of nature. You can't do much worse to a town in peacetime than drown it or blow it up.

ΩΩΩ

Dar wondered what he would do now. All of the road damage took his loaded van right out of the equation. Damn it to hell . . . he'd waited too long. Got sloppy and sentimental. He couldn't totally blame it on Dave, or BethAnne, but there was that. She knew he was upset about it. He had trouble sleeping now and was better off in his own zipped-up bag with his back to her. She made a remark about how he was acting bitter and morose that did not sit well. Everyone in camp was picking up on this. Dave knew the reason, and others like Dawn guessed at it and tried to cheer him up or at least provide a shoulder, but he wasn't having it. He didn't mean to be pissy, or to burn bridges, but the lost mobility was a severe blow.

The Schoharie ran brown for weeks, and Rick reported that its course and banks were "all screwed up for good." The West Kill cleared up more quickly, color-wise, but the topography of the creek bed and environs had been drastically altered in many spots. Where the lower feeder stream came in, the damage was massive. Along the main channel, raw banks of exposed brown earth would take years to stabilize, toppled trees across the water and along the banks would take their time rotting, and most disturbingly, the water did not seem to flow in a natural line anymore. It meandered in strange ways, familiar pools had disappeared, and the rocks were not *right*. How many decades or centuries might it take for all those displaced stones to look settled in again, and for the water to fashion a smoother bore down through them?

He came to the little beach where he'd caught the big trout and lain with BethAnne and it was nearly unrecognizable; blasted-looking and bereft of its supply of friendly sand. In a couple of locations at the end of long stretches rocks of all sizes had piled up in the tens of thousands like Queen Maeve's cairn. He clambered up one such mound and discovered a broad reddish stone stamped with unmistakable Middle Devonian fossil plant patterns, as well as a smaller gray one with sharp impressions of ancient sea creatures. Scattered debris from upstream homes and farms hung from branches in tatters and littered the shore, but it was nothing like the structural devastation so evident in the lower reaches of the valley as reported by Rick. Dar went down to fish the West Kill some days later, holding out little hope. How would a fish hang on in that torrent for so long? Normally you might think that some got washed down and others from higher up had replaced them, but the pre-mingled strands were very small to begin with. On the way upstream the woods were quieter than usual, as if a good number of birds and scolding squirrels had been drowned or driven out.

As Dar was squatting in a small hollow far to the side of the stream ruminating on these things, he thought he caught movement deep out into the woods. There was definitely a dark object out there low to the ground that seemed out of place, but it didn't move one iota during a long, hard stare, so he wrote it off as a stump. He rose to yank his pants back up, anxious to get away from the gnats and no-see-ums that were taking advantage of his temporary vulnerability, and when he stooped to bury the evidence moments later the blot was gone. He grabbed his rod and made haste for the stream bank, which was fairly low on both sides in that spot and did not require any scampering. In another case of bad judgment, and against the standard advice of Rick and Dave, he'd left his gun behind, and for the first time yet, his survival knife. If this was a person or a bear, he would lay low, look for movement, and pick the best escape route. If it was an aggressive or rabid animal intent on engaging him, his best bet was to get out into the water. That would either dissuade further pursuit or give him a good tactical position from which to brain it with a rock.

He leaned against the bank, looking out in steely silence for a good ten minutes, but nothing revealed itself. What to do now? It really didn't look like a person, and if it was an animal it was probably just passing through. Or the whole thing might have been a trick of the light. He crossed the water and continued with his fishing plans, imagining what it would have been like to stand there during the storm. He decided their home creek was probably in a little better shape than many others because there was nothing unnatural on or near it, save for the road that ran well above, and that seemed to have been constructed wisely, with good drainage culverts and riprap blankets. Dar was coming to a likely pool now, and he unshouldered his knapsack and began to bait the hook. Peripheral movement off to the right drew his attention, and what he saw gave him a big start.

An enormous black hellhound was standing on the opposite bank, just upstream. Dar knew his dog breeds fairly well, but he couldn't place this one. It appeared to be some unlikely combination of rottweiler, mountain dog, and great Dane. It didn't have an aggressive posture, he didn't see ribs sticking through, and it wasn't foaming at the mouth or anything, but the water was shallow there and it could have been on him in just a handful of leaps and bounds. Dar looked around for a good tree to climb or stout stick to swing, but there were none of either within quick reach.

"Good boy. That's a good doggie. How ya doin' today?" No response. The animal remained frozen and stone-faced. It had done the same thing back in the woods. He should have trusted his first instinct then. When Dar leaned down to get his bag, the dog backed up. Good. It was at least a little afraid of him. He calmly walked down toward the big pool ahead, which would offer more moat-like protection. The dog began to follow on the other side. When Dar selected the right size rock to do the job, should that be necessary, it backed up even more, this time showing a little fang. Objects had probably been pitched at this guy before, then, and he was comfortable commenting on the dog's gender because he could now see his enormous junk swinging around down there. He didn't want that to be the last thing he ever observed on this planet as his throat was being ripped out.

Dar moved on and the dog moved up. He studied the beast more closely as the range narrowed. There was a touch of dark brown around his muzzle and on his legs. At first he thought it was wearing a black leather studded collar, but the son of a bitch had a radio collar on, with a little black antenna! For all he knew there was a miniature camera attached. And it wasn't just a studded collar after all—it had large *spikes*. Who the hell puts a spiked collar on a dog in upstate New York? Come to think of it, the only place he'd ever seen one was in movies and on cartoon dogs.

Dar made his final approach to the pool, the cur mirroring his steps. This was ridiculous. He needed to resolve the situation and get back to brooding and fishing. He'd kept an emergency peanut butter cracker with him ever since hitting the road, all degraded inside its plastic bag by now. This was as good a time as any to use it. Dar carefully removed the intact center, scarfing down the crumbs.

A misty memory of a backcountry, big-river fishing trip with his pop and granddad suddenly bobbed up. Between neglecting to bring enough along, and the older man slipping and getting thoroughly soaked right up to his top pocket, they were down to just one questionable cigarette. His father had two single dry matches on the other side of the slippery river, and his grandfather the single smoke on his side. It was a novelty item in his tackle box, with "In case of emergency, break glass" on the side in red letters, so the cigarette was probably stale as hell if it was even a real one to begin with. They couldn't be heard across the rapids, but had made it clear to each other through hand signals that this was their only shot. His grandfather wanted to be the one to cross, but his father took the initiative. Watching this tiny event, with all the near falls, and the tension of trying to light it up in the breeze, and the awkwardness of sharing that shitty thing and the deep physiological relief they got from doing so—all of that was pure gold.

The practiced thrower flung the orange cracker backhand, calculating that method would frighten the mongrel a little less, thereby giving him a better chance to see where the morsel landed. But its mealy edge crumbled at the last second, and the cracker hit the water right at the dog's big wet stupid feet, spinning away down the current and through the pool he should have been fishing in already. Dar half expected a gargantuan trout to leap up with it. The hound sniffed the bank where a tiny crumb lay, and looked back at him quizzically. You know what? Come do your worst, big guy, thought Dar. I'm going fishing.

It went that way for the duration of the trip. The black dog shadowed him from the other bank, sometimes close enough to count the spikes on his collar but usually farther away. It crossed the stream once well behind him but retreated to the far side when Dar stared it down. Another time it appeared way up at the Powwow Spot, in profile like Rin Tin Tin. He guessed that the dog had ended up in the area as a result of the storm somehow. It seemed lonely for human companionship, but not trusting enough to commit. Perhaps with repeated contact and better treat delivery it would come around. Chances were that someone missed him. Or he could have belonged to a nearby wanderer or marauder. Dar was getting lower on the stream now, wondering if Blackie would follow him home, but he was suddenly nowhere to be seen.

This tale got a mixed reaction. Some thought they should try to take him in as a camp dog, with Andrew leading the call, while the brain trust was firmly against that. The barking alone would be a big issue, though it dawned on Dar that the cagey canine hadn't made a single sound the whole time. He had a word with Rick and Bennie later and asked them not to shoot it on sight. "Let's just see what happens," was Rick's reply.

ΩΩΩ

September was rapidly progressing, and the leaves began to mellow with yellow, singe orange, and bleed red. The stream took on a slightly retiring cast, the highest grasses and remaining flowers began to hunch their shoulders, bees seemed to slow down like they'd drunk too much trash can soda, and the first scent of autumnal decay was in the air. Everyone was apprehensive about the winter, and Dave and his top advisors were in final deliberations about squeezing into a smaller house up there somewhere, or relocating back to the cozy farmhouse toward the bottom of the road, which would probably be safer now since the big storm and the washed-out roads.

High nut season was beginning, and Sadie and Dave were adamant about harvesting them for bread and to store whole. They collected black walnuts first, pounding the hulls with rocks until their hands were stained black and letting the nuts cure for some weeks before cracking the shells for flour and meat.

Sadie spoke about the oak acorn harvest at assembly one night. "You all know what acorns look like, but you probably don't know what a great food source they were for early people, including the

Indians in this area. Harvesting them is pretty easy. It's fine to pick them right off the ground if they haven't been sitting there too long. You can usually tell by how fresh and bright they look. Just pop the little caps off and throw them in your bag or bucket. The nuts, silly heads, not the caps. If the branches are low enough, throw a rope up and shake them right down onto a big tarp. Some acorns contain weevils, and you want to get rid of those. It wouldn't hurt much to eat one, but let's not and say we did. Here's what you look for in a bad or weevily acorn. The cap should come off very easily. If not, discard it, far to the side so somebody else doesn't keep it. Same with any acorns that are discolored or have dark bands or spots. Small holes of any sort, chuck 'em. When we get the good ones home, we take the meat out, grind it up, and soak it to get the bitterness out. With that acorn flour we can make delicious flatbread and all kinds of things."

The crayfishing expeditions to the stream were replaced by nut parties, with almost everyone pitching in on all phases of the gathering and processing. This had something of a unifying effect after some of the recent hardships. It was closer than most of the farm work, and somewhat safer too, more under the cover of the woods. They also intensified their efforts to stockpile roots for coffee and leaves for tea.

In spite of their best intentions, not much had been done with the books up at the Ram House. Luckily the structure and most of its outbuildings sat high enough to survive what they now referred to as the Flood Storm. Dar had spent a couple sessions there with Liz. The house had a good manual typewriter in perfect working order. The new camp librarian thought it best to write down all the information on site, retyping it later into two lists by title and by subject, to include the author and date of publication, and placing these in binders. The most efficient way to do this was for someone else to read them off, and Dar was the best candidate for that, since he knew books, and since they were mostly his. Andrew had helped her the previous time, when Dar couldn't make it.

On this particular trip they were there to do some final sorting by category, and to decide which of the fluffier stuff already present in the house might be included. By the end they added nearly half of it. It was easy to classify most of these as bestsellers, or romance, or inspirational, but Dar hated to mix them in with his own selections, so they placed an asterisk next to those titles. He hugged a favorite paperback volume of D. H. Lawrence to his chest, probably from an old college class, and quoted Kafka. "A book must be the axe for the frozen sea within us."

All along Dar made little jokes and asides, like "Look, I'MOK— YOU'RE OK . . . must be a self-help book for Eskimos." They laughed uncontrollably over the title *Tour de France for Dummies*, not because that meant mannequins could race, but because it sounded like the Tour de France was for average bike riders. Two different-looking pieces of paper currency fluttered out of a copy of *Do What You Love, the Money Will Follow: Discovering Your Right Livelihood*, and they shared the same three thoughts in the same three seconds. We're rich! No we're not; money is worthless now. Hey, that isn't real money anyway! The first one was a very good mock-up of a million-dollar bill, and the paper even felt right. The second was attributed to the Socialist States of Amerika, with Hillary Clinton's picture on it, and zeros in all four corners. It was a fairly amazing piece of work, crammed full of insults, and printed in 2005 if that part of the hit job was to be believed. It was late afternoon already, and the days were getting shorter. They needed to wrap it up.

"Let's check upstairs," Dar suggested. "I know there's a few up there we didn't get yet. It would be nice to finally finish up with the notes so you can get the typing done." They went through room by room in the failing light, adding some keepers, and found themselves in what used to be the master bedroom.

"You ever wonder about these people?" Dar asked as he rifled though a small bookshelf and checked some boxes under the bed. As with so many of the houses they'd been in where there were no bodies, the family pictures were missing, their empty frames lying facedown on shelves and end tables.

"I missed you last time," Liz said in a small but clear voice.

"Sorry," Dar replied. "I was on a mission. Andrew did okay though, right? He's a bright lad."

Liz didn't answer. Her thumbs were hooked in her front pockets, and she was sliding her rear ever so slightly back and forth along the undulating curve of a beautiful bowfront dresser. Dar really still didn't know what to make of her, and this was a little confusing. He pulled the chain on a Victorian floor lamp with a fringed shade like he thought it was going to work, which got a small laugh out of her. "Not to be disrespectful, but I wish I could have ripped off all of this abandoned stuff and sold it in the shop. Ask four hundred for the dresser, for example, and take three. Buy low and sell high, though it often turned out the other way around." He began to investigate the closet more thoroughly.

"Wow, look at this," Dar said, pulling out a vintage knee-length yellow cocktail dress with black polka dots. It had spaghetti straps, a plunging neckline with a black border, and a black sash belt. "My mother would have been all over this one. I wonder where she wore it, around these parts. It looks fifties. Probably left over from her youth. And in one of the top forbidden camp colors too—bright yellow."

"I like the black crinoline peeking out at the bottom," Liz said.

"Is that what you call that?"

"Yes."

"Try it on." It just came out, but he let it hang.

Liz was silent for a few seconds. "Okay," she said, somewhat submissively.

"Let's find some shoes to go with it." The mistress's footwear was lined up in two rows of boxes in the bottom of the closet, and Dar unearthed a pair of black high heels. "I thought there might be matching polka dot shoes like you see in old print ads or movies, but these will do." He laid them on the bed, next to the dress, and everything seemed about the right size. Liz stared breathlessly at the clothes in the still, close room, and would not return his gaze. "I'll wait downstairs," he said.

Dar gathered the notes that Liz had taken and packed the books they'd selected to bring back on this trip. The typewriter had already been transported to the camp, along with a good amount of paper and some extra ribbons. They set it up on one of the worktables for a few days so anybody could play with it. Andrew in particular was fascinated. He couldn't wrap his head around printing as you went instead of at the end, not being able to save or send, the concept of having to start over again every time you wanted to make a revision, the weirdness of Wite-Out, and the ding of the bell.

As Dar finished packing, the high heels click-clacked just the way they should across the upstairs hallway and began their measured descent of the steps, filling the quiet house with that most erotic of sounds. He could see their thrust-up bottoms, like the discolored soles of upturned feet in more primitive times. She stopped at the bottom, with one hand on the banister and the other twirling a string of presumably fake pearls she must have discovered.

"Gorgeous . . . glamorous . . . ginchy. You wear it well." Liz remained silent.

"Up, okay?"

"What?"

"The dress."

Shyly but calmly, Liz inched the garment up, slowly revealing her white thighs. They were now the brightest thing in the silent darkening room, with the exception of an old bronzed baby shoe and empty oval portrait frame mounted on an equally lustrous stand up on the mantle that caught the fading fall light and seemed to summon its colors and glow with them from within. The camp cook was a thing of beauty in that pose, right there inside a real house. She seemed more like a willing wife than a lover or prostitute for some reason, hiking up her skirt for a GI on his first night back from the war, or sneaking a quickie in the den while little Tommy and Suzie were outside playing, or as a late-night reward after dinner with her trying in-laws. He was waiting for the panties and betting on their color when a wild patch of matting appeared instead, like ebony on ivory in that light. He'd observed the common trunks over the last few months, and there was the rare crown. Nice, and nasty, he thought. "Nice," he said.

Dar crossed over to the bottom of the stairwell and Liz fell into his arms. He kissed her deeply, bringing his strong left hand up under her slightly chubby ass while she unbuttoned his shirt and rubbed his coarse chest. One of her straps had fallen down. He followed that opening and kissed the top of her ample breast, suckling around a little clumsily as he was out of practice, and this was a different anatomy. His other hand ran up the soft thighs he'd just admired from afar and slid between her legs so much like a hot knife into pungent butter that he gasped. She exploded in no time at all, clinging on to him long afterwards, kissing his neck, and letting out little diminishing moans. He had never been with a woman much closer to five feet tall than six, and they fit surprisingly well together. This was almost as startling to Dar as the encounter itself.

After some time in this embrace, she finally sat toward the bottom of the stairs and gazed up at him with big green eyes that looked like smoky emeralds in the low light. "Down, okay?"

"Of course. I don't imagine those shoes are very comfortable."

"Your pants."

"Oh."

They took the riskier paved road back most of the way to make up for lost time, and would be lucky to reach the stream by true dark. "Liz," Dar began, as they prepared to cross their rural Rubicon, "that was . . ."

"Yes. Don't worry though. Say no more." And they didn't.

ΩΩΩ

October arrived. Geese were on the retreat, and a few monarch butterflies lingered before their epic journey to Mexico, perhaps tragically. The garden foragers picked the last of their new produce. It had been a successful season, especially for squash, green beans, tomatoes, celery, beets, carrots, and potatoes, and they calculated the harvest could be doubled in variety and volume the following year. The biggest problem had been minor droughts. Those were long hikes just to water plants, manually, and anything tender like lettuce wilted too quickly. They dug the last of the root crops and picked enough flavor-packed orchard apples to last through the winter. An old hillside root cellar had been discovered on one of the more remote farms, and some of the produce was transported there for safer keeping, as the entrance could be easily disguised under a pile of old fencing. Next year they would do some gardening right there, for greater convenience. A small pumpkin was brought into camp and decorated.

Dawn asked Dar if he could take her afield one day when BethAnne happened to be off with the foragers. It was getting a little chilly to fish, and he didn't feel like shooting anything, as so much produce was coming to the table now. The hunters were content with the occasional deer, turkey, or duck, and had been sparing other types of game. Dar suggested making a book run together instead. After the usual chatting on the way there, she asked if they could sit awhile.

"There's something I want to talk to you about," Dawn began. "I know this sounds weird, but last week I overheard Herbert telling Susan in one of their little sessions that BethAnne is pregnant. I didn't think anything of it at first, you know, but now I think I might see a little bump there. I know it's none of my business, and maybe it's not true, or it is and you know about it already, but I've been torn about mentioning it."

"Hmmm. Well my first reaction is that doesn't seem very likely, as we've been careful. She always has a little bump, and we *have* been eating better. And considering the source . . . Herbert said that to Susan?" Dar weighed Dawn's comments further for a moment. "Who else knows about this?"

"Well, I didn't tell anyone else, but other than that I can't say."

"Okay, thanks Dawn. I guess I'll have to look into that."

"You won't mention where you heard it, will you?"

"No, no, of course not." He gave her a big hug and they completed their errand.

Dar was still in love with BethAnne, but their relationship had cooled a bit since the Flood Storm. The embers were still there, but the spark was gone. He had a little trouble deciding if this was the normal result of familiarity, or if he had been too much of a jerk about not getting out in time and she was still annoyed at that, or if she'd just been using him all along. BethAnne was still making strong efforts to be a good tent mate, which he reciprocated. They were back into the sleeping bag sandwich, and still snuggled and had deep, intimate chats on occasion. She had finally confided in him that she'd had a miscarriage, but other than that she still didn't want to get into the details of her old married life. After they finished dinner that night and read a little together in the tent, they curled up in the customary co-fetal position. He rubbed her belly and could feel her tense up.

"Honey, go easy on me for asking, but is there any way you are with child?"

BethAnne spun around, and he could still see her flashing eyes in the final ambient throes of the roseate eventide. Her shoulders fell and she heaved a small sigh. "Possibly," she said. "Maybe. I've missed a couple of periods. I wanted to be sure."

So it was true! With Dawn's warning, and the time he'd had to consider such a momentous development, he was able to remain calm. "And I wanted to be sure I wanted to ask. That's wonderful news, dear!" He ran his fingers through her hair at the temples and stroked her cheek.

"Sorry, Dar. I wasn't sure how you would react. And I dread the camp finding out. You seem a little over me lately too. That's okay, though. We never said it was carved in stone. That was the deal."

"I could say the same thing," he responded. "You seem a little over me too. I guess we need to decide what to do. How to tell people. And then how to deal with it. It'll be a challenge. If there was any thought of staying in the woods, that wouldn't work out, would it?"

"Maybe they could set up a birth house, like they talked about having a virus house. A place where we could take our chances."

"Possibly, now that the roads are history, but the farm would be better, with lots of support. I bet Gwen would be a big help when the time came. Let's just tell everyone. How should we do it?"

"Nothing too dramatic, okay? I've been sick about that part and I just want to get it over with. What about tomorrow?"

"Sounds good. Maybe we should ask Dave to marry us. Just kidding . . . though we can if you want to. One question. Are you pretty sure? I thought we were more careful than that."

"Me too, but it doesn't take much I guess. I'm pretty sure though. If not we can say false alarm, no harm done. Thanks, Dar. I'm concerned about another miscarriage, but other than that, I'm ready. This will be a good thing, right? *La vie continue.*"

"Yes. I think you're very brave, and very sweet. Things will work out fine. Just be ready to pop those titties out quick whenever it cries. Maybe we should get some practice in."

"I knew I could count on your sensitive support," she replied in sardonic BethAnnespeak.

The announcement was made at breakfast, raising looks of concern amid the expressions of delight. As a courtesy, Dar had a quick word with Dave about it first. Dave confirmed that they had finally decided on the farmhouse—news that was very well received later that day—and he promised to accommodate BethAnne as comfortably as possible.

Premature snow fell toward the end of October, which really put a burr under everyone's saddle. They decided to ferry people, food, and campsite items down by truck as soon as it melted, and preparations began in earnest. They spent an entire assembly going over the farmhouse procedures and assigning rooms. The biggest non-security challenges would be the ever-present quest for food, and securing enough firewood for the stoves. A few rooms downstairs would be comfortable enough. Beyond that you would just have to stay active, bundle up, and cover up on the coldest nights.

Gwen, Bennie, Sadie, Dawn, Liz, Andrew, and Susan went first, as an advance contingent. Dave stayed behind to supervise closing down the camp, along with Cole, Dar, and BethAnne, and Herbert was scheduled to be ferried next. Andrew and Bennie would spend the next couple days picking up everything Dar and Cole piled by the roadside. The general consensus was that there was "too much crap," though once they got going it wasn't too bad. Dave compared this to a seasonal migration, and he was clearly in favor of moving back as soon as the snow melted. Rick would join them soon at the house, but he had some loose ransacking and reconnoitering ends to tie up first before new snow made that more difficult. Things were shaping up, and spirits were high.

As Dar was just dropping off to sleep, curled up behind BethAnne with his hand on her stomach, Herbert called from outside the tent.

Dar couldn't remember him ever being up there before in the daylight, let alone when it was pitch black. He stepped into his shoes, switched on his lantern, and opened the door flap.

"Herbert, what's up? Are you okay?"

"He's fine," came an unfamiliar voice. Dar had just been hoisting the lantern up, and he nearly dropped it in shock and surprise. There was another face just behind and to the side of Herbert's, like he had two heads. It was all crew cut, malevolent eyes, blacked-up chiseled cheekbones, and a gleamingly sinister smile over a camouflage collar. A serious gun barrel poked out, as if Herbert was holding it.

"I'm Max. Step out slowly, hands up. Tell what's her name to join you. Any funny business and I'll shoot both of you in one second flat, two at the most, her first. Is that agreeable, and clear?"

The cadet felt something cold under him, and looking down he saw that he was lying upon a large snake with a brood of little ones. He was quickly upon his feet, thinking he would rather take his chance among cannon balls than snakes.

The Frontiersmen of New York by Jeptha R. Simms (Albany, NY: Geo. C. Riggs, 1883)

SEVENTEEN

DAR escorted Herbert by the arm through the nearly empty campsite and down to the Commons, with BethAnne leading the way by lantern light and the stranger bringing up the rear. They were both shivering out frosty breath in nothing but bedtime sweats, trying to make sense of what was going on. As they got closer they could see Bennie sitting on the nearest worktable by the fire, which was much bigger than it should have been. He had an assault weapon trained on Dave and Cole, who were seated in the first row of benches. BethAnne looked back at Dar in wide-eyed astonishment, and Max gestured for her to keep moving.

"Good evening," said Bennie. "Glad you could join us. Before you do anything rash, Max and I are rated and ready to dispose of you right now, so stay cool. Anyone moves, we splatter *all* of you. Comprende?"

Dar exchanged glances with Dave. He looked proudly defiant yet resigned, like someone who knew the jig was up. Cole was off in his own world, and Dar could tell his mind was going a mile a minute trying to figure his way out of this one, whatever this one was. Max took position near the opposite worktable, putting the little band of seated prisoners squarely in the middle of any crossfire that might erupt.

"Bennie?" Dar implored, with a note of anger and desperation. "What's this about?"

"A fair question. I'll give you the abbreviated version. Your settlement days are over. The farmhouse is also in our control, under a larger group. We're going to take you to a better place, but we don't really need to. In other words, your best bet is to come along without any problems. I would be just as happy to shoot you. *Especially* you."

"I'd be happy to shoot most of you too," added Max. "Nothing personal, but it would make the transport easier."

"Transport to where?" asked Dave.

"I would say we're not going to play Twenty-One Questions," replied Bennie, "but I'm in an expansive mood tonight, so I'll tell you some of it."

"We are cold," Dave said. "We need coats first. And it's *Twenty* Questions, in case you ever have to use that again." Dar wondered why Dave was looking for more trouble with a remark like that, and concluded that they must have been verbally sparring already.

"Guess what, old man? There's a new camp rule you obviously aren't up on yet. It's keep your fuckin' mouth shut and stop telling me what to do. I've been sick of that since Day One. You and—"

"Bennie, c'mon," Dar interrupted. "BethAnne's shivering."

"Screw her," he snarled. "Oh, that's right, I guess you did already. By the way, do you know how bad I wanted to tap that all these months?"

"How bad?" asked Max with a leering smirk.

"Plenty bad. Max, you'll find some blankets in that big tent right behind us. Take the lantern. Hurry back." Bennie tossed a few more logs on the already enormous fire, illuminating the amphitheater even more and shooting sparks high into the night sky. The flames played across the worried faces of the five prisoners, though Herbert had a rather serene appearance, as if he didn't quite seem to get what was going on.

"I don't understand," pleaded BethAnne. "We took you in."

"I was here before you," Bennie responded, "though we both conned our way in. Fat Boy too, right Cole?"

"I ended up here by accident," Cole said. Max returned, throwing the blankets to Dar at the end of the bench and returning to his position on the other side of the fire.

"Okay, listen up," continued Bennie. "This camp has been targeted all along. Reinforcements will be arriving soon. By this time tomorrow night you'll be set up in new quarters, with real cots and roofs and everything. We have a little time to kill. I'll make a deal with you. I'll tell you everything I can, and then you can each tell me something surprising about yourself, while we're waiting. Something that really shocks me. Something to help make up for the boredom of bunker busting here with you whiny shit-for-brains all these months. Maybe I'll shoot whoever gives the most boring answer. I've emceed one of these before. How's that for an incentive?"

"We do not want to play any games like that," Dave said obstinately.

"I don't think he understands the New World Order yet, Bennie," said Max.

"He'd be the most boring anyway. Maybe I should just off him now and we can wait in silence. He deserves it for that John Denver concert alone."

"Go ahead," said Dave. "What use would you have for me anyway? I would not make a very good laborer, sex slave, or meal."

"Whoa," responded Max. "That's a pretty quick grasp of the situation."

"He wouldn't have made a good meal even when there was some of that going on," replied Bennie. "Scrawny geezer, always up on your high horse. You and that kitchen Nazi, and fruitloop Sadie, and Rick the human woodpile. I'd say to hell with everyone but the blood sample and the breeders, but it isn't up to me."

"I could use a change of pace myself," said Cole nervously.

"Me too," said Max. "How about we take a little walk while everyone else catches up on things?"

"Tell us," said Herbert. Bennie laughed.

"I gotta say, Grandpa, I did get a kick out of you, you flaky goofball."

"If we're going to find some things out anyway, I'd much rather hear it from you," Dar said.

"Well, once again, dipshit, it doesn't matter what you think, but I'll tell you anyway."

"Anything to eat?" Max asked.

"There's apples in that same tent. Look around and you'll find them."

The captives were squeezed together on the closest bench, as the seating immediately behind them was piled high with items that had been readied for the move. Dar calculated that anyone rushing up would be mowed down with ease. He might have made a solo dash for the woods at an opportune moment, but he was on the wrong side of the bench to pull that off, and then there was BethAnne. Having gotten a better look at Max in the light of the growing fire, he was unmistakably fit, and murderous-looking. Dar had no choice but to bide his time and learn what he could. His boots were loose, and he began to lace one up.

"No," said Bennie. "Leave those untied for now. Wait until we leave. And remember, no heroics, and no sudden moves. Everyone got that?" Just to illustrate the point, he yelled "Fire in the hole, Max," a second before letting off a quick burst into the night air, causing most of them to gasp and jerk back. Max bolted out of the tent with an apple in his mouth.

"I'll start at the beginning," said Bennie. "We've known about you from early on. When you—"

"We? The Cave Clan?" asked Dar.

"No, not the Cave Clan, but no more interruptions. Among other things, we call you the Dave Clan, as kind of a joke, which is what you are. When you first settled in the farmhouse, it was child's play to infiltrate in. And in case you wondered about the group that split off, they didn't get very far south, right Max?"

"Roger that."

"That was actually the first joint venture between our two bases. It went a lot smoother than this one has so far, with all the fuckups."

"You're jumping the gun there," replied Max. "We don't know what happened yet."

"I'd call you guys dispatching troops to the wrong county a pretty serious blunder, wouldn't you?"

"What can I say? It's beyond our usual range, and communications aren't what they used to be. You said the West Kill Creek that empties into the Schoharie Creek. *That* West Kill is way bigger than this one. There's even a third one over there by that name, the Little West Kill. It *is* a little confusing."

"Maybe you have a point. Schoharie County . . . Greene County . . . what's the difference? The important thing is that everyone knows no two creeks could ever possibly have the same name."

"We went by the map."

"Next time go by the book. Anyway, where was I? Oh yeah. There were several little settlements like this, all subject to what the chief calls 'colony collapse disorder.' Just for your information, you did some things pretty well compared to some others, and I have to admit I had a little fun here, on occasion, but it was a failed experiment from the beginning. One gun like this is worth an entire mountain of your hippie bullshit. We find it better to take field notes first before moving in. In this case, though, I was here *way* too long. This should have been wrapped up by early summer, but we had other priorities, the orders were slow, and then the Flood Storm washed lots of roads out."

"At the risk of speaking up again, how does the Cave Clan fit in?" asked BethAnne, still shivering under her blanket.

"I'll tell you how, biatch. We tolerate them. We keep an eye on them. And we keep them in check. And I happen to know that they want your ass real bad."

"Where are you based?" asked Dave. "What kind of leadership do you have? Are you military gone wild? Paramilitary?"

"Like I said, Moses, you listen while I talk. No interruptions. Actually, that's probably enough information. Let's play my game now. I call it Titillate or Die. It's kind of like Truth or Dare, but if *I* snooze, *you* lose. Let's start with you, and get it out of the way." Bennie lit up a cigarette, and gave one to Max. "We should be about even now with that one," he said.

"I have nothing to say," declared Dave.

"Really? No deep, dark secret or surprising fun fact you can share with us?"

"No."

"Okay. I'll get back to you. Maybe we can do a two-for-one. Dave and Gwen both lose because Dave was too proud to play. Gum on that for a while. Dar then. How about you? Or actually, ladies first. BethAnne?"

"Something shocking or titillating?"

"Yes."

"Okay. I'm pregnant, as you know, but Dar is not the father."

"Damn!" said Bennie. "You catch on pretty quickly. That's exactly what I'm talking about. But not so fast. Who is then?"

"Sorry, Dar," BethAnne said meekly, shifting her gaze down to the ground. "It's Rick."

"I don't know. Nice try, but he's not here to confirm that. I guess he'd be the logical one though, if that's true. It was plain to see he had the hots for you."

"It is fortunate for you Rick is not here," said Dave.

"Don't worry about old Rick, right Max? I'll play for him though and take his turn. Did you know that he had a little ladylove tucked away part of that time? He made regular visits there, to fill her larder . . . and to bring her food too." Max laughed wickedly. The captives sat in stunned silence as everything they were hearing sank in.

"Dark meat, too," Max added.

"Where did he give it to you?" asked Bennie, getting back to BethAnne.

"Does it matter?"

"Yes."

"In the woods."

"How often?"

"Just twice."

"Let's see," Bennie ordered, pointing his gun at BethAnne.

"See what?"

"What do you think? Up with the shirt. Let's see your belly once, sister, just to be sure." Dar began to rise but BethAnne pushed him down by the shoulders with surprising force, quickly doing what was asked and immediately covering up and sitting down again.

"All right. I see it. Nice. Congratulations. At least you don't have to worry about getting knocked up again any time soon. Okay, let's move on. Dar, your turn."

"So let me get this straight. If I give a better answer than BethAnne, you might kill her?"

"Even though she just admitted to shagging Bigfoot? The rules shift around the way I want them to. You might get shot for not trying at all, or for being an a-hole to begin with." Max slowly raised the barrel of his gun up from waist level and pointed it in the general direction of Dar's head.

"Okay. My biggest secret right now is this. Where I lived before I came here, I was in a house in the woods just before moving down into the cellar for the winter, and I shot my landlord from behind, right through the back and out where his heart used to be. He was waiting in ambush for me."

"I remember you telling us about that house. How do you know he wasn't just scoping you out?"

"Because all the shades were drawn. Usually, the only time I went outside was to dump my pee bucket or take a crap. He was waiting for me, but I happened to be in the woods already with my gun, way up behind him."

"I kind of like that one," said Max.

"Maybe he thought you were a threat to his family."

"Maybe, but I have half a feeling he packed them off somewhere, or even did them in himself. His house got hit by a road crew right afterwards and there was no sign of them."

"That it?"

"Almost. I dragged the body inside and tried to make it look like he died of the virus. I sat him in a chair facing the front door with his rifle in his lap, with a big coat and scarf on to help hide the damage. The body leaked down through the floor and smelled something terrible, then he froze over the winter, and then he thawed out again. I saw him on the way out and by then he looked a little like that big spaceman navigator in *Alien*, with a big hole in his chest and rib bones sticking out."

"The Space Jockey!" blurted Max. "I love that shit. We just watched that the other day."

"Did it work? Did it scare anyone away?" asked Bennie.

"I think so. They busted the door in but didn't enter."

"Is that where you got the piece, from him?"

"The P250? Yeah."

"Thanks for loaning that to me while we were moving into the house, by the way. I felt so much safer with it."

"Yeah, sure."

"Did BethAnne know about this?"

"Nobody did."

"Okay . . . pretty good. You're a back-shooting murderer who might have left starving chicks in the nest. See why I like this game, Max?"

"It ain't bad."

"We'll save Cole for last. Herbert, you're up. Do you follow what we're doing here?"

"Yes, I think so."

"Give it a shot then."

"I will. Without beating around the bush, and in terms that a brutal miscreant such as yourself and your colleague might understand, I am not of this world. I am one of a number of incorporeal beings who came here long ago, not so much to guide or observe, but to rest, and to absorb. It's special here. An extremely delicate balance. Most of you take it and everything else for granted. As things have greatly accelerated in a very short amount of time, some of us have switched out into different forms, and—"

"Is this guy from a mental institution?" interrupted Max.

"No," said Bennie, "he's just tetched. *Incontinent* being is more like it. He's a riot though . . . let him talk. What did you materialize from? Were you a wise old tree that could walk around whenever evil sorcerers threatened the land?"

"Were you one of those unopened fruitcakes that gets passed around at Christmas for years?" asked Max. They both cracked up at that.

"No. In a touch of cosmic irony, many of us chose the chambered nautilus for a vessel, well protected and connected at the bottom of the sea."

"And when did you come out of your shell?" asked Bennie, slapping his knee and wiping away tears of laughter.

"In my case, in the mid-1800s."

"And what have you been up to since then?"

"If I told you that, it would no longer be a secret of the universe."

"Is that it then?"

"Not quite. You said you've been keeping tabs on various settlements, but you are under watch as well. I only spoke in general terms about your base, but the exact coordinates are known."

"What's he talking about?" asked an alarmed Max.

"Pure twaddle. One of his buddies up the road a ways heard something about a base one time, years ago. That's all. As a matter of fact, folks, we have Herbert's remarks on that topic to thank for finally moving this operation up and getting me the hell out of here."

"I liked it here," said Herbert, "but we had to speed things along."

"You were reporting on us all along?" Dave asked Bennie. "How?"

"Mostly by leaving drops on some of those long ranger routes, and a couple of overnight visits."

A wild thought came into Dar's head from out of nowhere to pick up the garden gnome on the bench immediately behind him and hurl it toward Bennie.

"That black dog . . . was he spying on us for you?" Herbert asked in an agitated tone.

As Bennie and Max guffawed at each other over that, Dave and Herbert suddenly rushed the fire pit area. Their captors were taken completely by surprise. Herbert was on Max in an instant, landing a blow to his temple so severe that he lay there gasping. Bennie fired on Dave at close range, mowing him down and spraying bullets just to the side of BethAnne and Cole that tore up some benches and belongings. Realizing that the others were still seated and in a state of shock, he turned and began to fire on Herbert, who was just pushing himself up off of the dazed Max and beginning to pivot.

Dar considered charging forward but could see he would never bridge the gulf in time, and running for his life was not an option either. He whirled around, gripped the old gnome by the neck, took a few steps forward to improve his chances, and threw it at Bennie just as his smoking weapon was coming back around. The ceramic missile arced symmetrically hat over sandals and caught him full in the rib cage, cracking bone and gnome and sending Bennie reeling toward the fire. As he was gasping for breath and flailing around on the ground for his weapon, Dar closed the gap and followed up with a swift vicious kick to the head, but his untied boot missed its mark by a hair and went sailing up through the dancing circle of firelight and out into the dark woods. "*Jesus,*" he exclaimed, subconsciously realizing how comical this must have looked. Bennie was pulling the gun toward him now by the strap. With death just two feet and a few seconds away, Dar planted his left boot and launched a low karate kick designed to break Bennie's exposed windpipe with the ball of his bare foot, which it did. He quickly retrieved the weapon but was fumbling with it.

Cole charged up and instantly secured the other rifle. Both assailants were moaning and wheezing on the ground, and Max was beginning to gather his wits. Cole looked at Dar, stepped to the side in order to avoid ricochets off the fire pit, and unloaded on Max in expert fashion. Bennie was still aware enough to cover up after that, curling himself into a ball and gurgling some words they could not make out. Cole stepped forward to roll him over with his foot, but seemed to decide against taking such a chance. "I didn't think I should interrupt you before, Bennie, but I totally agree with you about the worth of a good weapon," and with a short burst to the back of the head that made a sick cracking sound he administered the same fate to the cowering infiltrator.

ΩΩΩ

Dar's ears were buzzing from the shooting, acrid gun smoke stung his eyes, and he was shaking with cold and fear. He looked at the bodies in disbelief, but there was no doubt that they were good and dead. The only signs of life came from two small plumes of smoke where their cigarettes had fallen in the cold mud. BethAnne ran up in shock herself, sobbing and shivering, and they hugged. Cole dragged the bodies out from underfoot, and next busied himself moving both guns to one of the tables. This was reassuring, as he was in a position to easily finish them off if so desired. They then turned their attention to Herbert, who was bleeding profusely but still stirring. The two men lifted him onto the other worktable and began to tend to his wounds, but he stopped them, asking for water instead. BethAnne brought a canteen from the stores tent and covered him with a blanket. His blood showed through right away. Dar checked on Dave but he was gone, perforated from gut to gullet. Herbert moaned, and then seemed to pass out.

"What on earth was that with Herbert?" BethAnne asked in a whisper from near the fire where she was trying to warm up.

"Did you see him move?" said Cole. "Was that pure adrenaline or what?"

"We need to get out of here," exclaimed Dar. "You heard what Bennie said about others coming."

"And go where?" asked Cole. "It sounds like down the road is out of the question. This whole county, for that matter, or region." The import of this rapid change of events was sinking in for all three of them. It had all fallen down like a house of cards. All that work and planning and hope.

"I don't know," said Dar. "We probably have a few minutes. Let's tamp down this fire and make up travel bags, quick! BethAnne—"

"On it. You see to Herbert." She ran back toward the tent with the lantern. Cole scurried off to his own tent, bringing one of the guns with him. Dar threw some water on the fire. Herbert stirred at the noise that made and grabbed his arm when he came back.

"Dar . . . listen . . . I was perfectly serious about the cabin I told you about. I had it built special. It has everything. Nobody left knows about it. There's a map . . . it's in my top pocket." Herbert's breathing was very labored now, and Dar didn't think he would last much longer. There was blood and tissue everywhere.

"I have it," Dar said, but the map was shot right through, and so soaked with blood that he could see it wouldn't even unfold. "It's ruined though."

"Never mind then. Listen carefully. One chance. It's in Hamilton County, above the town of Long Lake. You have a map for that county, right? Bring it. Go up Route 30. You know how . . . off to the side in the woods . . . whenever you can." He stopped for what almost looked to Dar like a moment of meditation, or extreme concentration, and then resumed. "Take a big shortcut on the Gilmantown road between Wells and Speculator. Take another by getting off 30 just after South Pond and cutting through the woods west and then north to Slim Pond. Slim Pond. Under any radar that way. The cabin is near the end on the south side. Look—"

"What about you?"

"I'll be all right, but you need to leave now. They're . . ." And with that, Herbert passed out again.

The map was a red rag of pulp. Dar threw it in the fire, cleaned his hands with canteen water, briefly considered looking for his boot, and hobbled up to check on BethAnne. Their knapsacks and the pack frame were out in front of the tent. "What do you have?" he asked.

"Your sleeping bag to share, some winter clothes, the stove and the white gas, the lantern and flashlight, the .22 and about a hundred bullets for that, if you think that's enough, water bottles, and some of the canned goods. You just need to get into these clothes and strike the tent. And there's your coat and better boots."

"Good. I'll tie things on rough for now and do a better job later. See if you can find any portable food in the kitchen and meet me back here." Hurling himself inside, Dar grabbed his northern maps, secured his belt knife from under the pillow, loaded up a pocket with more cartridges, and decided in favor of taking his basic fishing gear. His laptop would be like a dead weight, but he couldn't bear to leave it. He retrieved his van keys from the small box of personal possessions and pocketed Herbert's keys as well. His head was spinning, and he felt ill about leaving so much, but they had no choice. The library crossed his mind for a fleeting moment and he blocked that out too. BethAnne returned and they took the tent down together, carrying their gear back to the scene of the carnage below. Cole was just coming up with his own knapsack and sleeping bag.

"Herbert?" Cole asked Dar.

"Gone, I think, or close to it."

"I'm going to take his tent instead, okay?"

"Should we do anything with these bodies?" BethAnne asked anxiously. She couldn't bear to look in Dave's direction. Dar gently flipped him over, face down and away. He patted him on the shoulder, which already seemed stiffer.

"We should probably leave like right now," Dar said.

"What about that?" Cole asked, pointing to the other gun.

"Help yourself. You seem pretty handy with it."

"They're the same model. I'll keep this one and take all the ammo." He slung the remaining weapon far out into the woods. "We should see what these guys are carrying."

"Cole, stay if you want," Dar said urgently, "but we're outta here now. The question is, what about the others down at the farm?"

"No way. It sounds like they're done for one way or another. If you mean some kind of rescue attempt, that would be suicide."

"How do we know it wasn't just these two clowns trying to bluff us? Everything could be fine down there."

"Do you really think so, Dar?" asked BethAnne. "Did you hear what they were saying? They aren't really the clever ruse types. It sounds like they knew what they wanted to do with every one of us already. That was Bennie's job here."

"Yeah, and he rused us pretty good doing it. What if we just scope things out from the woods once, to be sure? I need to know."

"Sorry, lover," BethAnne said, "but I am not going down that way. We need to head in the other direction fast. I'll go alone if I have to. You can have the tent and the gun."

"I agree with BethAnne," said Cole. "I'm heading out."

"Where?" demanded Dar.

"I don't know. What about you?"

"West, eventually."

"Not west for me. I have—"

The three of them froze. They could hear voices coming up the trail from the stream, and strong beams of light bounced among the treetops leading toward camp. Dar motioned for them to follow. Cole shouldered the gun, draped his sleeping bag around his neck, and began to pull up Herbert's tent, but Dar yanked him away. They went right out along the Powwow trail toward the high spot above the stream where Dave had first explained the new facts of life to Dar. Halfway there, with no signs of pursuit, Cole pulled up short. "This is where I get off. I'll take my chances going up over the firebreak."

"South? Okay, man. Nice knowing you. Maybe we'll meet again."

"Yeah, like that's gonna happen," he replied. The two men shook hands. "And BethAnne, if I said you had a beautiful body, would you hold it against me?"

"Jerk," she said, giving him a quick hug. She shared some of their food, they wished each other well, Cole flicked on a little penlight, and he was gone. He was off the trail and less likely to be followed as a result, but he stood a good chance of getting lost or hurt. Even on their well-worn path the footing was treacherous, and Dar needed to use more quick bursts of the flashlight than he wanted to. They pushed ahead hard, stopping only to catch their breath and listen for pursuit.

"How could they find the camp like that in the dark?" Dar asked in a low voice. "They must have had help from somebody who knew how to get there."

"Yeah, from somebody like Andrew, probably at gunpoint. Or maybe Bennie just marked it somehow. Those jarheads live for that crap. And they're used to playing war games at night."

"Do you know something I don't?"

"Of course not. And look, Dar, I'm not going to debate this or second-guess it. There's like a ninety-nine percent chance we'd get killed or caught if we go back. And see this," she said, pointing to her stomach, "this baby that's yours, not Rick's? I'm not going to carry it in some *rape* room. *Got that?*"

"Okay, okay. Keep your voice down. Let's go then."

A traveler today may wander over Blenheim Hill and find frequent, though scarcely discernible traces of a population three times more numerous than that of the present,—depressions overgrown with briars, a cluster of lilacs, a clump of old apple trees, a large flat stone covering a hidden well, a grape vine growing wild upon the ground, a single rose bush—each betokens a habitation. Sometimes the rough wall of an old chimney, a cellar, or even the decaying timbers of a house tell of still later though abandoned homes. Family burial places, long unused, frequently unfenced and overgrown with trees, are to be found upon almost every farm. Headstones, where any remain, record family names long since forgotten. Some of these old plots have even been plowed over and the leveled ground no longer gives any trace of the graves beneath.

"Blenheim Hill" Series by Albert C. Mayham (Jefferson, NY: Jefferson Courier and Schoharie County Chronicle, 4/27/1905)

ΩΩΩ

The fact is new and seems strange to many that there should be in the North Eastern part of New York a wilderness almost unbroken and unexplored, embracing a territory considerably larger than the whole state of Massachusetts; a territory exhibiting every variety of soil, from the bold mountain that lifts its head up far beyond the limit of vegetable life, to the most beautiful meadow land on which the eye ever rested.

Long Lake by John Todd (Pittsfield, MA: E. P. Little, 1845)

EIGHTEEN

DAR AND BETHANNE were off the beaten path now, following moonlit rocks along the stream bank. They decided it was worth an extra few minutes to take their boots off and inch across the ice-cold flow, as they would be putting lots of miles on and needed to avoid chills and calluses. They made their way blindly uphill, pulling on saplings for help until the bank was so steep that they knew West Kill Road was just feet above them. Checking both directions for lights or activity, they crossed straight into the woods on the opposite side, taking care to leave no signs.

From there they headed in a due-north direction, holding hands and using the flashlight only when they felt they were about to tumble down a ravine or enter an impenetrable thicket. Dar gave BethAnne a rough description of the game plan, in order to keep her spirits up. The couple traveled for several hours until they felt they'd put enough distance between them and the campsite. They didn't bother setting up the tent, which would have been difficult, but they did drape it over their bedding for extra warmth, collapsing into deep sleeps.

BethAnne woke first with a jerk, as if from a nightmare. They had chosen a god-awful patch in the dark. Their limbs were sore, their faces were scratched, and they greeted the gray morning with frosty breath. All of their gear was pulled out onto a nearby bed of smooth pine needles, and Dar got it in better order while BethAnne prepared a little breakfast. She'd absconded with a good supply of jonnycakes and nut bread, a few apples, and what root coffee was left in camp.

They were low on water, but the stove came out and soon they were well fed and somewhat warmed. Dar checked his compass, and they began sheering to the east back toward Route 30.

"If they don't put dogs on us," Dar said, "I think we're off to a good start. Let's do this the way you did last time, but we'll keep to the thick woods whenever we can, and we should probably stay out of any houses. And don't get hurt. Watch your step."

"You told Cole west. Do you mean by way of your old house in that tiny town?"

"That was just in case he tells anyone or tries to follow. I'm thinking straight up. We have to beat the cold weather and snow."

"So tell me the North Woods plan again. What happens if Herbert is . . . if this doesn't work out the way he said?"

"I'm fifty-fifty on what Herbert told me. Normally I'd say a lot less, but he was so serious about it, and so lucid. His directions are only a county or two away from where I was originally heading, and I wasn't even sure exactly where I wanted to go, so I think we might as well give it a shot."

"What about the other crazy things he said to Bennie?" asked BethAnne.

"You mean his story? I'd say that was meant to throw them off so he could get the drop on them like he did."

"Yeah, and what about that? He never moved so quick before, and taking down Max like that. That was freaky."

"He got Dave killed doing that."

"I don't know. I think he realized we were goners otherwise. And when did they make plans to rush up like that? I didn't hear them talking. It wouldn't have worked though if you hadn't thrown the gnome just then. Great shot that."

"I guess we can go over all of that in the future. Right now we just want to get away, correct?"

"You're still mad about not going back."

"I can see your point, but I wonder. It's bugging me."

"Maybe they'll capture us soon and your curiosity will be satisfied."

"Whoever Bennie's or Max's people are, we are headed for Cave Clan territory now, though I know you don't want to end up in their hands either."

"I think we need to talk about this baby too, Dar. I don't think you believe I was lying in order to play Bennie's stupid little game. I swear to you—"

"You really wanna do this now?"

"I think we have to. We're at a crossroads here."

"All right. To be honest, if I'd been putting full shots into you, more often, I'd be more sure. I've been thinking of how you seemed to want this result, taking chances, and how I resisted. And what you said about Rick was so instantaneous too."

"You know I found Rick obnoxious."

"I don't necessarily mean out of attraction. I'm talking about procreation."

"Dar, I'm telling you the truth. You're being hurtful, and you're not giving me much credit. Look how quickly I got that over with, with Bennie. What the hell else did you want me to say? That I bring myself off when you're sleeping? That I stole a cookie when Gwen wasn't looking?" They trudged on in silence for a while. "Well, I can prove it to you for sure after the baby is born," she said, brightening.

"How's that exactly?"

"We'll see if it talks like him."

"I'm glad one of us thinks this is funny. I wonder where he's at right now. I can't imagine him going down without a good fight. He always had that cannon on his hip. I can't stop thinking about the others either."

"I know, Dar. Me too. Maybe they'll be okay. Sometimes you worry like crazy about someone, and then you find out that they're fine, or even doing better off than you are. I never thought that settlement would last forever, though. Bennie was right in a way. It was inevitable. You just have to put it out of your mind as best you can."

"I guess."

BethAnne stopped in her tracks and slung her knapsack to the ground. "I've been thinking about this hard. If you really need to go back, I'm okay with that. I could try to go on myself, or I could even wait here for a day or two if you want. I mean that. And if it wasn't for this baby, I think I'd come with you, Dar."

"No, you're probably right. From all indications, we'd get killed or caught."

"Did you want to talk about that other thing, with the landlord?"

"Maybe I just made that up, to play the game."

"Dar!"

"Okay. Sorry. I do love you BethAnne, and I'll try to protect you." He gathered her in for a bear hug, took one glove off, and rubbed some warmth into her cold, flushed cheeks. "Our odds are not very great though, especially on this trek. We'll have to keep our wits about us. It could be more of the same, as long as you understand that."

"What choice do we have?"

"Not much."

"So what were you saying about the plan? I wasn't following all of that last night."

"Yes. I was looking at the maps earlier. It's about a hundred and forty miles. If we can make ten or so miles a day, which should be doable, and nothing goes wrong, we'll be in that area in about two weeks. The middle third is the scary part. There's a lot of open farmland on either side of the road. Then there's the bridge across the Mohawk at Amsterdam. We can probably get around a traffic jam there on foot, if there is one, but there are bound to be people left in a city that size, and that's the natural place to get waylaid. I'd rather cross the river somewhere else by boat, but that probably won't be an option. We should do it very late at night, and then head upriver down near the railroad tracks, away from all streets and houses. According to the map, from there we can snake up through the cemeteries, bird sanctuary, and golf course in that area. After that, we can breathe a little easier when we get to the deep woods west of the Great Sacandaga Reservoir. He gave me two shortcuts after that, and then we'll be where he said."

"And this is all on Route 30? Why can't I get away from Route 30? What's up with that?"

"It's the Catskills-to-Adirondacks road, that's why. It goes three hundred miles south to north, from Hancock right up to Canada. I'll even be turning thirty on 30."

"Really? And the place?"

"I don't know yet."

"I mean the place we're looking for, wiseass."

"Above Long Lake."

"I think I need a name to hold on to."

"Slim Pond."

"You're sure it's not Slimy Pond?"

"Pretty sure."

"Well then, you'll be the king of Slim Pond, and I'll be your queen, and the mother of your child."

"We can be co-lairds, with a wee bonny bairn."

ΩΩΩ

For all of the worries and dangers, the journey went surprisingly well. The Adirondacks came into view quite soon after the lawn silhouette road barrier, lifting their spirits, as did a puffy, sunlit fog bank snaking above the Mohawk River. The virus must have taken an extremely high percentage of the human population after all. They saw a car on the interstate heading in the direction of Dan's last stand; they spotted headlights after skirting around Amsterdam from the heights above (and the spooky car-clogged bridge there that they practically crawled across would have halted the van anyway); they were challenged in open country by a pack of wild dogs that scattered when Dar dropped one; and they found a fairly fresh corpse on the shortcut road, a Gollumy character who was all skin and bones, with a head wound and rancid-looking bandages wrapped around one leg. The main challenges were primitive—physical strain, hunger, cold, and fear. As they transitioned from farmland to forest, there were some stretches where walking in the thick woods would have sapped too much time and energy, so they took their chances right on the road, ready to hop over the guardrail at a moment's notice. Dar caught a nice bass near the river valley and a few brook trout in the foothills for some variety in the menu, and late orchard fruit was still to be had. The signs turned tourist-rustic. They passed a game farm with all the gates open—causing Dar to privately wonder if they'd had any big cats—and a gigantic roadside woodsman smiled at them. The Flood Storm did not appear to have had as big of an impact up there. An occasional patch of dead sugar maple and red spruce stood on the acid-damaged western slopes of the highlands like the scarecrows from *Planet of the Apes*.

Dar was fairly familiar with Hamilton County in the heart of the Adirondacks, not far from the High Peaks region and nestled between New England to the east, Montreal to the north, and Lake Ontario to the west. It was the most sparsely populated county in the entire eastern United States, if he recalled correctly, with something like three people per square mile then, and it didn't have a single traffic light, which he knew for a fact. Given a century or three, it might have expunged its unnatural toxins and swallowed up its roads, railroad tracks, and structures.

Herbert's ten-mile shortcut through the woods seemed far too strenuous and risky. The weary couple stayed on Route 30 instead, passing through Long Lake in the dead of night. An access road led to the shore of the aptly named Slim Pond. It was a long scar on the map and in person, like no body of water Dar had ever seen. After a difficult four-mile hike along its flank they grew concerned about finding the Promised Land, setting up camp just in from the water that night to the eerie cry of a loon; something he'd been looking forward to hearing under less desperate circumstances. The expectant couple spent another full day searching around, to no avail. Their food was running low, and snow was in the air. Honking squadrons of fleeing Canada geese passed overhead. BethAnne asked Dar for the map, and she pored over it again while he skipped some stones.

"Are you sure he didn't say the north side of Slim Pond?"

"Positive. He said the south side, which is what this is. The other side seems more heavily treed to me. If there's a cabin, it's probably over here somewhere."

"And when he said go to the end, why would that necessarily mean the west end? I can see that if he was bringing us in off Route

30, but he meant to bring us in to the middle of the pond, from his shortcut through the woods, so it could be east or west to the end."

"It could be, but I don't think so, plus we looked good on both sides already."

"Right, but not as thoroughly as down on this end. I think we should either do that, or try the entire north side once, or give up and look for something else. I need to get out of this, Dar, and off my feet. We shouldn't get caught out in the snow either."

"I don't know, BethAnne."

"Tell me what he said again."

"I told you ten times already." She just stared at him, tightened the strings of her hood, and folded her arms. BethAnne's runny nose and cheeks were red, and a lustrous wave of honey-blonde hair curled along her neck and up the side of her chin. Dar sighed.

"The main things I remember are that it was all set up already, nobody else knew about it—though I don't see how he could claim that—and that it had everything we would need. At that point, he must have been thinking his map would show us exactly."

"And you never got a quick look at this map?"

"It was soaked. It wouldn't even separate or unfold for me. It was shot clean through too."

"Was there anything about it that looked like a map?"

"I couldn't tell. It just looked like a piece of paper."

"So it could have been some crackpot list, or an old letter from the friend he was staying with. And he told you about all of this when?"

"At the end. You know that."

"And the keys, the ones you never told me about until recently. When did that happen?"

"In the middle of the summer." Dar took the keys out of his knapsack and looked at them again for the hundredth time, but no clues were to be had.

"And what did he say then?"

"He just gave them to me, saying they were to his dream cabin in the woods, and that I should not let you know about them."

"*See*, you never said *that* before. He *told* you not to show them to me? He mentioned me by name?"

"Not by name, but he meant you."

"And he specifically said 'dream cabin'? I thought you said 'dream house' once."

"Something like that. Something kooky. I know . . . he called it his Robinson Crusoe house."

"Robinson Crusoe? Are you sure?"

"Yes. I remember now because he also borrowed that book from the library, after the keys I think, or maybe before. A nice reprint edition. I loved that one so much when I was little. *The Swiss Family Robinson* too, though that was written about a hundred years later. Weird how both of those use Robinson."

"Robinson, Robinson . . . *look*, there's a Robinson Pond right on the map, behind us on this side."

"That's a pretty common name. It could just as easily be Smith Pond."

"What's this other smaller one here right near it? It doesn't have a name."

"Probably because it's so small."

"Does it show on your other maps?"

"I don't know. I've only got the one other good one for this area. Let me see." Dar dug the map out of his knapsack and their eyes found Slim Pond together, traveling west along its southern shore.

"No . . . *friggin'* . . . *way!*" BethAnne shouted. Her echo came back across the mist-strewn water, startling both of them. "*Crusow* Pond, spelled differently. His Robinson-*Crusow* house!"

"Okay," said Dar, too nonchalantly. "That's a good sign."

"A good sign? Blow me! Do you think he means between them, or around them?" BethAnne asked.

"I don't know. They're only separated by two or three hundred yards. I got halfway up between them once, and partly around the other side of the bigger one. Let's take a look. We'll just loop around everything." They picked up their gear and headed back along Slim Pond before plunging through a bank of soggy brittle grass and into the late fall woods, strange substitutes for the deer hunters who might normally be up around those parts that time of year.

"That was brilliant, my little pilchard, but this still might not pan out. You know that, right?"

"Yes, Dardevle. I have a much better feeling about it now, though. Either way, don't forget the moral of the story. You should always listen to me."

They circled each pond closely. Both were choked with dead logs along the borders, a few hanging out in the middle where they were soon to be fixed in place like frozen alligators. These were not exactly azure jewels in the crown of the Adirondacks, as compared to Blue Mountain Lake and numerous others that graced many a coffee table book or wall calendar. But they had a wild aspect to them, and this whole area was dotted with such small ponds and lakes. The nearest of any size was Little Tupper Lake, home to a pure strain of heritage trout that went right back to the last ice age. The largest was Raquette Lake, which spawned a river by the same name that ran nearly 150 miles long. And if all this wasn't remote enough, the Tug Hill Plateau was not far off to the west if they ever needed to disappear even deeper, though you probably wouldn't want to winter up there in those record snows. Huge spruce trees and towering white pines in that area represented some of the last virgin timber in the country. Moose were common again, the wolf was back, pumas were pouncing in fast from the west, and with enough time the wapiti might even make its regal reappearance.

It was getting late now. The sky was a mixture of pale yellow and steel gray, lovely but foreboding. A few thick, widely scattered snowflakes began to fall. The first loops around the ponds had proven fruitless. The couple widened the net, pushing up well behind Crusow Pond. They were about to turn back not far from the base of a small elevation there when Dar noticed a long low line that seemed out of place. He put his rifle scope on it, but it was too dark out and he couldn't tell one way or the other. They had trudged through difficult terrain all day, BethAnne was weakening, and they would need to set up the tent and build a fire soon. He told her to stay put in a tiny clearing in order to save some steps, and that he would be right back. "Don't lose me, Dar," she said, just before he disappeared.

As he approached what looked like a small blowdown in the gathering gloom, it began to take on mirage-like form. He thought he could see eaves, and then a door. It was probably an old cabin or line shack of some sort, missing its roof. From fifty feet away he could see there *was* a mossy roof, and upon even closer inspection it turned out to be of colored-shingle construction, designed to blend in with the surroundings. It reminded him of the Gingerbread House in Tyringham, Massachusetts, with its flowing roof and organic form. Before he knew it he was treading on a firmly laid stone walkway and looking in through real windows, though they seemed to be made of some type of tough, low-glare glass he wasn't familiar with. Once he could make out furniture and a wood stove, he knew they might be home free. Dar knocked on the door, as odd as that felt, just in case it was occupied. The next minute was the longest of his life. He knocked again, louder, with the same result. He hurried back to BethAnne in the little clearing, dwarfed there by the dark hunched forest like Little Red Riding Hood and looking brave but forlorn.

"Bingo!"

"*Dar?*"

"I wouldn't kid you about something like that, honey. Come see. We're home, I think. Nobody answered the door, anyway."

They took to the woods and hurried back up toward the little house, as if it might magically fade away, never to be found again. They walked up the steps together and turned back at the front door to take in the view. Various bodies of far-flung water gleamed like pools of black mercury in what little light was left.

"Look," she said, hopefully. "You can see both ponds from here. Do you think this is it?"

"We'll know in a moment." The first key did not fit at all. The second turned perfectly.

Dar opened the sturdy, nicely constructed wooden door, which was curved at the sides like an old-fashioned barrel, locking it behind them with an authoritative click. He noticed large deadbolt locks top and bottom and fastened them as well. They were greeted by the familiar, soothing smell of pine paneling, and although it was chilly there was a surprising lack of mustiness. They laid their gear on the floor. "I should have carried you over the threshold," Dar said. He turned his lantern on and handed her the flashlight.

BethAnne took a few steps forward and drank it all in. "Shut . . . up!" was all she said. Normally Dar would have been on highest alert, should anyone be lying in wait for them, but he was oddly, overwhelmingly certain they were alone. No familiarly sickening odors told of old dead bodies either. They hugged deeply. Dar dabbed a cold-weather tear from her eye with his handkerchief and then held it to her nose, which she daintily blew.

The cottage was high-rustic in style, with lots of crafty flourishes. Just to the left was the slightly sunken living room, with the big wood stove Dar had noticed already, and multiple floor-to-ceiling bookshelves, which he hadn't, brimming with interesting bindings and dust jackets. He scanned them by lantern light and pulled one out with forest-green stamped boards and bright gilt spine lettering and decoration, including a nicely rendered shovel and pitchfork on the front cover. "*Talks on Manures*, published by Orange Judd in 1883. Nice."

"That would have been a good title for your autobiography," BethAnne replied with a giggle.

"How droll, dear. I see Burroughs too—both of them. And classic children's books, like *Minn of the Mississippi*."

The giddy couple moved on. The kitchen was just off to the right of the entrance, and even at first glance he could tell he'd never owned a nicer one, if masters they were to be. It was simple and smallish but out-of-a-magazine perfect.

"What does all of this run on?" he wondered out loud. "A generator, probably. I don't want to mess with that tonight though."

"Oh Dar! It's beautiful. And I think there's a porch out on this side." She opened up the small fridge, half expecting to find it fully stocked, looked inside the oven with the flashlight, and ran the tap water, which worked.

"Hey look, open plan," quipped Dar. "We can entertain our guests in the living room while we prepare dinner in the kitchen."

"Methinks you saw too many of those home shows on TV. There's a candle and matches on the counter, all ready to go. Should we light it?" asked BethAnne, as mirthful as he'd ever seen her.

"I guess, if you leave it here. We don't want to burn the place down on our first night. That would totally suck."

Heading straight back through the darker center of the cottage by lantern, the bathroom and a small bedroom were on one side and the larger bedroom was on the other. The layout wasn't radically different in design from Dar's old rental cabin, just more of a square than a long rectangle, but it was solidly built and highly superior in all respects. When they reached the master bedroom, Dar placed the lantern on the dresser. They hugged long and hard, and he stuck his hand down her jeans and rubbed some warmth back into her divine derriere. "Do you fadargalin' believe this?" he said. "Can you believe we are going to sleep in *that* bed tonight?"

"Pinch me."

"Hold that thought, dear. Let's see what else there is."

They opened a middle door in the hallway, expecting to find a closet, but it led down to a basement instead. Dar was shocked at that, as he didn't figure this type of house in such a location would have one. The hair stood up on the back of his neck, and he was on high alert again. As they descended the stairs the air was nice and cool, and he wondered how it stayed so dry down there. He flipped a switch at the bottom of the stairs, out of habit, and the lights came on.

"Whoa! Are you kidding me? Upstairs too then, probably. What on earth?"

"Dar?"

"I don't know what the power source is. There's no way it's lines, this far back. Maybe it's stored from a generator somehow. Maybe solar, though you wouldn't think so in these woods. Right now I don't get it."

They stepped out into the large windowless room and were further surprised and delighted to find extensive shelving loaded with food and supplies of all kinds! BethAnne let out a primal squeal of joy. Bin labels indicated stores of whole wheat and corn, oats, rice, beans, and sugar. There were separate shelves devoted to powdered and packaged food, canned goods from sliced mushrooms to big hams, bottles and jars in all sizes and contents, and on and on. All of the food was shelved in a central core, away from the walls. It would easily last through the winter—perhaps even a full year—and it would give them much more of a fighting chance, especially if they could start supplementing it early.

"How did they get all of this way back here?" wondered BethAnne.

"I don't know that either, but according to the map, this area was on private land. Maybe he had a deal with the owner, or was the owner."

A gun cabinet rested against one wall, with fishing poles and equipment next to that. "Interesting selection," said Dar. "Just for hunting. Nothing crazy." A large corner cupboard held medical supplies and vitamins, various types of personal water filters hung on hooks nearby, and a big empty freezer stood ready to serve. Mysterious boxes and crates were stacked in every empty space, and folders and manuals on a long oak table pertaining to the house and environs looked like they would be highly enlightening.

"I could spend a week absorbing all this stuff, with the bookcases for dessert," said Dar. "And I wonder what that other key is for too. Tomorrow though. Overload. Let's start a fire and get the chill off. Pick something out down here, okay?" BethAnne chose a can of black beans, yellow rice, and watermelon jello.

Amazingly, they had dim but sufficient lights upstairs as well, the toilet flushed, and the stove and refrigerator even worked once they were plugged in. Dar blew out the candle and pulled the thick, extra-wide shades down. Whatever the power source was, it seemed dedicated to everything but home heating, though the floors radiated a low ambient warmth. There was only enough warm water to last a few minutes, but it replenished fairly quickly. There was even an honest-to-goodness bathtub, though they were so tired and dirty that separate showers were in order, their first in a year, ladies first.

Dar fired up the wood stove while he waited his turn, and he could see how efficient it would be.

"There's a package of new razor blades in the medicine cabinet," said Dar after his shower, "and I saw more downstairs. New toothbrushes too. Nothing seems used. It's almost like a hotel. I mean, I don't see a single thing that says Herbert was here."

"You know, you're right," replied BethAnne, who was comfortably attired in a white terry cloth bathrobe and slippers, her hair wrapped in a towel. "Weird. What about the dressers?" They checked. There were new-looking clothes for a man and a woman, in a variety of sizes. Same with the closets, right down to some footwear and coats. The smaller bedroom even had clothes for boys and girls, including some baby items. "Talk about a fresh start!" BethAnne said.

Dinner was fantastic but anticlimactic, in a way, due to their sheer exhaustion. They kept the portions small to avoid shocking their systems, storing the leftovers in the fridge. Fridge! Leftovers! If only he could drift off to a little TV, thought Dar, and a cold beer would be damn nice too. Running on fumes, he threw another log on the fire, made sure both doors were still bolted, and banged on the bottom of one of the windows with an old hood ornament. It felt strong, perhaps even shatterproof. The couple slipped into bed, fastened on to each other, and had the best sleep of their new lives. "Just smell that pillowcase," was BethAnne's last utterance.

ΩΩΩ

Her first of the next morning, as far as he knew, was "Dar, breakfast will be ready before long." This was music to his ears, to the accompaniment of the percolating coffee pot. He realized where he was right away but still could not believe their good fortune. He asked if he could shave and shower first. Afterwards, they opened the curtains and strolled through the rooms together in the morning light. There was indeed a porch off the kitchen, fully loaded with firewood and kindling. Checking out the views, it really seemed as if they might be left alone in this place, raising one or more children and then growing old together—like Darby and Joan—backed up against the little hill in such a secluded spot and veiled so well by the surrounding landscape. They kissed and hugged, he rubbed her belly, she felt his cleanly shaven face, and he approached the kitchen table with its four chairs. Dar chose what would probably have been considered the head position, looking north out to the two ponds and the seemingly endless stretch of woods beyond, with most of the business end of the kitchen off behind him.

"What's for breakfast, my hyperborean honey pie? Fresh bagels?"

"How would you feel about powdered-milk pancakes, syrup, real coffee, but fake cream?"

"Get out!" He could smell the syrup as the plate approached.

"No, I won't get out. I've decided to stay."

"Nice pajamas, by the way. You look cozy . . . and radiant . . . and ravishing, I should add. We sure conked out last night, huh?"

"Yeah. Sleep good?"

"You bet." She brought his coffee over next, still spinning in the cup and swirling out creamy steam. "Did the newspaper come yet? I didn't hear Spot bark. It must be late. Why, when I used to deliver papers as a boy, I always blah blah blah."

"Very funny, dear."

The first sip knocked Herbert's comfy new socks off, and he could feel the caffeine muscle memory kicking in. Based on how many large cans of coffee they found in the basement, Dar could stop kidding himself about dandelion and chicory substitutes for a while. The look and smell of breakfast might have made him swoon if he wasn't sitting down, and he made quick work of it.

"You know, not to introduce any concerns on this first beautiful morning sweetheart, but I'm wondering if things are any better up here regarding possible neighbors. They've almost got to be, with fewer people, but who might be around? Locals that had hunkered down? Refugees like us? We have to hope for gentle people who want to rebuild in a better way, but who can also defend themselves. Peaceful and powerful. There were some interesting communities around here, in terms of the skills we'll need, unless things bounce back, which does not seem likely. Amish down by the foothills, around Ephratah and Stone Arabia, and the Mohawk Reservation not that far from here—Akwesasne. I guess there's little reason to believe they would have survived in large enough numbers to make a big difference though."

BethAnne stepped out of her slippers, and the gray tile floor felt cool on the soles of her feet. The cupboards held nice aluminum cookware, but the charming mother-to-be had used a thick, old, blackened cast iron skillet for the pancakes, a Griswold No. 5. She gripped it anew in her dominant hand and stole up behind Dar.

"One reason I mention that is because when we were scouting around yesterday looking for this apparent utopia, I think I saw some chimney smoke. I didn't want to worry you about it at the time. It was quite distant, just a wisp really, and it looked kind of friendly somehow. You never know though." Dar took the last bite of syrupy pancake and pushed his plate away. He cradled his coffee cup and leaned back in complete satisfaction. "Look at that," he said. "This year's calendar on the wall, for what's left of it, and a nice one too. Wondrous. He thought of everything."

It is interesting to contemplate an entangled bank, clothed with many plants of many kinds, with birds singing on the bushes, with various insects flitting about, and with worms crawling through the damp earth, and to reflect that these elaborately constructed forms, so different from each other, and dependent on each other in so complex a manner, have all been produced by laws acting around us. These laws, taken in the largest sense, being Growth with Reproduction; Inheritance which is almost implied by reproduction; Variability from the indirect and direct action of the external conditions of life, and from use and disuse; a Ratio of Increase so high as to lead to a Struggle for Life, and as a consequence to Natural Selection, entailing Divergence of Character and the Extinction of less-improved forms. Thus, from the war of nature, from famine and death, the most exalted object which we are capable of conceiving, namely, the production

of the higher animals, directly follows. There is grandeur in this view of life, with its several powers, having been originally breathed into a few forms or into one; and that, whilst this planet has gone cycling on according to the fixed law of gravity, from so simple a beginning endless forms most beautiful and most wonderful have been, and are being, evolved.

On the Origin of Species by Means of Natural Selection, or the Preservation of Favoured Races in the Struggle for Life by Charles Darwin (London: John Murray, 1859 first edition)